A MATTER OF PRINCIPLE

Alistair Barton

ZEST
PUBLISHING

Published by Zest Publishing
Ternion Court, 264-268 Upper Fourth Street,
Milton Keynes, MK9 1DP, United Kingdom
www.zestpublishing.com

British Library Cataloguing in Publication Data
A catalogue record is available from the British Library

ISBN 978-0-9574502-4-0

Printed and bound in Great Britain and Distributed Internationally by
the Ingram Content Group

Cover Adapted by Art Innovations
Typeset by Art Innovations
Set in Baskerville Old Face, 12

To my wife
Thanks for all your support.

CONTENTS

1. One   9

2. Two   26

3. Three   34

4. Four   52

5. Five   66

6. Six   102

7. Seven   134

8. Eight   153

9. Nine   169

10. Ten   182

11. Eleven   198

12. Twelve   210

13. Thirteen   227

14. Fourteen   240

15. Fifteen   261

16. Sixteen   279

17. Seventeen   304

18. Epilogue   323

ONE

Circular number 10/95 DfES

Annex

3 . . . . , an over-hasty or ill-judged decision immediately to suspend the teacher (there will, usually, be a range of options to be considered, only one of which will be suspension) when an allegation of abuse is made, can have a substantial, detrimental effect upon a teacher's career. It can, at the very least, prove to be a traumatic experience for the teacher concerned, for children at the school and their parents, and for other staff. Over-hasty or ill-judged action including a decision to suspend a teacher, can also be very distressing for any children concerned, who may feel responsible when they are not. A teacher facing an allegation of abuse needs to have confidence that agencies will act in a careful measured way when allegations are brought to their attention.

*L*en Jones suspended for allegedly assaulting a pupil! That was the news that greeted me, eight twenty five, Monday morning. The Staffroom was buzzing. Not a normal situation for a Monday. Normally one opened the door to a quiet, rather sombre gathering of teachers, most of them wishing they were somewhere else, one or two of them literally girding their loins for the expected forthcoming battle. But not this morning.

Various groups huddled in earnest discussion, an interesting reflection of the cliques that people form when thrown together at work. This was how I found them as I pushed open the door and walked in, my mind somewhat detached as I feverishly tried to plan the first two lessons. Perhaps planned was a rather grand term for the sporadic thoughts running through my mind, but Monday was often a case of survival, and this Monday was no exception. The weekend had been especially hectic and any plans for marking or lesson preparation had gone out the window by about two am. Sunday morning. The party had been well worth it, but the rest of Sunday had been a struggle.

"Hey Mike." A voice called and a finger beckoned, both belonging to the Head of History: Brian Stewart. Mike Sutherland, that was me. P.E. and Geography, six foot two, rugby fanatic and a New Zealander. One and the same really. I placed the pile of exercise books I had been carrying on top of one of the tables inside the door and threaded my way through the assortment of people, chairs and coffee tables littered with Times Educational supplements, paper cups and other paraphernalia, to where he was standing with two other colleagues. This was my clique: Brian Stewart, Robin Blair - Geography, and John Wheeler - English. I had last seen them early Sunday morning.

"Great party eh," I said, smiling at the memory.

"Forget the party, listen to this," Brian exclaimed. "Len Jones has been suspended."

All eyes looked at me waiting for my reaction. God knows what my face does but I've always felt that it betrayed me. "Yeah, I knew you'd be surprised. Hell, Len of all people."

"Wait a minute, wait a minute," I interrupted "what for and how do you know?"

"Well it's not certain but look around; we're all talking about it. Word's out somehow," replied Robin. "It seems Len has been accused of having it off with a girl in year ten, or something like that. At least that's what we've heard."

10

ONE

I thought of him. Len Jones. About my age, getting close to thirty, art teacher, married, had been on the staff for about six years, played occasionally for our staff cricket team, but really didn't mix with us socially. I couldn't see him interfering with a young girl, it just didn't fit the picture I had of him.

"No, there's got to be some mistake. I mean, I can't really see Len doing anything like that. Hell, we've all cracked on about his wife. Why bother, she's a real stunner."

"Damn right," Brian leered. "I'd give her one. Remember the end of term do last year, that black dress? Still plays on my mind." I thought back. A vivacious brunette with large captivating eyes and a wide mouth with bright teeth. Len had got himself a winner. And in that black, low cut dress, how we had envied him. I'd had more than a few improper thoughts after that.

"Well let's see if old Fields says anything," I said, "although I imagine it will be his usual waffle." I didn't have a great deal of time for the Head. On the odd occasion I'd had dealings with him, his manner, in my opinion, had been less than professional. My colleagues nodded their agreement. I watched as Jane Brown, the other half of my department, detached herself from a group of ladies on the opposite side of the room and moved across to join us. I counted myself lucky to have a member of the team who was both good looking and good at her job. We had once had a brief fling but decided in the end that we worked better together, rather than anything else. A shame really, for she was pretty. Blond shoulder length hair, reasonably petite, had a great smile and could sink the odd pint or two. A product of Loughborough, while I, she loved to remind me, was an inferior colonial from some sheep shearing university. We never shared our sheep I had reminded her.

"Hi Mike. I see you've heard the gossip. What do you think?" She eased herself into our group, an accepted member. Jane was, as we liked to refer to her, our 'titular' lad.

"I don't know Jane; I honestly can't believe that Len would do anything like that. It doesn't make sense."

"What's the verdict over there?" asked John, looking across at the group Jane had disengaged from.

"Well, what do you think? Mary's giving forth as only Mary can. She tried and convicted poor Len in about five minutes. Says that she always thought that he was odd and that it didn't surprise her at all. Some of the others agree. Don't you just love human nature. Jump on the band wagon and kick someone while they're down."

Mary Streeton, we all knew, was one of those people who seemed to ingratiate themselves with the hierarchy and spend much of their time making seemingly innocent remarks sound less than innocent. All unsubstantiated, all totally unnecessary. I often wondered what made people like that tick. I had been on the end of her tongue wagging once or twice and had not enjoyed the experience, and as such, I had no time for her. She was head of a small department but her capitation was significantly larger than it merited. Fair treatment? Rubbish!

The common room door swept open and all heads turned to watch Ian Fields and his senior management team stride in.

"This should be good," whispered Brian. "Oh sweet lips that never tell a lie."

"Good morning ladies and gentlemen, let us commence briefing."

The usual banal points were raised: Year seven history was on a trip to London to the Houses of Parliament. One of the school nurses was with them for medical cover. Had appropriate forms been completed regarding risk assessment?

"Of course they have," muttered Brian.

Computers were on the blink; the office staff was overloaded with work; . . . . I felt myself slipping away and wondered whether age was beginning to take its toll, as my attention span was certainly diminishing.

". . . . . And that concludes briefing." I knew that I had missed a couple of trivial points, but I was convinced nothing about Len had been

said. The senior management team swept out again, the impression of
unity and conformity very evident. I looked around the common room
at the other members of staff. It was almost comical if it wasn't so tragic:
Their faces a picture of bemusement and uncertainty.

"Well, that's a bloody great help," stated Robin. "Our esteemed leader
has once more reassured us." Voices began to rise again. I wandered over
to the substitution board to see if Len Jones was down as absent, and sure
enough, his initials were there: LJ - ill. To make matters worse, I was down
to cover one of his lessons. Damn it, I had too much to do. Just what I
needed to improve my day.

The rest of the day was just like so many before. Mondays came round
with monotonous regularity. P.E. on the hard courts had me wishing
I were a full time classroom teacher, or at least a better organised P.E.
teacher, as Jane had had the foresight to plan ahead and book the gym.
Barely into November and already bitingly cold.

"Mr Sutherland, Sir?"

"Yes, what is it Jamie?" I looked out through the P.E. office door.

"Well Sir, I've warmed the boys up and we're ready to start."

"Thanks Jamie." Jamie Lee, captain of the 1st XV and a brilliant
number eight. He seemed to have a natural instinct to be at the right
place at the right time and his running from broken play was awesome.
"I'll be out in a minute. Make sure that there are enough tackle pads out
from the store plus a supply of balls. And by the way, congratulations on
your County selection. Excellent and thoroughly deserved of course."

"Thanks Sir, I hope I can go a bit further this year," he smiled.

"Well you should do, and so should Simon and Keith. But as good as
you guys are, that was still a pathetic display on Saturday. We were lucky
to draw."

"I know Sir. None of us are happy about it. It won't happen again.
I mean Sir; even the mighty All Blacks come unstuck at times." He

grinned a big grin. "Just ask the Australians!" With that parting shot he headed back outside. The cheeky bugger. I finished my coffee. Quarter to four, and already the light was beginning to fade. Tonight should have been a fitness session, but I had gone against my instincts and opted for a bit of skills work, especially with the backs, whom I had felt, had let us down badly.

"Hey Mike," I recognised John's voice from down the corridor. "Wait up."

"I can't, I've got a practice and the lads are waiting and no doubt freezing. I've got to get on with it."

"You're mad," he yelled as he came toward me. "It's almost snowing, call it off, they'll thank you for it."

"John, you don't know these guys. We had an appalling game on Saturday and they as much as I, want to sort out a few things. Honestly, I can't stop. It's already starting to get dark."

"Yeah, okay, but give me a ring tonight. I want to discuss something with you." The tone of his voice intrigued me, but I didn't have the time to pursue it, and having agreed to call him, I shot out into the cold to be welcomed by the boys with a volley of good natured bantering: 'at last'..... 'good evening Sir'.......... 'we've just finished Sir'....... and so forth. All part of the special relationship that could be built up in a team. Those colleagues of mine who did nothing but teach, then went home missed out on so much of what it was all about. Sure enough, the constant interference from the various ministers of education had done little to encourage extra curricular activity, but teaching was more than just the national curriculum!

It was about six p.m. when I finally left school. My BMW was one of the last cars in the car park. This was my one real luxury, a Z4 coupe, way beyond most staff salaries but I was single, had come into a reasonable inheritance after my mother had died and I had always wanted to own a decent car. A light was still on in the Headmaster's study, so I booted the accelerator and roared out of the car park, tyres squealing: Childish but satisfying.

Out of the gates of King James I Grammar School, I turned left and drove towards the small Hertfordshire village I had grown so fond of since arriving in England. For me, Hertfordshire had encapsulated all that I had grown up dreaming of: Leafy lanes, hedgerows, green fields and lots of history. Welwyn village itself had its share of historical buildings, as well as its own Roman baths. It always fascinated me to be walking around amidst sites that had existed long before my own country had been discovered.

Traffic was light, so I made good time, and before long had reached the village and home - a modest three bedroom house I shared with two others: one a young executive for Rank Xerox, the other a company secretary. They helped pay my mortgage, we didn't socialise and kept ourselves pretty much to ourselves, for mutual convenience. Mark, Rank Xerox, had recently told me he was soon to be moving on, so I would have to start looking for another tenant or leave it to my very helpful letting agent. He had yet to let me down and in turn for a small percentage had always found professional people whom I could tolerate and equally, could tolerate me.

I let myself in. No lights were on. Flicked on the television in the lounge and moved through to the open plan kitchen to rustle up some dinner, dumping some geography books on the dining room table. I just had to get them marked tonight, as I had run out of reasonable excuses for year ten. Geography was my second subject and it gave me most of my evening work, so the rest of the evening would be a rather dull affair. Mark and Alison, company secretary, rolled in at different times and chatted briefly before going to their rooms. The living room was common ground. Whoever got there first had control of either the television or the stereo, and it was me tonight. I was trying to do some justice to some hydrology marking whilst watching a film, making the work take all the more longer, when the phone rang during one of the commercial breaks. John's voice was at the other end.

"You were meant to ring me." A statement

"Yeah, sorry mate, I got bogged down with some marking and was watching a bit of telly." It sounded a bit lame, but I had absolutely forgotten. School work did that to me.

"Yeah, yeah, I know, it's a tough life. Now you know what the rest of us spend our evenings doing. Anyway I want your view on something." He went on to speak of the rumours that had been circulating about Len Jones. "You know, we can't just sit back and wait for something to happen. We may never get told anything. You know what Fields is like. Everything secretive, so I thought that I would make an appointment with him in the morning and see if he has anything to say. What do you think?"

"I reckon you won't get far John, but equally I agree that something has to be done. What about chatting to one of the deputies first?" I asked.

"Funny you should say that. I cornered Davies at lunchtime and he clammed up completely. Wouldn't say a thing about it and then pressed me for my bloody department word banks. There's something going on though, I could tell by the way he spoke, and he couldn't look me in the eyes." He paused. "God only knows how he got the post. The guys got about as much personality as a wet blanket."

"What about chatting up Fields' secretary?" I asked. "She knows everything that's going on and a little bit more."

"No luck there mate, she's saying nowt. I've already tried. All I got was a rather supercilious reply that she was not able to disclose any information." John mimicked her quite well and I had to laugh

"Getting anything out of them is virtually impossible," I countered.

"That's crap Mike; you of all people should know that. Doesn't everyone have a fighting chance?"

"Well it depends on how far you are prepared to go. What you're willing to risk. There's no point going off half-cocked. Tread carefully. You know Fields doesn't like being questioned." I said.

"All the same I'll talk with him tomorrow. But I will be calm, you're right there. It would be just nice to know what's happening to Len. If he has been dismissed, the poor sod must be going out of his mind."

"What about ringing him and asking him straight off."

"Well I thought of that too, but I don't know his number, nor his address. Do you?" he asked.

"No I don't. I think he's somewhere over my way, in the Garden City, but to be honest, I'm not positive. It's bad isn't it, I know so very little about him," I replied. It was true. Len was a quiet, unassuming chap. He just seemed to get on with his life, not mixing with any of us. Yet that could be said about a number of the staff. We passed the usual pleasantries, had earnest conversations, heated arguments or whatever, but come 3.40pm we all went our different ways. Life was funny like that.

"Jesus, I don't know," sighed John. "This place is starting to get to me. I have to do something, Mike."

"Well, good luck mate. Let me know how it goes." I said. I hung up just in time to catch the last twenty minutes of the film, thinking how neatly everything got wrapped up and sorted out in the movie world, and then made a real effort to complete the marking.

Tuesday morning, cold, wet and grey. I hated grey days. I could tolerate rain, snow and even wind, but day after day of grey was too depressing. Even the drive to work through the lanes did little to cheer me and I arrived at school in a less than positive frame of mind. Year ten gave me a resounding cheer when I handed back their books and their good humour picked me up so that the lesson went pretty well. The weather seemed appropriate for discussing flows of water in a drainage basin. Robin, teaching in the adjacent room strolled in towards the end of the lesson, waving the kids down as they stood for him.

"Sorry to barge in Mike," he said "but I didn't catch you at briefing this morning."

"No, my lucky day for duty," I replied.

"Oh yeah, I forgot, break as well. Dining hall patrol - what fun."

"Cheers Robin, I was just starting to enjoy the day before you came in. I'd even got some of these guys working," I said, pointing at the students. They laughed in response. I found an appropriate exercise from the text for them to do and turned back to Robin. He was sitting, perched on my desk with his back to the kids looking at my whiteboard scribble.

"How can they read that?" he asked.

"They get used to it after a while," I replied. "Have you come in for any reason or do you just fancy a break from your class?"

"I always fancy a break," he laughed, "no actually I saw John first thing this morning and he mentioned that he had got an appointment to see Fields, about now." He looked at his watch. "He didn't have time to say any more as he was rushing back to his class and I just wondered if you knew what was going on. But then again, you weren't around this morning so I guess not."

"Well you're wrong actually, as it happens. He rang me last night." I replied. "He wants to find out what's happening to Len." I went on to tell him briefly about the phone call and Robin's eyebrows shot up.

"Blimey, he's jumping in at the deep end a bit. Fields hates being cornered, you know that. Didn't you try and stop him?"

"Not really, I suggested one or two alternatives but he had already explored those, and anyway what's the place coming to if we have to worry about asking questions. It is important Robin."

"Yeah, but all the same......." he shook his head in disbelief. "Anyway, I'd better trot off and see what my lot are up to. I'll see you later." He left the classroom and I got on with helping one or two of the pupils with the work I had set. The bell rang for the end of the lesson so I hurriedly set some prep, amidst groans, before dismissing them.

"The bastard. I'm so bloody angry I could thump him one!" Five thirty. Rugby practice finished for the night and I was tinkering on the computer in my office yet again. Windows XP It was all pretty straight forward. John had arrived at the office and had obviously wanted to talk. I had caught sight of him a couple of times during the day, head down, shoulders hunched, stomping along the corridor, everything about him suggesting a very angry man. It was still very evident in his present manner. I said nothing, just let the anger come to a head. "Mike, the man's a calculating, bastard." He clenched his fists and jaw simultaneously, raw emotion, controlled, but just barely. "I don't know....." he paused, fighting to contain himself, his eyes betraying the intensity of his anger. "I'll swing for him one day." He swallowed hard then after a further pause proceeded to tell me what had taken place at his meeting with the head. "You know what? He set me up on this. He bloody had everything prepared. I walked into his office to find the Chairman of Governors there. And not by chance, of that I am positive. Fields invited me to sit and then went on to say that Lord Grey would be sitting in. So I asked him why, but he wouldn't answer, just said 'I think Mr Wheeler, that there doesn't really need to be a reason. Lord Grey as Chairman has every right to sit in on any meeting'. Don't you think that strange Mike?"

"Well, it's certainly not usual John, I have to say, but I guess he is entitled to be there. Technically, he is our employer. But it is odd."

Lord Grey, a self made man, owned a construction firm among many other things, or so it was rumoured. A ruthless business man. Donated sums of money to the conservative coffers. His red face went with his blustering, belligerent manner. He used his title and his weight to push people round. I didn't envy John being confronted by both him and the Principal!

"Anyway, it got worse. Fields asked me why I wanted to see him, but I could tell that he knew. Mrs Pringle had obviously told him." (Mrs Pringle was the Head's secretary) "When I said I wanted to know if rumours I had picked up about Len Jones were true, he flipped. The guy went puce. He leant forward on his desk and gave me one of his stares and then proceeded to lecture me. I felt like a school kid." John spoke with disgust.

"What did he say?" I asked. I knew what he could be like.

"He accused me of interfering, of trying to turn the staff against him, of trying to stir up trouble. Where the hell is he coming from?" I said nothing. I didn't know the answer. John continued. "Then when I could finally get a word in I said again that all I wanted to know was whether or not a colleague had been suspended for allegedly assaulting a pupil and he went ape again. Threatened me with my job and asked me what right I had to question him, the Principal? What right? What are we in, a dictatorship?" John was most indignant with his treatment. "And also, why make such a fuss about a harmless question. Most Headmasters would be out to support their staff. All Fields said was that circumstances were such that measures had to be taken to protect the children. They were his first priority, but he wouldn't elaborate. And all the time, Grey nodded and agreed with everything said and suggested I basically just run away and leave the running of the school to those who knew how. I hate condescending, bellicose bastards like that." I could appreciate John's anger. His treatment had been appalling and showed a complete lack of man management skills by both of them. That didn't surprise me, it had happened before but it was interesting the way Fields had shown such anger when the situation didn't warrant it.

"I tell you what John. I've had enough of this place for one day. There are lots better places to talk in. What do you say to a pint?"

We drove separately to a nice little pub in the middle of the countryside: The Brocket Arms derived its name from the Brocket Estate onto which it backed. Inside was the English pub at its best. A huge welcoming fire, a low oak beamed ceiling heavily smoke stained, and a decent drop of beer. The fireplace was large enough to sit in, which is exactly what we did, and the stresses of the day in such convivial surroundings soon melted away. John was a decent bloke. He held a first from Jesus, Cambridge and was an intense, intelligent man who had had some of his stuffy edges worn off through his association with some of us lesser mortals. What I liked about him was his desire for fair play. John was the Othello of the English department, naturally trustful and besotted with his subject. An academic who was gradually coming down to earth. He had certainly landed with a bump today.

ONE

When we parted, much later than I had intended, he was much more mellow and rational. The realisation that not all fellows of high office were worthy of their placement, no longer such an affront. I drove back through the narrow lanes into the back of Welwyn, preoccupied with John's experience and frustrated that I could not think of what next to do. In the end I gave up and tried to put it from my mind but even sleep conjured up grotesque images of Lord Grey beating me into submission with a plank of wood, and Fields looking on, grinning slavishly. Most unsettling and I woke up early, not at all refreshed from my sleep.

"You're looking thoughtful Mike." I looked up from my desk where I had been arranging next week's rugby fixture. Not that I had done much. The combination of a fitful night's sleep and the thoughts I was entertaining were not good for concentration.

"Yeah. Hi Jane, how's it going?" She eased on to the stool beside me, the fragrance of Givenchy Amarige, slightly heady, lingering in the air, seductive almost. Very pleasant to the senses. I knew what it was because she had told me before. It had been a while since I had last enjoyed the company of a nice, or not so nice, female.

"Well, a penny for them," Jane demanded. She leant forward looking squarely at me. Bright blue eyes sparkling with good humour.

"Jane my thoughts are impure, indecisive and mixed up, and on top of that I had a lousy sleep last night. That aside, I'm fine," I replied.

"Well the impure thoughts intrigue me. You haven't managed to find someone at long last have you?"

"No, unfortunately not, and I think that's enough on that subject. As for the rest, I'll sort things out in time. Don't you get days like that?"

"More and more frequently. I'm putting it down to age."

I stared back at her. Age! There she was, young and attractive, in her Abercrombie and Finch tracksuit. How on earth had I managed to foul that relationship up?

"You're doing it again," she said.

"What?"

"You're staring. Looking through me."

"Tell me something. Have you heard anything more about Len Jones?" I asked, changing tack.

"Well, I've heard snippets, nothing substantial as you know."

"What have you heard?" I asked. "Everything seems to have gone hush, hush. As if it never happened. But Len has now been away for three days and all that the substitute board says is that he is ill. Fields isn't about to open up is he? And do you have any idea who the girl is supposed to be?"

"Well I think it is Belinda McKay. You know, the girl who joined the gym class last year." I couldn't place her. "She's in Ann Bryant's tutor base, dark hair, quite mature looking. She won the House junior tennis competition last term."

Got her! I could see her now. She had impressed me with her tennis and I had suggested she spend time on her serve to really complete her game. Dark eyes. That's what I remembered most about her, as well as an obvious awareness of herself and her sexuality.

"Yeah, I remember her. Good looking girl. Certainly looked older than her years, but seemed quite a nice kid. I hope nothing happened to her."

"Ann says that she has been absent from school for over a week, which doesn't sound too good. Look Mike, I've dug up Len's address." Jane spoke quietly, looking earnestly at me, her words loaded with a mixture of uncertainty and intent.

"How?" I asked. I had been thinking of doing the same thing myself but the effort of trying to find it had put me off.

"Well remember at the beginning of term we ran a raffle to raise money for some equipment?" I nodded. "Len bought some, in fact I think he won a couple of bottles of wine, and he put his address on the back of the

ONE

tickets. Anyway, I was digging through the filing cabinet this morning trying to locate some work sheets and I came across an ice cream tub jammed at the back. We all know how it got there, right?" She looked at me accusingly. She was right. I occasionally had a blitz and tidied up, ramming any loose papers or whatever else, into cupboards or files. It at least gave the impression of tidiness.

"I opened it and there was his name and address on the top of the pile. I don't suppose I would have gone through them because I wasn't actually thinking about him, but just to see his name there, it made me think. I've left the tub in the cabinet, second drawer down. I just wonder whether someone should go and see him. I mean, if he is innocent, he must be feeling so hurt and angry, and helpless. I couldn't cope with that......." Her voice tailed off.

By someone, I knew Jane meant me. I looked at her perched on the stool, knees hunched up to her chest, arms wrapped around them, biting on her thumbnail. A vulnerable figure. Jane wasn't just an honorary lad; she was one of the best.

"Jane," I said reaching out and laying my hand on top of hers. "How on earth did I let you slip through the net? I must have been mad."

"That's just it Mike," she replied softly, "you weren't really fishing." She stroked my hand as she talked. "You live for rugby, any sport. You like to go out with your mates, have a few drinks and end up with a curry. Or sit in and watch golf or whatever on the telly. That's not really me. I needed to feel as if we were heading somewhere. We just play different games, that's all. You're scared of being trapped, being committed and tied down, never to return to New Zealand." Had I been that transparent? "But you'll make someone a good catch one day Mike Sutherland."

"We could perhaps try again?" I said, acutely aware of the longing.

"Mike, we're good friends, I like that now and want to leave it like that. And don't look like that, it's pathetic, and it won't work."

The door burst open and Chris Williams, my second in the boys P.E. department strode in.

23

"Mike, uh sorry, am I interrupting a tender moment?" He spoke with a strong Welsh accent. Four years out of Bedford College, a good rugby man, we got on well.

"No Chris, not at all. Mike and I were just talking." replied Jane.

"Jeez, I'm glad he doesn't talk to me like that. You can never tell with these Kiwis. I was going to ask him something, but if that's what you have to do, then forget it."

I let Jane's hand go, stood up and faced Chris. "Now listen here boyo," I said in my best Welsh accent. "I haven't got time to stay here and be abused by you."

"Why does he always talk to me with a Pakistani accent?" Chris asked Jane, grinning.

"Yeah, accents were never Mike's strong point. He thought you were Irish when you came on interview. Anyway, I've got to go and take a lacrosse practice." She stood up. I made a quick decision.

"Jane, what we were talking about. I'll pick you up about six thirty from your flat and we will go and see if we can sort something out if you like?"

"That would be great Mike - thanks." She flashed a smile at Chris, waggled her fingers in a wave, picked up her lacrosse stick and left. We watched her go, admiring the view, and Chris raised a quizzical eyebrow.

"You're not starting up again, are you?" he asked.

"No I blew that long ago," I answered, "mores the pity. Come on, let's run the 1st and 2nd XV together today. I want you to take a session on the scrum machine to look at the binding on the front row. I actually thing Mackellar and Tate should swap and I want you to look at them." I wasn't great on front row play but my hunches often came off and Mackellar seemed to me to be more of a loose head prop than tight head. Chris had played as hooker, in fact still did, when he got the chance and I valued his opinion.

"Yeah, okay, although you're usually right. I actually came in to see what you had done with the pads for the machine," he replied.

"I put them in the store cupboard. The rain cover keeps coming off so I thought it best to put them away. If we could both do that from now on it would save them." I said. We moved out of the office via the back door that led straight on to the pitches. I had managed to get that and a staff shower put in when I was appointed and both had proved very useful.

The boys were making use of their free time throwing balls about and drop kicking over the posts but when they saw us approach, moved towards us to hear what the session had in store for them.

TWO

I was, unusually, on time for Jane. She lived a few miles away in Kimpton, a small linear village with no obvious reason for its existence. Jane lived on a modern estate surrounding a green not far from the attractive church which commanded much attention. She lived there with two other teacher friends from college, one teaching in Harpenden further to the North West, the other in St. Albans. It was Jane who answered the door.

"Good grief Mike, you're on time!" Her voice registered a degree of amazement. "You were never on time when we were going out."

"Well there you go Jane, some things do change." I hadn't in fact been home, but had showered and changed into fresh clothes at school. Jane was dressed simply in a pair of jeans, a light coloured blouse and a dark waistcoat. The black against her fair hair was most effective.

"Just wait a mo' while I fetch my coat," she said. "Come in if you want."

"No its okay, its best if we get a move on," I replied. I would have loved to have gone in and enjoyed her company, much more than talking to Len, for I was rather apprehensive at that prospect. On top of that, it was cold on the doorstep. A real bite in the air, the sky filled with pale glittering stars. There would be a cracking frost tonight. It was with some relief that we were finally in the car with the heater full blast.

Two

"I take it you do have his address?" said Jane.

"Whose address? I thought we were just going out for a drink."

"Don't play the funny boy with me Sutherland. You do have it?"

"Yep, 46 O'Neill St, Welwyn Garden. I think I know where it is." I knew the city reasonably well, although it wasn't a place I frequented socially.

I drove down through the lanes into Welwyn, over the little bridge by the graveyard and up and over the hill to the roundabout. From there it was straight forward, following the Mimram River under the massive railway viaduct and into Welwyn Garden City. With minimum fuss, we found the street and slowly moving along located number 46 on the right. The orange street lamp outside the house lit up a typical new town house, semi detached, red brick, two up, two down. Len's old Volvo was parked in the drive.

It was Len who answered my knock. He pulled the door open and stared blankly at us. I heard Jane draw in her breath, for an obvious reason. He looked terrible. Unshaven, hollow eyed. His longish hair lank and unkempt, no longer in the pony tail that had been the talk of the staffroom for several years. He continued to stand at the door staring blankly at us, no acknowledgement, and no animation. All very disconcerting.

"Len, hello. We thought we would come over and see how you were." I said rather lamely.

"Yes, yes, I'm alright thank you." His voice was rather brusque, slightly agitated. He held the door ajar, one arm down, one arm resting against it, using it like a defensive shield.

"Can we come in and talk Len?" Jane said quietly. His eyes flicked back and forth, looking at one then the other of us.

"Len we've come because we thought you might like some company. We know you must be having a pretty rough time." I could see that he was struggling to come to a decision but all the time the door was slowly closing. I knew that if I moved forward it would shut completely. A soft voice from beyond called out.

"Who is it Honey? Who's there?" I seized the moment.

"Mrs Jones, its Jane Brown and Michael Sutherland from King James. We just wondered if everything was alright."

There was a moment's pause, and then a quiet determined voice.

"Len open the door for our visitors." Rather like a little child, Len responded. Mrs Jones appeared in the hall. A very drawn and sad looking lady, with none of the sparkle that she had shown at staff get togethers. She had a little dark haired child in her arms, and further into the house another little voice was calling 'Mum, Mum' over and over again. Len stepped back from the door and mumbled for us to come in. We passed through into a dimly lit entrance hall, the stairs leading off from the left covered down their middle by a rather threadbare brown carpet which matched the one we were standing on. There was a sound of thumping and crashing and the little voice calling for her Mum finally appeared through the door leading from the kitchen. Another little tussle haired girl, this one probably about four years old. She came towards us, peddling frantically on her trike, a trailer half full of building blocks knocking against the walls, and pulled up with a start when she saw that her Mum was not alone. For a moment she stared with big brown eyes, then with a great deal of manoeuvring and bumping turned her chariot around and headed off in the direction from which she had come.

"You've got your hands full there," I said to Mrs Jones as the trike careered out of view. She smiled rather sadly back.

That's Sammy; she's a real bundle of energy." She gazed fondly down the corridor then looked back at me and I couldn't help but think how attractive she was, her high cheek bones, dark eyes and wavy brunette hair still captivating. "Come into the lounge please," she said looking across at her husband. "Would you like a cup of tea, or coffee?" We both said yes to a cup of tea and were directed into the smallish living room. It was simply furnished: A tired two seater settee, plus two small armchairs and a television in the corner. In contrast the walls were richly adorned with paintings from still life to landscapes, to my eye quite stunning, a richness and intensity pulsating from them. Holding pride of place above the small mantelpiece was a large portrait of a young Mrs Jones, strikingly beautiful with long shoulder length hair cascading and blending into the dark backdrop. The deep wine colour of her dress adding to the dramatic effect. I loved paintings, knew nothing about them, just enjoyed them for what I took them to be, and some of these, I thought, were excellent.

"These are superb," I said looking around the room. Mrs Jones smiled with pleasure.

"Yes they are, aren't they? I think Len has a lot of talent."

"Len did all of these? How on earth have you found the time Len?" I turned to him aware that he had been hovering on the fringe of the conversation. He looked directly at me for what seemed a long time and I wondered whether he was going to answer then taking a deep breath he slowly replied.

"Holidays mostly, it's a passion of mine."

"I think they are excellent." Jane's voice piped in. Len turned to her.

"Thank you. I have a lot more time on my hands now, don't I?" His wife made a dismissive, almost irritated gesture but I took the opportunity to speak.

"Look Len, we know something's afoot, but true to form at King James, nobody is being told anything nor is likely to be. Jane and I, plus a lot of others, were concerned, so we thought we would come and see if you were okay." He shrugged his shoulders and let out a great sigh. It said a great deal. He rubbed his eyes with his hand, massaging the eyelids and walked from the door to sit down. Nothing was said. In the quiet that had descended upon the room I could feel his anguish and then his body began to shake as long shuddering breaths engulfed him. His wife sat beside him wrapping her arms around his shoulders in a protective cocoon much like a mother comforts her child, rocking gently side to side and making comforting noises. Jane looked across at me and gestured toward the door and we quietly made our move, not wishing to impose upon their privacy. Mrs Jones looked up.

"Please don't go!" she implored, her eyes bright with tears. "This is the first time Len has shown anything, or allowed me to console him. Please stay - sit, please." The little girl that she had been holding was looking on inquisitively, tugging at her fathers trousers and trying to squeeze in between them. Jane stepped forward and swept her up and began to talk to her and amuse her and in no time she was chuckling away. I waited, and spent my time studying the paintings. I was captivated by their quality. At last Len spoke.

"I'm sorry, I feel a bit of a fool. It's just that these last few days have really got to me." He wiped his eyes with his sleeve.

"I guess it must be hell, but what has happened?"

"Nothing!" He stated firmly. "Absolutely nothing. I was teaching in the art room on Friday afternoon when the headmaster's secretary came for me saying that the Head wished to see me immediately. When I got up to his office I was ushered into his study to find Lord Grey and a tearful Belinda McKay there. God, I never expected what was coming next. Fields launched into attack straight away, stating that I had breached the professional code of ethics, that I had brought shame upon my teaching colleagues and that basically I was a disgrace and not worthy of the trust that everyone, especially he, had of me. Grey stood there nodding grimly. When I managed to get a word in and ask what they were on about, all I got was even louder abuse until finally Grey stated that I was being suspended pending further investigations for sexually assaulting a minor, Belinda McKay. That certainly knocked the wind out of me. Sexual assault. It sounds horrific doesn't it? I was absolutely stunned. How dare they accuse me of something like that. How dare they!" His voice shook with anger as he fought to control his emotions. "Anyway, it seems this impropriety took place on Thursday night after school in the art room. Unfortunately I was in the art room that evening and I was alone with Belinda. Great isn't it. I can't even deny that. And there I was thinking I was doing her a good turn. How ironic! One good turn leads to a suspension! I'm her tutor; she asked to talk with me after school."

"No one else around I suppose?" I asked. Len shook his head.

Two

"No such luck, just the two of us." He bit his top lip, reflecting on his naivety. In all fairness he had probably done what most of us would do, but it had only been at the start of the new term during one of our compulsory in service days, that we had listened to a guest speaker go on about the dangers of one to one contact behind closed doors. In this day and age it seemed we were opening ourselves up to the very thing that Len was now experiencing. Young girls fantasized and sometimes we became the victims of their fantasy. If you had to meet a child alone it was prudent to tell a senior colleague. Statistics had shown that only 0.1% of all staff were found to be guilty of any offence against pupils. Not particularly high, but any percent was too high. The Children's Act had placed a duty of care on staff and any allegations that were made had to be investigated. And that was the rub. Allegations could be made by vindictive pupils or disturbed ones and the machinery would be set in motion. But where did that leave the teacher? Innocent until proved guilty did not seem to be part of the package, not when children were involved. They were suspended on full pay while things were sorted out. By then the stigma was attached. Even if there was no case to answer the allegation remained on file once the police had been informed. Tough. One had only to look at Len and see exactly how tough it was.

"It's a load of lies," Len continued "I tried to speak to the girl but she just started crying and Lord Grey escorted her out of the room. I couldn't even speak with her and find out why she was making it all up. They wouldn't let me even question her! Why would someone want to do this to me and my family?" He looked stricken. "What chance have I got? Everyone believes the children. You remember what happened to that P.E. teacher at Watford? He claimed he didn't molest that boy but even when they eventually cleared his name the damage had been done. The school wouldn't take him back. You tell me, what chance have I got?" He shook his head despairingly. What could we tell him? He was absolutely right. It was pretty much all stacked against him and there was little succour we could offer. I could see that he knew this too.

We drove slowly back to Kimpton, neither of us with much to say. The visit had left an unpleasant taste in my mouth. Why would the girl go to such lengths? It didn't add up. Perhaps Len was lying, although I would have put money on it that he wasn't. On an impulse, I had pulled into a pub car park. We were in the little village of Codicote and the thought of a bar snack and a pint had seemed a great idea.

"That was awful Mike, I didn't enjoy tonight at all," Jane said. "Len didn't do anything I'm sure of that. Aren't you?"

"You know what they say though Jane; no smoke without fire." I stopped her before she could jump to Len's defence. "But I don't believe that for one little bit. I'm pretty sure that He is the innocent party. Another drink?" She nodded and I made my way to the bar and waited. One barmaid and a reasonably full bar. I felt somewhat guilty thinking of Len's predicament whilst here I was enjoying myself. My thoughts were interrupted by a commotion across the room. An unpleasant looking young man, obviously the worse for drink was yelling abuse at a girl seated across from him. His language was particularly graphic and the girl, embarrassed at the scene they were creating stood up to leave. As she did so, he slapped her with his open hand, the crack of it clearly audible in the hush that had descended. Her reaction was surprising for she launched back at him with her fists flailing, screaming obscenities in her rage. He staggered back, warding off her blows and tripped, falling back across the table where Jane sat. She sprawled on the ground and I moved quickly to help her up before she was caught in the middle of things, then grabbed hold of the girl, clamped one arm around her and held her back as Jane got to her feet. She struggled for a moment then collapsed into tears and I sat her down then turned to see if Jane was okay. The young man was on his feet and had begun to move purposely towards the girl.

"You slut," he mouthed. "You'll be sorry." The fight had gone from her. The sudden rush of anger fuelled by the blow had dissipated, and she sat cowed.

"That's enough," I heard myself say. I looked around the room for support but the rest of the crowd stood still, watching. Great. He was a fairly big chap, but going to seed. His cropped hair and bull neck enhanced his malicious demeanour. "You've had a bit to drink, you've made a scene, why don't you lighten up and leave. You're not hitting that girl again."

32

"Piss off," he sneered. "I'll do what I want. This has nothing to do with you."

I turned to the barmaid who was standing helplessly behind the bar. "Where's your boss? Get him in here." She shrugged helplessly.

"I'm on my own at the moment; he's gone out for a bit." Marvellous. The last thing I wanted was a brawl. I wasn't a great one for fighting, not off the field anyway, and it had been a while since I had thrown a punch in anger.

"Well now, what are you going to do?" he asked. He stepped towards me and I waited as he came forward. "Get out of my way you interfering bastard," he snarled. He came in close and I guessed he liked to use his head. It was like slow motion. His head came up as I moved back and down and I threw a hard punch to his soft paunch. He wheezed hard and before he could recover his breath I hit him with another, slightly higher and up under his rib cage. He sunk to the floor retching and whooping in large gulps. I stepped back and looked around the bar. Thankfully, no-one was wading in to his assistance.

"He's all yours," I said looking at the girl. "He shouldn't drink so much."

She smiled wryly. "Yeah, fanks, he's okay when he hasn't. Thinks he can do wot he likes wif his father being ti'led and all." She spoke as though the letter 't' had no place in the alphabet. People began to talk again, the odd bit of laughter, one or two wry comments breaking the tension that had mounted. I turned to Jane who was standing with her back against the bar, her eyes open wide.

"Come on, let's get out of here. I've had enough for one night." She took my arm gladly and we stepped outside into the car park and the crisp night air.

THREE

"Action man eh?" Robin's voice piped up. "Gallant Kiwi to the rescue." We were striding down the corridor, dodging kids on our way to class. Great practice for honing in on your side step technique. I had resisted suggesting it to the lads for it would, I was sure, have ended with accidents along the way. I remembered back to my youth when I would sprint along the sidewalk dodging one way and then the other, much to the consternation of the pedestrians. Robin's comments jolted me back to the present.

"You know, the bush telegraph in this place is truly amazing," I replied. "Who needs faxes or computers, just rent a staffroom."

"True, but come on, fill in the detail."

"Haven't got the time at the moment Robin, I'm late for tutor base, again. I'll catch up with you later. Plus I need to talk to you about something else, okay?"

"Yeah, okay, reserve me a table at lunch!"

What a joke! Lunch in the dining room was an experience to be missed. Queues of children, volume on full, jostling for the culinary delights of our kitchen ladies, which to be fair were pretty good. Jamie Oliver would have been pleased with what was on offer.

"So where do I go from here then?" I looked across the table at Robin as he digested the news about Len. The noise in the dining hall had abated somewhat, only the last stragglers being fed, whilst most of the staff had retreated back to the sanctity of the staffroom.

"Jesus, I don't know Mike. It doesn't sound too good. The poor guy must be at his wits end."

"He wasn't looking too good, I'll say that. It's not a very pleasant thing to be accused of, is it? And no matter what, word is bound to get out. Some of the old gossips here won't keep it to themselves."

"I don't really see what you can do. Look what happened to John when he asked questions."

"I know that, but to sit and do nothing doesn't seem right. I'd hate to think that no-one was bothering for me."

Robin took a sip of his coffee and grimaced. "There's more bleach in this cup than there is coffee. God knows what it's doing to my insides." Robin enjoyed a good cup of coffee and what we got in the dining hall certainly wasn't that. "So you think you should speak to Fields then? He won't like it you know."

"What the hell, he's just another bloke."

"Not quite though is he? He can make or break you. If you cross him it won't do your promotion prospects a great deal of good."

"That's a reason for not helping someone? Come off it Robin. We don't work like that surely. We don't have to be a bunch of yes men for God's sake."

"Mike, sometimes I worry about you. For a grown man you can be so naive." He looked at me and grinned. "This is the land of the Old Boy network. Screw one and you've screwed the lot."

"It's been a while since I had a good screw," I laughed. "I'll go and see what Fields has to offer." I stood up, leaving Robin shaking his head in disbelief, and emptied the remnants of my meal into the bucket on the trolley. It hadn't been wonderful this time.

Robin called out, "Let me know how you get on. It could be interesting." I waved back in acknowledgement and continued on out of the dining hall.

The school office was situated in the old part of the school, of mock Victorian splendour, the architecture slightly over the top, but magnificent to the eye. Nothing spared to create the impression of grandeur. The Cotswold stone must have been shipped in at enormous expense. At the top of the stairs I popped my head into the secretary's office.

"Any chance of seeing the Head?" I asked. She looked up from her computer, a tight faced woman, our Mrs Pringle, very much the Principals first line of defence. Getting past her was hard work.

"Mr Sutherland, I'm sure you know the Headmaster only sees members of staff by appointment, first thing in the morning." She primly admonished me.

"Yes I do know that Mrs Pringle, but there are times when we have to see him outside the designated hours." I tried to reply civilly.

"Well I'm afraid there is no chance of seeing the Headmaster today. If you had taken the time to read the weekly calendar you would have seen that he was out at a meeting this afternoon." Her reply was rather curt and she turned back to her computer.

"Excuse me, Mrs Pringle, but I haven't finished yet." She looked up, staring owlishly through her glasses. "As it now seems that I can't see the Head today, perhaps you would put me down for tomorrow morning."

"I shall have to check the diary," she replied. I stood waiting; leaning against the door in a manner I knew she would find irritating. She fussed, clicking her tongue in a tut tutting way, like an old hen pecking at the grain, and eventually turned back to me with a disapproving look.

"It seems the Headmaster does have a vacant spot," she said.

"Indeed," I replied with a half smile. It wasn't lost on her and she flustered at the faux pas.

"Eight fifteen tomorrow and mind you're prompt."

I left her with a curt nod of thanks. It never ceased to amaze me how people needed to use their position to show their power. My father had always said that real power lay in not having to use it.

Fields sat at his desk, positioned in such a way as to command the room and indicated for me to sit down. A desk on blocks and an elevated chair. I smiled inwardly at the psychology behind it.

"Now Mr Sutherland, what can we do for you?" He spoke with a reasonably pleasant voice, as he shuffled some papers on his desk.

"Well Headmaster, I'm a little concerned." I replied.

"Oh yes." He looked up. I had caught his attention. "What about?"

"Len Jones actually." That certainly got him!

"Now look here Mr Sutherland, according to Mrs Pringle, you told her you wanted to speak to me about some P.E. equipment. Unless you have something to say to me along those lines, I suggest we terminate this meeting." His face had reddened considerably, not a happy man.

"I do find it amazing Headmaster that you cannot bring yourself to talk about one of your staff. He's been a colleague of ours for some years. We want to know what's going on, I think we have the right. Rumours are rife, it's not healthy. It does absolutely nothing for staff moral. On top of that we are all covering his lessons."

"Oh, so your concern stems from extra work does it Mr Sutherland?"

"No it doesn't, although the point is a valid one. But what I want to hear from you is whether he has been suspended and if so, for what exactly?"

"Suspended? What makes you think that? It could be that he is ill at the moment. Have you not thought of that? I can't be expected to react to every rumour that is started. I have more than enough to keep me occupied as it is. I would suggest you and your colleagues spent less time gossiping and more time concentrating on your lessons!" His voice rose in anger and he thumped his desk to emphasise the point.

"I think," I deliberately kept my voice calm, "that your meeting with John Wheeler, and with Lord Grey there, further fuelled the fires of speculation. I know Len Jones has been suspended and I know why. What I find puzzling is why it has to be such a cloak and dagger situation. Surely it would be in everyone's best interest to be informed. I saw Len the other night and I know for a fact that he would certainly like the staff to know what is going on. So why can't they be told?"

"How dare you question my actions. I'm in charge," he shouted. "You have no right, no right at all. I do as I see fit, and I do not have to answer to the likes of you."

"But it's not just me. And what about Len? Who speaks for Him?" I replied quietly.

"Don't interrupt me; I haven't finished yet," he blustered. "You had no right to see Mr Jones and you will not see him again. He is under investigation at the moment."

"No right! Who are you to tell me what I can and can't do outside of this place? That's my business, not yours. If I choose to see Len Jones there is nothing you can do to stop me." I turned away and walked towards the door, before I said anything more.

"Don't you walk out on your Headmaster," he shouted, and as I slammed it shut I could see Mrs Pringle in the adjoining office looking uncertain and startled and I knew full well she had heard everything. That was fine by me. I winked at her and went down the stairs, outwardly calm, inwardly seething. Who the hell did he think he was? And what the hell had I accomplished? I had changed nothing, been told nothing new and had antagonised the Head. Like it or not, I couldn't really afford to do that.

THREE

Fields and I basically ignored each other, but I could tell that I had been blacklisted, for the senior management team appeared awkward in my presence and the number of substitutions I found myself doing had increased noticeably. That must have been the case for others remarked on it as well. I saw Len off and on, either with Jane or one of the others. I was concerned for him, for he was losing weight and taking very little care of himself. He tried to immerse himself in his paintings but even with that, he lost interest.

With Social Services snooping about, we were finally told what was going on. The way it was presented left us in no doubt that Len was guilty: Case closed! What happened to innocent until proven guilty? The young girl presented as an innocent child whose trust in adults had been completely destroyed by Len's actions. Len told me, after about three weeks, that there was a case against him which would be heard in the district court in a month's time. Unfortunately for him, he was not a member of any teaching union, so any legal representation would have to come out of his own pocket. It was all a pretty grim affair. The fact that the press had got hold of some information, further increased the tension he was living under, and this tension began to erode at the very heart of his existence. A photograph of him with his little girls on a picnic made its way into the local review. The caption, 'It's No Picnic for the Child Who is Molested' and a grossly overplayed story line, resulted in hate mail arriving through their door and verbal and physical abuse when they went out. When I asked Mrs Jones how the press would have got hold of the photograph, she had no idea. Strange. Someone had obviously sent it. The phone interrupted some sixth form essay marking. Two hours without a break on Christaller's Central Place system was doing my head in, to the point where I was looking for any excuse to stop. There had to be more to life than spending the evening marking essays. I kept cursing myself for my inefficiency, why did I always leave things to the last minute?

"Hello." I answered.

"Oh God, Mr Sutherland, I'm . . . I'm so sorry to bother you, but it's Len, he's in a dreadful state." Lara Jones almost on the verge of hysteria, speaking quickly. I talked quietly to her, calming her down and eventually she managed to convey what had happened: Len had gone out to the local wine store and had been set upon by some thugs. I told her to ring the police and the ambulance, and that I would be straight over. It wasn't quite the excuse I had been looking for.

I grabbed the car keys from the bench in the kitchen, pulled a hoody over my rugby jersey, slipped on some trainers and stepped out into the cold night air. I never saw nor heard them waiting for me. My eyes were still adjusting to the dark, when I felt the searing pain explode across my back as I turned to pull the door shut. Christ it hurt. Before I could react, arms grabbed me, pulling mine up and behind me. I struggled to get free and as the third person loomed in I lashed out with my feet, catching him low, but not enough to do real damage. I couldn't make out who they were for their faces were covered by balaclavas, but my actions only increased their intent to do me damage. The one I had kicked snarled a few obscenities before wielding the baseball bat he was carrying with deadly effect across my thighs. I bit my lip to stifle the cry which threatened to escape, and tasted blood.

"That will teach you, you nosy bastard," he growled. I could hardly hear him, the agony was so intense. He struck again, the pain exploding across my ribs and I felt them crack. I groaned and sagged against the restraining arms.

"That should do it; he's learnt his lesson," said one of them.

"Not yet he hasn't," snarled the baseball batter. "I want this guy hurt. Let him go." The two behind me released their grip and quickly stepped back. Pointless really for I wasn't up to doing anything, barely able to stand but determined not to give them the satisfaction of seeing me fall.

"You're a brave man with a bat and a couple helpers." He moved in close and something in his manner triggered off a memory process but before I could grab it, my face seemed to explode, my nose crunching under the impact of his forehead. I knew that I had seen it coming but had not been able to do anything about it. Why had I known he would do it? Now I was falling and in the blackness that was beginning to engulf me, I heard his voice.

"Not such a big shot now eh? We don't like pricks whose friends are fuckin' paedophiles. Keep away from Len Jones." To accentuate the point he delivered a thumping kick into my body, but by this time my defence system had finally cranked into gear and I drifted off into oblivion.

"Thank God, you're alive." A voice. A safe voice. I moved. Bad mistake. Alarm bells jangled as my nerve ends locked up in a spasm, and into darkness I fell.

"You okay?" Mark's voice. What a bloody stupid question! I certainly wasn't going to answer. "No I suppose you're not. Stupid question really." He looked down at me with concern. "What should I do?" I didn't have, nor did I know the answer. This was new territory for me. Injuries for me had always been on the rugby field and if they were bad enough the St. John's ambulance men took over with their omnipotent bucket and sponge. Damned if I felt like that at the moment. "Perhaps I had better call an ambulance." He stood up to go.

"No." The effort of that one word cost a lot and I clenched my teeth as the pain racked through me again. He stood there, watching and waiting. I didn't feel good but I was not going to be taken to a hospital in an ambulance. Whoever had done this was not going to get that satisfaction. Pretty irrational thinking really, but for me it was a case of pride, and I needed something to cling to. I don't know how long Mark stood by me waiting, quietly, not saying a thing, but it seemed an age before I could bring myself to speak and tell him the gist of what had happened, and some time after that before I could summon the courage to try and move. It hurt, and I nearly blacked out a couple of times but I was now beginning to function a little better and with a few self directed insults at my manhood, got myself sitting up.

"You don't look too good Mike, we should get you to hospital," he said, concern written all over his face. I spat out some blood and went into a coughing and retching spasm which did nothing to improve my overall well being. "Jesus, Mike, is that blood coming up or is it from your nose and mouth?" I hated to think and hoped it wasn't from inside, but the way I felt.... "Why?" He looked at me almost accusingly. Fair enough I guess, it wasn't common practice for the likes of us to be set upon without good reason, but in this instance I wasn't sure that the reason was good enough. "Have we been burgled?" Much greater concern.

"Jeez Mark. . . . . .No I don't think so." I spat some more blood. I'd have a damn good try to find out though. I didn't like to be beaten, in both senses of the word. It had been too easy and it made me feel impotent. Held and assaulted. A horrible feeling. More than that, it made me feel angry, illogically angry at myself. "What you could do is get me a blanket or something," I said between clamped teeth. "I'm freezing cold and shivering hurts." He took himself off inside and after a while returned with a blue travel rug and draped it round me.

"There's nothing that seems to be missing," he said with obvious relief. "I had visions of all my DVDs having been taken." He smiled and then looked a little guilty. "Sorry, but I've got such a collection now, I'd hate to lose them." Quite understandable. I would have felt the same in his position.

Cold was not such a bad thing. It stopped the blood flowing. I didn't know how bad I was. Breathing hurt a bit. I knew some ribs had gone, but that wasn't too big a problem. I was pretty sure nothing had punctured my lungs. There didn't seem to be any light pink frothy blood, and I vaguely remembered seeing a war film where they said the guy was a 'gonner' because he was coughing that up. I seemed alright in that respect. The phone rang and Mark went back inside to answer it, returning with the hand piece and handing it to me with a shrug, pre-empting my question.

"Hello." I didn't need to say any more, as the voice on the phone rushed into a torrent of words.

"Thank God you're alright. I've been worried sick. I didn't know what to do. It's my fault. I'm so sorry, so sorry." Her voice rose in hysteria; Lara Jones. "He said he would rape me in front of the children and that Len would get another hiding unless I called you. He even said that my children weren't safe. . . . . . I didn't have a choice . . . did I? Oh God, I'm sorry." She sobbed into the phone, distraught and shocked.

"Its okay, its okay. You had no choice. I'm alive, there's no harm done. What about Len? Is he alright?"

"I'm not sure." She broke down again. "They hit him with a baseball bat so many times. Said he would never assault young girls again. They dragged him into the house and made me and the girls watch. He was bleeding badly but they kept hitting and kicking him. He's just lying here. I've called the ambulance but it hasn't come yet. That was twenty minutes ago. Why hasn't it come?!"

I tried to placate her, telling her that they would be with her as soon as possible. She wanted to know what to do with her children. Could they go with her to the hospital? If not, who would look after them? I wasn't up to all this but the rage I felt when I thought of those kids having to watch their father being brutally beaten overcame any self pity I was feeling. I said I would sort things out, rang off, then dialled Jane.

"What's the problem?" she asked when she came to the phone.

"Len's been badly beaten. Can you meet me at his place?" I replied. "Mrs Jones needs someone to look after the kids while she goes to the hospital."

"Oh, that's terrible. The poor family. Is Len okay? Anyway, I'll leave immediately. Hey, you don't sound too good. Everything alright?"

"Yeah, thanks. I'll see you there." I pressed the power off button, not wanting to discuss me. Next call Chris Williams. Incredible, he was at home.

"You're lucky boyo. I was just off out for a pint. What's the matter?" I explained very briefly again, and asked if he would mind driving his clapped out old banger over to pick me up.

"Bloody cheek," he replied. "I'm not so sure I'll come now. There's nothing wrong with old Daphne. Give me twenty minutes. Anyway, what's your problem? Why aren't you driving? Been on the bottle or has that fancy German car started playing up?"

I didn't answer, just said I would be waiting for him. It was all I could do: sit and wait!

"Christ almighty, what happened to you?" Chris's old CV 5 had barely stopped in the drive before he was out. He looked shocked and that more than anything, made me realise I must be looking a bit grim. He looked me up and down. "You look like shit on the outside Mike, but what about the inside?" I attempted a shrug.

"I'm not sure, apart from a couple of ribs. I know I hurt, but a baseball bat tends to have that effect." Chris raised his eyebrows. "I'll have to wait and see. Listen, I'll explain all on the way over to Len's place. By the way," I said pointing to Mark, "That's Mark, he lives here. Mark, meet Chris, he works with me." They shook hands and then proceeded to carefully manoeuvre me to my feet. They both fussed a bit, and were keen to see me to the hospital, but after some strong protestations on my part Chris conceded to drive me. I let him take my car, which brought a smile to his face, but it was more for my sake, as the seats reclined much further and allowed more comfort. I filled him in on the detail and also let him know that apart from a driver I was also looking for a body guard. He didn't seem to mind, which pleased me, for in my weakened state I couldn't have warded off a toddler, let alone a bastard with a baseball bat.

When we pulled up outside the house, Jane's car was already there. Chris went on in to see what was happening. When I eventually made it to the front door I was sweating profusely despite the cold. I leant against it to get my breath and wait for some strength to return to my trembling limbs. The pain in my left leg was intense. I knew I was doing things wrong, that I should be icing, compressing and elevating it. At least I was moving it.

44

I'd spent long enough drilling it into the 1st XV. But practicing what one preached wasn't always possible. Chris had left the door open, and I could see patches of blood on the carpet of the floor and smeared down one of the walls. I was still staring at it when the kitchen door opened and a man walked through.

"Good evening Sir, can I help you at all?" He had the typical policeman's rhetoric.

"I'm a friend of the family. Mrs Jones rang me to say that her husband had been badly assaulted. I came with my colleague, the big welsh chap." He nodded all suspicion receding.

"You don't look too good yourself Sir. Have you had some of the same treatment?" The last thing I wanted was a long quizzing on what had happened.

"No nothing as bad as that. I just had a bit of an accident." He waited for me to continue but I wasn't about to give him the satisfaction.

"Well then, perhaps if you do have anything to report you will come down to the station." He wasn't happy with my explanation, but knew that he would get no further, so with a curt nod he brushed past me, the contact triggering off a fresh wave of pain. He turned and peered at me again. "Are you certain there's nothing you want to tell me?" There was, actually. I was sure he had deliberately knocked into me, but insulting an officer of the law was not the most prudent course of action.

"If I think of anything I'll be sure to look you up, ah . . . ?"

"It's Carmichael Sir, D.C. Carmichael, and you are?"

"Mike Sutherland. You can find me at King James."

"Thank you Mr Sutherland, and might I suggest you see a doctor." He smiled, turned on his heel and made his way down the path.

I gingerly entered into the hall and opened the living room door. Jane was sitting on the settee, her arms wrapped around the two small girls.

She was reading them a story from a big book resting on her lap. All around her was chaos. Paintings lay smashed on the floor, books and cushions were strewn about and the television in the corner had been wrecked, the hole in the screen a gaping wound. Jane stopped reading and looked up, and the little girls on seeing me began to cry, drawing closer to Jane for reassurance.

"I'm sorry I didn't come out to you Mike, but these wee girls have had an awful time and I thought it best to be with them. God, Chris told me you weren't feeling great, but not why. You look like death. Was it the same lot?" I nodded.

"Someone thought I was being too friendly with the wrong type of person and decided to educate me in the error of my ways." Chris picked up the overturned armchair and gestured for me to sit and I gratefully acceded. "I guess I learnt my lesson." I smiled wryly.

"I'd like to teach the buggers who trashed this place, a thing or two." Chris muttered. "These were fine paintings. And that copper didn't seem too bothered." He almost implied that it was to be expected, that if someone went round molesting school girls they got what they deserved. When I asked him, what about innocent until proven guilty he just laughed and told me not to be so naive.

Jane put me into the picture regarding Len, although it was difficult to elaborate in front of the children: The ambulance had finally arrived and the medics had been extremely concerned with his condition. Mrs Jones had gone with them and Jane had volunteered to remain at the house for as long as she was needed to look after the children. I asked Chris to ring the local rugby club for I knew the club captain would still be there after training. He was a doctor and a damn good bloke. He got through to him and when he explained that I wasn't feeling great he promised to come around to the address as soon as possible. Make sure he had some tape I told Chris.

Chris pottered round picking up bits and pieces while I sat as comfortably as I could. Jane managed to keep the girls entertained, the smallest one finally falling asleep on the sofa. By the time Peter James arrived from the rugby club, the place was looking a lot more ship shape, but even so it didn't take great powers of observation to see that something had gone on.

"What's happened here then?" he asked as he stepped into the living room, casting his eyes around the bits of debris that still lay strewn about. "Were you part of this Mike?"

"G'day Peter, no... it's a long story, I'll get round to filling you in sometime. I won't get up if you don't mind."

"Fair enough. Let's have a closer look at you then." It took a while and although I tried the tough act, one or two times his prodding fingers caused me to catch my breath.

He looked up at last. "Basically you're a mess Mike, and damn lucky not to be worse than you appear to be, although goodness knows what's happening internally. You've got serious bruising on your thigh, probably a severe haematoma, massive bruising on your stomach and back, at a guess a couple of ribs gone, maybe more, not to mention your nose. Sorry Mike, tape won't do. I'm not strapping you up before you have been checked over good and proper at the hospital. You have been well and truly rolled over. Not very pleasant I would imagine." I shook my head. "Look, I don't know what's happened, but obviously someone's got at you and someone else here as well. This isn't your place or Chris's that I know. Is it yours?" he looked at Jane.

"No. It's a chap from school." I went on to tell him what had taken place and when I had finished he said nothing, but insisted he drive me to the hospital.

A couple of hours later, after being X-rayed, strapped up, handed out some pain killers, I was ready to leave. Peter had gone to find out any news of Len, and returned grim faced.

"You okay?" he asked.

"Yeah, thanks, pretty much as you diagnosed. All sound inside." "Right, good," he nodded. "Look, um your friend wasn't, well he wasn't so lucky Mike. He died on the way to hospital. They couldn't revive him. I'm sorry."

I didn't say anything, couldn't think of anything for a moment. My mind had gone blank. I felt as though I had been slugged by another baseball bat. I saw images in my mind which passed by, unbidden, but there all the same, like a video on fast forward, as Len Jones flickered by, on the cricket field, in the staffroom, with his kids. I saw the picnic shot as clearly as if I had been there. What a waste, what a sad end to a talented life. This wasn't the way it was supposed to end.

He drove me back to Len's, declining to come in, insisting that he still had a lot to do. I thanked him for his help, and made my way slowly to the door. It was opened for me by a very serious looking Chris.

"Mike, have you heard . . . .?" he began.

"Yeah," I interrupted him. "Not too good is it. How on earth do you know?"

"Len's sister in law rung from hospital. She came over from Watford. It's pretty devastating isn't it? Are you okay?"

"Yep, I got off lightly didn't I? This is way out of my league Chris. It just doesn't make sense. What's going on?"

"I've no idea Mike. Obviously someone took exception to what they believed Len had done and decided to take matters into their own hands." Chris replied.

"The right sort of person doesn't go around beating up people, nor do they go armed with baseball bats. They obviously planned to hurt us both. I don't suppose they expected Len to die." I limped on into the house, the painkillers doing a reasonable job, and into the kitchen to be met by an older looking Mrs Jones. The same intense eyes, slightly high hollowed cheekbones, framed by similar dark glossy hair.

"You must be Mike," she said softly, offering her hand. I nodded. "I'm Anne Wilson, Lara's sister." I shook her hand. "How are you? Jane told me you had been beaten up as well."

"I'm fine thanks. And I'm really sorry for what has happened." I shrugged awkwardly, and she laid a hand on my arm.

"Thank you for all you have done. You have been very kind, you and your friends. I know Len was grateful." She smiled sadly. "What a waste of life. Those poor wee girls." She shook her head in disbelief.

Jane came into the kitchen her eyes red and puffy. She laid a hand on my arm and asked how I was. I told her I was fine, and over a mug of tea the four of us sat and talked about everything and anything.

When Chris finally returned me and the car back to my house I was still feeling wide awake. Sitting quietly in the dimly lit lounge, nursing a crystal tumbler of Irish malt, and listening to the soft sounds of a Katie Melua C.D., I tried to make sense of it all. Len Jones had been set upon and killed. Murdered really. For what? Because they disliked child molesters? By taking the law into their own hands, they had committed a more serious offence. Where was the sense in that? There wasn't. But did there have to be? That presupposed people behaved rationally, which of course they don't. And what about me? Lara Jones had been made to ring me to get me out of the house so that I too could be beaten up. Why? Surely not just because I had befriended Len? There were others as well. Would they get the same treatment? How did they know where I lived? Try as I might, I couldn't fit the jig-saw together. The combination of pain killers, whiskey and a baseball bat finally got the better of me, and I drifted off to sleep.

It was the sound of movement that woke me. It was dark, although the table lamp was still on. Five a.m, and a headache from hell. More small noises. Someone moving behind me in the kitchen. My heart picked up the tempo, and my mind reluctantly churned through some disturbing possibilities. Surely someone hadn't come back again! I felt completely knackered and my head thumped incessantly. Voices, very soft. I tried to lever myself up out of the armchair and instantly regretted it. The muscles had stiffened up; the painkillers had worn off, but blowed if I was going to be beaten again, sitting down. Oh to be like one of those guys on the tele. They were invariably beaten up or shot, but could still fight their corner. Not me though. It was only the fear of being set upon again that got me across the room to the fireplace. I grabbed the wrought iron poker from the grate and only just made it back behind the door, when it opened, blocking me out. I heard a voice.

"There's a light left on. I'll just switch it off." I didn't recognize it, or the figure moving into the room. As I lifted up the poker, it clanked against the door handle. The intruder spun round.

"Christ," he croaked. "Who the hell are you?" His face was ashen and he was breathing quickly. At least I'd frightened him.

"What are you doing in my house?" I asked, partly a question, partly an answer.

"Your house?"

The second person came through the door and stopped suddenly, looking at me with staring wide eyes.

"Hello Alison," I smiled wryly. "I take it he belongs to you?"

"Mike meet Andrew, Andrew meet Mike with the poker." Andrew the intruder raised his hand in greeting.

"You gave me a helluva fright," he said, a tentative smile beginning to form.

"Sorry," I replied, "but I was asleep on the chair and I thought we had intruders."

"Mark told us what had happened," Alison said, looking at me critically up and down. I was doing much the same, for she was standing in a black negligee, a pretty sight indeed. "Your eyes seem okay," she said laughing and aware, "but the rest of you doesn't look too good. I did leave a note on the message board."

We had a system which worked well. A little wipe clean board on the fridge which was for any messages between us, such as common shopping, money owed, telephone messages, or as was the case now, an extra staying over. It avoided awkward moments and I would normally have checked it when I got in. I hadn't this time.

FOUR

I spent Friday recuperating, nursing the bruises with ice packs - frozen peas in small bags did the trick. Three times a day for twenty minutes. By far the best way to get things mended. I telephoned the school as soon as the alarm bell shattered any further chance of sleep. I told them I was ill, and then left some work with Robin. I felt I owed him an explanation, but kept it brief. The news about Len Jones silenced him for a moment. I asked him if he would make an announcement at briefing, if the senior management failed to do so, and he said he would. I rang off, and then dialled Chris who promised to see that the rugby squads were sorted out for Saturday. That done, I hobbled off to the freezer, iced up and retired to bed to watch some pretty uninteresting stuff on television.

Saturday dawned bright and frosty. One of those sunny autumn days that lifted the spirits and made one so grateful to be alive. A poignant thought. The oak trees across the valley were clinging on to the last of their leaves, their dark twisted branches standing out in contrast to the light blue sky. Not a breath of wind. It would be a great day for rugby. Tendrils of mist reached upwards from the river like outstretched fingers. England on a fine day. You couldn't wish to be in a better place. The stillness creating a canvas scene. I had never known days like it. It was just a pity they weren't more frequent. As a kiwi, I had fallen in love with this place: A gentle countryside. Whilst I missed the rugged mountain landscape of my homeland, I had been won over by the soft greenness of the trees and hedges of the south of England. It was a landscape of history, of people who had successfully blended their settlements with the surrounding landscape. It was a pity that the more modern building estates didn't measure up quite as well. Just a pity some of the people didn't measure up that well either. 'Never trust a Pom, son,' my old man had once said to me. A bit harsh that, I had thought, and had continued to do so, for I had met some pretty good people in my travels. Like anywhere else, it was just the odd few who spoilt it for the rest.

The ice packs had done a pretty good job in as much as I could move adequately. Experience had taught me to get things working as quickly as possible. Letting nature take its course took too long. The body responded to a bit of encouragement. I hung on to the window sill and proceeded to stretch, starting with my calf muscles first because they were the least affected. No problem, just a little stiffness. Heels off the ground, then back onto the ground. The rest of my body protested strongly as I put myself through my home made routine. I had been knocked around quite a bit in my playing days and was used to a bit of bruising, but this was a bit special. I had to go easy on my ribs, the movement there restricted and sore, but I kept at it, working into a gentle sweat, but definitely improving in mobility. Half an hour later, I ran a small bath and sat looking down at my body. It didn't look great. Massive blue bruises virtually everywhere. I wasn't too worried about those, but my left thigh was hurting but not showing any sign of bruising, and the last thing I wanted was a calcified haematoma. Nothing I could do though but keep on icing.

I did a lot of my thinking in the shower or the bath. It was the place where I planned my first XV training and game format. Amazingly, after all that had happened, I found myself drifting back to the familiar. Razor in hand I gingerly scraped around my face and thought of the big match to be played in the afternoon. Watford Grammar was a solid team in all departments and they played in black! Any team playing in a black strip deserved respect. I tidied up the missed bits in front of the cabinet mirror. My face was not one to draw admiring glances from the ladies today: black puffy eyes stared back at me, separated by a nose that was swollen and crooked and a mouth that looked a touch lopsided. Still, I wasn't out to impress.

But it did, for the boys at least! One thirty and a home game. As they walked up the corridor towards the gym I could see their faces, make out one or two comments, but could do little but return their smiles.

"Good afternoon Gentlemen. Trust you're fit and well?"

"Yes Sir," came the chorus of replies. I opened up the equipment cage and gingerly tossed out a couple of balls.

"You okay Sir?" Jamie Lee asked. It was a captain's duty really, to ask after the health of the coach.

"Yeah thanks Jamie. Just had a bit of an accident, that's all. Nothing to bother about. Get the guys stripped. I'll be in shortly." We had our routine. Meet an hour before kick off, change slowly in the gym, go out for a pitch inspection and warm up, then back in for a team talk. It seemed to work. Ground staff flagged the pitch and put the post protectors up. All the duty team had to concern itself with was the filling of water bottles and the laying out of kit.

The second XV, and colts began to stroll in, followed shortly afterwards by Chris Williams. He ran a critical eye over me.

"You alright?" he asked.

"Not too bad thanks Chris." I replied. "And thanks also for your help the other night."

"Oh that's alright boy, I'd do it again for another drive of your machine." He grinned, and then it faded as he spoke again. "That wasn't good what happened was it? Someone will have to catch those buggers. Robin spoke up in briefing you know, and there didn't seem to be much sympathy evident. Fields didn't even add anything extra. Can you believe that? But I'm sure he knew." We chatted on, directing the opposition to the changing rooms, brewed up a cup of coffee in the P.E. office and shared it with the various masters who came with their teams. After fielding a bit of stick from them over my appearance I escorted the society referee to his room, then went into the gym. The lads stopped passing the ball about and sat down waiting for my talk. I built it up slowly installing in them the pride and passion they had to feel when pulling on the school strip. Rugby was as much about skill and strength as it was about having the want to win, the will to commit oneself wholeheartedly. I left them with Jamie to finish off, and walked out onto the field.

A largish number of parents and other interested spectators gathered around the field, but I couldn't see Fields himself. Nothing peculiar in that. For a school that boasted a fine sporting record, he seldom appeared to cheer the teams on. I walked slowly across the turf, nodding to familiar faces, many of them obviously curious, but too polite to ask. The roar of the fifteen chanting out the count of ten, blasted across the ground. The opposition huddled in the centre looked up, and as they did the counting stopped and the team strode out purposefully from the gym doors. They were greeted with shouts of support from girlfriends and fellow students.

"Come on King James. Come on the Kings." They looked impressive in their black and gold strip. I moved on to my usual spot behind the goal posts and proceeded to watch as the game unfolded. It turned out to be a cracker, forwards and backs combining to play fast, open rugby. Player supporting player, the ball kept in hand, the rucking fast and furious. By the final whistle, we had pulled off a good victory, a last minute try from a well worked double switch with the fly half, allowing the centre to carve his way through a struggling defence and score, 15 - 10.

"Well done lads." I walked into the gym, amidst the sweating bodies in various stages of undress. Jerseys lay strewn across the floor, tape abandoned in small piles.

"Jamie, superb, well done. A great win." He grinned.

"Thanks Sir. It was a tough game and we've still got a few things to work on, but it's coming."

"Yep it is. We can work on a few areas next week. Support around the base of the scrum is one of them. But a win is a win, and this was a good one." I moved around the boys talking and joking with them. Pete Brown, the diminutive scrum half flipped the match ball to me then asked the question which had been waiting to be asked since first they saw me.

"Sir, what's going on?" The gym went quiet. He stood in front of me, hands on hips, a towel wrapped around his body. I could see a couple of angry stud rakes across his ribs.

"In what way Pete?"

"Mr Jones, Sir. There are rumours flying about the school, but that's it. Do you know anything?"

"What have you heard?"

"Well, that he's dead, been murdered, and that he was trying to have it off with one of the girls in the school."

"I see. The first part is correct, but as to the second, I can't tell you, because I don't know, but I will tell you this, I think it is highly unlikely." I could hear my voice sounding angry, though I was trying hard not to be.

"I'm sorry Sir, I'm not saying that I think he did anything," he stumbled on, but looked me squarely in the eyes, "it's just pretty hard to take on board. I mean, Jonesy was different, had some pretty crazy ideas, but we reckoned he was a straight guy. He caught some of us smoking a couple of years ago one lunch time. Didn't report us, just sat and had one of his roll ups with us and talked about how stupid it was to smoke. Didn't he Danny?"

Danny Boyd, fly half, lightening quick off the mark, could sell the most preposterous dummy and slip through a gap as quick as you could blink,

56

smiled a little sheepishly. "Yeah, I don't think I bothered smoking after that, in fact that was when I decided I would try out for the firsts. He even suggested that I should. Said he'd seen me playing in some of the house matches and thought I was good. Did you know he used to play Sir, when he was younger?"

"No I didn't Danny, in fact, I didn't know much about Mr Jones. He kept himself pretty much to himself."

One or two of the other boys piped up with their own observations on the person that I had come to know for such a short period of time. Their recollections added a further dimension to that private man.

"Who would want to kill him?" Brian Grieves, fullback, asked. Do you think it was on purpose, or a mistake?"

"That's a tough one Brian. I don't think they meant to kill him, just teach him a lesson, and rough him up a bit."

"What happened to you Sir? I mean, you look a bit of a mess," Jamie piped up.

"Let's just say I met with a problem," I smiled, "and I'm not about to discuss it now. Listen, standing about here is not doing any of you any good. Get into the shower and clean up. Remember to ice anything that hurts, you know the score." They knew it so well that they often called me the Ice man. "Monday, in here for fitness. I'll see you in the dining hall in twenty minutes. Well done chaps. A good win. Almost kiwi style rugby there. . . . . almost!" I grinned at the derision that the comment raised, and walked stiffly out.

It was a day that somehow seemed fitting for a funeral: grey skies, stark leafless trees pointing heavenward. We walked under the wooden archway and into the churchyard. Haphazardly arranged gravestones were dwarfed by a large crypt which occupied a central plot. It had certainly seen better days. The roots of an old cypress fir had caused it to tilt forward in a seemingly drunken manner and large cracks ran its length.

"I hate funerals and churches," Jane said "It's all so final and depressing." She almost shuddered. Our feet crunched loudly on the gravel of St. John's pathway.

"Well it is, isn't it? It's not my favourite place to be. I'm not a great fan of funerals either."

"Poor old Len, I can't believe he's no more. It's such a waste Mike."

"Yeah it is." I agreed. We walked up the steps and into the quiet coldness of the church. There weren't many inside but I could see a few familiar faces from school: Robin, Brian and John had managed to make it; Fields had not been too impressed with us expecting time off. He of course, hadn't bothered to turn up, but had sent one of his deputies to fly the flag. At the back, Lord Grey sat impassively, with one of the other Governors, or so I guessed. I looked at him, and he returned my stare, neither one of us acknowledging the other. This was not the place for the irreverent thoughts I was having. Love thine enemies and all that sort of thing was what was expected here. Not likely!

A grim Christ hung from a cross from the ceiling at the front of the church, and a bronze eagle cast its unblinking eye from the pulpit. Most funereal. Along the front row of pews, Mrs Jones, her two wee girls and her sister, plus other family members sat dressed in black. Jane squeezed along the pew to sit with the others and we waited quietly. There were muted whisperings, and then the deliberate tread of feet as the coffin was carried in, a single wreath lying on the top.

The priest spoke pretty well of Len and told us a little more about the man that we never really knew: I had not seen him as a steam train buff.

Jane and I followed the funeral cars to the graveyard overlooking the village where I lived. A pleasant spot, if a graveyard could be called that. It had a great view, but I wasn't convinced that the residents could make use of it. Most of the others had headed back to their respective jobs, but I thought it only proper to see Len completely put to rest. We stood around the hole in the ground, in the drizzle, watching a box being lowered;

containing what had once been a happy family man. Finished. No more. I declined Mrs Jones's offer to return to the house for some food and a drink. I didn't really feel like making small talk and the cold was making me feel sorry for myself as I started to stiffen up.

"Come on Jane," I said, "lets go and warm ourselves up beside a big fire and drink to the memory of Len."

"Okay, but where?" she asked.

"The Brocket. It's got a good open fire. They claim it is haunted. Who knows, perhaps Len will join us."

"You're the limit Sutherland, how can you joke like that?"

"Practice," I said, "years of it. Let the dead bury the dead and all that. It's my way of dealing with these sorts of things. That way, it doesn't get to me."

"That's a little insight into Mike Sutherland not often seen. A touch of the real McCoy," Jane replied.

"Yeah well, there you go." I wasn't about to argue. It was too cold and I hated being where I was, visibly being reminded of my own mortality.

The fire at the Brocket gave off much needed warmth as well as a pleasant aroma of smoky wood. It was hardly crowded. An old couple sat in one corner and to my surprise the only other occupants were Lord Grey and his friend. The only good thing about that was that they hadn't taken the seats closest to the fire. It was great to be able to sit in the chimney. I ordered a couple of drinks, a dry white wine for Jane and a malt for me: the best possible way of getting rid of any chill. We chatted about anything and nothing although Jane was keen for me to tell her what I still proposed to do about clearing Len's name.

"You can't just let it lay, Mike. He may be dead but surely we should do something to try and help his wife and leave her with his good name intact at least?"

"Why me? I'm still feeling the effects of the last little escapade. What does it really matter now? In a couple of months the whole thing will be forgotten and we will be getting our knickers in a twist about some other issue." I shrugged, and took a small sip, enjoying the warm glow as it slipped down.

"Well, if that's not the limit!" An angry Jane. "I thought you at least would have wanted to do something. I can't believe that you can just sit there and quietly state that the whole thing is dead and buried, along with Len. I credited you for something better than that."

"Yeah well I'm afraid I'm not the knight in shining armour type. I can't see the point of pursuing something that is all finished with."

"What about the guys that beat you up? Don't you want to know who they were? I mean, they're wandering about scot-free. Doesn't that bother you?" She leaned forward and looked closely at me, knowing full well that that aspect really bugged me. I didn't like being bettered and I had already decided to do something about it, although quite what, as yet, I didn't know. Police work, I had always believed, should be left to those who were best able to do it. But then again, I had never been set upon and that had tended to alter my view. I didn't answer her, just swilled the whiskey around in the tumbler, watching it almost cling to the side. What could I tell her anyway? Inside, the old emotions of anger and frustration welled up. I had never learnt to live with injustice. It got to me.

"You're not saying anything Mike, but you're thinking things. I know you better than you think I do."

I laughed. "Jane, let it lie will you, let's just enjoy a quiet drink." I raised my glass. "Here's to Len, wherever he is."

"But that's just the point isn't it Mike, he's in a hole in the ground." Jane was not one to let the issue go. She raised her glass with a sad smile. "To Len, may he rest in peace?" The peace was interrupted as I found myself looking up into the eyes of Lord Grey who had appeared at our table.

"Mr Sutherland, Miss Brown, it is Miss Brown isn't it?" He paused as Jane nodded. "I trust you won't mind my interrupting you, but I'd like give you both a word of advice. It's this business of Mr Jones. For the sake of the school it would be in everyone's best interest to let it be buried with him. There's nothing to be gained from stirring up bad memories." He smiled an obsequious smile, no warmth in his eyes. My loathing for the man took on an even greater intensity and I stood so that I was on equal terms with one of England's noble class. The old feudal system had a lot to answer for if this was all they could muster at the head of the flock.

"Now wait a minute . . ." I started to say, but he cut me off, with a dismissive shake of his arm.

"No, Mr Sutherland you wait a minute. I'm not going to allow you to cause trouble over this. As Chairman of the Governors it is my responsibility to ensure that the school continues to run smoothly and continues to be successful and I know the Principal is very much of the same mind."

"I bet he is. Anything to keep up appearances eh." I was shaking with anger. "If you cared one jot about the school you would do all you could to look after the welfare of the staff, instead of just running rough shod over them. You never attempt to get them working with you, you just dictate the terms, knowing full well that Fields will follow .Some of you people really take the biscuit." I sat down in disgust.

The man seemed lost for words, but the expression in his eyes spoke volumes and I knew that I had touched on a raw nerve. He continued to stare down at me in undisguised hostility, then turned abruptly away, striding angrily out of the bar, his colleague hastening out after him. I could feel my heart pounding away and I knew I'd done myself no favours.

"You okay?" I looked at Jane and nodded. "I don't think you've won a friend there," she continued. "You have to be careful Mike, he's a powerful man and he didn't like the way you spoke. When you let rip, you don't hold back, do you?" She shook her head in amazement.

"I know." Old enough to know better but still not able to overcome the innate desire to stand my corner. It had got me into trouble enough times to suggest that adverse experiences would generate new behaviour patterns, but so far nothing could overcome my initial gut reaction. My Dad had called me a hot head when I was younger. I don't suppose you can unmake yourself. A man's got to be what a man's got to be I guess. I knew that there had been a few less bullies in my school as a consequence. "I've never been very good at being told what I can and cannot do." I took hold of her hand and gently squeezed it, "I think Len's name has to be cleared."

It's easy to be wise with hindsight, and looking back now, the decision to do something to clear Len's name came not from a noble gesture to help ones fellow man, but from a real dislike of being told what I should or should not do. That decision was to cost me, but then as I said; it is always easy to be wise after the event.

Having taken the path of action, spurred on by what educational psychologists would describe as emotional and behavioural disorder, I didn't actually have a clue how I would go about it. Whilst Ritalin might nullify the symptom, it could do nothing for the cause.

Life in school reverted to type, as the excitement generated by Len's death, and my beating died down. The bruising turned a dirty yellow brown and the cracks began to mend. Social Services and the Children's Act was no longer the topic on everyone's lips, although their autocratic manner had ruffled a few feathers. And anyway, hadn't we seen enough evidence in the papers and on the television, to suggest that perhaps they didn't really know what they were doing. Field's damage limitation exercise, at the expense of a colleague, ensured that the schools Open Evening went smoothly. I found it ironic that even I did all I could to make sure that the displays I put on in the gym were of a high standard and would reflect well on the department. Professional pride I guess. The number of prospective parents remained high, in spite of, or perhaps because of, the local press coverage of all that had gone before.

The appearance of Belinda McKay back in school opened up the wound again and caused some consternation.

FOUR

Robin stormed into my class from next door bristling. He waved year nine down as they rose to their feet. "What the hell am I meant to do Mike?" he asked. "I've just bowled into class to find Belinda McKay there."

"I guess there's nothing you can do, you're going to have to teach her, just like the rest of us." I replied.

"God, that's marvellous, bloody great. We bury a colleague who has been accused of all sorts of improprieties, his wife still suffers the stigma, and this girl can waltz back into school as though nothing has happened. Where's the justice in that?"

"Justice! Don't be stupid, that's a concept, not a reality. You haven't got a choice Robin. And anyway, we don't know that she wasn't telling the truth."

"Well that's rich Mike, are you saying now that he could have in fact done it?"

"You know better than that Robin, but you do have to look at these things from both sides. What if she was assaulted? You can't refuse to educate her for that. The problem is that we are all convinced that Len was innocent. But what if?" I left the question hanging. I was pretty certain that Len had been innocent but like it or like it not, there was always an if with things like this. The old adage 'no smoke without fire' was a difficult one to extinguish. And let's admit it; the Social Services did little to dispel it. The problem was that, with Len dead, there was no way of getting his name cleared, allowing us to kick up a fuss and try to get the Head to move her to another school. Not that I thought we would have much success there anyway. It appeared there wasn't much comeback on a kid who made up stories, no matter how damaging. A lot of it came down to finances. Schools couldn't afford to permanently exclude pupils, for when the child went, so too did the monetary value they represented and most schools had already spent or accounted for that money. Great system?

"This place sucks." Robin shook his head in disgust "I guess I'd better get back, but I'm not happy." He strode out of the room and from the back of the class I could just make out the muted whisper of one of the lads, "Old

Blair's in a stress." I let it go, there was no point in highlighting the fact, and anyway, the observation was pretty accurate. But equally it was worth getting his mind focused again.

"Ah, Larson, you've obviously finished. I want you to outline to the class the difference between volcanoes on destructive and constructive plate boundaries." Got him!

The beginning of December brought with it the usual cold north east winds and the promise of the winter's first snow from the grey uncompromising stratus clouds that hung so oppressively above. But not only did it bring that, it also brought one of the major clashes of our rugby calendar, a fixture that had been set back in the beginnings of our school and one that was fought with real passion. Honours were fairly even, but having suffered a defeat at Berkhamsted's hands last year I was determined not to undergo the same thing again. The biggest problem I found over here was that it got dark so quick which meant there was very little time to practice once school was finished in the afternoon. We were working on sponsorship for some floodlights but that would take another season and so for now one of the best sessions we could have was a work out on the hard courts. I found this was an excellent means of improving handling: double touch in a confined space. I was watching them now. Young lads, moving at pace into space, wrist flicking their passes, calling for support, joking and ribbing each other. It was a great way of getting rid of the day's tension and a good build up for Saturdays match. Yesterday had been the tactical session. I had spent some time going over lineout drills, an area in which we were a little weak. It was crucial that we got it right and won our own ball. That and of course quickness to broken play was the means to our success. Recycle the ball quickly and you gave the backs the opportunity to actually run onto it with confidence and pace and the game today was one that cried out for open running rugby.

"C'mon Sir, we're one short and we're getting a pasting," Richard the loose head prop yelled. He tapped the ball with his foot and sent out a long spiralling pass toward me. I caught it and set off up the court drawing one player before popping an overhead to my support and through he went. "Oh well done Sir," someone shouted, "Silky skills for an old timer." The banter was there but so to was the desire to win and the contest hotted up. I left them to it, the aches and pains of my recent skirmish still not to be ignored. After fifteen minutes I called it a day. The light was abysmal. I gathered them around and stood amidst a body of players, steam rising from their shirts in the cold night air.

"Okay chaps, that's it until Saturday. No parties on Friday night I trust." I looked around at them as they all shook their heads.

"No Sir," Jamie Lee spoke for them all, "Not on Friday, but we are going to get absolutely ratted on Saturday night if we win. It's Sally White's eighteenth up at the rugby club. Should be a good do. Food laid on as well." The guys murmured their agreements with one or two remarks slightly on the knuckle about that hopefully not being the only thing laid, but I let it pass for I knew they were feeling a little hyped.

"Right then, go and shower before you catch cold. But remember, parties are only any good if you win, and we can win, but it will require each and every one of you to be playing at your best. I want to see you hit those guys in tackles that would make the Samoans come to us for lessons."

FIVE

It was tight. Neither side showing any particular weakness in their game, but the tackling of the King James' boys was awesome. The sort of total dedication that I had asked for. We were driving now, sweeping over the broken play as man and ball had been crunched to the ground in one of those body jarring hits, the ball spilling to the deck, to be cleaned up by our outside centre, and as he was wrapped up, he was supported by the loose forwards who kept the momentum going. We took it to the floor, our rucking infinitely superior, and out it came. Pete Brown instinctively glanced toward the blind, noting that our fullback was moving into the attack, and in an instance the ball was spiralled into the waiting hands of the blindside winger who was surging forward. As he drew his man, he flipped the ball inside to the outstretched hands of the fullback and the race was on. Brian Grieves was at full pace now, just his opposite number to beat. I watched as he slightly altered his line of running to angle in towards the defending man and saw the indecision in the defenders face as he was forced to slow his momentum in case Brian cut back inside. At that precise moment, Brian straightened up, kicking off his inside leg to swerve away from the outstretched arms, and run in unopposed behind the posts. Poetry in motion. You can teach kids the basics, make them better than average players, but timing, balance and the ability to read the game were innate. I couldn't help smiling, and the lads on the field were on high, slapping palms as they moved back into their half. I looked up as a loud voice yelled across from the other sideline.

"Sort it out Berkhamsted, what a load of rubbish. What the hell are you doing?" The voice came from a well dressed man in a black coat, and as the game unfolded, he proceeded to yell abuse at his team, the referee and my own boys. I found myself at one stage standing beside my counterpart, Cliff Davies, a quiet mannered man, with a good knowledge of the game.

"Who's the chap making all the noise over there?" I asked, gesturing towards the touch line.

"I'm surprised you haven't come across him before. We have to suffer him on too many occasions I'm afraid. He never contributes a great deal of positive advice. He's an old boy, never played for the firsts, although he likes to tell everyone that he did. He's one of our more prominent gentlemen now. He's running for parliament and using his father's name to help him: Your chairman of Governors, Lord Grey."

What a turn up! It seemed I was never to be free of them, come school, pubs, or playing field. "Great, he seems to have inherited his father's charm," I replied.

"Oh yes, he's done that alright. Even as a junior he was quick to point out who his father was, and look out anyone who confronted him. He was a right little bugger, needed putting in his place. Hasn't improved with age. Told me a few times that I didn't know my job, and that he should have played for the firsts. Unlike his brother, Peter. Now there was a talented boy. His father tried to muscle in on the scene and it took our Head to intercede and make some strong protestations before I was left in peace. I don't envy you having him as a chairman."

"You're not wrong there. We're not each other's favourites at the moment. I've been told he's not the best person to cross."

"And you're still employed! He must be getting soft. God, how did he drop that?" Cliff grimaced in frustration, as the ball spilt from the fly half's hands, putting an end to what had been a promising phase of play. From the scrum, we secured position and Danny Boyd made good the line with a thumping kick, sending the Berkhamsted boys back towards their line. Half time came with the score at seven points to three in our favour and I spent the break emphasizing our strong points and encouraging the boys to continue to take the game to the opposition. We had the game if we could keep the pace of it to our advantage. What we could not afford to do was let the bigger lads slow it down and hold us up, for we simply could not compete with their strength. And that was pretty much the key to the whole affair. We made them react to our strategy, hustling and bustling them, and when the final whistle had blown we had pulled off a great victory: 17 points to 6. Most satisfying.

I joined Cliff and the parents in the dining hall, post match. The talk was as expected: aspects of the game played over, dissected and improved upon. I looked up just as Lord Grey's son strolled into the room and watched his air of arrogance and authority, instantly taking a dislike to his manner, probably tempered by my dislike for his father. I would have guessed his age to be roughly the same as mine, but the obvious signs of good living were to be seen in his paunch and face.

"You haven't done much with that bunch of no hopers Cliff," he smirked. "I mean, good grief, in our day we would have slaughtered King James. Hardly worthy opposition, surely?" He stood looking down at Cliff, waiting expectantly, and gave me an unseeing fleeting glance.

"Well now Eric, that's not strictly true. King James have always proved difficult, and as you are aware, I'm sure, the honours are pretty even over the last few years, if not in their favour," he replied quietly.

"You must be doing something wrong then Cliff. If this were politics you wouldn't stand a chance of re-election on your performance." He looked about him, smiling widely, his rather loud, cultivated, public school voice, rising above the general chatter, ensuring him of the platform he desired. One or two parents looked on uncomfortably. Cliff didn't appear to be too bothered, seemingly impervious to the implied insult.

"Thankfully Eric, this isn't politics. It's sport, the game where on the day, the best team wins. Better still, its rugby, which at this level thankfully, is still unsullied from the input of money or other extraneous influences. Not like politics," he smiled slowly. Eric Grey's face coloured perceptibly. "How is your campaign going?" When Cliff had his opponent on the rack he certainly liked to stretch the point. "I don't think you've met the coach of the opposition team, your father's school in fact, have you?" He turned to me and I watched the eyes focus. "Mike Sutherland, Eric Grey."

"I know your father," I said. I could see that he had heard of me. At least the Grey family didn't suffer from a lack of communication. Just a lack of propriety.

"Mr Sutherland," he acknowledged, recovering his composure. "Well, you know what I think. We should have won. Your boys played quite well, although I would call it spoiling play. Father said you had developed that style over the last few years; that colonial influence, he called it. Some of us purists despise what is happening to the game. Even Mr Davies is trying to adopt it at Berkhamsted!" He stared at me intently, his confidence much in evidence again, back on his stage. Oh well, I wasn't his father's favourite person. I might as well keep it in the family.

"Cliff tells me you played second XV rugby. I'm not so sure that that gives you the necessary credentials to speak with any particular authority on the specifics of the game. I often find that with politicians, prospective or otherwise. They seem to have this inbuilt belief in their own importance and often speak through a hole in their head." In for a penny, in for a pound. The colour was returning to his cheeks again, and I could see some of the parents were taking an interested back seat.

"Now listen here," he attempted to interrupt.

"No, you listen here," I continued, "what you and your father suggest is spoiling play is actually an exciting open style of running rugby involving the whole team, not just the eight or nine that you so called purists would wish to see return. Let me put it another way. Rugby is like a democracy, the whole team has a say in the play. I much prefer that to a plutocracy. Don't you? I'm not so sure that I've seen your father grace our playing fields anyway, which perhaps takes me back to one of my first points." I stopped, and stared intently back at him, watching his jaw clench and unclench, his eyes, narrow slits in an angry face. Emotions close to the surface. I had the distinct impression that he was close to losing his equanimity. With visible effort he turned on his heel and strode out of the hall, not looking one way or the other.

"You've not made a friend there Mike. Phew, in his younger days he would have set upon you. I thought he was going to as it was. He never liked being confronted. Almost got sent down on a couple of occasions. Only father stepping in saved him. I'm not so sure you've done the wisest thing putting him down like that. He won't forget. He could become a powerful man."

"Sod him, chaps like that get on my wick. They strut around thinking they're bigger and better than all the rest. Sometimes they need putting in their place. And anyway, he's not up for my constituency."

"Fair enough, but all the same, keep a watch. I've known him long enough to know that he's a vindictive character. Personalities don't change that much from school days, high office or otherwise."

"How exactly does one get to run as a member of parliament?" I asked. "How does a guy like him get the chance?"

"It's like you told him. It's a plutocracy out there. The rich and wealthy look after themselves." Cliff replied.

"But not for the liberals or the Labour candidates. They don't have that kind of support."

"You seen the papers lately? Anyway, you don't think he's running for them do you?" I shook my head, smiling. "Oh no boy, his posters are all blue, through and through."

A couple of the parent supporters edged over to join us, balancing cups and plates as they stood. I didn't know them but Cliff obviously did. My lot were down the other end of the hall. I would have to go back and join them. It was only politic. An appropriate thought, that. Cliff introduced me. The taller of the two, wrapped up in a green wax jacket with matching green corduroys and Hunter Wellingtons, spoke first.

"A most enjoyable game to watch. We would have, of course, liked to have seen the result reversed, but, well done. Your boys play a fast game, and unlike some of our supporters, we like it."

"Thanks," I said. "We always enjoy playing this fixture."

"Don't let the likes of Mr Grey put you off," spoke up his friend, similarly attired. "He has a charming way about him. We have to suffer him all too often. I couldn't help but hear parts of your conversation with him and I think you gave better than you got. Not many manage that, I might add." An affable man and his manner was equally pleasant and relaxed. Another Lord, Lord George Alexander. The country seemed over run with them.

"Thank you."

"It's George by the way. We don't stand on ceremony here, not in rugby circles. Isn't that right Cliff?" Cliff nodded. "Now tell me Mr Sutherland."

"Mike." I interjected.

"Fine. Now tell me Mike, is that an antipodean accent I can faintly detect?" I nodded. "And I would say, being brave, and looking at the way your boys played today, that you are from New Zealand, yes?" I nodded again. "I thought as much, didn't I William?" He turned to his companion. "We were remarking on the style of your play and I was pretty certain then, and when you yelled at your players a couple of times I was fairly positive." He seemed quite delighted. "But you have to be careful; some of you chaps don't like to be mistaken for the other." He chatted on, obviously a keen talker. "I say, did you think my son played well? I can't really ask Cliff that, it puts him in an awkward position." he winked at me.

"Well, that's a bit difficult. Which one was he?" I asked.

"Oh, yes, right, he's that fair haired lad chatting away to that delectable young lass over there," he said, pointing across the hall to a good looking youth whom I immediately recognised as the opposition scrum half. He was right too, the girl was gorgeous. The memory of Len flashed across my mind. Damn.

"He's good. Good awareness and quick hands." His father beamed. Obviously a proud Dad. It was good to see. "I like the way he delivers to his fly half. I can see you are a keen rugby man George, did you play yourself?"

"Yes, I dabbled a bit. Loved it."

"Dabbled, he says," Cliff chimed in, "He certainly did that. A very modest man is George. An Oxford Blue and an England trialist. That's not a bad bit of dabbling in anyone's book."

"I'm impressed," I said. "What position did you play?"

He laughed. "Would you believe it, I was a wing three quarter." He patted his stomach. "I think I've lost a little speed."

"And now you have a son who is dead keen. That must be most satisfying."

"Indeed. I'm reliving my youth with Gavin. Bit unfair really. William here is the same, aren't you William?" His companion nodded: William Townsend-Smythe, an eminent surgeon, well respected and known in the right circles, as I was to later glean from the conversation. His boy had played well as hooker. William was also a Blue. This was grand company that I was keeping. "I would like to see Gavin do well and make it all the way to the top, something I would have dearly loved to have done. My eldest lad John didn't take to the game. A bit of a disappointment. A bit too much like his mother. Intelligent and sensitive. Damn well made sure the next lass I married came from sporting stock."

"Come now George," William butted in. "You would have made it if it hadn't been for your accident."

"What sort of accident?" I asked.

"I parted company with my Harley Davidson. Mangled my leg a bit. Mangled the bike as well. That was it, end of any thoughts of serious rugby.

It doesn't really prove to be a problem. Things mend, but opportunities pass by. I occasionally get a twinge when I'm out and about on the farm in the cold, but that's about it."

"You have a farm? What type? Arable, mixed?"

"Actually I have a pedigree dairy herd, but also have land under cereal crops as most farmers in these parts do. A far cry from your part of the world. I actually spent some time out your way looking at what some of your countrymen were doing, cow cockies I think they were euphemistically called, yes?" I nodded. "They had some fairly advanced techniques then. I came back and incorporated them into my own setup. Do you know the Taranaki area? Great people."

"No, I'm afraid not. I hail from the other island. My Dad owned a sheep station, the sort of occupation everyone thinks we all do in New Zealand. We lived near Lake Wanaka. Did you get down that way?"

"Only a very brief whistle stop tour I'm afraid. Flew to Christchurch, then went inland. Loved the Southern Alps. Now there's some real mountain scenery. And the lakes. Beautiful. Got to Queenstown and Lake Wakitipu, is that anywhere near where you lived?" He asked.

"Not too far away. Sort of just over the hill, the Crown Range, and into the Cardrona Valley. A bit out in the back blocks, but a fantastic place to grow up."

"I bet. Why on earth did you leave? My memories of it are those of paradise. Does your father still farm?"

"Yes, he's still going strong. My younger brother has gone into partnership with him. I guess I moved on because I wanted to see what the other side of the world looked like, and my rugby playing days like yours, had come to a premature end. Nothing to stop me doing the big overseas experience."

"I see, and you say you played. To any particular level?" He looked keenly at me. What could I tell him? That I had been selected for an All Black trial, only to be at the receiving end of a good kicking which damn

73

near finished me a week before the trials took place, and that I had been tipped as a certainty. I still smarted at the unfairness of it all, but in some respects, that was what you took on when you took to the field. Luckily I was spared from giving an answer, for his son appeared with his girlfriend and interrupted our conversation.

"Pops," he said fondly, a big smile spreading across his face, "I'm taking Victoria home, then we're heading out to a do. Jeremy's got a party organised, so don't wait up, okay?"

"Do I have any say? Just be careful. No drinking and driving."

"Get real Dad, you know me better than that. If I drink, Victoria can drive me back. That's the only reason I take her out. She's teetotal."

"You rat," his girl laughed, playfully punching him on the arm. If that was the only reason he took a stunner like that out, then modern youth were getting their priorities wrong. They waved goodbye, his son stopping quickly to talk with Cliff, before sweeping out. Bright young people with bright futures ahead of them. Lord Alexander turned back to me and apologised for the interruption. I could see that he was a father who was clearly devoted to his young protégé.

"No problem at all," I replied, "and I too must be making tracks. I've spent very little time with my own boys' parents. They will be thinking I'm neglecting them, and especially after today's performance. Sorry Cliff." He shrugged good naturedly. One had to be philosophical in sport. The mighty could be vanquished or equally so, could vanquish. There never was a recipe for guaranteed success. I turned to Lord Alexander and extended my hand. "It was really good meeting you. I'm sure we'll meet again. County sevens perhaps?"

"I hope so," he said taking my hand and firmly shaking it. "I would like to talk rugby with you, and indeed talk sheep farming in New Zealand. Who knows, I could even be convinced to try out with some pedigree sheep on the farm. Why not come over and visit the place? I'd love to show you around." He snapped his fingers, "In fact I've got just the idea, lunch tomorrow, why not eh? What do you say?"

FIVE

What did I say? I said, "Yes."

I woke up looking forward to the day's prospects. Silly as it might sound, the chance to walk around a farm again and get back on the land was a real thrill, but it had opened up a void I thought I had closed for good. I guess one can't completely shut off one's past, no matter how hard one tries. There were memories there that I thought I had extinguished.

I showered, dressed quickly and grabbed a bite of toast with my coffee, not instant; because this was Sunday and Sunday demanded filtered coffee. The sun was streaming through the kitchen window, building up the heat in the room. Alison joined me as I was halfway through my second cup, looking most comely in her bathrobe.

"Mind if I join you?" She asked, sitting down beside me at the breakfast bar.

"No, not at all, be my guest," I said as I grabbed a mug and poured some coffee from the percolator. "You're up early for a Sunday. What's the problem?"

"Does there have to be a problem?"

"Usually, I don't often see you up at this time of the day on a Sunday." She held the mug in both hands, elbows on the bar, staring into space. "A penny for them."

"Decisions, don't you just hate them?"

"Well, you can't really avoid them. It's one of the perks we get when we become adults. We get to make our own, and not have our parents making them for us. So what big decision has come along to disturb your sleep?" She didn't say anything for a moment, just sat there sipping at her coffee.

"This is good," she finally said, "What is it?"

"I've no idea. I picked it up at that little coffee shop in the Howard Centre the other day. The lady said it was good stuff so I took her word for it.

It certainly cost enough. The name is probably printed on the bag. So come on Alison, tell your caring landlord everything."

"That's just it; my caring landlord might not be for much more." She smiled ruefully. "I'm pregnant." That was a bit of a bombshell.

"How? No forget that, I think I know how," I said in response to her wry smile. "Andrew?" She nodded, her eyes filling.

"What am I going to do? Back to that decision thing." She sniffed, searching in her robe for a tissue. I got up and walked across to the bench and pulled off some of the kitchen towel for her. "Thanks"

"What does Andrew say; I take it he knows?"

"Yes. He wants to marry me."

"Well, what you feel about that. Do you want to marry him?" I wasn't very good at this Oprah Winfrey type stuff.

"Yes," she said, emphatically, "I do."

"So what's the problem? It seems to me you've already made your decision. Go for it girl. He strikes me as a pretty decent chap." I patted her arm. She gulped, sniffed and wiped her eyes.

"He is, but that's just it. He's so decent he might be just asking me to marry him because I'm pregnant, and I don't want that."

"Have you asked him whether that's the case?"

"Of course, but he's not likely to say so is he," she bit back.

"Fair enough Alison, but it boils down to trust in the end. There are no iron clad certainties in life. It's all a bit of a gamble. You've certainly proved that. But I bet in your intimate moments he told you he loved you." She blushed, looking down at her bare feet.

"Well, there you go. We're not all bad you know. Some of us say it because we mean it, and not just to ensure that we can make it. You have to trust that Andrew is like that. I bet before this all blew up, you did believe him when he told you. Right?" I squeezed her hand. "Marry him."

"Oh God, you're probably right. Why did it have to happen?" Tears spilled from her eyes, splashing upon the breakfast bar, as she struggled to come to terms with the situation, until it all got too much and she collapsed, sobbing uncontrollably against me.

Breakfast ended up taking a lot longer than I had intended, but when I finally got away, Alison was more composed and setting about to put her life together with Andrew. Good luck to them both, they would need all they could get, but I was pretty certain that Alison had found herself a good man. It looked like the house was going to be pretty empty for a while. Mark's move was imminent, and now Alison. My agent would be rubbing his hands in glee; the prospect of two new contract fees.

The drive to the farm took over half an hour. I could have done it in less, but there was no hurry. The farm was near to the little hamlet of Great Gaddesden, just off the A4146, which ran along the valley of the river Gade. I had travelled this way a few times, but not enough just to take it for granted. I loved the way the countryside could change so quickly just by turning a corner. I turned off the road at the signpost which identified the farm: Coverdale Farm Pedigree Holstein Herd, G. W. Alexander esq. The road up to the house was lined with oak trees which really must have looked impressive in the spring and summer when in full leaf. A couple of hundred yards up the drive it opened out to expose a large rambling farmhouse, barn and other buildings. Unlike a lot of farms which seemed only to be strictly functional, this had the look of one which complimented efficiency with an aesthetic quality. Most pleasing to the eye. I pulled up beside a Range Rover, my tyres crunching on the gravel, the sound quite loud in the stillness of the morning. As I stepped out of the car, I was greeted by two black Labradors, which had come from the direction of the barn. They gave me the once over, sniffed my legs, then seemingly satisfied that I posed no threat, wandered off to sniff the car and leave their mark on my tyres.

"Oy, Nelson, Jonah, get out of it!" I recognized the loud voice of Lord Alexander, and he appeared from the open doors of the barn, attired in a pair of stained blue coveralls, wiping his hands on a greasy cloth. The two dogs slunk away from my car, the younger of the two unable to contain itself, started to nip and worry away at the older one, which snarled back, teeth bared, tail wagging. Off they went, careering across the courtyard and out of view.

"Michael, good to see you. You had no trouble in finding us then? Excuse the state of me. Having a bit of trouble with one of the milking machines. Not up your street is it?" He extended his hand and shook mine firmly.

"Sorry." I shook my head.

"Ah well, never mind. I'll just tell Ronnie to keep at it. He usually gets things sorted out in the end. A good man is Ronnie." I followed him back into the barn, really a converted workshop and garage. To the side, a silver Mercedes was parked along side a silver Golf.

"Yours?" I asked.

"The Mercedes is, yes, but the Golf's Gavin's. I wish he would spend as much time at his studies as he does cleaning and polishing that thing." He gave a resigned shrug, and then stepped across to talk to a man who was engrossed in his work. I couldn't make out exactly what it was he was trying to do but George seemed pleased enough when he came back over to me. "What did I tell you? The man's a genius. Come on, come and meet the wife." He steered me out of the building and we strode across to the house, the dogs once more joining us, walking beside their master in what was obviously their accustomed place. "The young one there," he said looking down at the sleek black velvety coat of the smaller dog, "we got from up in the Yorkshire Dales. Comes from working stock. The owner was a Game Keeper. Good chap. Breeds them small and tough. Gavin called this wee fellow Jonah, after that awesome wing you had in the All Blacks. We hope he doesn't grow as big." He bade them stay as we went inside, into a large, bright kitchen. A large Aga range occupied a good part of one side of the room, the rest tastefully decorated with pine furniture, an enormous table and pine dresser being the main feature pieces. "Virginia, we have company." He yelled, then turning to me asked, "Would you like a cup of coffee?" Without waiting for a reply he moved to fill the kettle and switch it on. "Take a seat."

As I sat down, a very pleasant looking lady entered the room from the door on the opposite side. She had straw blond hair and a face which radiated bonhomie.

"Ah there you are Ginny, cup of coffee? This is the young man I was telling you about. The Kiwi. Michael, I would like you to meet my wife."

I stood up and looked into clear blue eyes and took her offered hand.

"How nice to meet you!" She said. There was a slight lilt to her voice, I took to be Irish, for the timbre was soft, all adding to the image of this most elegant woman.

George left us to freshen up, and his wife sat down with me and chatted away. George and she had met whilst he was in Eire looking at stock. 'I trust I didn't fit into that category', she laughed. She was originally from Cork, but after a quick courtship, had married George and departed for England. She had certainly been a great catch, for her beauty and elegance was so very obvious.

By the time her husband had returned, showered and refreshed, I had learned much about his family, his wife, the tragic circumstances of his first wife's death, and she had found out more about me than I normally disclosed.

"Well now George, you're looking better," she greeted him. "Michael and I have been having a good chat. Did you know he was an All Black trialist?" I grimaced, "But was severely injured. Took a kicking to the head and had to give up. Isn't that a shame?" She patted my hand. George looked at his wife, an amused smile on his face.

"Ginny, you're a marvel. You could entice confessions from a priest."

"I'm sure I don't know what you mean," she replied with mock severity.

"Yes you do. You learn more about people in five minutes than some of us do in a lifetime. Watch it lad, she'll explore and dissect your inner most thoughts if you're not careful. Just as well I returned when I did."

"Oh George, you're a caution. Michael and I were just chatting. Did you know that he hasn't spoken to his father for several years, nor been back to New Zealand?"

"See what I mean Michael. Lulled into a sense of security. She'd make a great interrogator." He obviously knew his wife and damn it, he was right. I had said more to this remarkable woman about my life, than to anyone else in this country, and I had just met her. Frightening.

George took me for a guided tour of his 500 acres. I was impressed by the obvious efficiency of it all. He pointed out one field which stood in contrast to the ordered neatness of the rest and told me that it was set aside. Paid not to farm it. E.U. bureaucracy at its worst. And things weren't getting any easier for them, what with subsidies being removed and quotas imposed and the worry of BSE. George went on to state that they were lucky compared to others, as the farmer down the road was diversifying, setting up a golf course, although he thought it would prove handy.

The Sunday roast still lived on at the Alexander's, accompanied by Yorkshire pudding and fine claret. Conversation was in full flow with young Gavin extolling the virtues of the current England team, when the dining room door opened and a younger version of Virginia Alexander breezed in. Dressed casually in jeans, cream roll neck, and red gilet, she cast a pretty picture. I reckoned she was in her mid twenties.

"Lucy darling, how lovely, I didn't know you were coming home this weekend." Virginia stood up and hugged her daughter.

"Hi Mum, Dad. I just wanted to get out of London and breathe some fresh air. Hey Gav, how's school?"

"Okay thanks Luce. I'm still there, surviving."

She turned in my direction and coolly assessed me. A very confident lady, this.

"Hello," she said. "I'm Lucy."

"Excuse our bad manners Michael, Lucy let me introduce you to Michael Sutherland," George cut in. "And as you have probably worked out, this is our daughter Lucy. She is a solicitor in London." I nodded a greeting. "Michael is a teacher over at King James. I met him yesterday when Gav's team played them over at the school. We lost. Michael came from New Zealand, off a farm, and I thought he might like to have a look around this one. If you want to find out anything else about him, you will have to cross examine him yourself, or ask you mother, who has already done a pretty good job." He turned to me and added, "It came as no surprise to any of us that Lucy would go into law; she's her mother's daughter."

Space was made at the table for Lucy and she joined us for the meal. The conversation was full of cheerful banter, and whilst I felt slightly distanced from it, I equally felt privileged to be part of it. It had been a while since I had sat down with a family for a meal, and this was one family which was very close. The parents admiration for their children was very obvious, but so too was their respect and love for them. You could see it in their body language and hear it in the conversation. The little touches, the laughter and the willingness to listen made for quite a remarkable family. George may have got himself a pedigree herd, but the pedigree of his own family was worth a lot more and spoke volumes.

I left them, later than intended, having spent a much appreciated day, with the echoes of their invitations to return, ringing in my ears.

The mundane side of life however, kicked back into place. We were winding up for the Christmas break, and that meant GCSE mock exams, marking and the interminable reports. Exam invigilation in the hall, amidst the ever present sniffing and coughing of students suffering winter colds, did give me opportunity to reflect, not on the weighty issues of life, but the more immediate and seasonable question: What was I doing for Christmas? The prospect of spending one on my own was not one I relished. I knew where I would like to spend it; cocooned in the company of the Alexander's, but short of inviting myself, and I am sure, being accepted, there was little hope. The 'Lads' were all heading to their respective family homes, and once again extended an invitation for me to join them, but I had invaded their families too often when I needed some company. Even Jane, bless her, had asked if I wanted to spend Christmas in Leicester with her and her family. It came as a surprise to realize that the feelings for Jane that I had recently rekindled had now been snuffed out by the constant thoughts of one Miss Alexander.

Interviews for a new Head of Art were taking place and made me realise that Len's life, his existence in the school, was about to be totally erased. What sort of life was his wife having? What kind of Christmas would they experience? I resolved to ring her, and left the exam hall determined not to be forever bemoaning fate.

Fitness in the gym found the first XV in high spirits. Saturday's game had been our last for the term. A good way to go out and their mood infected mine, so that by the end of the session I was back in a positive frame. I rang Lara Jones from the P.E. office. A rather lack lustre voice answered the phone.

"Hello."

"Mrs Jones?"

"Yes?"

"Mike Sutherland. Just thought I'd give you a ring to see how you are." I paused, no reply. "Mrs Jones?" Still quiet. "Are you there?"

"Yes, sorry, yes, yes I am, Mr Sutherland. It just hasn't been a good day. Some days just seem to get on top of me and I just don't know what to do." Her voice sounded distressed and I thought I could detect the sound of crying.

"Well, I am sorry. It can't be easy. And I'm not sure there is anything I can do to help, but if there is, please let me know. Perhaps I could come round and visit?"

"Oh, um I, I guess that would be fine." Not entirely convincing. Rather hesitant, which I found a little strange. Perhaps I was just being ultra sensitive. In the background, I could hear the sound of the children, then the sound of a doorbell, then no sound. All had gone quiet. "I'm sorry Mr Sutherland, I'll have to go. There's someone at the door. Thank you for ringing." She rang off and I was left listening to the dialling tone, and feeling a little puzzled by her manner. My ego had taken a dent, for I had felt sure she would be keen to see me.

End of term came with a rush and all the usual goings on. My form base were decent enough to present me with a fine bottle of scotch for Christmas and I promised not to open it until the actual day, with side bets on that I wouldn't be able to keep to that, by some of the doubting Thomases at the back. The staff function proved to be as successful as many of the other ones had been: staff and their respective partners standing around in their usual groups discussing the usual problems, only this time at a later hour with a glass of cheap table wine and a paper plate of food, instead of coffee and a biscuit.

The senior management and guests occupied the far corner of the staffroom, suitably divorced from the ordinary masses, with recognizable bottles of wine and china plates. Ah well, life in the economy section at least provided better company. With the wine flowing things eventually loosened up and despite ourselves we began to enjoy the evening, our corner much the loudest and probably the most puerile, but it was great to feel the holiday mood taking effect.

"A toast to absent friends." Jane's voice broke the mood of optimism. She stood up, a trifle unsteadily, raising her glass high and we all followed suit. Her voice had carried far enough across the room for others to hear, and that coupled with the fact that our entire group were standing, temporarily silenced the rest of the gathering. "To Len."

"To Len," we replied. I could see that some of the gathering were looking on uncomfortably. Too bad. Unfortunately I couldn't see what was happening down at first class! "To friends," I added, "without them, where would we be?" We all stood up again and solemnly toasted ourselves, the wine a catalyst to our emotions.

"So, what are you going to do over Christmas Mike, if you're not coming down to us?" asked Robin. "What have you got lined up?"

"Not a thing mate. Just a drumstick on my own, a good bottle of plonk and a relax in front of the tele. Who knows, The Sound of Music might be running again."

"What, you mean you're going to be on your own for Christmas day? You can't do that, look, come down with me. Mum will stick another potato in the pot."

"Listen Robin, I've crashed all of your Christmases at some time or other, and you've all been really beaut, but I can't keep doing it. Even Chris invited me down for welsh rarebit."

"Bloody cheek, my old mum works magic with the turkey and ham. You don't know what you'll be missing boy." Chris assumed an air of mock indignation.

"Listen guys, I do know what I will be missing, believe you me, but this time round I'm going to quietly sit at home. And I will be fine, thank you." I said in response to one or two raised eyebrows. "For Poms, you're okay people."

"Well thanks, coming from you, that's a real compliment. Just how much have you been drinking?" Brian asked.

"No, actually, I think I'll call in on Lara Jones before Christmas and see how she's getting on. She sounded a bit uptight when I rang her. It feels like I've almost forgotten them anyway, and this won't be a very happy Christmas for them." The others nodded soberly, obviously feeling much the same as I did. Loud laughter, somewhat inappropriately timed, emanated from the other end of the room. We looked up to see Lord Grey, his arm draped around Mrs Pringle's shoulders, a little the worse for wear, attempting to dance, his glass of wine spilling everywhere.

"Typical," muttered John, casting a disparaging look in their direction. "Who said God was on the side of the righteous? It doesn't look that way from where I stand." I had to admit he had a point: "I think I've had enough for the night, and I certainly don't want to have to stay here and listen to the likes of him." John drained the contents of his glass in one gulp. The others were doing the same, the night coming to a close.

The first day of the Christmas break was blissfully wasted in bed for most of the morning. The afternoon saw me doing a complete cleaning of the house. We all lived busy lives and what the house got was a pretty superficial dusting now and again, just enough for us to be reasonably satisfied with its state of cleanliness.

I didn't have much reason to do any Christmas shopping, and couldn't see the point of buying myself a present and waiting until Christmas day to unwrap it. As far as I was concerned, Christmas was not for those who were on their own. I didn't even exchange cards with my family. I hadn't spoken to my brother or father since my mother's funeral. I had said it all then in a passionate outburst, beside the grave as we filed past and threw in the customary dirt onto the coffin. As far as I was concerned Mum had no right to be there, and they were to blame. The Sutherland family wasn't a family anymore.

Welwyn Garden City on a Saturday afternoon. Food shopping needed to be done. Always such a busy time. Mums dragging complaining children back and forth, looking hassled. Shop assistants looking harried, everybody in such a rush. I was watching one young mother with a couple of little girls when it struck me that now was as good a time as any to visit Lara Jones. But before I did, I needed to hassle a shop assistant myself.

Lara Jones looked terrible. Where as once she had been a stunner, she was now unkempt, no obvious pride in her appearance at all. Her clothes were all crumpled and her face looked puffy, her eyes ringed with black smudges.

"Mrs Jones, hi. As I said on the phone, I thought I would pop over and see how you are."

"Mr Sutherland, yes . . . come in." She stepped back from the door and gestured for me to enter. I stepped into the hall. Her two little girls clung like limpets to her dress and as I put my hand down to ruffle one of their heads, she flinched and stiffened. Christ, the little kid was scared stiff. It was dark in the living room, the curtains pulled. She switched on the light and asked if I would like a cup of tea. Whilst she was out making it, I looked about me. No new paintings hung on the hooks where Len's had been before they had been slashed about. No photo of Len was anywhere to be seen. I thought that a bit odd. Mrs Jones came back with a tray, minus the two little girls, and handed me a mug of tea.

"I see you haven't put anymore of Len's paintings up yet," I said for starters.

"No, I just haven't got round to it," she replied. "Anyway, most of them were destroyed." All the vitality of the woman had disappeared. Everything seemed to be mechanical.

"You should, they really were very good." She said nothing, just sat there staring at her tea. "How is your sister, does she get across to see you much?" She nodded. This was hard work. I had expected her to be coping better than this, but she was obviously still very distressed. Her little girls slunk into the room, not daring to make eye contact with me. They sat huddled together, a sorry picture. Nothing at all like the family I had met when Len had first been suspended. I had brought in with me a bag, and I reached across for it. "I hope you don't mind, but I thought the girls would like a little Christmas present to put under the tree, or whatever." I leant across to hand out the wrapped gifts that the shop assistant in John Lewis had informed me was all the rage this year. The girls shrunk back, obviously afraid. What the hell was going on?

"Thank you very much Mr Sutherland, what a lovely thought." She whispered to the eldest girl, who tentatively edged towards me and received the presents. No big smile, no thank you. No anything. Mrs Jones eyes were filled with tears and I could see that she was struggling to keep her emotions under control.

"Oh, it's nothing. They haven't had much of a time of it of late. I guess they must be missing Len a lot." She didn't say anything, so I ploughed on. "It may be a stupid question, but are you alright?" No response, just silence. "I know that when my mother died I was extremely angry and I did some pretty stupid things, but in the end you have to get on with living. Len was a good chap. You should hold on to that. Don't let gossip destroy what you both had. You have two lovely daughters; Len would want to see them grow up happy and confident." I paused. Mrs Jones sat very still, tears running down her face. Very quiet. I sat, looking at the happy family that once had been. Why would anyone have wanted to destroy them? It made no sense. If only people thought of the knock on consequences, before they launched into something. You could never just hurt one. There were always others involved.

"Did you . . . do you really believe that Mr Sutherland?" Mrs Jones voice broke the silence that had descended upon us. She stared at me, desperately.

"Yes. Look, I didn't have a lot to do with him at school, but I've heard good things spoken of him by pupils. If anyone has their finger on the pulse, then they have. They know who is okay and who isn't." I went on to tell her what the guys in the team had said about him. When I finished, the tears had started again.

"Thank you," she whispered. "Thank you for telling me that. It means a great deal. Oh Len, what have I done?" She rocked back and forth on the sofa, arms tightly folded. I didn't know what to do or say. What had she done? Probably nothing. I imagined that she had had some doubts about her husband. For God's sake, in her position that was only natural. We weren't all blessed with unshakeable faith. I stood up to leave. The best thing I could do was leave her and let her sort her emotions out. She looked up. "Don't go just yet," she implored, "I have something I would like to give you." She left the room, returning after a while with a parcel wrapped in brown paper. "This is from Len," she said. "He would have wanted you to have it. It always amused him. I found it with some of his stuff in the attic." I looked at the parcel she held out for me, intrigued. "Open it when you get home." I took it from her, thanking her. I was pretty sure I knew what it was. "Thank you Mr Sutherland." She took my hand. "Thank you for coming." She rubbed her eyes with her other hand and shook her head. "What a mess! Why did it happen?" There was nothing I could say. I didn't know the answers. Sometimes there weren't any.

Death had a way of having the last say. This time it was my father's. He died of a heart attack whilst out on the farm, died doing what he loved best. God rest his soul, the old bugger. Sixty five made of iron. Far too young. I thought he would last forever. In spite of everything, I felt robbed of the chance to square things up, and that feeling surprised me. I had convinced myself that all of that was a thing of the past.

The phone call came from my brother in the early hours of the morning. No one rings with bad news midday. It seemed that Iain had dug my number out from a cousin I still kept in touch with in New Zealand. We kept the call short, neither of us prepared to bury the hatchet that ill will had created, even with Dad no longer there. Iain said that the funeral would be in the week between Christmas and the New Year if I felt like turning up. I said I would think about it and then he rang off. I spent the remaining hours before day break reminiscing, dragging up the memories that I had tried to bury. Dad had been a great father when I was a kid: Had driven me miles to rugby games, had always been there to support me. I wasn't so sure I had paid him back in kind. He had been my fan club and critic, there to build me up when my confidence had taken a hammering, and there to keep my feet on the ground when all and sundry were singing my praises. The fact that we were too alike to climb down and make our peace had kept us distanced, now for eternity. By dawn I had decided to go and bury the old sod, and hopefully bury a lot of the anger that had eaten away at me for so long.

Another phone call woke me from a fitful sleep, mid morning. This time a welcome call, the voice at the other end belonging to Lucy Alexander.

"Hello, Michael?"

"Yes?"

"It's Lucy, Lucy Alexander. Look, I got your number from Dad. This is going to sound a little forward, but you did say the other day that you would quite like to see where I worked, and well, we're having a Christmas party here on Friday night, so I just thought you might like to come along. I know it's short notice, the fact is, my partner and I have just split . . ." Wonderful, I was a last minute thought. But, what the hell, last minute or not, I was a thought all the same. "Hello, are you there?"

"Yeah, sorry. Good to hear from you."

"Perhaps that didn't come out as it should. I really would like you to come to the party with me."

"I'd love to come Lucy, believe you me, but I'm going back to New Zealand for a couple of weeks." Typical, the chance to take her out and I have to turn her down. Nice one Dad.

"Oh." Could I read a lot into that? She sounded disappointed; I hoped it was because she would be missing my company and not just a partner to go with.

"I actually hadn't planned to head back. I got a bit of bad news. Got a call during the night from my brother. My father has just died." Saying it sounded so final.

"I'm sorry Michael." Her voice was soft and gentle, not really what I needed. I wasn't good at handling compassion; it brought the defences down.

"Yeah, well. . . . ," I couldn't add anything more. I could feel myself starting to choke up. I took a deep breath, swallowed a few times and willed the tears to go. There was no noise at the other end of the phone, but I knew she was waiting for me to continue. I forced myself to get control. "He died of a heart attack. My brother said it was instant, nothing anyone could do."

"I truly am sorry Michael. Sorry that I rang at such an inopportune time," she apologised.

"Don't be silly, how could you possibly know it was a bad time to ring, and anyway, I'm delighted that you even thought of me. Tell you what; if you are free tonight, how about having a meal with me?" Sutherland was pushing his luck here a bit, but it got the desired result.

"I'd love to. Where?" Good question.

"How about I meet you from work? You probably know some good places and I can sort out some travel arrangements before I meet you." We arranged a meeting time, spoke a little more, and then said goodbye. I padded round the lounge, feeling extremely good. The effects of last night had gone and my mind raced with thoughts of what I had to do. Alison had left a message on the board saying that we were out of toilet paper and bread, and would I get it please as I was the one on holiday. Mark had scrawled a profanity beneath that which didn't speak highly of the teaching profession, and put the time beside it: 7:30 a.m. Too bad.

I showered quickly, dressed and headed into the village to pick up the articles Alison had requested. Another grey day, the cloud low and thick, but somehow it didn't seem so bad. The chance of some time with Lucy had put a shine on it, in fact had blotted out the bad news, and I felt a little guilty about that. I knew, however that my father would have laughed and told me not to be such an idiot. He had always believed in taking opportunities when they came. Life was all too short. Chores done, I left my own note to the effect that I would be home late as I had a date, and not to wait up, and headed down the A1 carriageway into London.

Lucy looked stunning. I had successfully arranged my travel details with a popular travel firm, had had a look around the city which I hardly ever bothered to do, then walked to the Haymarket where we had arranged to meet, outside New Zealand House, where else! She was standing there, black coat wrapped around her, a red scarf high on her collar and her blond hair finishing the picture. This was some girl.

"Sorry I'm late, I went further than I had anticipated," I offered, by way of apology. She turned towards me and smiled, her whole face lighting up.

"Actually, I think I'm a little early." We stood looking at each other. She raised her eyebrows and smiled a little nervously. I took the initiative.

"Come on, let's go and have a drink. I'll take you to the pub I worked at when I first came over here." We set off down Pall Mall, and the chatter began to flow after a slightly hesitant start. Lucy was an intelligent woman, quick to laugh. The sort of person who could put you at ease, and I guess, lull you into a sense of security, then pounce. Great qualities for her job. We walked up St. James and crossed into a little street running just behind the Ritz. On the corner stood a little pub known as the Blue Post. It was here that I had spent some memorable days and nights, my first introduction to London life, and I had enjoyed the cross section of society that frequented the bar, from office workers, to croupiers, to barrow boys. I pushed open the door and guided Lucy in, expecting to be hit with nostalgia, but the place had changed, the bar seeming noisier and more smoky than I had remembered. Lucy had a white wine and I ordered a pint of Guinness for myself. We were lucky to find a table at the back, and squeezed in.

"Cheers," I said. She raised her glass.

"Cheers. So what have you done in London then?" She sipped at her wine, gently swirling the glass in her fingers between each sip.

"Just being a bit of a tourist again. I shot up Regent Street before I met you, to have a look at the lights. Not bad. It's the first time I've seen them since coming over here. It's a great atmosphere, I love the way the shops are all done out, and the pubs too." The Blue Posts itself was regaled with tinsel and streamers and added to the festive spirit.

"Did you get your flight booked?" she asked. I nodded. It hadn't been easy. I had got virtually the last seat on a Singapore Airlines flight, leaving in a day's time.

"Yep, I fly out early Thursday. Straight through, only a quick stop over at Singapore for a couple of hours."

"I'd love to fly across the world."

"Well, if I could I would get you a ticket and you could come with me," I said, half in fun.

"Maybe next time. I'm so sorry you are going back for such a sad reason," she replied. I looked into her eyes, God she was beautiful. She had removed her coat and scarf, to reveal a simple but smart black dress, the v of the neck cut perfectly to offer a suggestion of her figure, and I found it difficult to stop my eyes from straying. "What are you thinking?" she asked, bringing me back to my senses.

"Honestly?"

"Yes, why? Is it so bad you can't tell me?"

"No, actually I was thinking of how extremely pretty you are," I replied, watching her reaction and seeing a hint of colour come to her cheeks. "You did ask?"

"Perhaps I didn't expect such an honest reply. Are you always so forthright?"

"I guess so. Can I get you another drink?" Her glass was empty and she continued to fiddle with it.

"Please." I pushed my way to the bar and ordered her another white wine. "So where do you suggest we eat then?" I asked as I sat down again.

"Well, it depends what you like to eat really." She replied. She took a sip of the wine and waited for my reply.

"Anything and everything. From fish and chips to McDonald's, to Indian and Italian. We New Zealanders are not very discerning with our tastes.

Lamb or mutton normally does the trick." I smiled. It wasn't quite true, but it fitted the popular image.

"With Anchor butter, no doubt," she laughed. "Anyway, I took the liberty to book us a table at Mulligans. It's Mum's favourite place to eat whenever she comes to London. Says it takes her back to her youth. You should enjoy it too. The Irish stew is probably made from New Zealand lamb."

"Sounds good, what time are we booked for?" The table was for eight, which gave us about an hour to kill. It wasn't the weather for walking the streets window shopping, so we sat it out in the pub amidst the smoke and the general hubbub. She told me she had gone to Exeter University, got a first in Law, then got a job with her current firm, because of her father's connections. Somehow, I couldn't see a law firm keeping her on if she hadn't proved her worth, connections or not. She had just finished with her boyfriend of eight months. He had according to her, been interested in vintage cars, his work and her when he could fit her in. She had just had enough of fitting in last. What a fool he must have been. They still saw each other simply due to the fact that they worked together. Well, if I had anything to do with it, there wouldn't be much reason for them to want to start up again.

We made our way along Piccadilly and up the Burlington Arcade, until we came to the entrance of Mulligans. The bar downstairs was crowded, but the restaurant was upstairs, and although busy, was reasonably quiet. I could understand why Mrs Alexander enjoyed coming here, for the food, although quite simple, was beautifully prepared, and tasted superb. We took our time, enjoying each others company in the convivial surroundings. I was reluctant to have it come to an end, but like all good things, it had to. I drove her back to her flat in Wimbledon and saw her to her door. We had already agreed to see each other again on my return. She offered her cheek and I kissed it, a light perfume filling my senses.

"Goodnight Michael, thank you for a lovely evening. I hope you are able to sort things out when you get back to New Zealand. You and your brother have to set things right, your Dad would want it like that." She said, more like an older sister, than anything else. "Ring me when you get back." I said I would, and left her, feeling on the top of the world. A world which certainly had its ups and downs.

They must have got out of their parked car just as I was getting out of mine. I didn't at first see or hear them, my mind still occupied with thoughts of the evening I had just spent. It was only as I turned to look up the street that I registered their approach, my brain taking in their purposeful intent and the dark balaclavas which hid their faces. Shit, not again. Images of the last time flashed before me. This time I could see no baseball bat. Thank God for that. They had cut off any flight of escape into the house, as they had split up. Both were fairly heavily built, both darkly dressed and both wearing leather gloves. Gloves would save knuckles I thought wryly.

"I take it you're not making a courtesy call then," I said to the closest guy. He said nothing, just came on in silence. Oh hell, this time I wasn't going to wait to see what they could dish out. There was no way I could take them both on; perhaps I could do something to one at least. I turned quickly, and sprinted towards the furthest one, catching the one beside me by surprise, but I reckoned on speed and a thumping good tackle as being my only advantage. It had done damage on the rugby field in earlier days. The guy I was racing towards looked up, and made to meet me, his fists swinging up on guard, but he stood no chance. My blood was boiling, all the pent up anger of the last few months coming to the surface. This one was for Len. I hit him hard and drove him backwards, the air coming out of him in a whoosh as we landed with a crash. As he struggled to get up I kicked him hard between the legs and he let out an anguished cry, the fight going from him as he clutched himself in agony. Good. That would teach him. I turned in time to see the other one approaching warily, the way he moved suggesting he was a lot more practiced in this type of situation than his friend. He wasn't going to rush in, and the blade in his outstretched hand cut silent slices of air. I bent down beside the retching figure on the ground and grabbed his head.

"If you continue to come towards me I'll crack his skull," I spoke a little breathlessly. It was all I could think of.

"Do what you like, I don't much care. The stupid tosser should have sorted you out. It's his problem." The balaclava spoke in a deep voice. Great. Now what? At least I could get a look at one of them. I ripped off the balaclava of the man I held, to reveal an unknown face. It was a face I would remember though: Pinched and rather acne ridden and capped with mousy blond hair, undercut at the sides. I put him at about twenty.

"Ya can't do it can ya," sneered the other guy. "So what are ya going to do now mate, because I'm thinkin I'm gonna cut ya up a bit? Then maybe you'll learn to keep away from certain people, and stop asking questions. It's not liked. And if you don't, we'll come back again until you learn to keep away."

Keep away from who? I didn't have a clue what he was talking about. At least he wasn't thinking of doing away with me permanently.

"Look, I don't know what you are talking about. Who do you want me to stay away from? And why?" I couldn't see any point in getting roughed up if I didn't know the answers.

"You keep away from Lara Jones, as if you didn't know. We were told to teach you a lesson so that you would remember. So teacher, you're gunna get a lesson," he laughed.

"What is it about low life's like you?" I asked standing up. "You talk big and tough when you have a weapon in your hand. But without it, you're a waste of space. Whose dirty work are you doing? Obviously someone who hasn't got the bottle to do it himself. Acne face here," I said pointing down at the lad on the ground who was making desperate efforts to sit up, "wasn't up to much. I can't see why you would be much better."

"Think what you like teacher, but from where I stand you look a bit scared to me." For a thug he was quite astute. I couldn't think of anything I could do. Fighting guys with knives wasn't something I had made a habit of. I guess this was to be my initiation. His knife was swishing hypnotically from side to side, then suddenly he lunged forward. I just had enough time to jump out of the way, before he lunged again. Damn, too slow, the blade cutting through my jacket into my arm. A horrible feeling, but no great pain, yet.

"That's for starters," laughed the balaclava man. "Want some more?" I said nothing, but could feel the warm stickiness of the blood running down the inside of my arm. "C'mon hot shot, let's see what a big rugby star can do then." He urged me forward, mockingly. How did he know about me? Apart from disarming him and beating the answers out of him, I couldn't see how I was going to find out. And for the moment the odds on me doing that were certainly long. We continued to circle each other. I contemplated making a dash for the house, but realized that I had little chance of getting the key in the door and inside before he caught up with me. Pity the house didn't unlock like the car. The car! I grabbed my keys from my pocket and hit the panic button and was rewarded with a strident repeating horn and flashing indicators. The move took balaclava man by surprise and he swung round to assess the new situation. It was now or never. Before he had time to turn back I was on him. I punched him hard on the side of his head, hard enough to make me wince as the skin over my knuckles split. He staggered back, dropping the knife, mouthing obscenities. I hit him again, as he turned, a crunching blow to his nose and it cracked sideways.

"Fuck you," he mouthed, spitting blood.

"Not tonight, thanks." I replied sucking in the air. I moved forward all set to hit him again, but luckily the fight had gone from him, and he backed off, still obviously groggy. A light had come on in my house, and in the one next door. Amazing, people did respond to car alarms. A pyjama clad Mark opened the door.

"Mike?" he said peering into the night light.

"Yeah," I answered, relieved to have some friendly company.

"You alright? What's going on?"

"Ring the police will you," I yelled. "There's a thug here trying to knife me." Mark hesitated at the door, then he must have remembered the previous occasion and was galvanised into action, disappearing without adding another word. Good. Balaclava man had retreated away from the noise of the car, and away from trouble, which suited me. He yelled a parting comment.

"I know where you live teacher boy. Watch out. Next time I'll bloody do you." I refrained from replying. My arm was starting to hurt which was pretty much standard reaction once the danger had past.

Mark reappeared in the doorway, golf club in hand. From where I stood it looked to me like my three wood. He looked around and a little hesitantly stepped out toward me, stopping when he saw acne face still on the ground.

"What did you do to him?" he asked looking down at the pathetic figure still clutching his testicles.

"I would have thought it was fairly obvious," I replied, smiling. "I booted him in the nuts, hard."

"Jesus Mike, you could have done some serious damage to the poor guy."

"I'm sorry Mark, next time I'll pat him on the back and tell him to be a good lad and leave. What the hell was I meant to do? There were two guys out to beat the living daylights out of me. And you didn't exactly bring out my three wood to invite them for a game, for Christ's sake." He looked at the club in his hand and smiled a little sheepishly.

"Yeah, you're right. It's just when you see someone a bit distressed, you can't help feeling sorry for them." He looked closely at me as he spoke and his eyes wandered over my arm and I could see them dilate slightly. "You're bleeding." Almost an accusation.

"Yeah, I am. I hope you feel sorry for me as well, because it hurts like hell." I pushed the alarm button and the car went quiet. "I'm going inside to get something to put on my arm. Would you mind waiting out here for the police?" He didn't look too keen, but nodded all the same.

"What do I do if he tries to do something?" he asked, gesturing towards acne face.

"Practice your swing," I replied, and left him.

By the time the police arrived I had managed to staunch the flow of blood on a temporary basis, but I knew the cut would need stitches. All in good time. Mark brought them through the front door and into the kitchen where I stood at the sink, shirtless. One of them had acne face with him. The poor guy still looked in agony, and the arrival of the law had not done anything to improve his state of mind. They pushed him onto one of the kitchen chairs and then turned to me.

"You don't look to good Sir, you'll have to get that seen to." said one of the officers. I looked closely at him. It was the same policeman that I had seen at Len Jones' following the last incident.

"It's D.C. Carmichael isn't it?"

"Yes Sir. Have we met somewhere?"

"I met you when you were called over to a house of a colleague who had been beaten up. We met at the door." I answered. He looked at me closely and I watched as the recollection dawned.

"Right, yes I remember you now Sir. You seem to have your fair share of trouble." I went to answer but his colleague interrupted.

"Right now, I'm Sergeant Coombe. I wonder if you would be good enough to give us a statement. Then I think you should get yourself to outpatients and get that cut seen to. What exactly happened?" I proceeded to tell him everything, and they interrupted on a number of occasions to clarify points. Acne face was taking much more interest in what was being said and had developed a very morose down trodden manner. They questioned Mark as well, and when Alison wandered into the kitchen they politely stood for her and asked her some questions as well, but there was nothing that she could tell them. However, through some clever encouragement they managed to get Mark to discuss the first incident and he painted a very accurate picture, if not a somewhat uncomfortable one for me, as I had no wish to go through that again. They looked at me accusingly and asked me why I had not reported it to them. How could I explain that it had been a personal humiliation and one that I had wanted to sort out for myself? I could see as I tried to explain, that they were not particularly sympathetic.

"I think it would be in the public's best interest if matters like that were reported to us Sir," Sergeant Coombe gently admonished me. "How can we get the likes of those sorts of people off the streets if the public don't keep us informed? Obviously it is far too late now, but it does give us another angle on the case of your deceased colleague. You see Sir, we are still trying to sort that one out, but as yet we have not managed to uncover any leads." Fair enough, I guess he had a point. I just hadn't wanted to share what had happened to me with anyone at the time, and afterwards I had thought there was very little point in making a fuss.

I managed to tell them one or two bits of information which they seemed to find interesting, especially the fact that the men had been clad in balaclavas last time. They turned on acne face with renewed interest and I could tell that he would be in for a torrid time at the station for the rest of the evening. I promised that I would call in, in the morning and help with their enquiries. They seemed satisfied and with that they escorted acne face out the door. I dressed again and drove myself to the hospital and waited the usual hour or so before being seen, stitched and sent home. Sitting in a hospital waiting area with the odd assortment of people that it seems to attract at that time of the early morning, was not the most riveting way of spending my time. There were the usual drunks, the ones you couldn't quite work out why they were there, and a young mother with her crying baby. The literature was non existent, and I had little to do but think. What a night it had been! Initially a very pleasant one with Lucy, which now seemed an age ago. But then the latter event Why would anyone want to warn me away from Lara Jones? What possible reason could there be? It wasn't as if I was getting close to discovering who had beaten Len and me up. I had absolutely no idea. But this was getting to be a bit of a regular occurrence and one I could certainly do without. I suppose it was good that the police were now involved, they might find out what was happening. I hoped they would. This was not the type of life I was accustomed to.

When I woke the next morning, my arm felt like it had been set on fire. I had thought that the stitching would sort it out, but if anything it had made it worse. They had given me some pain killers to take, and I gladly succumbed. When the pain had eased, I set about packing. I planned to travel light, but as usual, by the time I had finished there was more in the case than I had intended. I left the usual sundries to pack away at the last minute and congratulated myself for being so well organised. It was only when I dashed out to the local chip shop for some lunch that I saw the brown package, from Lara Jones that I had left in the car, and later on the kitchen table. With slightly salt and vinegary fingers, I unravelled it to expose a painting of a hunt scene with a difference. I could now appreciate what Lara had meant, for I too couldn't help but have a bit of a laugh. The central theme of the oil painting was of a master huntsman being unseated from his mount, whilst dogs and other horses milled about. A picture of great commotion and activity, and a rather odd subject, yet it did have a sense of appeal. The look of concern on the other huntsmen's faces was well captured, and the almost disbelieving expression on the unseated rider spoke volumes. There was such vitality and colour on the canvas that I knew I would hang it in the living room. It would certainly be a good talking piece, and would be a real memory of an excellent artist.

I wrapped up Christmas presents for Alison and Mark, in her case, a bottle of perfume, recommended by one of the shop assistants I had hassled at John Lewis. In his, two free introductory golf lessons at Knebworth Golf Course, with a note on the gift voucher complimenting him on the way he held my three wood and that he showed great promise. I also knew that he wanted to take up golf but had never quite got round to it. I put the parcels under our small artificial tree to join the others that were there, some of them coming from the kids in my tutor base, as well as the lads in the 1st XV. There might not be any perks in teaching, but there were rewards.

SIX

*H*eathrow near Christmas was jam packed with holiday makers heading out to somewhere hot. I joined the queues of waiting travellers, and waited. Whilst others cursed and complained, I enjoyed the chance to soak up the atmosphere. I hadn't done enough of this. I had got too involved in my own little world and forgotten that there was a much bigger one outside. I knew I wasn't travelling back for a holiday, but regardless, I couldn't help feeling excited by the prospect of visiting home again. Flying economy class for over 24 hours with a brief stopover at Changi Airport is not everyone's idea of pleasure, but I was enough of a kid to still enjoy the novelty. Even the food seemed acceptable, if not the timing. I was not one for sleeping on aeroplanes and the recent press over deep vein thrombosis kept me jiggling my legs like a Parkinson sufferer and travelling the length of the plane on numerous occasions, much to the consternation of the passengers beside me.

My first glimpse of the coastline of New Zealand filled me with an excitement I had not thought possible. What is it about mankind and his attachment to his homeland? How do you rationalise that? Over the centuries men had risked their lives to save their nations. I didn't know how this embedded feeling became instilled within each of us, but I knew without doubt that this was my country I was peering down at. I watched as the landscape unfolded. Early summer, but the Southern Alps still cloaked in snow. Magnificent peaks, carved up by glistening rivers that threaded their way down towards the coast to the fringe of flat land: the Canterbury plains that they had made and finally over Christchurch city and my first point of call. It was as if my system had gone into overdrive. Senses picking up different yet familiar smells. The air had its own quality, a quality which pervaded more than just the nose, triggering a whole response, a reawakening. And I loved it.

I made my way through customs, enjoying the familiar twang of the accent, and once through, located a car hire firm, before steering my newly acquired Honda Accord south towards State Highway 1.

Familiar sites brought with them a rush of memories. It seemed the closer I got towards home, the stronger they became. Different places had their own particular relevance and I could see in my minds eye, my parents, Iain and me at different stages of our life. They had been happy times. Damn it all, I was going to miss the old man dreadfully. I wish I could have told him. A bit bloody late now. But not too late for Iain. That was a sobering thought. Easier to deal with the unattainable than have to face what I had basically run from. To err is human, to forgive is divine. The trouble was: I had never felt much like a saint.

I stopped off at the coastal town of Timaru and found a suitable motel overlooking Caroline Bay, a pleasant spot dominating the centre of town. A chance to catch up on some much needed sleep and delay the inevitable. But like everything, the inevitable eventually arrives. In my case a little later than need be. I had taken the road inland from Timaru, stopping off at various points along the way before eventually driving out of the tussock hills of the Lindis Pass and up towards Wanaka, a beautiful little town on the edge of a glacial lake, humming with the summer holiday makers. Then, on up the Cardrona Valley towards the homestead. Things had changed a bit. Dad had obviously gone with the flow and looked towards deer farming as a viable alternative to sheep, but what was really surprising was the money they must have spent on constructing a ski field, obviously quiet over these summer months, but the home paddocks had been converted into a large car park and ski complex. George Alexander would love to see this type of diversification, I thought. Meeting Iain again was a strained affair, but his wife Catherine (I had heard that he was married, hadn't got an invite) worked hard to keep the peace. He had got himself a good wife. She made sure that I was comfortable, had even moved their little daughter, my new niece from her bedroom so that I could once more occupy my old room. Whilst the décor was now different, closing the door on the first night home took me right back with an almost suffocating emotion so that all the hurt that I had carried these last years over whelmed me. I lay there half hoping that my parents would come through the door and wish me good night, as they had always done when I was a kid. Mum had always liked to go through a sequence of prayers, Dad a gruff 'sleep well son, don't read too late' and a tussle of the hair. I spoke more to them that night than I had done for years.

Over the days leading up to the funeral, my brother and I gradually sorted our feelings out. Time heals wounds, as talking helps understand. A couple of late night sessions where the beer and the talk flowed, helped us put to rest both our parents and our animosity. It was wonderful to belong again. Iain recounted the events which led to Mum's death. He had needed the closure, had carried the guilt for so long. Whilst I had been the one to rant and rave and look for blame, perhaps I should have understood their grief as well. It appeared that she had driven Dad and Iain back from Wanaka following a rugby match when they were both the worse for drink. Mum was not a confident driver at the best of times, and I imagine that she had been reluctant to have to drive. Late at night on an icy stretch of road, they had skidded and overturned and Mum had put the steering wheel through her chest. I guess mine had been an illogical reaction, but I had been extremely close to her, and had felt robbed of saying goodbye. I knew what Dad and Iain could be like once they got to drinking and they knew Mum had not liked driving. I was angry that they had put her in that position, but emancipation was a little slow in coming to the back blocks, and Mum was not one to make a fuss.

It was sad saying goodbye to the old man. He couldn't have had a better day for it: hot and dry. The sort of weather that found him striding about in a pair of old army khaki shorts, with a black vest covering his leathery skin, head covered with a Stetson style hat.

He had a good send off. He was a well liked man, had been active in so many of the clubs that rural life offered. From an elder in the church, a Master in the Masonic Lodge, to Captain of the bowls club and Chairman of the Rugby club. The church in Wanaka was full to overflowing with the cross section of society that he had mixed. Iain spoke well of him, recounting the many adventures of his life, so that at times the church rocked with laughter as his exploits were remembered. Dad had been a colourful man, embracing life to the full, never taking half measures. We threw a wake in the woolshed, dug a pit for a hangi, and once the food was covered and cooking, proceeded to follow his example and drank to his memory, no half measures allowed.

As I flew out of Christchurch, I felt more at ease with the world than I had for a long time. I had spent some good days fishing the lake, with Iain, had gone deer shooting with Pete, cousin, long time confidant from boyhood through University, and hunter extraordinaire. Joined them both with their wives for some memorable nights, found myself wanting Lucy to be there with me. Knew without doubt how completely she would fit in.

London was grey, cold and extremely busy. A stark contrast to what I had left behind.

Lights were on in the house and as I walked in Alison greeted me with a hug and a kiss.

"Welcome back," she said, releasing me from her grip.

"Thanks, it's good to see you looking so full of the joys of life," I replied. "Things are obviously working out, yeah?"

"Yep," she grinned, "Andrew and I have found a nice little place just up the road. It's lovely. Mum's taken the news pretty well, considering." I knew that that had been worrying her. "In fact, she said she was looking forward to becoming a grandmother. Can you believe that?" she asked incredulously. I had met her mum on a couple of occasions and quite frankly, I couldn't. "We've even set the date for the wedding, and Andrews's folk have been super. So, its good, isn't it?" Again a big smile.

"Certainly is. I'm really pleased for you." I squeezed her hand.

"There is just one other thing though Mike." She hesitated and I wondered what was coming next. "I was hoping you would give me away." She looked questioningly at me. Alison's Dad had died a number of years ago.

"I'd be proud to," I replied. "When did you say the date was?"

"I didn't, but it is in early April, so you won't have to miss any rugby either!" I grinned, and made out that the thought had never crossed my mind. "So anyway, enough about me, how was your trip home? Obviously the weather was good, because you have a disgustingly healthy tan, for which I hate you. I'm soon going to be fat and white, like a big basking whale." I told her all about it, over a decent cup of tea. I had missed that. The tea back home hadn't tasted as good. I told her about my brother, his wife and family, the funeral, then the lazy days on the lake, swimming and fishing. It had been a necessary opiate, a chance to recharge flagging batteries.

"It sounds idyllic, why on earth have you come back?" she asked.

"It is, and I'm not sure. Probably to keep an eye on my tenants," I answered. "At the moment I have a strong desire to pack up and head back, but life isn't that simple. I know that I would miss a lot of the things I like over here, once I went back, so I guess I have to work out exactly what I want." I had spent a lot of time weighing up the pros and cons of both places. With Dad no longer alive, Iain had asked me to consider coming back and taking on a partnership with him. The ski business was thriving, drawing in Australian and Japanese tourists with money to spend. It was an attractive proposition and I had told Iain that I needed some time to sort things out and think about it. In our new found fraternity, he was more than willing to allow me as much time as I needed.

I crashed willingly into bed, the twenty six odd hours of flight taking their toll and slept the sleep of the innocent, not emerging until some twelve hours later, once again to look out onto a cold grey winter's day. One day of holiday left until it was back into school. I had no plans, apart from stocking up on some very necessary provisions. The cupboards were looking bare, Mark had obviously been too busy to do much in the way of shopping while I was away, and Alison had been caught up in her own world. I took the opportunity of driving past Len's home, on the off chance that I might see Lara, but I didn't really feel like making a formal visit. That side of things had seemed very unreal whilst I was away. Iain had expressed his anger about what had happened when I had talked with him, in much the same manner I had felt. The whole escapade seemed unreal, and for the moment I didn't feel like entering back into it again. I told myself that it had nothing to do with the threats that had been levelled at me, but deep down I wondered if I was just kidding myself. Driving past her house brought everything back so vividly and it was with a sense of guilty relief that I could see no sign of her. I had hung the painting of Len's in the living room first thing in the morning. Why had that painting amused him so much?

"Well it's obvious you didn't stay in this neck of the woods." Jane was the first to greet me as I sauntered into the staffroom. "Where did you pick up that tan? And all the time I was feeling sorry for you and wondering what you were doing for Christmas. I can see I needn't have bothered." She sounded a little piqued. It was funny how a tan could irritate. I guess it represented an escape.

"Hello Jane, good to see you again."

"Hi Mike, did I sound envious? I'm sorry. It's just that you look so healthy. Where have you been?"

"Yeah Mike, it's obvious you didn't have a white Christmas, wherever you were, or have you started sunning under a lamp?"

"Not yet Chris, although there are days when I'm tempted. How are you mate? Have a good Christmas? Was Santa generous?"

"Yes, yes and yes actually, but perhaps not as good as yours."

"Well I'll tell you what; we'll spend the first part of the inset discussing my Christmas, because I don't feel like spending it discussing curriculum matters, okay?"

"Fine by me boss," said Chris, picking up his notes and heading out the door. "See you in ten minutes."

I checked my own pigeon hole, chatted to the "Lads," who also gave me a hard time until I gave them the run down, and headed off to the P.E. office. Chris and Jane expressed their sympathy over Dad's death, listened with some astonishment at what had happened to me prior to flying off to New Zealand, and requested a quick disrobement to convince them that I wasn't delving into the realms of fantasy. The scar still looked quite raw and probably worse than it really was.

"What's going on?" was Chris's reaction. "What silly bugger's mucking you about, and why?"

"I wish I knew, but I haven't got the faintest notion. Obviously it's all tied up with Len's death, but I can't understand why. I mean the guy is dead, so what possible harm can there be in talking with his wife. It beats the hell out of me?"

"Perhaps she's having an affair with someone, perhaps she already was before all this blew up," Jane offered. "It does happen you know," she replied in response to Chris's and my reaction.

"Yeah, and it's always the man's fault," Chris said in mock disgust.

"Well I guess it could be a reason. Perhaps someone is worried that she might tell all, although I can't see how that would be a problem. I mean, it's not exactly a crime is it?" I couldn't see any reason for what had happened. And I had certainly spent long enough trying to sort it out in my mind. It just didn't make any sense. I guess there were a lot of things in life that you could say that to.

"What will happen now?" Jane asked. "They know where you live. What happens if you go back to see Mrs Jones?"

I shrugged, "I guess I have to be careful late at night."

"Will you go back to see her," she asked.

"I guess so. She gave me a painting that Len had done and I want to know why she said it had amused him so much. And anyway, I'm not too fond of being told who I can see and who I can't. I don't like being pushed around."

"Well be careful Mike. Next time it could be really serious. Don't be the hero."

"There are no worries on that front Jane. You're looking at one of life's natural survivors. I'm fast. If there's trouble, get out on the double," I laughed.

"Unfortunately that isn't really the case," she replied. "Don't forget, I know you Sutherland."

"I couldn't forget that," I interrupted.

"No, let me finish. As I was saying, I know you. You have this thing about not being pushed around. A sort of, nobody mucks Mike Sutherland about, attitude. Isn't that right Chris?" she said, turning to him. Chris grinned one of his slow smiles. I had seen him smile like that to pupils who were giving him a hard time, and then watched as he systematically destroyed them. A hard man. You didn't muck Mr Williams about if you wanted a quiet time. This time however the smile went all the way to the eyes.

"I call it kiwi arrogance," he answered. "You know, the I come from God's chosen land, attitude."

"Oh come on, that's a bit steep," I protested. "I'm not like that at all. You're making me sound like an Aussie."

"Oh yes you are," they both replied in unison. I decided at that point to direct our thoughts more to matters concerning the department. It seemed safer territory, and the rest of the day dissolved into discussion on GCSE mock results, rugby fixtures and lacrosse and netball matches.

With the pupils back in school, the Christmas break was quickly forgotten, almost as if it had never happened. New Zealand seemed a long way away both in miles and time, and if it wasn't for my new P.E. kit that I had purchased over there with the distinctive logo, much to the envy of the boys, it would have been easy to believe I had never been there.

Period two and I was running late. It was one of those mornings. I raced down the corridor towards the Geography block knowing that Robin would offer some witticism as I went passed his room. As I shot round the corner I collided with a pupil coming the other way.

"Whoa, steady on, you're on the wrong side, are you okay?" She had knocked into the armload of books I was carrying and had taken a bit of a tumble.

"Yes Sir, thanks. Sorry, it's just I'm late for my lesson." She picked herself up and brushed the dust off her skirt.

"Where are you meant to be?" I asked.

"I should be in art Sir, but I had to see the Head." I looked at her more closely. I hadn't seen her since before the incident. She wasn't as vivacious as I remembered, in fact looked rather drawn and dowdy. Where had the spark gone?

"You're Belinda McKay aren't you?"

"Yes Sir." She seemed a little embarrassed that I knew of her. I wonder why she had seen Fields.

"I thought so. Last time I saw you, you were shaping up to be a good wee tennis player. Have you kept that up?"

"Yes Sir." Her face lit up for an instance, before fading just as quickly. "I have been practicing indoors, or I was until recently, at the sports centre, but I haven't much bothered for a while now." Her voice trailed off. Not a very happy little girl.

"You had better hop off to lessons before you get into trouble." Strike while the iron's hot. I stopped her as she made to move off. "I want to see you at lunch time if you don't mind. P.E office, okay?" Her eyes widened slightly. I had the feeling she knew what it was that I wanted to talk with her about. I hadn't known that I would, but the chance encounter was too good an opportunity to miss.

"Yes Sir." A disconsolate reply and I watched her walk away dejectedly. I was dabbling in a minefield and I was pretty sure that if I put a foot wrong I would be dealing with a lot of flack.

"You what?!" An incredulous Jane. "Have you lost your senses? Mike, she accused Len of trying to molest her when he was alone with her in the art room. And you told her to come to the P.E office."

"Yeah, I know, but we're almost always in the office together at lunch at some stage or other."

"What would you have done if Chris or I or anyone else hadn't been there? Did you think of that? And Fields will go spare if he gets wind of this."

It was break time and I had managed to catch up with Jane in the office. She stood leaning against the filing cabinets looking at me as though I was a complete idiot.

"You know what he said to the staff at the end of term." I didn't need to be reminded. In one of his outbursts in briefing he had warned of the dangers of harassing pupils, and although no names had been mentioned, it was obvious to all and sundry, that we were to leave Belinda McKay alone and to let her get on with her schooling. Robin had sat at the back snorting in disgust, which had not gone unnoticed by the senior management team, and had evoked a heated exchange of words and a public dressing down. Fields had much to learn about handling people.

"I was sort of hoping that you could be around actually." She stared at me for a moment before taking a long drink of her coffee. Those blue eyes of hers flashing back to me.

"Mike, you're the limit. Not only do you want to get yourself in trouble, you want to drag me in as well."

"Come on Jane, it's not like that at all. I simply want to talk with her to find out what really happened to her. You were the one that got me in to this in the first place. Remember?" She nodded her head slowly in acceptance. "A couple of months ago in this office, you found Len's address, we went and saw him, went to his funeral, and when I suggested that was the end of it all, you got in a stress. And at the moment it all seems to have been a bit one sided. I've been beaten up, knifed and threatened. And I don't know why. That little girl might have some answers. I need you there Jane so that I don't get accused the way Len did, and you want to know what happened don't you?"

"Okay Mr Sutherland Sir, you've made your point." Jane's face had reddened a little and her eyes burned a little more fiercely. "I'll be there."

"Good. Thank you." I stood up and lightly punched her on the arm.

"You can be pretty bossy you know, just don't come on too heavy handed with her. I've got to go. I've got a couple of girls wanting to see me." I watched her disappear out the door. I had upset her a little, but she was a resilient person and I knew she would bounce back.

"Come in," I yelled in response to the knock on the door. It was pushed slowly open and Belinda McKay walked hesitantly in. I had not had that good a look at her when we had bumped into each other in the corridor, the lighting not being that wonderful anyway, but I knew that my impressions had been correct. She was nothing at all like the girl that I had given some tennis coaching to. The sparkle had faded and she stood uncertainly before us, a rather dejected, plain young girl.

"Put your bag down if you like and have a seat." She did it all rather automatically and sat in the chair I had pointed to. "Miss Brown is here just so you don't feel too uncomfortable." Jane nodded a greeting. "You've had lunch have you?" I asked. She nodded. "Good." I paused, uncertain how to continue. Belinda herself gave me the opportunity I needed.

"Sir, what did you want to see me about?" She asked the question in a timorous voice and I had the distinct impression she was extremely nervous, almost afraid. But why?

"Well Belinda, it's no secret that it was you who was implicated in the affair over Mr Jones, and I just wondered . . . ." I got no further. She sat bolt up, panicky, bewildered and agitated, and protesting strongly.

"It's not true Sir, I wasn't having an affair with Mr Jones." She looked from Jane to me, her eyes darting back and forward in distress. Jane made moves to comfort her as I quickly tried to reassure her.

"It's alright Belinda, that's not what I meant. You've just misinterpreted what I said. What I meant was that it was over you that Mr Jones was suspended." It didn't sound a great deal more comforting, but it did have the effect of calming her down a bit. "I was hoping you could tell us what did happen with Mr Jones." I was out on a limb here, but the question had been asked. We sat in silence for some time, and I watched as she fidgeted with her cuffs, obviously trying to come to terms with some inner turmoil. She breathed a big sigh, and began to shudder, tears spilling down her cheeks. A sad little girl.

"It's okay," Jane said. She went over to the cupboard and grabbed a handful of tissues and handed them to her. "Here."

The poor girl was utterly distressed. Great racking sobs shook her whole body. We waited and after some time the storm abated. She sat looking down at the floor.

"I can't tell you," she said in a small voice.

"Can't tell us what?" Jane asked.

"Anything."

"Who told you that?"

"They said I must not discuss anything with anyone, except my parents, or there would be trouble. They said it would be in the best interests of Mr Jones. And now look what has happened!" Her voice rose. Close to hysteria, and the tears, always close to the surface, spilled over again, splashing down onto her hands which lay tightly clasped on her lap. She didn't seem to notice. We let her cry, waiting for her to find her own time. And then it burst. "They killed him because of me. I didn't want him to die. He hadn't done anything wrong. He was only trying to help me. He hadn't done anything. They saw us talking together in the art room. They killed him!" Her tear reddened eyes stared blankly into space, almost as if we weren't in the room. Christ, what was happening here, what the hell had we opened up? I looked across at Jane, her face was grim white, the implications of what Belinda had said had obviously not been lost on her either. She caught my eye, then looked towards the girl, who seemed to have withdrawn within herself, rocking slowly back and forth, arms folded tightly across her chest, oblivious to everything.

"Mike, what's this about?" I didn't have an answer. Hell it wasn't what I had expected at all. This was dynamite. She sat perched on the chair, seemingly oblivious to the both of us. Withdrawn into herself as though seeking refuge. It was all a bit alarming.

"Shit Jane. Look at her. What the hell do we do now? Belinda?" I shook her shoulder, but there was no response.

"Mike," a panic stricken Jane. "We have to get her to the school nurse." I nodded in agreement, but then thought of a better alternative.

"No, bring her down here. I don't want the kids to see her in this state." The door of the office opened, interrupting any further conversation.

"Afternoon fellow sport enthusiasts, how goes it?" Chris stopped in mid track his eyes focusing on the cocoon like figure of Belinda. He turned back to me, eyebrows raised. "Jeez, what gives Mike, what's the matter with her?"

"She's basically blanked out. Shut everything out, doesn't want to deal with the thoughts she's having, I would guess, but I'm no psychologist." Chris looked questioningly at me. "It's Belinda McKay," I said by way of explanation. "I bumped into her this morning and decided to ask her a few questions about Len Jones. I guess it was too much for her. The poor kid must have been under enormous stress, but this makes things a little tricky. Fields will go ape."

"Bloody ballistic I'd imagine. You know we were told to leave her alone." He looked at me almost accusingly.

"Yeah, but it doesn't get us any answers does it, and what has happened? Bugger all. Not a bloody thing. I know how this looks. Shit! I didn't expect her to go like that. But it all seems to have been swept under the table. The need to know principle gets up my nose." I could feel myself getting annoyed. "It was a spur of the moment thing, but it did prove one thing."

"What?" he asked.

"That there is more to all this than first meets the eye." Chris looked a little quizzically at me.

"How do you make that out?" He looked back at Belinda, who still rocked gently back and forth, still heedless of her surroundings. He shook his head slowly. "You could have dragged up unpleasant memories which she was trying to suppress," he added. "Hell Mike, she could be in real trouble."

"Whatever," I answered, still feeling a little irked, "but what of Len's family? Who helps them, who keeps the trouble from them? Absolutely no one. They haven't got a father or a husband to look after them any more, and what's being done?"

"Mike." Jane's voice cut into my tirade. "I think Chris would understand things a bit more, if you told him what Belinda had said." She was right, of course. I took a deep breath, and let the tension ebb from me and then filled Chris in with the details. His response was much as mine had been, and he looked again at the girl.

"That's dynamite Mike. What are you going to do now? Why would anyone want to set Len up?" My thoughts exactly. I didn't have an answer, couldn't even begin to think of one. I shrugged my shoulders and rubbed my temples. I could do without this. Jane had knelt down beside Belinda and was talking softly to her, gently rubbing her hand. I couldn't make out what she was saying, she just kept quietly speaking. We watched, wondering whether it would have any effect, but the girl just kept curled over in a semi foetal position.

"I don't think I'm getting through," she said, standing up and looking at us. "I think I'll go and get the nurse."

"No," I said quickly before she took off, "it would be better if you stayed here and Chris or I went." I didn't want anyone getting hold of the fact that she had been left alone with two male staff, in her state. We were in enough trouble as it was.

Mrs Johnston was a fairly forthright lady, and not one to be messed about. She had been with the school most of us reckoned, since it was built, dishing out TCP, and very little sympathy, to many a poor pupil attempting to duck out of a lesson.

"Right then," she boomed, bustling into the office, Chris tagging on behind, "what's been going on? Not another one of your boys injured again Mr Sutherland? I'm sure I don't know what you do to them." She stopped, her gaze resting on Belinda. "Dear, dear," she tutted, "the poor lamb, what's happened here?"

"I think she's basically gone into a sort of coma," I replied. She looked sternly at me and I found myself rushing to explain, like a transgressing little school boy. She had that effect on me.

"I think we had better get her up to the surgery and call the school doctor. I don't like the look of this." She knelt down beside Belinda and talked to her, telling her what we were about to do, but she might as well have been talking to a brick wall for there was not a flicker of response. Chris and I lifted her up and carried her along the corridor and up to the surgery, aware of the inquisitive stares of other pupils. News of this would be around the school quicker than wildfire. It wouldn't be long before Fields had something to say. Thank God he was out at one of his consortium meetings. Having left her in the care of a fussing Mrs Johnston we made our way back to the office.

"What now Mike?"

"Good question. I think I'll wait until I hear what the Doctor has to say."

Mrs Johnston got back to me just before school finished to say that the Doctor had seen Belinda and had had informed her parents that she should be admitted into hospital for observation. Time would tell, but for the moment there was no change in her condition. She then went on to say that in future, should I have questions to ask pupils, perhaps I should learn to be a little less imposing so as not to scare them witless!

"Michael?" Lucy Alexander.

"Lucy, great to hear from you. I've been thinking about you, you know." Quite a lot actually, but I hadn't wanted to rush straight to the phone on arriving back.

"Thanks for the postcard." I detected a slight coolness in her response. I waited, and the pause grew longer. And then it came. "Why haven't you rung me? I wasn't sure if you were back or not. Then Gavin had to return to school, so I assumed you must be. Or you hadn't come back at all."

"I'm sorry Lucy; I got back a few days ago and seemed to have been snowed under with things. And I didn't exactly know how we stood, I mean, you might be back with your barrister friend again."

"Listen Mike Sutherland, if we are going to be going out, then we need to sort out a few ground rules." This sounded good, and like an idiot, I realized I was grinning. She proceeded to ground me in the required procedure, and the banter became frivolous, the tension evaporating.

I rang off much later, feeling positive for the first time since my return. I had even managed to discuss what had taken place in school and in good lawyer fashion Lucy had offered advice. Free, well almost. There was one stipulation: I had to take her out for dinner over the weekend. I thought I could manage that.

I knew the following day would prove to be a difficult one, and when I was summoned to Field's office immediately after briefing I was prepared for the worst. I looked in on Miss Pringle.

"I hear the boss wants to see me," I remarked flippantly. "Is he in there now?"

"Mr Sutherland, I have been told to ask you to wait downstairs until you are summoned. So if you wouldn't mind." She pursed her lips in her usual tight way, turned back to her computer, and pretended to be busy typing a letter.

"Okay, give us a yell when he's ready, but don't blame me if year nine runs amok. They're in the gym on their own." I left that as the parting shot, and slipped down the stairs to the general office, satisfied that at least I had caught her attention, for I had seen her reach for the phone. Very shortly afterwards, I was summoned back up.

There had been a time when I found entering the head's office a daunting experience, but not now. If you truly respect someone, then you don't like being reprimanded by them. I didn't particularly care what Fields had to say to me.

"Mr Sutherland, Mrs Johnston informs me that you were the last person to speak to Belinda McKay. I wonder what you have to say about that?" He sat back from his desk, waiting.

"Yep, it's true, I did speak to her yesterday, and yes she did go into some sort of shut down. I'm sure Mrs Johnston filled you in with the details. I believe she called the ambulance and went with her."

"Yes she did," he replied, a little quickly, a sure sign that he was agitated. "And what I fail to understand is why you talked to her in the first place, when I had specifically instructed the staff that they were to leave her alone, and secondly why you didn't go to a senior member of staff immediately, once you realized there was a problem? A situation like this does not reflect well on the school. If anything gets out to the press it will be your neck on the line. I hope you realize that. If you go charging into affairs which do not have anything to do with you, then you must face the consequences. Do I make myself clear?" His voice had risen slightly. Deja vous. Sod it.

"Loud and clear." I countered feeling my heart beginning to pound. My blood pressure was taking a hammering these days. "Basically, Headmaster, I talked to Belinda McKay because the opportunity arose. I can't sit around and pretend that nothing has happened, that it's all finished. I see a sad little family struggling to come to terms with the loss of their father, and I see this girl in school, and you know what?" My own voice was going up now, "I think it stinks." He started to speak, his face visibly reddening. This was old territory for the both of us. I ploughed on. "If she can't handle what has happened, if she feels guilty because nothing actually did happen, then great. This whole bloody set up does nothing to protect the teacher, and we all know kids tell whopping stories. So if you want my opinion, she's blanked out because she can't face the reality of it all."

"I gave explicit orders for her not to be questioned. You have gone right against that. You have absolutely no right to do so." He banged the desk to enforce the point. "That poor girl has had an awful experience, and you have just brought it back to her. I will not have you flagrantly disobeying what I have said. Do you understand that Mr Sutherland?" He stared angrily at me.

"Oh, I understand all right, but there's something not quite right here. I'm not sure who exactly it is you are trying to protect." Fields looked stunned, his face puce, then he visibly collected himself and launched into the attack.

"I'm not sure to what it is you are alluding Mr Sutherland, but I don't like your tone, nor what you imply. I have tried to protect no one but the poor girl," he shouted, standing up in his rage.

I stared down at him, loathing him for being the type of man he was. "That's about the extent of it," I shouted back. "You didn't give Len Jones or his family one bit of help or advice. You just left him. There was never any support. He didn't belong to a Union, he had nothing. You could have offered advice, made it all a bit easier for him, but you didn't. As far as you were concerned he was guilty." I stopped in disgust, and tried to calm myself down. The fact that Belinda McKay had actually said that Len had done nothing was not something I wanted to share with Fields just yet. Knowledge is power and this was knowledge I had no wish as yet, to share. Len had died because a girl had lied about him. But why she had lied needed an answer. Who were the they she had referred to?

"If you understood anything about procedure in these matters Mr Sutherland," Fields voice cut across my thoughts, "you would know that my hands were tied. I had to follow the book..." I went to cut in, but he overrode me... "And the book says that anyone under suspicion must be removed immediately from the premises." He made a gesture with his hands, a bit like Pontius Pilot washing away his responsibility, I thought.

"That may be the case, Headmaster, but at any time did you bother to check his story out? Did you ask him to tell what had been going on? Did you give him a chance to speak out for himself? Or was it just a case of telling him to go because of what you had heard? You could have been a bit more compassionate."

"When someone has been accused of molesting a child in my care, I am not in the habit of being particularly compassionate. Surely you are not suggesting I should be?" He added, a little smugly, obviously feeling on safer ground.

"Well, I would like to think that I would be," I replied. We had both come down from the ceiling, the initial duelling done for the moment. "Everyone deserves a chance."

"Yes, well it's easy to be idealistic and so on when you don't have to answer to the decisions that you make, but I'm afraid the buck stops with me, and I can't jeopardise the school's position, on a whim. Rules are rules." His voice rose again.

"Rules are made to be broken," I countered. "They are a purely utilitarian devise for the good of mankind as a whole. But sometimes the rules can be bent to help man as the individual."

"Then that is where we differ again Mr Sutherland. Society relies on the acquiescence of rules for its very survival. If people choose to ignore them, or bend them, then society collapses."

"Are you telling me that you have never bent a rule, never done anything wrong?"

"That is hardly the issue here," he replied a little impatiently.

"But surely it is Headmaster; you bent the rules when you got rid of Len. Belinda McKay never complained of anything. Someone made the whole thing up and you reacted to it. She was never even questioned until later. That's bending the rules." Bugger it, I hadn't meant to say anything but it shook him, I could tell, but I had to give him credit for the way he composed himself.

"And how have you come to that conclusion?" he asked.

"Because the girl said so herself before she became traumatised," I replied.

"Well, of course she would," he said, "she was obviously frightened and told you what she thought you would want to hear. Surely even you can appreciate that?"

"What I saw was a disturbed young girl. What I don't understand is why she was feeling like that."

"I think the only confused person was you Mr Sutherland, so let me make you clear on one issue. You will not question the girl again, ever, nor will you continue to make trouble over this issue. It's finished, and I will not have you bringing the good name of this school into disrepute. Should I hear of any instance where you have gone against my orders, then I will have no option but to bring you to a disciplinary hearing with the Governors. And that Mr Sutherland is that. I suggest you run off back to your lesson and do what it is you do best. Teach. Leave the running of the school to those who are best suited to it. Thank you." He turned away and rummaged in his desk, the meeting obviously over. Arrogant and patronising. Two qualities I didn't much admire. I walked to the door, and turned back to him before leaving the room.

"Someone's lying here, and it is either you or the girl. I intend to find out one way or the other. The truth has a habit of coming out in the end." With that, I turned on my heel and strode out the door before he could reply.

It seemed a long week one way or the other, and I was glad to see Saturday appear. I just wanted to be away from school, and I was looking forward to resuming the rugby. It was always a bit of a hit or miss affair first game back after the break, the boys willing in spirit, but weak in body, when it came to keeping fit. I hoped they hadn't lost it too much. County matches had finished during the first week of the holidays, and I had missed two of the games, but was pleased to hear that on their performance in those two games, Jamie Lee and Brian Grieves had been chosen for higher honours; at divisional level. Great stuff. I was delighted for them, as I was for Lord Alexander when I read the team sheet which showed that young Gavin had also been selected. I was in no doubt who would be the more pleased of the two of them. And with that in mind I rang to congratulate them both. He was thrilled that I had phoned.

"What do you think of that then?" he asked. I told him that I thought it was great and thoroughly deserved, and I could almost hear him purring with delight.

"Well, we're pretty pleased at this end." He had no need to tell me. I could hear it in his voice. "I spent a bit of time over the break with Gavin helping him to speed up his delivery, when he wasn't with his young lady. I've told him that too much sex would go to his legs, but he assures me not to worry, that when he's with her, he doesn't want to speed up his delivery. Cheeky bugger." I could hear the pride coming through his words. "Mind you, he does know how to pick them." I thought back to the first time I had met them both, and had to agree. "So how was Kiwi land? Did everything work out alright?" I told him it did, and then he suggested that I come over for dinner again on Sunday. "That okay with you Ginny?" I heard him yell, "and bring Lucy with you. I hear you are going out for dinner tomorrow night. God knows how you can afford her. She has expensive tastes, that young girl of mine, gets it from her mother."

"Well, if my savings get too depleted, then I'll suggest we go Dutch, or McDonald's. I can just about afford the latter on my salary."

He laughed. "In this liberated age, why not suggest she pays. Knowing Lucy, she would probably like the idea."

"I'm not quite there with that yet," I replied, "so I'll just have to struggle on till the pennies run out, and then see what gives." I found George Alexander a very easy man to talk with. He had the knack of conversation, making the trivial seem interesting.

Saturday was hardly the conditions to inspire fast open attacking rugby. The pace of the game slowed in the mud. We did our best to keep to our game plan, but in the inches deep mud, playing it out wide wasn't the easiest. Bishop Stortford had a big pack, were well coached, and they had enough outside to threaten us. We employed a system of 'lost cause' ball, which simply meant that we did not commit all and sundry to the mauls and rucks, if they had taken it in, but rather hung the forwards off, ready to pressurise when the ball came out. It worked. They hit and drove anything back over the advantage line all day and we eventually scrambled out the winners 18 - 15. A most satisfying victory.

Lucy had driven up from London early afternoon. I had left her with directions to the house, and by the time I had returned to the school on the coach with the teams, had the designated pint with Chris at our usual, discussed the days play and returned home, she was already there. I found her in the kitchen, sitting talking to Alison, a mug of tea in her hands.

"I take it you two have met then?" I said as I walked through the door. Alison smiled.

"Yes, Lucy has been telling me all about the work she does."

"Boring her probably," laughed Lucy. Alison shook her head.

"Not at all. She's obviously very good." She smiled knowingly at me, and I tried to ignore it. "I've told her about my predicament. She's a very good listener. I found myself telling her everything." She looked almost bemused by what she had said and I found myself smiling.

"Don't worry about it Alison, it runs in the family."

"How did the rugby go," Lucy asked, "Did you win?" I nodded my head.

"Yep, we sure did. It was a tough game, but thankfully we came through in the end."

Alison spooned some coffee into a mug, filled it with boiling water and handed it to me. "Well, at least that will put you in a good mood. You should see him if the unthinkable happens and his team loses," she said to Lucy, "not a very good sportsman really. He gets all morose."

I poured in a bit of milk, grabbed a stool and sat with them, choosing to ignore Alison's comments. What chance would I have of defending myself against the truth anyway, in the presence of a barrister? We chatted for some time, interrupted only by the arrival of Andrew. With introductions made, I grabbed a South African merlot, and we moved through to the living room. Andrew mentioned our previous meeting there and after some pestering I had to explain to Lucy what exactly had gone on. Alison added more detail when I left it out, and in the end, I ended up telling them the whole story. Lucy connected that, with the business at school with Belinda McKay and was horrified to hear of the further attack outside my house. We spent some time discussing possible reasons for all this actually happening but no one in my opinion came up with anything plausible. The whole thing seemed totally unrealistic anyway, like something out of a book, and not something that I should be part of.

With the wine consumed we eventually decided to eat out together at the Indian in the High Street. It felt good to be out as a couple.

When we returned to the house, they said goodnight as they wanted to be up early to have a look around some show homes to get ideas for their own home.

"They're a nice couple," Lucy said as they left the room. "I really enjoyed tonight, thanks."

"My pleasure Mademoiselle." I looked down at her, sitting on the floor cross legged, relaxed and soft, and fought the impulse to kiss her. The intuition of the Alexander women was obviously most acute, because she looked up at me and smiled, the gentle light of the fire accentuating her features.

Here I was, too close to thirty for my own liking, and my heart was hammering away like a kid on his first date, and the stupid thing about it was I felt like I was on my first date. Her hand enclosed mine and she made up my mind, gently pulling me down onto the floor. I could feel her breath on my face, smell her, and then I was tasting her. Lips so warm and moist and pliant. My mind raced through possible outcomes, further adding to the heady excitement and it was some time before we finally came apart.

"Whew," she whispered, her face flushed. "I had better go while my reputation is still intact." She lay with her head resting on my chest and I leant forward and lightly kissed it.

"You don't have to you know. You can stay."

"Don't tempt me Michael. I'm not old fashioned at all, but don't you think it's a little soon for us to be jumping into bed. Much as I would love to, the way I feel at the moment. I want you to want me, but not just for the sex."

"Lucy, without a doubt I want you. And yes, I would very much like to be in bed with you, but you do mean more to me than just that." She went to interrupt. "No, listen. It's stupid for you to drive all the way back to Wimbledon or home at this hour of the night, so stay, but not in my bed, unless you get a change of heart, but in the spare room."

"You don't have a spare room Sutherland. And I was just beginning to think that the age of chivalry had not died in New Zealand." She whacked me on the leg.

"Hey, steady on. You pack a big punch there. You might have bruised me," I protested.

"Don't forget it either. I was brought up in the country, and we country girls can look after ourselves." She punched me again just to prove the point, and I was convinced.

"If my learned friend would hear me out, rather than resorting to bar room tactics, then she would realise that the offer I made was wholly upstanding." She looked quizzically at me and I went on to explain that Mark had left, moved on by his company at the start of the New Year. It was a shame really, for I had begun to appreciate him as a friend. It happens when one shares some interesting moments together. And hell, we even used the same club. In our case a three wood!

"So you see madam prosecutor, in this instance you hadn't actually researched all the information. The defendant pleads not guilty to ulterior motives, although accepts that they do lie close to the surface, and should the opportunity arise, he may find himself incapable of resisting the temptation." I punched her lightly on the chin, and she bowed her head in mock acquiescence.

"Mr Sutherland, forgive me for my mistake. Is there anyway I can make it up to you?" I went to reply with the obvious, but she cut in . . . . "Apart from that."

"Well, let's see. How about putting the kettle on and making us both a cup of tea?"

"Agreed." She sprang to her feet, kissed me quickly on the lips then disappeared into the kitchen. I lay back in the chair listening to the noises she made as she searched through the cupboards, looking for cups and tea bags, humming a tune I recognized but couldn't put a name to. It felt good, right, to have someone like Lucy to share the house with. We talked into the night, and as the fire died, and the glow of the embers faded we kissed goodnight on the landing and went our separate ways. Damn. I lay awake in my double bed thinking of her in hers, wearing one of my pyjama tops, and had some trouble getting off to sleep. I hoped she was having the same problem. I did quite like the fact that she hadn't been too easy, or at least that was what I was trying to tell myself as I finally drifted off.

"Nice to see you again Michael," George Alexander greeted me as I stepped out of my car, "and you too daughter." Nelson and Jonah did their customary inspection as I shook his hand. He looked searchingly at me as he continued. "Did you have a good evening last night?"

"Very good, thanks George, good food, excellent company. You have a fine daughter." I knew to what he was alluding, but I thought I would let him suffer. I guess if I was a father, I would be considering the same sort of things, regardless of my daughter's age. Lucy, however, rescued him from his plight.

"Oh Dad, you're so transparent. I'm nearly twenty seven. I'm a woman who makes her own decisions in life. You have to let go sometime." George nodded in capitulation. "And anyway, sex is to be enjoyed, and provided you respect one another and know what you are going into, then there's no great sin involved. You told me that when I was going off to University." She stared challengingly at him.

"You're absolutely right Lucy. It's just that old habits die hard." I stood by listening. Good for old George. A liberated Lord, almost.

"Well this time my Lord," she replied in a posh accent, "you need not worry. Michael is a true gentleman. I stayed at his place, but in his spare room, so my honour, whilst hardly intact, remained unsullied on this occasion." She stared defiantly at her father. He stared back, then laughed.

"Sorry Love and apologies Michael. Just call it a father's prerogative. Last time, I promise. Anyway, come inside. It's too cold to stand out here and chatter. Cup of coffee?"

The rest of the day proceeded much as the previous time, although this time I felt more a part of it, accepted into their closeness. Someone liked by their daughter and therefore liked by them.

They were keen to listen to my time in New Zealand, upset for me that my father had passed away, but delighted that Iain and I had made things up. George was particularly interested in the family's foray into diversifying the farm. We were lucky with its position, for that part of the country received fairly regular snowfalls throughout the winter, assuring its success, so much so that Japanese and Australian skiers were beginning to arrive in numbers.

"Your brother has asked you to join him in the business?" Virginia asked softly, returning from the kitchen with a large steam pudding. She placed it carefully on the table and gently patted my hand as I nodded. "I'm so pleased that you have both managed to sort things out. What will you do?" That was the sixty four million dollar question and everyone joined in, offering their views, throwing up problems and solutions. George was very much in favour of me taking it on, trying to railroad the others with his comments, but his wife, quiet and unflustered, allowed him his time and then reminded them all that it was my decision and one that only I could make. She was right.

Lucy directed the conversation towards the incidences that I had been involved with during the last term at school, detailing events with remarkable clarity. When she had finished, George, elbows resting on the table, a glass of wine in his hands looked across at me.

"That's pretty odd. Have you any idea why?"

"Yes, actually, but not who is involved." They looked intrigued, and I went on to explain. "I managed to keep hold of one of them who had tried to attack me, until the police came. I'd never seen him before. Just a hired thug I'd guess and not a very good one. I haven't been back to the police, so I don't know what they got out of him." I would have to check. Perhaps if it had been important they would have contacted me.

"So why," asked Virginia.

"It's all to do with the dismissal of a colleague last term." I went on to explain. When I mentioned Lord Grey's involvement, George visibly sharpened his attention. "What I can't work out is why it is so important to someone that I keep away from Mrs Jones. Fair enough, warning me the first time. I can almost understand that. People get a little emotional when it comes to child offenders."

"Alleged offender in this case," Lucy quipped.

"True, but still, people don't worry about that. For some, suspicion means guilty." Lucy made to protest but I cut her short. "No, not for the likes of you or all of us here, but there are elements in society who react on gut instinct and don't actually think things through."

George nodded in agreement and then spoke. "Quite right, you've only got to look at the hysteria that mobs get into to see that, but I agree with you, two times doesn't sit quite right. There's more to this I would say, at a guess." He reached behind him to a small side table and took the box of cigars. "You don't mind if I smoke one of these things, do you?" he asked me. "It's one of the few infrequent pleasures I have left in life." I shook my head. "Perhaps you would like to join me?"

"Why not? Thanks. I haven't had one of these for a while." Lucy looked disgusted, wrinkling her nose.

"Well, if you two are going to pollute the air, Mum and I might as well clear up in the kitchen. Gav, you can help if you like."

"Thanks for the offer sis, but I think I'll head out for a while, if that's alright with you pops?" His father nodded, his head almost lost in the smoke he exhaled. "Cool, I'll see you later then," he shook my hand, yelled a parting thanks to his mum for the meal, and shot out the door towards his car. I inhaled a deep breath of the sweet smoke. As a rule I didn't, but on the odd occasion it was nice to smoke a good cigar.

"Don't discuss anything interesting until we get back," his wife had ordered before heading towards the kitchen. George however took scant notice of his wife on that front. He sat across from me, looking through the haze of smoke, grey eyebrows furrowed in thought, blue eyes piercing the fog. A formidable man this, not one to be messed with.

"Lord Grey eh?" he said, "not a chap to mix with. I told you that before. They are not known for their finesse. He got his knighthood for service to the community, but no one seems to know exactly what service it was; apart from giving big donations to the Conservative party." I must have looked surprised for he continued. "I'm as blue as the best of them Michael, but I cannot abide underhand actions. You get where you get through honest endeavour, or not at all."

"Yes and no," I replied. I didn't really believe what he was saying. I agreed with it, but then, how far did you take it? The world had always rewarded those who best fit the circumstances of that time. Many of the peerage had received their titles through dubious circumstances, if history books were to be believed. Was it fair that their descendents should continue to reap the rewards that went with the title? George heard me out before replying, not the least upset by my comments.

"Good point. I can't really offer a good argument. Titles now are for the duration of that person's life, not to be handed on from generation to generation. My title however, will get handed on to Gavin when I die, so he will as you say, continue to reap the rewards of the title, as I have done. But the title itself doesn't bring with it wealth or work. It brings a degree of status I suppose, in this country. It gives you access to certain clubs and so forth, but I still have to milk the cows each morning. They don't care who I am. Quotas are still a problem to me, the same as it is to every other farmer."

"What sort of title does Lord Grey have?" I asked.

"Unfortunately, I would imagine, much to the chagrin of his eldest son, it will disappear when Grey himself does. Knowing Eric Grey that must really eat away at him. He loves to be important, which is why he is running for his constituency."

"And using his fathers position to help no doubt," I interrupted, "which therefore does give him an advantage, surely? It's back to that old title thing."

"You know, you are probably right. I can't see him getting there on his own. I'll concede on that one." George took a long pull on his cigar and watched the plumes of smoke billow up towards the ceiling. "Funny isn't it, the way a family turns out. You can never guarantee your genes. Look at old Grey. He must be so disappointed with his progeny. You haven't seen his youngest have you?" I shook my head. "Well, he's a real case. Been nothing but trouble right from the start. Didn't acquire any of the family charm, limited as it is. Got kicked out of school and hasn't done anything with his life. Turned out to be a bit of a thug."

It couldn't be possible. My mind was racing, thinking back to the incident in the pub when I had gone with Jane. This would be too much of a coincidence. But what had the girl said, something about his father being titled?

"What does he look like, this younger son?" I asked. "He isn't a ginger headed mulish looking character, is he?" George nodded his head, somewhat surprised.

"Don't tell me you've come across him as well. I trust you didn't do anything too outrageous. He's definitely bad news. Would have been put away a few times were it not for his father."

"It's that old privilege thing again," I reminded him. He looked suitably abashed. "Actually, if it is the same guy, then I have definitely alienated myself from the whole family." I went on to explain the circumstances of our meeting. He shook his head again.

"Have you got a death wish?" I smiled, but he didn't seem to find what he had said to be particularly amusing. "Listen Michael, this is no joke. You have made an enemy of a particularly unpleasant family. They are all capable of doing you damage, in their own way. The youngest is the least subtle, Eric particularly sadistic and cunning, but of them all, watch out for the father. Seriously." He could see my sceptical look. "It might not be a coincident that all your troubles have begun since you came in contact with them." It was food for thought, but in this day and age, and happening to me?

"How come he retains a title then?" I asked, "if he is known to be a criminal."

"Knowing and proving are two different things altogether He has power and can use it, and he has money and uses it. I would imagine that he thinks he is beyond the law."

"That may be so, but what has it got to do with me and with what has gone on at school? It doesn't make sense. I can't really see that he is connected with any of this. I'm sure it is a case of unfortunate circumstances."

"What unfortunate circumstances?" Lucy entered the room, latching on to my final remarks. She looked from her father to me, waiting for an answer. I briefly explained what we had been talking about and she looked concerned.

"Michael, you must be very careful."

"That's what I've been trying to tell him," said George, "but he's not convinced. See if you can convince him."

"Look, don't you think we are being just a little dramatic? There is nothing that can be proved." I wasn't convinced that we weren't making a mountain out of a molehill.

"If you consider the timings of these incidences against you, doesn't it seem all a little coincidental?" Lucy asked.

"No, not really. I can appreciate that it obviously has to do with the Len Jones incident. But I refuse to make the connection between that and Lord Grey. Yes, I might have hit his youngest son, and had words with his other one, even had words with him, but I can't for the life of me imagine that there is anything more to it than that."

"Well, perhaps you are right," conceded George, "but all the same, it wouldn't hurt to be cautious, whoever is involved." I agreed wholeheartedly with all he had to say. I certainly didn't want anymore damage done to me.

It was a good day, and it was with some reluctance that we said our goodbyes. Lucy had to pick her car up from the house and get back into London to prepare for a case later on in the week. I promised to ring her frequently, one of the ground rules, and booked in for Saturday night, this time in London. The week couldn't come round quick enough as far as I was concerned.

SEVEN

I had once read a quote saying, 'procrastination is the thief of time'. I liked it, and was honest enough to appreciate that in many instances, I had been guilty of great robberies. It was in this frame of mind that I decided to seek out the McKays and talk with them. Belinda had yet to return to school. I felt responsible.

I got hold of the appropriate register and managed to dig out her address and Monday evening saw me finish fitness training and set off to find her parents armed with the appropriate street map. Hatfield was one of the first generation New Towns to be built just outside London. Like the rest of them, it was characterised by certain uniformity in its housing. Why was it that planners lacked so much imagination? Was it purely money, or a certain lack of concern? It was a pity they hadn't taken more of a leaf out of Ebenezer Howard's book. Hatfield could at least boast a large shopping complex, The Galleria, an impressive design built over the motorway. I bypassed it, heading further south towards the railway and the old town centre, finally locating the street, after a few wrong turns. Here the houses had a little more character. They were of an older age, had a little more history

Six thirty in the evening, and not much sign of life. I banged on the front door, having tried the door bell first, which didn't seem to do anything, and waited. I was finally rewarded with a response, and the door was slowly opened to reveal a rather mousy looking woman, who peered out apprehensively.

"Mrs McKay?" I asked.

"Yes?" she replied timidly, looking suspiciously at me.

"Hello, I'm Michael Sutherland. I teach at King James. I wonder if I can talk with you for a moment?" She visibly started at the mention of either my name or the school's. I couldn't quite tell which.

"My husband is not in at the moment," she rattled out, and went to close the door. I managed to put my hand on it and gently resist her efforts, watching the panic grow on her face. Damn, this wasn't what I wanted to happen.

"Mrs McKay, I have come simply to see how Belinda is getting on. You can tell me that. I don't need to talk with your husband." I could read the indecision on her face, but I couldn't appreciate why.

"I don't know," she flustered. "My husband said I was not to talk with anyone. I don't know what to do." She stood there dithering, and I took the initiative before she reached the conclusion that I knew she would make.

"Your daughter has been through a pretty torrid time these last few months, and quite simply nothing seems to really ring true." I could see her growing concern, but pressed on. "As a result of what your daughter said, one member of staff was suspended, and then beaten to death." She gasped, a tiny sound, but significant, I thought. "When I talked with her the other day, she started to say something about being made to say things, and quite frankly I would like to know what she has said to you." The pressure on the door became stronger, more urgent.

"Let go of the door," she pleaded. I maintained the resistance.

"You heard her, let the door go." I swung round to face the owner of the voice and found myself looking at a fairly rugged character, about my height, thinning hair, unshaven and a little overweight, the boiler suit he was wearing looking slightly strained in places. The door accelerated shut with a bang. "What the hell do you think you're doing?" he growled. "Who are you, and why are you bothering my wife?" Mr McKay. Well, well. Not a particularly nice looking chap. He stood there aggressively, waiting, his arms hanging down by his sides like great big meat cleavers.

"My name is Sutherland. I teach at King James." I didn't have a chance to say any more. My name and King James was like a red rag to a bull and he moved menacingly towards me, meat cleavers swinging up.

"You bastards have ruined my daughter. Piss off, or I'll break your bloody neck," he mouthed. I stepped backwards wanting to avoid any confrontation.

"Look Mr McKay, all I want to do is talk with you both. There's no need for any violence."

"Talk. I'm effing sick of talk. That's all you and your type do. You talk and talk until the likes of us get completely fooled, and then you take advantage of us. Just like you did to poor Belinda!" He stopped, the rage in his face abating, replaced by one of utter anguish. "What the hell have you done to my poor wee girl?" I thought this was the chance I needed.

"I've no idea Mr McKay. Could we not try and sort something out?" I watched the indecision, the turmoil of thoughts he was having and then at last his arms dropped to his sides and his shoulders slumped and he turned back towards the house.

"You'd best come in then," he sighed. I followed him back up the path, and reflected on how close I had been once again to resorting to violence to protect myself. Life was filled with stressed up people. Some one was certainly screwing these poor people about. He took a key out of his pocket, fumbled a bit before he found the key hole, then unlatched the door and pushed it open. I followed him in. His wife came out of the kitchen, stopping in her tracks when she saw me.

"Stephen?" She looked across at her husband in an enquiring way.

"It's alright. I just want to hear what this chap has to say. I've had to listen to all the other buggers so I guess one more won't hurt too much. At least this one is the first to have the balls to confront me in person."

"Stephen! There is no need to use that type of language in our house," she admonished him. And he had the grace to look suitably sheepish.

"Sorry," he muttered, "but I've had it up to here listening to oily voices on the other end of the phone telling me what I should and shouldn't do. And my little girl is in all sorts of bother because of it. What's your name again?" he asked turning back to me. I told him and could see him committing it to memory. "I'm going to have a beer. You can have one if you want." It wasn't the friendliest invitation I had had, but I took him up on it all the same. He motioned towards the sitting room and we went in to a plain room, the walls painted a light creamy colour, magnolia I guessed. I sat down on the two seater settee and looked around me while he went into the kitchen. I could hear his wife talking urgently to him and listened to his occasional grunts. There wasn't much of a chance for him to say anything else. I reckoned that she had the measure of him. On the wall over the gas fire hung a picture of the family. Four faces staring intently in the direction of the camera, three smiling, but the young lad standing beside Belinda seemed to be sneering, almost as if that was the nearest he could get to a smile. I assumed he must be Belinda's brother. The photograph had been taken some years before, for Belinda smiled a gappy smile, her two front teeth nowhere to be seen.

Mr McKay came back into the room clutching two pint handles of beer. He passed one to me without a word, and I thanked him. He grunted. The atmosphere whilst chilly was decidedly warmer than it had been. He took a long pull on his pint, then looked directly at me.

"Right Mr Sutherland, what's going on?" He lay back in the armchair, placing his drink on the side table and reached into the top pocket of his overalls to fish out a packet of tobacco and papers. All very much automatic. "Don't mind if I smoke in my own home do you?" A statement rather than a question, really, but I shook my head all the same. I watched him deftly shake some of the tobacco onto the tissue and roll it one handed into a more than acceptable shape. I had never been able to do that, having tried a number of times when I was a kid. It was one of those things that cowboys always seemed to do, and as boys we had been impressed. Mr McKay was every bit as good, and although he didn't have a six gun in his other hand, he still got full marks.

Starting a conversation can be a difficult thing. You know what you want to say, but not exactly how to say it. I felt very much like this, this time. There was nothing for it but to launch in, which is what I did. I told him about Len Jones' suspension, his death, my involvement and my increasing antipathy toward certain people at the school. He could appreciate that. Several times he interrupted to clarify a point and then at last, satisfied with all that had been said, he spoke.

"At last a straight up guy," he wiped a bit of froth from his moustache. "God knows, I thought they were a thing of the past."

"No," I put in, "there are still some of us about, it's just that we don't make it to the top."

"Huh, top!" he snorted in disgust, "in my book it's always the scum that floats on top." He had a fair point. "Bloody politicians. They're all at it. What chance does the small bloke have?" I nodded, finding myself almost warming to the guy. "They have the money and the means to buy their way out of trouble. They're all the same."

"Oh that's not quite true," I argued. "There are some good ones out there." I thought of George Alexander and his family. They wouldn't allow anything dishonest to go unpunished. Stephen McKay shrugged, not convinced. He sat staring across the room lost in thought and I had the feeling that he was coming to a decision. About what I didn't have a clue. He took a deep breath as if to blow away the indecision, his eyes wandering back towards the family portrait.

"Damn you boy............" I couldn't make out to who he was referring, but the anguish was plain to see. He ground his cigarette savagely into the glass ash tray, still staring at the photograph. I felt he was oblivious to me. "Jimmy was a good lad." His voice surprised me; I hadn't expected him to start speaking. "What makes a good lad, bad?" Now that was the sort of question that had been debated by mankind down through the ages. I didn't have an answer. Possibly genetic, probably environmental. But at the end of the day the child had to make a choice. In my book they had to shoulder some of the responsibility. Our society was too keen to look everywhere else to lay the blame. Teaching had taught me that kids themselves knew right from wrong. Some just chose to ignore it. Why? Now that was the real question. "We gave him everything. His mother worked all hours to give him the best education possible. He was a bright boy, and we wanted him to be able to have a chance to compete with those who were more advantaged. We sent him to a prep school and he did well, but as he grew up he came to despise his background. He hated not being one of them. He wouldn't invite friends back to our home because he was ashamed of us. His mother did cleaning jobs for the very people he was mixing with and he hated it." He paused, looking back up at the picture. "It got to a point where I began to hate him, my own son!" The admission shocked him. He had finally spoken his thoughts. Thoughts I imagined that he had bottled up for years. Not a healthy thing to do. I should know, I'd done it myself. I made placatory gestures, but he carried on as if he wanted to unburden himself. "He got a scholarship to Haileybury and boarded there and we saw less and less of him. He would come home during the long breaks and make it very obvious that he had outgrown us. It destroyed his mother. He had been her pride and joy, the ungrateful little sod."

I looked up, seeing for the first time Mrs McKay standing at the door, tears running down her cheeks, her hands wringing a tea towel, tighter and tighter. What a sad family!

"Stephen, what are you doing?" she asked softly.

"It's got to be said love. We've carried it too long." He answered her just as gently, and she moved towards him, to stand beside him, not entirely convinced, but willing to support her husband whatever. I waited, unsure of what they were going to say next. He looked back at the photograph. "Jimmy began to mix with the wrong sort of company. There were one or two boys there who had it all, but didn't have much in the way of respect for authority. All cars, girls and drugs. Jimmy found that pretty exciting. He wouldn't listen to us; he bloody looked down at us..." His voice choked with emotion at the memory. Shocked and hurt. His wife patted his arm in support. He gathered himself and continued. "Then it happened. He was at a party, got pretty high and raped a young girl. Can you believe it? My own boy." He stopped again, taking a deep breath. I imagined that I was the first person outside the family to actually hear this. "He came to us not long after it had happened. He came asking for help. He hadn't done that for some time. What can you do? You have to look after your own, don't you?" He wasn't looking for my support, merely stating what was obvious to him. Yes and no, I reckoned. It depended on what one had done. You couldn't harbour a murderer, could you harbour a rapist? That was a tough call. Blood is thicker than many things, but rape?! He must have seen the look on my face for he spoke again. "Yeah, it doesn't sound good does it? Keeping quiet about such a horrific act. Lord knows, if anyone had done such a thing to Belinda I would want to castrate them or beat them senseless." He stopped, suddenly aware of what he had said.

"Is that it then?" I asked. "Is that what happened to Len Jones?"

"No, God help us, it wasn't like that at all." He buried his face in his hands and let out a large sigh. His wife beside him looked on sadly. After a moment or two, he spoke again.

"You know, if it had been like that, I don't think I'd have really cared. He would have deserved it. But the poor bugger didn't deserve it. He didn't do a thing!" It was out. Belinda had been right. God almighty, what was happening here? Len had died for no reason? The enormity of it almost took my breath away.

"Why?" It was all I could say. Stephen McKay shook his head and said nothing. The cigarette he was rolling trembled in his hand, spilling tobacco on the floor, before he brought it to his lips to seal.

"Why?" he answered, "because some sick bastard is blackmailing me." The anger in his voice was plain to hear. "Someone knew about Jimmy and the rape and threatened to spill the beans. After all these years! And just when he was finally sorting himself out. He's got a good position in a big company and looks to be heading for big things. I couldn't let him down now."

"How was it, that he was never identified anyway?" I interrupted.

"He told me that he wore some sort of hood. God, can you imagine hearing that sort of thing from your own son?" Hoods, balaclavas. I loathed the thought of them. Had seen enough of them these last few months and despised the cowards who had to hide behind them. "I haven't told Jimmy anything about this. We didn't want to upset him." Yet how much upset had that boy created for everyone else? He looked up at his wife, and she stared back. Two sad people, paying for the mistakes of the child they had spawned. Personally, I was developing a distinct animosity toward him. His moment of unbridled sexual aggression had adversely touched the lives of many people. I would very much have liked to upset him. But then again, he wasn't my son.

"What happened to the girl?" I asked. I had imagined that she would have got over the incident and carried on with her life. How wrong I was! Stephen McKay winced, and looked guiltily at me, his wife turning her head to stare across the room.

"She ah, she," he paused looking decidedly awkward. "She ended up being unstable and had to be put in a home." Silence. There wasn't anything else to say. The son they had protected had done a lot of harm. The consequences of his action had ripple effects which transcended beyond that time. It is always the same. Nothing exists in isolation.

"I, I mean we, ah, we have contributed donations towards her treatment." Mrs McKay spoke without looking at me, the shame so very obvious. Money was not atonement for sins. It was a bit like indulgences: sin now pay later. But what else could they do? Life always threw up difficult circumstances; I couldn't sit in judgement of them. They had paid for their son's sins over and over, and would go on paying for it for the rest of their lives. But who was responsible for blackmailing them? That was the real question, for behind that lay the answer to the attacks on me and the murder of Len.

I spent a good part of the evening with the McKays. They told me that someone had phoned them one night and let it be known that he knew all about their son's indiscretion. The voice had gone on to say that there was only one way that it would not be made public, and when they had grasped at that straw they were told that Belinda would have to pretend to be sexually assaulted by one of the staff at King James. When they protested, the voice hung up and they had spent some time in utter trepidation expecting the world to collapse around their son. A day later the voice had called back and by then they were ready to agree to anything. Good tactics on behalf of the blackmailer. Belinda had to be told of her brother's involvement. She had taken the news badly, had stopped eating and her mother worried about anorexia. Christ was it any wonder. The poor girl was carrying the welfare of her whole family on her shoulders and probably protecting a brother whom she despised. No wonder she had traumatised the way she did. She was still in hospital and seemed to be making some progress. The nearest they could describe her condition was that she had chosen to blank out part of her memory, like selective amnesia. Stephen McKay lived in fear that she might end up like the poor girl that his son had raped. When I said that I wanted to dig deeper and try and find out who was responsible, their main concern was that their son didn't get implicated. They were prepared to go on paying the price. No one had contacted them since Len had died. That had to be good and they didn't want anything more to happen. I said I would be careful.

There was a message from Lucy on the answer phone when I got in, asking me to ring and demanding to know where I was.

"Hello?" God I loved her voice. Silky smooth with that little hint of a good public school.

"Lucy, it's me, Michael."

"Hi. I rang earlier just to see how you were."

"I'm fine. Got your message on the answer phone. How are things with you?"

"Good. Listen, thanks for a great weekend. I really enjoyed myself. And thanks for the bed."

"Any time." I meant it to. Just hoped that she would find room for me in it.

"Michael?"

"Mmm?"

"You've gone quiet."

"Yeah, I was just thinking. Say, how about this weekend? Anything planned? I mean, you're dragging me down to the big smoke. What are we going to do when we get there?"

"It's a surprise." She laughed. "I think you'll enjoy it." I pestered her for information, but to no avail, all I got was the typical lawyer 'no comment' bit. I then went on to tell her about my visit to the McKay's and what they had confessed.

"Oh Mike, you have to be very careful. Perhaps you should go to the police. They would know what to do. What can you do?" Her voice was full of concern. She was right of course. The sensible thing would be to go to the police, but I didn't want to drop the McKays in it, at least not yet.

"I don't know what I can do, but I know what I can't, and that is to involve the McKays . . . ." Lucy tried to cut in, but I cut her short. "No, listen. I sort of promised them that I would not implicate their son in any of this."

"But Mike, he's guilty of a horrible crime. He should be castigated." She spoke it passionately, solicitor and woman, both horrified at the prospect of such a crime going unpunished.

"Technically you're right of course," I agreed, "but I can't go back on my word to them. As far as I'm concerned, their son can rot in hell - he

143

sounds a supercilious self centred bastard who has caused a lot of hurt to a lot of people. But I don't particularly want to hurt his parents even more. If there is a way of making him pay for what he had done, I will try my best to see it happen." The image of him sneering at the camera was still fresh in my mind.

When we finally hung up, Lucy still wasn't convinced that I should be doing anything at all, but was at least happy that I had promised to go to the police to see if they had found out anything about the chap I had handed over to them.

"Hey Kiwi, where are you hiding yourself these days?" It was Brian Stewart: History. He looked up from his desk in the quiet room, surrounded by books. "Bloody marking. The bane of my life. You would think someone could come up with a better system. Use one of those supermarket checkout scans. Something like that. Hey, that's not a bad idea." He grinned. "I might have come up with something there, what do you reckon?"

"I reckon you should stick to history." Brian made an appropriate gesture.

"Are you sure you are allowed to make those kinds of signs here," I joked. He doubled the number of fingers.

"Anyway, Sutherland, where the hell do you get to these weekends? You missed a hell of a good bash on Saturday night over in St. Albans. A friend of a friend." He answered in response to my question.

"Fat lot of use telling me now. Why didn't you say something during the week?" I replied.

"Nothing was definite then. It just sort of happened. We were all at the pub and it took off from there. But you haven't been at the pub these last few weekends buddy. So what gives? You going monkish on us, or have you picked up some other habit?" He grinned at his own joke.

"Ha, ha. Very droll."

"No, c'mon Mike, what gives? I know you buddy. We go back a few years. It was you that would drag all of us down to the pub whenever the chance arose. And now you're not there. So that can only mean one thing. Who is she eh?"

"What the hell is this? Ignatius Loyola time?" I countered.

"Oooh. Throwing some history at me eh? It must be pretty juicy then." Brians grin grew even wider.

"You're clutching at straws Stewart." I shook my head, but knew that I hadn't convinced him.

"You reckon. Don't forget Mike, I was around when you and the fair Jane were having a fling. It was frightening. You were almost domesticated before you saw sense and came back to the pack. The signs are looking a bit similar." He said wagging a finger at me.

"The old imagination is working overtime Mr Stewart." I left him to his books and moved through to the staffroom. A free lesson. I had stacks of work to get on with, but couldn't get down to it. I felt I was party to a lot of incriminating information, but I didn't know how to put it to best effect. It was damned frustrating. There was nothing new in my pigeon hole, nothing new on the notice board, and no-one new in the staffroom. Twenty minutes of free time left, I decided to head back to the P.E. office and ring the local police station. I asked for D.C. Carmichael and was surprised to get put straight through. Catching up on paper work, was his reply. I told him why I had rung and waited while he typed something up on the computer.

"Right Sir, I have it in front of me now. Not that there is a lot to tell. He's a one Ronald Harrow, seemingly of no fixed abode. A real down and out. A bit of a pathetic specimen really. Seems he was approached by the other character you had dealings with and offered a sum of money to help out. Doesn't know the chaps name, was scared witless at the thought of confronting him, more scared of that, than the prospect of getting into

145

trouble with us." He paused, and I imagined he was taking a further look at the screen. "Oh yes, he didn't get his money. Naturally a bit upset about that, and was considering citing you for grievous bodily harm." I snorted in disbelief.

"I sincerely hope you are joking," I replied.

"Not at all Sir. He seemed quite serious in his intention. The, uh, person in question complained bitterly about his privates. He was concerned that he might be ruined for life."

"I bloody hope he is," I replied angrily. "The sod was out to get me. If I've put an end to any future cock up on his part, in any respect, then well and good." I could hear him laughing at the other end of the phone.

"Yes Sir. Well, you'll be pleased to know that we managed to convince him that it wouldn't be in his best interest to proceed along those lines, although there are no doubt, lawyers prepared to act on his behalf."

"The law's an ass." I snorted.

"Mmm," he replied non committed. The conversation didn't reveal any startling information. They hadn't managed to find out anything more about the other chap with the knife, although they had been given a description of him, of sorts, by acne face. As far as he went, they had cautioned him, then released him, for he had not done anything: Committing a crime was solid, intention to commit, not quite so. I asked if anything more had come to light over the Len Jones incident and drew the same blank reply, with the usual line that they were proceeding with their enquiry and still had a few leads to pursue. I hung up feeling that I wasn't much better off than before I rang. Still, I had learned that one Ronald Harrow was often to be seen occupying the streets of Welwyn Garden City. If the need arose, I would keep an eye out for him and perhaps see if I could squeeze something more from him.

The afternoon games period left me little time to dwell on the issues that were pressing. A session with the sink group of the junior form, who had a strong reluctance to play rugby, would have tested the patience of a saint, and it was with much relief that I watched the firsts come out to begin their practice. Routine now. Boys becoming men. Jamie calling them together for the warm up, the peppering of the goal posts coming to an end as they finished their last kicks and headed off round the field. These were the last few weeks of school rugby for some of them. I hoped we could finish it on a high note. Then the sevens season would be upon us. Different but no less demanding.

"Come on Phillips," I yelled at the back of the waddling prop. "You look pregnant from this end."

"Sorry Sir," his voice trailed back through the growing gloom. "I'm still feeling the effects of Saturday's game." He continued to jog slowly on. I caught up with him and ran beside him.

"That guy was a good prop. Gave me a right going over. He bored in so much I thought I was going to pop out like a cork. Couldn't do a damn thing." I smiled at the annoyance in his voice. He was a good old grafter and no slouch as a prop, and from where I had been standing, I would have said that the honours were fairly even after the game. His man too, would have been sporting some aches and pains. I jogged amongst them picking up their mood, listening to their staccato comments as they puffed along.

"Hey Sir." Danny Boyd glided up beside me. "My Dad said he saw you the other night at the Indian." I knew what was coming next. Nothing could be kept a secret. "So who is she Sir? Dad said she was well tasty." I knew Danny's father, a London accountant with a big firm. I couldn't imagine him using such phraseology.

"Well Danny, she's okay." I replied. He waited for me to continue but I said nothing more, just carried on jogging.

"Is that it Sir? No clues?" I shook my head. "Oh that's not fair. The boys are dying to know. So's Mr Stewart. I had him this afternoon, and when I told him about Dad seeing you he was dead keen to find out more." Damn. I bet he was. I would be in for some stick now.

"Well Danny, you and the boys and Mr Stewart are just going to have to dig up some more info. For I'm certainly not going to tell you." He continued to pester me, and right throughout the drills the boys kept it up.

"Right lads, I'd like you, if at all possible, to put your mind to more important things than my social life, and start thinking about Haileybury this Saturday." The name of the school brought with it an image of Jimmy McKay. "No game is easy, and this one is certainly not the exception." We went on to talk tactics, suggesting game plans for wet or dry conditions, then got on to the squad session, finishing in the dark of the cold misty January night.

We travelled in convoy, through Hertford, following the road up the hill towards the A10, turning at the large roundabout towards the distinctive dome of the school. It was strange how the old emotions never quite left you. I could feel the nerves beginning to twitch. A great feeling, adrenalin beginning to pump. I regretted with some passion the fact that I was growing old. Too old now for a real game of rugby. In my mind there was no real substitute, and I missed it like crazy. While coaching gave me a buzz, it wasn't a substitute for the real thing. I had realised that when I had dropped acne face to the floor. That had felt good. Action at last. Perhaps there were a lot of us out there. Old players put out to pasture who still needed to let off steam now and again.

The game went pretty well to plan. We kicked off on a dry pitch, on a sunny afternoon and soon had them camped on their line, due in no small part to the actions of Phillips the very prop who had been waddling through the practice sessions. He had taken a loose ball from the lineout and stormed twenty to thirty metres brushing off the opposing players like flies, before finally being lowered to the ground. With the support quick to get to the break down, we had recycled and passed it along the backline, the miss pass to the wing enabling him to make ground before being pulled down five or so metres short of the line. Jamie Lee was first there, blasting through and beyond the ball, leaving it for Danny Boyd to pick up. One quick look, and he then he was through the gap of players, burrowing, and bumping, before diving low over the line. 5 - nil. It was good stuff; nothing could beat a fast fifteen man game.

Unfortunately, Haileybury hadn't read the script and with five minutes of the game left we were trailing 17 - 15. It had been an absolutely storming encounter, spectators from both camps totally caught up in the atmosphere, the volume of noise impressive for such a game. I looked up as the whistle blew shrilly, and watched the referees arm rise in the air. Penalty to us. Players killing the ball. Thirty metres out, but near the sideline. Brian Grieves stepped up and indicated to the referee that he was going to take a kick at goal. This was it, the time when all the hard work comes down to one man. His was the responsibility to lift us to victory. I watched him go through his routine, take a big breath, shake his arms to relax and then step in to kick the ball. Watched as it sailed towards the post, a beautiful place kick. Watched it as it slid narrowly past the left hand upright and over the dead ball line. Heard the whistle for full time. Felt the disappointment. Listened to the roar rise from the spectators on the other side of the field, in stark contrast to our parents muted applause. Looked across at the boys. Heads down, Jamie Lee walking across to his fullback to console him, the action strangely moving me, and I could feel myself blinking quickly in a vain attempt to remove the emotion. Bloody old fool. God I hated losing, hated it with a passion, but it had been a great game, one equally contested, a game which could have gone either way. I felt a hand on my shoulder and turned to find David Morgan, their coach, extending his hand in sympathy. Welshmen seemed to coach in just about every school I had come across. For the most part they were a great bunch of guys, who still remembered with great fondness their days as welsh schoolboys. David was an excellent ambassador for his country.

"What can I say Mike? A real nail biter. Great game. Shame one side had to lose. But, just glad it was yours." He laughed, clapping me on the shoulder as he spoke. "We owed you that for the last couple of years anyway."

"Yeah, but it still hurts," I replied.

"Good. You don't experience it enough."

We walked back together towards the changing room, exchanging comments with parents and players alike. The battle done, we now all shared in the camaraderie of the game.

"Tell me David," I said as we stood in the dining hall drinking coffee, "How long have you been here?"

"Years boy, or so it seems. Why, why do you ask?"

"Do you remember a student called James McKay? He must have been here about six or so years ago?"

"McKay, James McKay," he mused staring into space. "He rings a bell." He took a big gulp of his coffee, put the cup back on the saucer and clicked his fingers. "Got him, yeah Jimmy McKay. Had an attitude problem that one. Not one of our better students. Do you know him?" I didn't want to go into details.

"Know of him. I don't suppose you can remember who he kicked around with can you?" It was a long shot, but it seemed pretty logical that whoever had been blackmailing the McKays, either knew their son fairly well, or knew of someone who had told them what had happened.

"Kicked around is a fairly good choice of words. There were three or four of them. Pretty much constituted the school bully team if I remember correctly. Names though, that's harder. I don't know about you, but once they leave, most of them fall into obscurity, unless they played for me, which I know for certain those guys didn't." He continued to stare ahead, oblivious to the noise around him: a large hall filled with boys jostling for their plates of food, not too dissimilar to the game they had just played! "Let's see. McKay and Holden, Gareth . . . . , no, Craig Holden. Nasty piece of work. He was one. Rich kid gone sour. We kicked him out for doing drugs. Parents kicked up a fuss. Threatened all sorts of things. Claimed he had been victimised. Couldn't buy themselves out of that one though. Too much proof. Got a feeling it was his good buddy McKay who grassed him up. They had fallen out over something. Lovely." He grinned a fleeting grin. "No one was sorry to see that guy go. McKay got a bit of a beating from the other two though. Really roughed him up. Put him in hospital for a while. When thieves fall out eh. Jeez, not the most impressive time in our history. McKay, Holden, Marshall, yeah he was another. Big brute of a chap. Didn't have two brain cells to rub together. He and, who was it now? He and Dalton Murphy, all muscle from the feet up." He paused. That was one long shot that hadn't paid off. The names didn't mean a thing to me. Still it had been worth the question. Back to the drawing board. "Anyone you know then?" He asked. I shook my head, and although I could see that he was intrigued, I managed to steer the conversation in a different direction.

"What have you got planned tonight?" Chris Williams sat beside me on the coach as we headed back to school. It was dark already. Tonight, now there was a thought. I didn't have a clue what Lucy had lined up. I didn't really care. Just being in her company was good enough.

"Not really sure," I answered truthfully, almost.

"How about a beer then?"

"I'll have to do a rain check on that," I replied. Chris gave me a quizzical look.

"What are you up to? The Mike Sutherland I know doesn't turn a beer down. Are you ill? Brian's right eh? You've got a bird. Don't deny it Mike. Who is she?" What the heck, it would be obvious soon enough. And anyway I wanted to show her off at some stage. Chris listened as I explained, adding the odd comment, asking the obvious, but impressed with her pedigree. "Moving up in the world," and "High flier now, always thought kiwis were flightless," and other such witty repartee were quick to be stated. When we parted he gave me a big grin, clenched his fist and raised his arm in a rude gesture and hoped that I was taking the necessary precautions.

Jamie Lee turned to me as he stepped off the bus. "Sorry boss. We wanted that one." He shrugged his shoulders in resignation. Pete Brown followed him out echoing the same sentiments, and one by one the boys dismounted, Brian Grieves unable to look directly at me. Stupid. I stopped them from walking off, and we stood in a huddle, young men I felt proud to know, and told them so. Told them that they had played a wonderful game, told them that with the bounce of the ball going their way the result could have been different, told them that there was nothing to be ashamed of, and clipped Brian Grieves lightly across his head and told him not to be such a silly ass. No one blamed him for the loss. Certainly not me. The others murmured in agreement and I watched as Brian lifted his head to face them squarely again. The way it should be. "But listen you dozy buggers; Monday's fitness is going to be hell, just in case you think I'm going all soft." There were loud groans, but wide grins as well, and they departed in a more buoyant mood.

EIGHT

*L*ucy's flat was a smallish affair, but as expected, beautifully decorated, capturing a mood of light and warmth in soft yellow and pale blue. She guided me towards the sitting room, a coal fire burnt orange in the hearth throwing a further sense of warmth through the room. I sat on the settee and stretched out toward the fire. Bliss.

"Drink?" She asked having offered her mouth up for a kiss as I sat down.

"Love one, thanks. Whatever you've got," I answered in reply to her question. She stepped out and returned carrying a bottle of red wine and two glasses, and sat down on the floor in front of the settee. I eased down to join her. She lifted the bottle up for my inspection.

"See, New Zealand," she said proudly. I looked at the label. Montana Cabernet Sauvignon. A pretty safe bet. Reds were getting better, but the white wine was to International standard. However, Lucy knew me, knew my taste. I loved red wine.

"Perfect." I reached for the cork screw and opened and poured us both a glass. "Cheers. So, what have you got planned for the night then?"

"What would you like to do?" She asked throwing it back at me.

"Truthfully?"

"Yep."

"Well, this actually. This is just great. I could sit here all night and just relax. Anyway, what are we going to do?"

"This. I hoped you would want to. I've got the meal all planned." She looked at me, slightly uncertain, vulnerable and very desirable. I leant forward and put my hand gently behind her head and pulled her toward me.

"Lucy, you're marvellous." She smiled in delight and kissed me and then jumped to her feet just as I was warming to the task.

"Got to check the meal," she said and dashed out of the room.

We sat in the kitchen. Candles on the table, chicken in tarragon sauce and sherry vinegar. Mouth watering, followed by strawberry Romanoff and port. She made an excellent hostess and I told her so and was rewarded with a big smile. We left the dishes and retired to the living room, the quiet sounds of a CD playing in the background.

"Michael?" She lay with her head against my chest as I sat against the settee and I could smell the pleasant fragrance of her perfume.

"Mmm?"

"Would you like to stay the night? I don't have a spare bed!" She looked up at me and we stared into each other's eyes. I could see the humour in hers. This was some girl. I could feel my heart thumping in my chest. I wanted her very much.

"Are you sure it's what you want Lucy? You know I'd love to stay the night with you."

"Yes," she said with feeling. "Come on Sutherland, take me to bed." Her voice had gone all husky. I stood up and swung her into my arms.

"Guide me oh thou great Jehovah." She giggled, pointing her toes in the direction we were to go, going through into a small hallway. I turned into one room only for her to tell me it was the spare room.

"I didn't think you had a spare room," I said. She giggled again.

"I lied."

I pushed open the door into what was obviously her room, soft cream, large bed, soft lighting. We said nothing as I lowered her gently onto the bed. Like novices we fumbled with each others clothing, all thumbs. She was every bit as beautiful as my mind had imagined. Her breasts were accentuated by the pertness of her nipples, the little goose bumps around the nipple itself having nothing at all to do with the temperature. She lifted up to help take off her skirt, which when slowly removed revealed a scanty thong beneath, the satin black fabric stretched over the mound between her legs. I looked into her eyes and she smiled back up at me, her hand guiding mine back down to cover the very area I had just been looking at. I gently tugged at the thong and slowly removed it so that she lay there, soft downy hair shaped in a strip, accentuating her femininity. I felt my boxers being removed, felt her hand encircle my erection sending me into an involuntary spasm, before releasing to gently pull me down to her. Nothing frenetic. We took our time, discovering and awakening responses, until she opened her legs wide and guided me into the soft and pliant warmth that was her. Wrapped together we finally completed with a shuddering intensity. Bliss. We lay together talking and finding out more about each other, sharing the intimacy and enjoying the pleasure of being close together until the mood changed and we made love again, more physical, more urgent, before drifting off to sleep.

"Good morning." I opened my eyes to focus on Lucy standing beside me, a white bathrobe wrapped around her carrying a breakfast tray. "Fancy some breakfast." She looked at me almost shyly, offering a gentle smile.

"Mmm, yes please. It's been ages since anyone has offered me breakfast or anything else, in bed." I grinned back at her and watched the smile widen across her face.

"Mmm, I did detect a certain interest, like a kid with a new toy." She placed the tray on the bed and deftly removed the robe before slipping beneath the quilt, the vision of her slender naked body arousing interest again. She was some new toy. I moved my hand under the quilt.

"Breakfast!" She said with mock severity. "And anyway the tray will end up on the floor. You pour while I butter the croissants." I did as I was told and we sat in quiet companionship reading the Sunday Times, sipping tea and dropping crumbs over the bed. I loved her little ways; the brushing back of her hair when she leant forward, her darting tongue as she licked her lips for the crumbs, the screwing up of her nose as she read things in the paper that she obviously did not agree with. I kept waiting for the man on the side to yell 'Michael Sutherland, come on in your time is up' it felt almost unreal.

"What are you thinking? Michael?" I realised Lucy was talking and looked over at her, looked into those eyes and felt I should pinch myself.

"Just that this is so good, how do we know that it is for real?"

"What?"

"How do we know that what is happening here is not just a dream?"

"Because I'm with you. I can say things which your so called dream has not yet dreamt up. And anyway, I know it isn't," she replied with certainty. "What brought this on, this 'how do we know we exist' stuff?"

"Cogito ergo sum. Descarte. Nothing really." I shrugged, feeling a little awkward. "It's just that I would hate to wake up now and find out that it was only a dream."

"You're an old romantic Mr Sutherland." She leant across and pecked me on the chin. "You've got yourself a problem you know. Leave me now and I'll drag you through the courts and sue you for everything possible." It sounded good to me.

The morning slid by and a good chunk of the afternoon did as well, before we finally climbed out of bed and showered and prepared a meal together, then we sat with plates on our laps and a glass of red wine and watched some film or other on the television. But like all good things it had to come to an end and with great reluctance I said goodbye and left the warmth of her company and home and drove through the cold streets of a quiet London Sunday evening back to my own house.

One of the things Stephen McKay had given me was an address where his son could be contacted. He had done so rather reluctantly and only after I had managed to convince him that it might help Belinda if everything was cleared up as quickly as possible. That had swung the balance but he still held out until I had yet again sworn that I would not go to the police. The bonds of a family ran really deep and seemed to brush over any malfeasance.

Whilst most of the time my mind was occupied with thoughts of Lucy as I drove towards home, it occasionally drifted back, unbidden, to images of Len Jones and his family, little kids deprived of a father, a wife deprived of a husband. I felt guilty and angry at the same time, guilty because I was on top of the world, having the love of a beautiful and intelligent woman, angry because Len had died for no reason and was unable to do so. And yet it wasn't for no reason. Every action has a cause. It was just a matter of finding it. I knew that I owed it to him to do my best. I loathed injustice and unfair play, hated the bad guy winning. The tricky part was pulling all the pieces together to form a picture. I had this jig saw of events, of incidences, one off activities which in their isolation seemed pointless. I had to sort them out. Had to solve the puzzle.

The house was quiet, no sign of Alison. No doubt she and Andrew were out somewhere. I went straight to the phone and punched the number for information and gave the bright sounding operator Jimmy McKay's name and address. I was in luck. He hadn't gone ex-directory or cable.

The voice on the other end belonged to a woman who informed me that Jimmy was out and wouldn't be back until late. Did I want to leave a message? No I said, thank you, I would try again some other time. He's not often in she had replied, sounding a little annoyed, or so it seemed. From what I had learned of Jimmy McKay she should count herself lucky. I rang off, poured myself a splash of whiskey, ran a bath and soaked for an hour. A time to think, to mull things over. By the time I finally emerged I thought I had one or two ideas which might be worth pursuing. Certainly frightening if they proved true. I was going in at the deep end, teacher turned detective. God help me.

11.30. She had said he would be in late, so I dialled again, this time success. A rather abrupt voice answered and I tried to match it to the photograph that I had seen at the McKay's.

"Yes, who is it?"

"Jimmy McKay?" I answered. There was a slight pause.

"Yes."

"You don't know me but I know your parents." No reaction. I ploughed on. "I would very much like to meet with you." Another long pause. Finally.

"Why?" Almost belligerent. "Listen buddy, I don't know who the hell you are and I sure as hell have no desire to meet with you. I couldn't give a friggen toss whether or not you know my old folks. What do you want to talk with me about? Them?" I had no trouble matching the voice to the sneering photograph now.

"How about a case of unlawful entry Jimmy." I could almost hear his brain whirring away. "Get the picture?"

"I don't know what the shit you're on about and quite frankly at this time of night I don't really care to find out. Goodnight."

"Fair enough Jimmy, but before you hang up just let me say this: Karen Thomas. My name is Mike Sutherland, should you wish to get back to me I'm on 01438 897661." I hung up. Two could play his game. I had just heard his protestations at the other end as I put down the receiver. His father had divulged the girls name just before I had left them. I was sure it would get young Jimmy thinking. I hoped it would get him sweating. Ten minutes later the phone rang.

"Mr Sutherland?" He didn't sound quite so self assured this time round. I told him again that I wanted to meet with him, not to discuss his parents but to discuss someone else and suggested that as he had mentioned his folk perhaps it would be a good thing for him to visit them on Wednesday evening and that we could meet at The Crooked Chimney afterwards at about 9pm. No argument. How would he recognise me he had asked?

I told him not to worry, that I had a fair idea of what he looked like and that I would see him on Wednesday and left it at that.

Fields had once again thrown a spanner into the works by announcing that he and the Governors were reviewing the position of rugby on the sports calendar following an accident to a young lad over the weekend in a rugby related incident in a school up north. What Fields didn't tell the rest of the staff during briefing was that the accident was purely a freak one, that the boy had fallen awkwardly over his own feet and landed on his neck, paralysing himself. Horrible, but it could have happened on a football, hockey or any other field. Another chance for the anti rugby lobby to swing into action. Fields had little love for the game but because of deference to tradition had maintained it. This was probably just the chance he was looking for. More as a way of getting at me I felt, but then I was a bit prickly over issues of that sort.

As promised, fitness training went ahead and true to my word I gave the boys what for, finishing with the mandatory bleep test which put an end to most of them. As they lay about on the gym floor gasping for breath I told them what the Head had said about the possible future of rugby. Immediate attention, immediate anger and I watched as they dragged themselves up ready to do battle.

"Whoa. What's this? A moment ago you were all dead beat, unable to go on. Now look at yourselves."

"Were you serious then Sir?" panted Pete Brown.

"Yep, but I don't think it will come to much, well I hope not. But doesn't it tell you something. If the motivation is strong enough you find the energy. Remember that lads."

Wednesday evening. I had spent the afternoon outside on the games field with the team playing league. There were things that we could learn from the game, like lines of running and support and defence patterns.

The boys enjoyed the change and with the season winding towards completion and the sevens season approaching; this was as good bridge between the two games. Prudence had taught me not attempt to compete with them, as the ball moved quicker down the line and my legs and lungs had long ago decided what was reasonable for a man in my condition. It was time I did something about that.

8:30. I had managed to get an hour of marking done before driving to the pub, it's name derived from the distinctive shaped chimney which rose above the tiled, wisteria clad roof. There were, surprisingly, quite a few people there. How they managed to get out during the week I had no idea. They were probably the same people who were first to criticise teachers for their easy life, yet I knew very few who managed to get out on a week night. I sat in the corner, nursing a Guinness. From here I could look at all those who entered. It had often been a pastime of mine when I had time to waste, to try and work out what people were and imagine their lives and I found myself so engrossed watching a young couple at the other end of the bar, I had him down as a young farmer and she as a receptionist that I missed seeing Jimmy McKay enter. I was suddenly aware that there were two new arrivals ordering a drink, one of them obviously the chap I had planned to meet but equally obvious was the fact that he had come with support. A fairly solid looking individual who looked like he knew his way in a brawl. Possibly a bouncer at a night club. I looked at my watch. 8:40. Interesting. Jimmy had had much the same intentions as me: to get in early and watch who was coming and not disclose the presence of his companion. Cunning. The boy had survival instincts. Whilst he had matured and got fatter in the face, he still had the same arrogant look that I had seen in the photograph. I watched them pay for their drink and move down to the other end of the bar, around the corner. That solved the problem that I thought I would be faced with, which was how to get out without them noticing so that I could enter again and let them think that their plan had worked. I downed the remains of my drink and departed back to my car and sat listening to Chiltern radio bang out a variety of songs, my mind racing over the possible scenarios which might eventuate. I wished I had had the foresight to bring Chris Williams along for company. I would, it would seem, have to become a lot more worldly wise if I were to survive in the game which I had set in motion. How could I possibly use my knowledge of their being two of them to any advantage? As much as I racked my brains I could think of no possible way, save that any intervention from another party would not come as a shock to me.

9:10. Let them wait. Get them fidgety. I sat for another five minutes and was rewarded with the sight of Jimmy coming out of the pub on his own, to stand and light a cigarette whilst gazing up and down the road. A car slowed down, indicating to enter the car park and I watched Jimmy casually flick his cigarette away and turn back into the pub. A good time for me to move. I locked the car and made my way back, ordered another drink and looked around me. Jimmy was sitting where I had expected to find him but I couldn't see the other chap. Ah well, he would be somewhere. I strode over to his table.

"Jimmy McKay?"

"Yeah and you're bloody late." A charming character. I didn't bother offering my hand but sat down opposite him.

"Yeah, well there you go. But I'm not here to talk about time; I want to talk about one Karen Thomas. Okay?"

"What about her?" He didn't seem too phased. I looked at him; his well cut suit, large gold wrist watch and bracelet. City boy with money and very little in the way of a conscience. His poor parents; hard working, no frills and a conscience that had kept them working to pay for the care of the girl their son had raped and to pay for the blackmailer that their son knew little about. My dislike of him grew more intense. "What are you looking at?" he demanded, the belligerent tone there to be heard again.

"A low life perhaps," I said quietly. He went to say something then thought better of it. "Listen to me," I said leaning forward. "I have better things to do with my life than sit here with the likes of you. But your little act of criminal lust has had a number of knock on effects, so you just sit there and listen to what I have to say. For one, you have a sister in hospital in some sort of traumatised state because she has had to carry the brunt of your misguided pleasure and from the looks of you, you couldn't give a shit. Secondly, rape carries a prison sentence and unless you behave I might just point the law in your direction. I'm sure they and the family of that girl would love to see you behind bars." He took a pull at his drink and placed it down deliberately on the beer mat in front of him, rocking it back and forth.

"So, what do you want? I guess you know my old man. What do you do? Work with him? You look the type. You know, manual labourer. I suppose he got pissed one night and blurted out everything about his boy who had been the pride and joy of his family but had erred. I knew he couldn't keep it to himself. I shouldn't have said anything. Dozy old bugger. Never was up to much." He took another long gulp of his drink. I breathed in deeply, fighting the urge to punch him. "So, I guess you want me to pay you some money to keep quiet eh? Keep you in beer money or something like that. Jeez the company my old man keeps." He sneered contemptuously at me and sat back waiting for me to say something.

"Listen you piece of sleaze, there is nothing I would like to do more than run you off to the police station. You have destroyed an innocent girl's life and quite frankly I'd love to destroy yours. Unfortunately I had to promise your father that I wouldn't say anything to the police. As far as possible I will stick to that." He sat back in his chair and looked to be reassessing me. "You've made the mistake of thinking that everyone works from the same base level as you. You think that if you flash a bit of money about it will buy you out of any problem. That everyone wants money. Well not me buddy. I want fair play. Quite honestly I think what you did warrants castration! However, that's not the issue. As I said before, your little act has had a number of consequences and I want to know whether you have any answers. It's obvious that you have very little respect or time for your family. They're beneath you, right?" He looked down at his drink and said nothing. "Beneath you. That's a good one. Well let me tell you something. While you've been living up the good life in the big city, they've been forking out all their hard earned money to ensure that their little boy continues to enjoy himself. Makes you wonder who's beneath who eh? For some time now they've been paying off a blackmailer, someone else who knows what dirty little deed you did. And I can tell you something else. It wasn't your so called dozy bugger of a father that told whoever it is, so he can be blackmailed! So, question? Which one of your illustrious pals knew what you did?" He said nothing. Just sat there for a while, the hubbub of background pub noise suddenly seeming loud, probably contemplating how he was to extract himself from this situation with the minimum personal damage. I couldn't imagine him being particularly perturbed about his parents predicament.

"No one," eventually came his reply. "No one knew."

"Well someone did, didn't they?" I asked sarcastically. "So give it some more thought. Dalton Murphy maybe?" That got a reaction. He seemed to visibly blanche. "Or what about Marshall?"

"Who the hell are you? How do you know those names?" He looked a little sick. Not quite the unknown quantity he thought he was.

"You know Jimmy, I bet if you were to bend your mind a bit more you might come up with the name. What about Craig Holden? He sounded a bit of a dirt bag and from what I hear, wasn't too keen on you at the end. Did you brag to him at some stage? Perhaps you were too high to know who you spoke to." He looked almost dazed, like someone had physically punched him.

"I can't tell you anything, I don't remember much about it," he said. "I don't know who knew about it. I might have talked, but I don't know. You have to believe me." He sounded almost desperate and looked quickly around the room.

"What a pity! I want some answers. The quicker I get them the better. You have a sister in hospital. She's there because she has carried the guilt of your action with her and was forced to falsely accuse someone that I knew, of doing something similar to her. He's dead now. He was beaten to death! So you're linked up with it you see." I could see that he was able to make the connection which intrigued me. This boy knew something, more than me. He turned again, looking anxiously about him.

"What's the matter. Lost your friend?"

"What?" More shock.

"You know, One Dalton Murphy. The guy you came in with." An enormous long shot but it found the mark. He sat bolt upright, his hands beginning to tremble.

"How..... who told.......?" He spluttered.

"As I told you on the phone, I had a fair idea of what you looked like. I also had a description of your cronies. That guy seemed to fit the picture. Funny that you should keep in with them, considering the beating they gave you. Bit odd don't you think?" He said nothing, looked deflated. "What were you going to do? Give me some money then wait until I got outside and do unto others what you had done to yourself?" I could see that I had pretty much disclosed their plan. Murphy was no doubt outside waiting for me to show. "So tell me Jimmy, why are you still with them? I would have thought you would have wanted to get as far away as possible from the likes of them and Holden. Unless they have some kind of hold over you. That's it isn't it?" He said nothing, just sat there staring into space, then slowly he cracked.

"I'm caught whatever I do. I don't want to go to prison. I don't want to be beaten again. I still have nightmares. They hit me with baseball bats until I thought I was going to die." Tears streamed down his face. "I can't take that again, just can't. I didn't know what I was doing. Craig gave me some substance, said I had to take it, said I would enjoy the reaction. So I did. I don't remember much after that. It was all like I was in a mist looking down at myself. I could see me on top of this girl, she was putting up a real fight, but I was winning, forcing her legs apart. I was wearing a balaclava. So were the others. I didn't even know who she was. They were saying that she really wanted it, was hot for it. I thought she did. I hardly knew she was screaming. And that was it. I didn't know I was doing it. I couldn't feel anything." He stopped and wiped his eyes. All arrogance gone. I liked him better like this. "When I got the chance I grassed on Craig. I didn't want to rape anyone. He set me up. But he's got me now. Shit, I even work for his Uncle's company."

164

EIGHT

"So, for some reason they have kept tabs on you. Do you have any thoughts as to why this might be so?" I asked. I couldn't think of any myself. Many of the conclusions I had arrived at in the bath the other night didn't seem quite so relevant now. Still, there was a lot to untangle. It was a bit like trying to unravel a knot: You get one bit done only to find out that you have created a knot which seems worse than the one you had started off with. It was like the many fishing trips with my father when I was a kid. The fishing forever punctuated by frequent stops to sort out the tangle that my reel had become and his very patient attempts to fix it, one step at a time. I guess I would have to take a leaf out of his book and try the same approach. With a pang, I realized that he was no longer there beside me to help me. I missed him and I sorely rued my over sensitive reaction to what had happened. Damn but I wished I could turn the clock back. . . . .Jimmy was speaking again.

". . . . . at university. Craig somehow had managed to swing it so that he was also eligible for entrance. He had gone to another school after Haileybury, Berkhamsted I think. God knows who wrote his UCAS." I sat up with a jolt. "I got a hell of a shock to find him in the same hall of residence as me. I almost quit then, but he seemed to ignore me and wasn't at all like I thought he would be. Then something happened in the Hall. There was this issue over a girl. She claimed that Craig had tried to have sex with her, raped her I guess. She went to the police. It looked like he would be sent down and quite frankly I was pleased. I had never felt that comfortable with him about. I kept expecting something to happen. I guess it did, but not quite in the way I had expected. Craig came to me and told me that I was to vouch for his story, that he had been with me on that particular night and that we had been to the cinema and if I didn't then sure as hell, if he went down, so too would I, for my indiscretion at school. That was it. What could I do? The slimy bastard has had his hooks in me from then on, every so often calling in a favour. And he knows I won't do a thing to stop him." He stopped. There wasn't anything more to say. As he had said, he was caught in a vicious circle. But why this latest pay back? And what had he told the others to make them bring Murphy along: That someone else was trying to do the same thing to him as they

165

were doing? I didn't get a chance to ask, for I was suddenly aware that we had been joined at the table. Murphy stared down at me, for a moment I felt that he had been shocked to see who Jimmy was talking to but I might have been wrong. He turned away and spoke to Jimmy.

"You finished with this dick head? Shit, you've been nattering on for bloody hours. What gives? I'm fuckin' freezin'." His voice was deep and gutteral and enhanced the image of a tough man. Jimmy flapped a bit, managing to reply that I was in fact a friend of his fathers and that there wasn't anything to worry about but I could see that Murphy was less than convinced. I decided to add my bit.

"I take it you are one of Jimmy's mates then?" I asked innocently. He turned slowly, acknowledging my statement.

"Yeah, something like that, we go back a bit."

"So, did you come here with him or did you just meet up by chance?"

"Whatever." He turned back to Jimmy, his conversation for the moment over with me. There was something about him. You can disguise a face, a voice, but it's hard to change the mannerisms of a lifetime and the way this guy moved and held himself sent tingles up my spine. I knew we had met before. The last time, he had held a knife in his hand. No wonder he got a shock seeing me. Obviously Jimmy hadn't mentioned my name. I watched him talking, watched the hand and arm expressions saw the bent nose, knew I was right. What could I do with it? If I told the police Jimmy would end up being found out. Wished I hadn't made any promises to his parents. What was the smart move? Murphy knew who I was. Knew that I was connected to Len Jones, knew that the stakes had suddenly gone up. This wasn't just a problem for Jimmy to sort out. This obviously went further. It wouldn't take the brain of Britain to realize that I would be able to put one and one together and make the connection between them and Jones. Time to see what was going to happen.

"Right then Jimmy. I can see you and your mate have a bit to catch up on, so I'm off. Think on what I said. Your father's struggling at the moment, seems in a bit of a tight corner. Wouldn't hurt to bail him out."

Jimmy looked a little puzzled but it was all I could think of which would justify our meeting. I watched him slowly latch on and nod as I stood up to make my way out. For a moment Murphy and I locked eyes as he stood barring my way. There wasn't much warmth in their expression but after a moment, he looked away and turned aside.

"Cheers," I said as pleasantly as I was able to, then made for the door at the end of the bar and out into the car park which was thankfully well lit. No one followed.

As I eased out onto the road I glanced back towards the pub and fancied I saw a figure coming out. Too late. I turned right for a short distance before taking the road down through Lemsford and on up the old A1 to Welwyn. I spent a good deal of my time after that wondering what had made me take that road and not the more widely used A1 M. I didn't have an answer. And I wasn't one of those who prescribed to the theory of predestination. Kismet, destiny, or Karma were not things I believed in. I drove up the road because I had made an unconscious decision to do so, nothing else.

I booted the BMW and reveled in the surge of power as I shot up the hill towards the pub at the top. My mind raced over the events of the evening. What had I stumbled into? What had seemed a totally senseless death, by thugs who took little pleasure in sex offences, now seemed to have further dimensions. Where did that leave me? My dabbling was not going to be tolerated and the closer I got to finding out the answers the more likely I would end up like poor Len.

Over the top, past another pub, lights blazing, car park full, a popular place for the young scene. Didn't take much notice of the headlights in my rear vision mirror, some ignorant person who didn't have the manners to dip his lights. I flipped the mirror onto night driving, cutting out the glare then shot round the first of the corners. The car following was close, too close. Silly bugger, driving like that could cause an accident. Put my left foot on the break while I kept the other on the accelerator. That usually did the trick. But not this time, he was hanging in close. Down the hill we went, the bridge over the motorway appearing as we swung out of a left handed turn. Shit! What was he playing at? The car had come along side. I looked across, couldn't make out much in the dark, just a dark figure. Then all hell broke out. One part of my brain screaming to me that he had turned in on me, the other part directing my hands as I fought to control the car. Who was this maniac? Hold the wheel. Christ, listen to the noise. Metal tearing. Oh hell I'm going through. Engine racing, screaming. No resistance. Was I screaming? I wanted to die in New Zealand, not here. I knew in that moment where my future should be. Then there was no moment, just an incredible shock shattering finality, intense pain blossoming over my body. Nothing.

NINE

They told me afterwards that I was incredibly lucky to be alive. That it was some kind of miracle that I escaped major injury. I thanked the manufacturers of my BMW and lady luck. Kismet? Who knows?

Darkness punctuated by stabbing pain, stabbing lights, and a crescendo of noise. What was going on? What the hell had happened? Where was I? I moved. Bad idea. . . . . . . no pain, no lights, no noise.

Voices. Who they belonged to I truly didn't care. Memories came flooding back. My car. I had been in my car. I opened my eyes. Couldn't see a thing, couldn't focus. Why couldn't I focus? Could feel the onset of panic coming on. Breathe deep Sutherland. That's a start. Michael Sutherland. Me. More voices. More bright lights. But why didn't I feel right? Moved my hand to explore. Could tolerate the pain. Couldn't feel anything with my left hand. Everything disoriented. And such pain in my back and neck. Intense pressure. That wasn't right. I couldn't budge, couldn't move. And a steering wheel. The damn thing seemed to be attached to my chest, stopping me breathing. More panic. Shit Sutherland get a grip you big girl. Voices closer now, discernable.

"Hang in there mate, you'll be okay, there's help on its way." A man's voice. I tried to speak. Could only cough. Needed to spit. God I'm choking on blood.

"You alright mate? You'll be okay. Keep your eyes open. My wife has phoned for an ambulance. Shouldn't be long now." Tried to answer. Oh Christ I hope not. Sheer panic overtook me. I didn't want to die. I wanted to live. I thought of Lucy. I wanted to spend more time with her. I wanted to see my brother again. I wanted to see the Southern Alps, see the lakes. Sod it, it was not my time yet.

"Hold on lad. I can hear the sirens. They're almost here now. It's going to be okay. Hold on." His voice seemed to be going, fading into the background. 'Don't leave' I begged silently. 'Please don't leave me whoever you are. I don't want to be alone in here.' I stretched out, groping in the blackness which was engulfing me. Nothing.

Voices. Quiet voices. I opened my eyes. Bright daylight, bright room. As my brain slowly engaged gear I realized that I was in fact in a hospital ward. Thank God I was alive. Unconnected thoughts became connected. I had been given a second chance. Breathed deeply. Could smell. It didn't matter that it was an antiseptic hospital smell. It was good. I took stock of my immediate surroundings. Tubes of plastic appeared to hang down from a stand like octopus legs. I followed them down and saw that they entered into me. Great. I had no idea what they did. It didn't seem to matter. A time to think. I had time. Wasn't that great. So close to not having any. What had happened? Had it been deliberate? I had an uncomfortable feeling that it had. The image of Murphy standing at the pub door clutching something to his ear left me in little doubt that he had been talking to an accomplice who had been waiting. It didn't need much guessing to put a name to the other fellow. That pleasant gang of ex public school delinquents. I tried to piece it all together but quite literally my brain hurt and I gave in to the waves of sleep which washed over me.

D.C. Carmichael sauntered into the ward, the first person aside from hospital staff to see me. I had no concept of day or time. It just felt suspended in this institution. Whilst there was a rhythm to it, it lacked identity. Endless shifts of nurses monitoring and observing, all merging together.

"Good morning again Sir," he said. So it was morning. That was a start. "We seem to have a habit of meeting in the most trying of circumstances." What could I say? He was right, but then when else did you meet a policeman? "Right then, are you up to answering a few questions?" I didn't have a chance to answer for he kept right on. "You know, you seem to live a charmed life, never quite coming out as badly off as you deserve."

"Thank you. I see I have your full and total support," I replied dryly.

"Perhaps it came out a little wrong. What I meant was that considering the situations you have been involved in, your injuries have not been as great as perhaps they might have been."

"Yeah, you're probably right, but you should see it from my side."

"Yes Sir, I'm sure you are right. It can't be very pleasant. I'm afraid your car is a complete and utter right off." I tried to shrug. The car was the least of my worries. I would get it sorted. "You know, you were extremely lucky. I have to hand it to those Germans. They know how to build a good car. In many others, I'm afraid we wouldn't be talking now." He paused and looked down at me. I said nothing. I had already offered a prayer to whoever it was up there that listened. "Yes . . . . . . right now. . . . . , let me see, perhaps you could fill me in with the details if you feel up to it?" I nodded. "Good."

I had run the scene through my mind over and over again, each time more convinced that the accident, hadn't in fact been an accident at all. The dilemma of course was to convince D.C. Carmichael that it had been, for the present at least. I wasn't sure where that stood me; holding information back was a criminal offence I believed. Lucy no doubt would update me on that. I filled him in with the details he needed to know, missing out that I had in fact been at the pub, telling him that I had become aware of a car following rather closely behind as I headed up the B197 towards Welwyn. Told him how the driver had pulled over to overtake and had somehow connected with me. D.C. Carmichael listened, made notes in his notepad then looked at me a little askance.

"Tell me Sir, do you think it was an accident?"

I did my best to look bewildered. ". . . . . well, ... , yes. Of course. Why? I'm not one of these victims of road rage am I?" I asked. He stared, added a little more to his notepad, sucked on the pen for a bit then spoke again.

"Road rage eh? There's a thought. Tell me, why is it that whenever I see you, you have been in some kind of incident? And yet you tend to underplay it."

"Just my way I guess. You make it sound like a lot of times. What is it? Twice now?"

"On my reckoning, three times now Sir. If you remember, the first time was at the home of that colleague of yours after he had been beaten." I said nothing. "And then there was the knifing, now this. It's not your everyday normal existence now is it?"

"Put like that, it does sound a little bizarre," I agreed. "So what do you infer from it all then?" It would be interesting to hear his assessment. D.C. Carmichael was nobody's fool.

"Well Sir, I was kind of hoping you could tell me." He paused, tapping the pen on his front teeth. I waited. "But it seems that you are either disinclined to say anything or in fact have no real idea what has happened. So, I'll run this by you and you tell me whether it makes any sense. Alright?"

"Fine," I agreed. I felt damned uncomfortable. I leant across to the bedside locker to pour myself a drink of what I had earlier discovered was tepid water. D.C. Carmichael beat me to it and handed me the half full glass. "Thanks."

"Pleasure," he said. "You're not too good are you?" Good was a fairly general term. Good in comparison to what? He had already informed me that I was Good, because I was lucky to be alive. Yet he was right,

I didn't feel good, in fact I felt bloody lousy. The steering wheel had crushed my chest causing internal bleeding. A rib had punctured my lung. Apparently I was lucky not to have broken my neck. I broke my clavicle instead, along with my left humerus and dislocated my knee, had severe bruising in a number of places and my back hurt like hell, like I had been beaten with rubber hosing for several hours, or a police truncheon. The doctors had been quick to point out how remarkable the body was, how accommodating to stress it was. I took their word for it.

"Well Sir, I think that you have got yourself caught up in some sort of circumstance which you may or may not know anything about. I'm not one to believe in coincidence. Statistically, it just doesn't hold water. Therefore on that premise, these 'situations' have occurred because you are acting as the catalyst." He waited for a reaction on my part but was disappointed. "I would like to bet that it is all connected somehow with the first incident. What is it? Are you attempting to be some kind of avenging angel, a modern day vigilante? Mmmm?" I continued to stare back at him. "Because if you are Sir, then I must strongly caution you against such action. Leave police work to the police."

"Tell me then," I replied, "just how close are you to finding the people who murdered Len Jones?"

"At this point in time Sir, we seem to have come to a standstill on one line of enquiry but there are other lines to pursue. Unfortunately, the young lass who was helping us has been hospitalised, comatosed. Her parents have put it down to stress and until we can talk with her again then I'm afraid there is little we can do."

"So what you're really saying is that you are stymied, going nowhere fast."

"I think that's a bit harsh Sir. These things do take time you know. Police work can be tedious but we normally get our man in the end."

"Just like the Mounties," I replied somewhat facetiously. He said nothing but slowly put his notepad and pen away and retrieved his hat from the bed. After a moment he turned back to me and spoke.

"I'm not convinced you've told me all that you know or suspect but for the moment I'll let things rest. Just let me remind you that withholding information is actually a criminal offence. If you do know anything which may be important to our enquiry then I do urge you to come forward with it. I'll say goodbye for the moment." He turned on his heels and strode off. Not a very happy policeman our D.C. Carmichael. I couldn't blame him; he knew that something was afoot. I would have to watch out. Jeez, life used to be so uncomplicated. Why me? What if I just forgot about everything? Ignored what had happened? Would I be left alone? I didn't know. What had I got myself involved in? Which ever way I turned there seemed to be more and more people whose lives were affected, like a net being cast, gathering in more unsuspecting souls along with those others, the ones who knew, who had thrown the net in the first place. Why?

In a place where time seems to stand still, where the abnormal becomes the norm; the meals at such early times, the clockwork programme of shifts, the visiting hours, the constant monitoring and prodding, there was time to try and piece the events together. I didn't know whether I was guilty of exaggerating the detail, but the picture I formulated did nothing to restore my confidence in the good nature of mankind.

Lucy and family, at different times and occasionally together were regular visitors. Virginia brought brightness, warmth and some good home cooking, George, humour and a hip flask, Lucy a tonic for an ailing patient: love and soft lips. They all brought their fears and it didn't take them too long to voice them. I listened and tried to put them at ease. They were right of course, but I couldn't let them see that I agreed with them. Not yet anyway. I had things I wanted to do once I got out of this place.

Chris and the 'lads' from school also made their presence known, much to the obvious delight of some of the staff, but not the staff nurse who visibly bristled every time Chris's welsh accent boomed down the corridor.

"Another bloody holiday. These kiwis can't stand the pace. Terms only been going a few weeks and you've cracked. Leaving me to do all the rugby as well eh? What's going on then Mike?" He looked serious. His first visit and I could tell he was shaken by what he saw. I told him everything I knew, within reason. He had been there before and deserved an explanation. "So you think you were deliberately pushed over the bridge?" I nodded and he looked shocked. "That could have been murder, do you realise that?" The thought had crossed my mind many times. It was most unsettling. "Why would anyone want to kill you? What is it about Len Jones that would lead to such extreme action? I mean he was after all, just a school teacher?"

"Well, there are a couple of things I think have triggered this off. The one factor which I can't quite place is why Len Jones was involved in the first instance."

"Care to elaborate?" Chris asked. He had pulled a chair to the bedside and leant forward, elbows propped upon the bed. I shook my head.

"Not just yet. I want to get out of here and do a bit of digging and see what I unearth."

"You be careful Mike. At the moment you seem to be digging your own grave. These guys are playing for keeps. You don't really know who or why and like Len, you're just a teacher." He didn't need to add the last bit. It was implied in how he had said it: Len was dead.

Chris was a regular visitor. He kept me informed of goings on at school, gave me blow by blow accounts of the training of the firsts and following their next game on the Saturday called in to give me a full account of their victory, accompanied by Jamie Lee the captain. I was keen to get out, but was informed by the doctor that it would be a couple of weeks before I was ready for the move. Most frustrating. Whilst the visits were the high points of my confinement, I was eager to leave and counted the days down like a prisoner.

It was Lucy who picked me up when the big day finally arrived. She had borrowed George's car and once I had been wheel chaired to the exit and the doctor who had been in charge of me had said his goodbyes, tempered with advice, and the staff nurse had seen me off, I manoeuvred my crutches with reasonable ease, I was almost practised with them following the last incident, and followed Lucy out towards the car. God it was good to breath in some fresh air and feel the coolness of it. Virginia had insisted, on her last visit, that I was to recuperate at their home and no amount of protesting would alter her mind. I didn't like imposing myself upon them but Lucy took pains to put my mind at rest as we drove back to the farm. Whilst I didn't yet feel 100%, just to sit and listen to Lucy chatter on about her latest case and look out at the changing landscape filled me with a deep appreciation of life.

I spent a further two weeks in their care, cosseted by Virginia and doctored on good malt by George. I was made to feel like part of the family and they gave me a free run, or in my case hobble, of the house. George told me I should use the time constructively. He didn't push too much but I could tell he was keen to know what was going on. All in good time. He introduced me to his computer and suggested I get acquainted with it, told me that Gavin had got them linked up on the internet and if I wanted, I could go surfing on it!

I learnt more about computers in that two weeks than I had during my entire life. Frustrating at first. My knowledge somewhat limited, as Jane had often taken great delight in informing me. I didn't feel inclined to read through all the copious literature which went with it, but in the end realized that it was perhaps the best way. It always seemed strange to me that with the computers supposedly taking over, you still had to use a book to work out how to use them!

I spent hours slowly typing up my thoughts: The how's, the why's, the who's. I thought I had a pretty good picture of the first and the last but struggled to come up with much for the one in the middle. George had given me my own disk, on which I copied everything but left nothing on the hard drive. I didn't want Gavin to stumble across it, nor Lucy. I knew what her reaction would be. I was healing quickly. Virginia's motherly attention was by far the best medicine. They opened up their home to visits from my friends and gave them the same five star treatment I was receiving.

176

When Lucy managed to visit, George and Virginia diplomatically left us with space for ourselves. I knew I was recovering when her presence left me feeling a little frustrated. Her 'steady on Sutherland, you'll do yourself a mischief', left me in no doubt that I was on the mend. We managed to grab secluded moments together and during one of those times with the sitting room to ourselves, Lucy poured her heart out.

". . . . . . . I really thought I had lost you, you know," she whispered nudging up close to me on the settee. "It was horrible. When I first saw you I couldn't believe you would survive. You looked such a mess." She took a deep breath, fighting to control the emotion which she must have denied for so long. "I would hate to lose you." I wrapped my good arm around her shoulders. We had learnt through practice how to sit.

"I remember not wanting to die." I looked down at her. "I remember thinking of you, thinking how unfair it would be to lose out on not seeing you." She smiled. I also remembered thinking that I wanted to head back to New Zealand. It was prudent not to mention that at this particular time. Anyway, if I could swing it, I wanted Lucy to come back with me. ... if. Time would tell, but I had known at the crash that I wanted her to be part of my life.

"Mike?" Her voice interrupted my thoughts.

"Mmm?"

"A penny for them. You were miles away. What is it?"

I smiled and shook my head. "Nothing. Just thinking back to the crash I guess." I stopped talking. I hadn't liked the experience. Had found a side of me which had discovered serious fear. Didn't like that. Made me feel less like a man. Couldn't voice it yet.

"What is it Mike? What are you holding back?" She stared intently at me, chin thrust forward, scrutinizing, waiting for me to continue. "Mike, it would be better to talk than to bottle things up you know. Mum thinks there is something troubling you as well. Dad, well Dad's Dad. He thinks you should be just left to sort yourself out. Time will heal and all that sort of thing. But, I'm not going to just sit and watch you." The Alexander women were certainly something.

"It's nothing, truly." I leant across to kiss her but she drew back.

"Nothing. I know you, better than you know yourself. Don't give me this nothing business."

I didn't want to say anything yet. There would be time later. "Lucy, for the moment let's drop it." She went to interrupt but I stopped her. "No, listen, all in good time. I promise I will tell you. It's just something I want to come to terms with first. Okay?" It was not in her nature to drop it, partly her training, partly her genes but for whatever reason, she remained quiet. Almost!

"Well, just make sure you do." That was her last voice on the subject and we went on to talk of other things. She did tell me that she had gone to the site of the crash. The car had been removed but the bridge had part of the side missing . It had made her feel sick to think that I had come crashing over that onto the A1M below. "God you must have been terrified," she had remarked so acutely.

Towards the end of my stay I found myself alone with George. Virginia had popped out to a Woman's Institute meeting 'on flower arranging' in the village hall, and Gavin was out at the cinema with his girl. George and I sat in the lounge, comfortably ensconced in his large brown leather chairs. As soon as his wife had driven off he had made for the drinks cabinet and pulled out one of his decanters of whiskey.

"Got a taste for the Irish," he laughed, "and not just their woman. This is good stuff. No doubt you will keep me company."

"No doubt at all, thanks very much." He had good taste. We discussed the relative merits of various whiskies and found that we had a pretty similar palate. George liked to lie back in his chair, shoes kicked off, ash tray within easy reach. It hadn't taken long before the cigars were out and we were lost amidst the clouds once again.

". . . . . . . .That wasn't an accident was it?" One moment we had been talking about cattle, the next, his observation on my crash. He said nothing else, just lay there staring up at the smoke he was blowing circles with, rather like a big kid. I said nothing for a moment but my mind was racing. I desperately wanted someone to talk to, to have someone else apart from Chris objectively consider my conclusions. I couldn't think of anyone better.

"I don't think so." His eyes tracked down from the smoke to meet mine.

"No, I thought as much." He shifted in the chair, hitching himself forward, eyes beginning to blaze. "It's all that business isn't it?"

I tapped some ash from my cigar. I liked the way it sat in curled layers. "Yeah, I reckon. I can't be positive, haven't got any real proof but there's too much coincidence. Hell George, ever since this Len Jones thing, I've been plagued with bad luck."

"Bad luck my toe. I told you before, you mess around with the likes of Grey and you are bound to come off second best."

"So you say, but I've no way of knowing whether of not he has anything to do with it. I can't see any connection and the crash, well hell he wasn't anywhere around."

George snorted into his glass. "Come on Michael, don't be so naive. You're not in the back blocks now. Money talks, jobs get done. Any kind of job. They all have their price."

It didn't make any sense. What was it about me that was important enough for someone to want to get rid of me? I didn't know anything that warranted such extreme measures and I told George so.

"Perhaps someone thinks otherwise," he replied. I could see George was fairly convinced in himself that Grey was behind it all but it didn't sit well with me. Certainly there was something going on with Jimmy McKay and the dubious connections he had. But where did they fit in the

179

great scheme of things? Perhaps there was a connection between them and Grey. It was possible that Holden had met up with one of the Greys at Berkhamsted. It seemed the most likely possibility. I guessed I could make a few enquiries and find out whether or not they did. George voiced my thoughts. "There has to some connection. Someway that this all fits in together. If you sit there long enough Michael, I'm sure that you will come up with something. Every action has a corresponding reaction. Without a doubt Len Jones has been the catalyst to all this. What did he do? Why did he trigger off such an eventful set of reactions? That's the key to all of this you know. I'm convinced of it." He was in full swing now. I could see his mind racing over as he tried to come to grips with the solution. "You've got to get out and ask a few questions boy. That should stir a few things up. Yes that should do the trick."

"Fair enough George, although for the present, that might just prove a little tricky." I pointed to my crutches. "I'm still hobbling around like an old man. Hardly the dashing sleuth."

"Mmm. You have a point there. But I tell you what. I can help here. I've got a Governors meeting at the school this week. Young Grey will be there as well. Seems he's managed to get himself on the board. Not a good step for the Collegiate in my opinion. Anyway, I'll have a little chat with him. See what kind of reaction I get." He sat back in his chair and puffed vigorously on his cigar, looking very pleased with himself. I could see that he was really getting into this. He needed to understand that it wasn't a game. He had told me often enough that there were some pretty unsavoury characters about. It was my turn now.

"Just what sort of things are you going to say George? You can hardly front up to Eric Grey and tell him that you think he is into something corrupt, or that you have an acquaintance who suggests that he might be dabbling in murder. It wouldn't go down to well." George looked back at me as if I was some kind of patronising idiot and spoke quietly.

"I think I can handle it Michael. Give me some credit for diplomacy."

"Yeah, sorry George, concern really. If you are right in your assumptions then these guys are pretty hard cases. It's not a game to them."

NINE

By the time Virginia had returned we thought we had pretty well sorted out some kind of action. Whether it would blossom into anything fruitful remained to be seen.

TEN

*G*etting back to school was hardly a home coming, but it did feel quite good and familiar. After fielding off the initial and expected questions it didn't take too long to slip back into the routine. And not much longer to catch up with the gossip, although surprisingly, there was scant of that. Getting back to school had also initially proved to be something of a challenge. With the car written off, I had come up against the slow wheels of the insurance company who seemed reluctant to make any hasty decisions concerning my replacement of it. Once again I was privileged to have the aristocracy working my corner. A few well placed calls from George soon got the ball rolling and within no time, I was the proud owner of a newly registered BMW. Black as before. My first journey in it took me back to the scene of the crash: In broad daylight with a lot of nervous looking in the rear vision mirror. Stopping on the bridge and looking down at the busy A1M below left me with a cold chill down my back and immensely thankful that no one was in fact walking on my grave. I had been lucky.

I had spent a good part of my time out, contemplating my life, my future. It was a new experience. I considered myself one of the original drifters, not especially motivated by anything, just a collective desire to enjoy life, to work to live, rather than live to work. What did I want out of it? What could I reasonably expect? Tough questions. I was beginning finally to formulate some answers. It was just a matter of prioritising

TEN

First XV training was a step in the right direction. Of all the things I had missed it had been this which I was chomping at the bit to get back to. They had continued to perform well, as expected, the only disappointing aspect for me was the fact that the fifteen season had come to an end a week before I got back. I felt robbed of the moment, cheated out of what was rightfully mine. It was good to see the whole squad turn out that first Monday, like a welcoming committee. I let them throw the ball about, and whilst the session was relaxed, the mood was recreated and we began to plan for the sevens competitions.

Chris's explosive entrance into the P.E. office as I was about to head home, was unsettling.

"Shit, shit, shit and shit," he said with great feeling. I looked up, tempted to say something smart about his command of the English language, but thought better of it as I saw the look on his face.

"What's up?"

"Bloody Fields." I waited. He stood in the room, too agitated to sit, breathing heavily. "I've just spent the last hour or so arguing with him and he won't budge. The guy's two bricks short of a load in my opinion. Mike, while you were away he got together a working party on health and safety and rail roaded them into agreeing that rugby was too dangerous for the school to continue with, as its official winter sport." That was news. Boy was that news. And here I had been thinking that there had been very little of any consequence happening whilst I had been absent.

"Jesus, Chris why the hell didn't you say anything sooner?" I could feel the anger beginning to grow. "Why did you see him tonight and not me? Come on mate, we don't run the department this way. Did Jane know of this?"

He looked a little sheepish and nodded. "Yeah, in fact it was her suggestion that you should be allowed to just ease your way back in without too much hassle."

"You must be joking. When did you plan to tell me? Or were you going to surprise me next season with some soccer posts! I'm spitting tacks They

183

can't just alter the tradition of the school without due consultation. It has to go to the Governors and be ratified before Fields can do anything. And I would have thought that they would then discuss it with me." I could feel the anger inside. One thing after another and now this. What I couldn't come to terms with, was that they had all remained quiet for the entire day. Fair enough, they knew I would be upset, that was an understatement, but now it just left me seething for another night. Chris had started to speak again.

". . . . . . it was Mike." I hadn't caught what he said.

"What was?"

"The Governors, or probably more correctly, Lord Grey and a select few, rubber stamped Fields proposals. Fait Accompli."

I snorted in derision. Grey and his protégé were becoming too much a part of my life, and all of it bad. "Were you involved Chris? Did they talk to you or Jane? Involve you in the decision making, anything?" Chris shook his head.

"Jane queried the rumours that she had heard, but Fields dismissed her, stating that decisions being made at management level had very little to do with her. To give her her due Mike, she stuck at it, but Fields showed his usual hand, threatening to terminate her contract if she continued to question him. It sucks Mike. There has to be something behind this."

"He couldn't do that. I hope she got her union rep involved. It would be unfair dismissal."

Chris nodded. "Yeah, apparently he said that as well, but did go on to say that should she leave she probably wouldn't get a great reference."

I was sure he was right. As for Fields, I couldn't think what he was up to. I was paranoid enough to consider that it was simply a way of getting at me, but then if that was the case it would surely have been better to wait for me to return then confront me with the decision. "I think I've had enough for one day Chris. You know, I actually missed the place while I was away. Crazy isn't it. . . . . . Fancy a beer?" He nodded "Good, so do I."

We made our way out into the cool night air and drove toward the "staff" pub, so called because it was reasonably patronised by a number of us. Tonight proved to be no exception and as we walked through the door into the warm smoky atmosphere, a cheer went up from the table in the corner.

"About bloody time Sutherland. Your round."

"Cheers Brian, I'm glad I came now." The rest of them laughed, their mood one or two pints the better than mine. Robin eased himself from behind the table.

"Here I'll give you a hand. You're still a bit of a walking wounded."

We stood at the bar, the young girl behind it quick to fill up the pints, Robin as equally quick to dispense them, and me a touch less eager to pay for them. A round these days cost a small fortune. Still, I reckoned I owed them. They were good friends, had been quick to visit me in hospital and see to it that I was okay and as I had been out of circulation for a while, it was only fair that I stood them a drink.

As was the case with a gathering of teachers, discussion centred around the pupils, their discipline or lack of it, work in general, pay in particular and the government in despair. We had just finished toasting Fields and his latest little gem of a decision when the Len Jones affair was once more brought up, the mood sobering, the name like a wound still to heal. Some one asked a question of his wife. I replied that I hadn't seen her for some time so I had no idea how she was getting on. I told them that she hadn't appeared too good the last time I had seen her though. Had any one else dropped in on her? No comments, a few guilty looks, most of us realising that while good intentions were there, circumstances overtook us. It was the way of the world, all busy, busy.

"Why not organise a rota then," piped up Chris, "A visit per week."

There were murmurs of agreement and one or two voices against the idea. John in particular felt it was the wrong way to go about things. People should visit because they wanted to, not because of a rota. It

185

seemed indecent he said. His voice and those of the others who agreed with him were over ridden. As Chris had come up with the idea, he drew lots to see who would go first. It was John. Wasn't it often like that? To be fair, he took it well, although to add insult to injury it was unanimously decided that as he had won the lottery, he should buy the next round.

"You bastards," was his response, as he eased himself out from behind the table, to the hoots of the rest of us.

It proved to be a good night. I hadn't really spent much time in their company over the last couple of months, a point noted and commented on by the 'lads'. To the effect that I would lose my status if I didn't get it sorted. 'And bring your bit of stuff along too', had been Brian's delicate contribution.

The first couple of weeks of teaching came and went. I hadn't managed to confront Fields as he had been out of school on some sort of conference. So it was all pretty uneventful. A weekend to look forward to, no rugby, very little marking. Alison was making her first steps towards married life, shifting out some of her things to the new home they had found in a nearby village. The wedding was drawing closer.

"So tell me Andrew, are you all set for the big day?" I asked him as we sat around the table tucking into cheese on toast. Alison looked up, searching his face with her still vulnerable look.

"Damn right," he replied positively reaching out for her hand and gently tapping it. "I can't wait until Miss O'Neal becomes Mrs Young. It's going to be great." Alison smiled a wide beaming smile and I couldn't help but think that they were two very lucky people. Maybe in time, just maybe I could be committed to some one like that. If she would have me.

"You must come and see the house when you have some time Mike. It's starting to take shape. Andrew has been working like a Trojan. He's completely refurbished the kitchen and bathroom and what will be the baby's room." She stopped there and blushed.

"You're obviously marrying a handyman Alison. Good choice. Hey listen Andrew, before you two leave for good, how about doing a few odd jobs around here?"

"I'd love to Mike, but I've got enough to keep me busy in our own home for the next year or so I reckon. Sorry."

"Well it was worth a try." I shrugged, laughing, got up and made the tea and brought it over to the table and we sat together, sipping at the hot mugs. I told them to leave any dishes, as I had nothing better to do and they were soon off back to their house. Without a doubt I would miss Alison. From tenant to friend. She was a nice person and I liked the man she was going to marry.

I finished pottering about the house and decided that I might as well get out. We were running low on a few commodities and with Alison busy with her own life, it was down to me to get things sorted. I drove out to Tesco's on the round about near Hatfield, grabbed a trolley and set about doing what I wasn't really designed to do. As I pushed my trolley through the throng of people I found that I was queuing at the delicatessens beside Mrs McKay. She looked up at me, not registering at first and I watched as the dawning realisation took hold.

"Hello," I said, "How are things?"

"Mr Sutherland?"

"Yes. How's Belinda?" The poor kid was still not back at school. Jane had said that she had heard that she was back at home but still not a hundred percent.

"I thought it was you. I'm sorry, my mind was miles away. Belinda? Well, she's home but as you know, she's still not back at school. The poor mite has really suffered. It's a terrible business, just terrible." She put a trembling hand to her face and crumpled, tears welling up and over, running down her cheeks.

"Look, I'm truly sorry Mrs McKay. I didn't mean to upset you." I put my hand out to comfort her, but she stepped back, determined to sort her emotions out on her own.

"No, no, I'm fine." She held her hands up in front of her like a shield. "It just seems like there is no way to turn, no way to win. Stephen seems to have gone into a shell. After you talked with him he really seemed positive. He said that at last there was someone fighting our corner. But you haven't been in touch since and as the days went by he's just stopped hoping that something would happen. Jimmy called to say that he had met you and that he was sorry for the pain he had caused us, but then he too has not been back in touch. It's just too much. Stephen has even got to the point of thinking that it might be best if he spoke to the police. It's tearing him apart. Where have you been?" The last question an accusation. They needed help. I had breezed into their life, seemed to offer a solution, if not a solution, a hope, but had failed them.

"I've been laid up for a while, in fact, I've only got back to school a couple of weeks ago. Tell your husband not to despair. I'm trying to sort things out. I truly hope Belinda can make a full recovery." Her mention of Jimmy disturbed me. The fact that he had bothered to ring his parents suggested to me that he was finally experiencing pangs of guilt and developing a conscience. Having made the first reconciliatory steps, why hadn't he been back in touch? There was no way his parents were going to turn their back on him now. So what was happening? "Would it help any if I popped around and saw your husband?" It was all I could think of. I didn't see how it possibly could. In some respects I was the perpetrator of their current predicament. To my surprise she latched on to my offer like a life line.

"Oh please. Thank you. That would be wonderful." Her face lit up in hope. God knows why. I couldn't offer salvation. I left her with the promise that I would be in touch. She seemed so grateful. I couldn't understand why. Desperate folk, desperate to cling to someone.

Having information that was so important to so many people and not being able to do anything constructive with it was proving to be a real mental burden. To whom did I owe what? What could I tell Len's wife? That he hadn't committed any crime, that someone had made the whole story up for some reason? What reason? Would that help her? It wouldn't bring her husband back. How would she feel knowing that he had died because of something that he hadn't done? I couldn't see that it would make her feel any better, and yet to clear his name, let people know that he was not some kind of sexual pervert would be a blessing in itself. But then that would drop Belinda McKay in it and her brother's part in this would be exposed, something I had promised them I would not do. Should I distort the cause of justice just because of my word? It was a moral dilemma. I owed them nothing. If I spoke up, then the loose ends might get tied up. So why didn't I? I didn't have a rational answer. Life is never that clear. This was the indecisive part of me - that and a certain sense of honour: a man's word and all that sort of thing. I had wrestled with this conundrum for weeks and still hadn't got a submission. Yet I had, I thought, at least some sort of justification for what I was doing. As it stood, Belinda was in no state to be questioned. I had no doubt at all that were her brother to be pulled in, he would deny everything. The fear of those behind him ensured he did nothing else. And they would end up scot free anyway and I didn't like the sound of that. The loose ends wouldn't be tied up at all. They would merely make a slip knot for the real culprits to escape the noose.

One of the big stores next to Tesco's was advertising good deals on all sorts of electronic equipment so on impulse I stepped inside and took a look. It didn't take too long before I had a salesman attached to me like an extension, speaking a language I could make little sense of. But he could see that he had an interested prospect. My time at George's home had aroused a latent interest and the possibilities of owning my own lap top meant that he didn't have to work very hard. He had made the sale before I even walked through the door.

Saturday night, Sunday morning. Like the Alan Silitoe novel suggested, I poured over the literature which went with the computer and finally managed, after much cursing and frustration to get it up and running. I converted what had been Mark's room into a sort of study. While the money would always come in handy, I hadn't had the chance to sort out another occupant and really, I didn't know if that was what I wanted. I had hung the painting that Len had done, above the desk, partly for inspiration, partly because I liked it, but mostly for Len. It intrigued me. One of the few paintings left untouched by the thugs who had killed him, left untouched probably because it had not been easily accessible. The colours were vivid: bright red hunting jackets, amidst a throng of dark and chestnut horses who seemed unphased by the frenetic beagles. Most of the large canvas however, centred on the unseated rider, captured in his moment of dethronement, the bay wild eyed and rearing, the rider looking shocked, but somehow familiar. That was it. He looked somehow familiar, but I couldn't quite tell why?

The news of the death of Lara Jones came as a complete shock, leaving a sense of numbness and disbelief. Such tragedy for that family was too much to comprehend. I was outraged, angry. Felt in desperate need of doing something. I resorted to something that I always had done since childhood: run. Ran until the sweat drenched my body in the cool night air, ran until my aching muscles began to seize, and my breath grew ragged and painful, the saliva drying and turning sour in my mouth. I chased the demons. Cursed the gods of injustice and cried out loud in my anger and self imposed exorcism, until I could run no more, the physical and emotional hurt leaving me drained.

I had failed them. I had not been there for Len when he needed me and now Lara Jones had given up on life.

Her sister had rung with the news. When she had said her name I was at first unclear who in fact she was, but the mention of Lara Jones had evoked a memory of a lady not too dissimilar to her sister. It seemed that Lara had left the children with her for the day, had driven home, mixed herself a cocktail of spirits and sleeping pills and pulled the plug on her life. Had she appeared distraught I had asked? Not at all, her sister had replied. In fact if anything more calm than in recent times. Calm because she had at last found a way out, I thought.

"Oh no," the thought had obviously crystallized in her mind as well, and I could hear the quiet sounds of muffled sobbing at the other end of the phone. I waited, not wishing to say anything, not able to say anything. Feeling wretched. "Your name was by the phone with your number," she finally spoke, "with a sealed envelope. She must have wanted me to phone you." Christ, why hadn't she just phoned me herself? I might have been able to help.

"I've got it with me. I didn't want the police seeing it and asking questions or opening it. Lara obviously wanted to write to you and therefore you must see it. Can I send it to you?"

"Of course," I replied.

"I was the first to find her. I had gone back to pick up something for the kiddies for they had asked to stay the night and Lara wasn't answering the phone. I let myself in and there she was, just slumped over on the sofa. So peaceful. But all alone. Oh God." The voice broke again and uncontrolled sobbing filled my every sense. How hard it must have been for her!

I took the news with me to school, not pleased at all to be the bearer of sad tidings, feeling slightly depressed and slightly hung over. George had rung. Lucy had spoken with him following my call to her and he suggested that I drive over. Kind gesture, but I felt little like talking, more like crying and more like beating the crap out of those responsible. Sometime during the night I pledged to them both that I would do everything in my power to see that the bad guys were caught. What was the point of it all if good didn't win in the end?

I knew before I made the announcement that very few people would show much concern. It hardly caused a ripple and got lost between the deputy's reminder about the forthcoming curriculum area meetings and the bursar's demand for greater care and consideration of her cleaning staff. Both obviously weighty matters. Poor Lara was dead unlucky!

Morning break however saw the gathering of the 'lads' and we occupied our corner of the staffroom. I told them of the phone call and the tragic way that Lara had gone. Jane, bless her, latched on to the children. They were alright I told her. Their Aunty was looking after them, and probably would continue to do so. John muttered that he felt desperately bad because he had not managed to see her. Didn't we all.

"I can't believe that the police haven't been able to find the culprits. Perhaps if they had, this wouldn't have happened." Jane spoke her thoughts.

"Dozy lot, couldn't find their way out of a paper bag." Chris was less than complimentary. "The only time they seem to really get off their jacksy is when one of their own gets done." Not strictly true, but in this instance there didn't seem to be a great deal going on.

One had the sneaking feeling that they weren't too bothered about a so called sex offender. Chris ploughed on, feet up on one of the coffee tables, a cup of coffee balanced on his stomach. "Come on Mike, you know the score. Look at you, you've been on the receiving end of this a couple of times at least now, what have they been able to tell you?" Not a lot I had to agree. But then, I hadn't let on to them or my friends that the car crash was probably deliberate as well. I hoped Chris would say nothing.

"Give them a chance, they might come up with something," Brian added. "Although I guess it becomes more difficult now. I mean the children are hardly going to be able to remember anything more that is relevant, are they?" He looked around at our faces, but who could disagree. In their current state it would take a rather heartless person to try and put them through it all again. "So that's it then isn't it. Fucked!" He placed his cup down on the table with a bang, causing one or two in the staffroom to look up in our direction. I knew how he felt, in fact we all did. I was the only one however who was party to information which might have prevented it. It didn't make me feel any better.

"It seems that we're the only ones who give a shit anyway," Robin added looking across the room. "Look at them. Not a care in the world. How quickly they forget."

"The human survival instinct." John added. "Forget about death and it doesn't happen. That way we all keep our immortality."

"Bullshit." Chris was always subtle. "They just don't give a toss. Their little lives are too important for anything to get in the way. Look at little miss busy body over there. Fussing over someone, anyone who's flavour of the moment." We all knew who he meant: Mary Streeton. And true to form she was listening with apparent rapt attention to the chaplain, nodding and smiling, nodding and smiling. "Christ, look at her. Like a bloody character from Enid Blighton," growled Chris.

"You read?" John looked amazed. The rest of us laughed, and Chris grinned, lunging out at him with a playful slap. "Steady on you big thug,"

Our little gathering was interrupted by the very same person we had been talking about.

"That was a terrible business you spoke about, Michael, this morning. The poor lady. She must have been so depressed. That dreadful business with her husband must have left her so ashamed." She looked down at me, waiting for my reply.

"You mean Len? I'm not so sure Mary, it could have been that she simply missed him; felt that no one was there for her, felt helpless, who knows."

"Oh no. I'm sure she must have been horrified at the thought of having a husband who could carry out such a nasty assault on a young girl. I'm sure I would have felt worried for my own children." The nodding had started again.

"Well Mary, your remark is a bit flawed." I sat up, removing my feet from the table and looked back at the typical school spinster. Chris always referred to her as the dried up old prune. Juiceless. It wasn't a very nice description, but I thought he had it pretty right. "For one, if I remember correctly, Len was temporarily removed from school while the incident was being looked into. The headmaster has to do that with any member of staff, when such unfounded allegations are made." I deliberately emphasised the word unfounded and saw that it had hit home. "Secondly, you haven't got any children."

"None that we know about anyway, eh Mary!" Chris butted in, full of his usual irreverent banter. There were one or two smirks.

"Oh," she directed a withering stare in his direction, but to give her credit, ignored the comment doing little more than stiffening her posture, as if the added height would enable her to impose greater authority.

"You know Mary, everyone's quick to condemn. We're good at that, but there aren't many good Samaritans amongst us. That poor lady needed comfort, needed reassurance, and we all failed her." I looked around the gathering, noted their slow nods of regret, knew how they felt. "Did you ever bother to see how she was coping?"

"Well, I hardly knew her. I didn't like what her husband had done. Didn't think it was my place to check up on her," she replied in something close to a fluster.

"It's not your place to come to unfounded conclusions either," I replied coldly. "It's people like you who do more damage, whispering vicious gossip to other's who are always only too keen to hear the worst. Lara Jones was inundated with hate mail from people who thought like you, then suffered the pain of watching her husband basically being beaten to death in front of her and her children's eyes. No one says much about that. It seems to me we conveniently forget how to practice what we are forever ramming down people's throats." I was aware that the room had gone quiet, that the private conversation between Mary Streeton and our group had suddenly become public. Her face had reddened noticeably, but she had no answer. She continued to stare directly back at me, but this time I felt unchristian enough to revel in the delight of at last having her at the receiving end of my tongue. I too could appreciate an eye for an eye, tooth for a tooth. Without comment she turned on her heel and strode purposefully away.

"Whey hey, way to go Kiwi," howled Robin. "That's a first, shutting old Mary up. Note that for the Guinness Book of Records." He slapped his leg in glee. "Bet you get your wrists slapped though. It won't be long before the Head has a wee word with you. They're like that you know." He crossed his fingers.

TEN

"Not literally I hope," Brian shuddered in mock horror. "Don't know who I'd feel the most sorry for."

The letter from Lara Jones arrived through my door next morning. I hadn't given it much thought. Getting ready for school was hard enough. It was with a load of the usual uncalled for drivel that seemed to fall on the floor: Double glazing circulars, Reader's Digest. I sat at the breakfast bar as Alison flitted back and forth, scraping butter on toast and slurping fresh orange, glowing. Two weeks away from marriage, a few months from motherhood.

"Last few days of work coming up," she beamed, "I'm not going to miss that for a while." She spooned out some honey and spread it over the toast.

"Lucky you. Just think, I've got years of it ahead of me." She tutted in sympathy, but in all fairness she was being swept away in a tide of optimism and excitement. And who could blame her. I slit the envelope and pulled out the letter. With it came a couple of old newspaper clips. I opened the first, slightly faded one and read the caption. 'Oxford Blue Scores Classic Try', with interest. Jesus, Len Jones had been a rugger player of some ability. So typical of the man to remain quiet, never commenting on himself or the 1st XV. A real enigma. And yet he had turned his back on it all. The article had gone on at some length about the real talent England had to look forward to. In a class of his own. I wondered what had happened. The answer came in one of the other scraps of print, along with some glowing reviews of the work he had done for a local society's art weekend. What a waste.

The other rugby clipping was about one of those tragic incidents that people like Fields would refer to in support of a total banning of the game: A university game which had come to an abrupt end as two players had collided in a head on tackle. Leonard Jones, the article went on to say, was in hospital with damaged cartilage's. The student who had performed the tackle, one Peter Grey, had been paralysed from the neck down.

Surely not! Sweet Jesus. Too much of a coincidence. Len Jones, Peter Grey, Lord Grey. Did he have another son? A son who had been deprived of a full life? Whoever he was I knew now why Len had given up the game.

"You look as if you've read something pretty important." Alison stopped by the breakfast table and looked at me quizzically. "Everything alright?"

"I'm not sure. If it's what I think, then there's a whole can of worms about to spill over."

"Care to elaborate?" she asked.

"Not yet, there's nothing really conclusive that I can tell you. It's all tied up with the Len Jones business."

"Who's the letter from then?" She asked, not to be put off.

Letter! I'd forgotten all about it. With the host of thoughts scrambling around my brain, I'd not given it a thought. I picked it up, not really wanting to read a dead woman's last thoughts.

'Dear Mr Sutherland!' it read. 'I know that you will find the newspaper clippings of interest. My Len was a man of tremendous talent. How I could ever have doubted him I just don't know. I have no excuse, just feel so ashamed of my part in his death.' I paused, took a deep breath and continued to read, vaguely aware that Alison was still hovering waiting to see what it was all about. 'It was just seeing photographs of him with little girls which made me flip. I didn't even know where the photographs had come from, and I was too shocked to ask Len. The letters even suggested that my own girls were at risk. I couldn't think straight and Len had gone into himself, he wouldn't talk to me, just shut himself off. Then someone rang me and said that he should be given a lesson to stop him from behaving the way he did. I told them where they could get hold of him.' The writing had visibly deteriorated. I couldn't bear to think why. 'God forgive me Mr Sutherland, for I cannot forgive myself. I know Len would not have done what was said. I just as much murdered him as those thugs did. I don't know why they wanted him hurt, or who wanted him hurt. I wish I did. Len kept saying the whole thing was a conspiracy against him because of that newspaper clipping, the fact that Lord Grey's son had been so seriously injured. I don't think he was right. I hope one day you can find the answers. Len spoke highly of you. Said you were an honest man, not likely to stand for any nonsense, and not one to bow and scrape to those above you.

I shall miss my wee girls but I know my sister will love them dearly. She and her husband never had any of their own. What kind of mother would I be? I helped kill their father.'

That was it. Nothing else. Such a sad cry for forgiveness. I couldn't rid myself of the picture of a lonely lady, drinking herself into oblivion, totally destroyed by the events which had overtaken her. God rest her soul.

"What is it Mike?" Alison sat down on a chair beside me and I wordlessly handed over the letter for her to read, watching the passage of emotions flit across her face.

"Oh Mike," she whispered, her hand covering her mouth in despair, "the poor woman, oh how sad." She stared sightlessly at the letter, shocked. "What does it all mean. Is she . . . I mean . . . Has she died?" It was as though she didn't want to say it, or hear what might be the answer. I nodded. Alison bit her trembling lip. "But why?"

I told her very briefly, although in most respects the letter had said enough. What was I going to do, Alison had asked? What could I do, I had replied? Alison was convinced that the police should be informed but I told her that for the moment I was going to keep it to myself for the simple reason that I felt Lara Jones deserved it. I didn't want it known that she had played some part in what happened to Len. In my view she was simply a victim of tragic circumstances, someone who had been callously used, the consequences of no particular importance to those that had used her. At that moment I wanted more than anything to be able to clear her husband's name.

ELEVEN

"Any chance of finding out the address of Lord Grey?" I propped up the hatchway of the general office and directed my question to one of the secretaries. And waited. Finally, and with no apparent sense of urgency she looked up from the screen which seemed to hold her in rapt attention.

"I beg your pardon?"

"I was wondering if there was any where, where I could find out Lord Grey's address. Like the prospectus or whatever."

"I'm sorry Mr Sutherland, but I've not got any of the addresses of the governors. They are kept with the headmaster's secretary." She smiled apologetically and I smiled back. There was more chance of Scotland winning the world Cup, than there was of getting any information out of her.

"Well, I thought as much, but it was worth a go. Thanks anyway Gill; I'll just have to resort to some other course of action."

"I am sorry," I nodded in understanding, knowing full well that if she could, she would be the first to help. There had been times when she had stayed behind to help me with PE circulars or make calls to arrange fixtures or whatever. I went to speak but she beat me to it. "I don't know whether you are aware of it or not," she whispered conspiratorially, "but you're not the most popular person on the staff with one or two people."

I grinned. "I bet. And I bet it's a toss up between your boss or mine as to who thinks I'm the worst." She looked amazed. "It comes from speaking your mind." I added, "It's a bit of a failing of mine."

"Well, I've told them that they are wrong. When they were talking about you over coffee one morning I told them that you were a very good teacher and one who cared for people. I told them what you did for my Adam; how you did everything to help get him into the fire service, writing his reference, taking him to his first interview. You know, when friends of mine ask what school I think they should send their children to, I say King James partly because of you, because you don't talk about doing things, you just do them."

"Thanks a lot Gill. But don't go sticking your neck out. You have to work here you know. I can fight my own corner if the need arises."

"I don't doubt that. I think they're a little bit frightened of you actually." She hunched her shoulders and nodded, looking like a little sparrow.

"Oh I wouldn't think so," I replied intrigued.

"No, it's true. Mrs Pringle says you're a bad influence, that you don't know your place in society and that you don't have the proper respect for the headmaster. But I can tell by the way that she speaks that she is really a little bit afraid of you."

I laughed. "Well there's a turn up for the book. It's normally the other way round. Anyway, thanks. I'll have to think of another angle."

"Have you tried the telephone directory?" she asked. Good grief, it's amazing how the most obvious solutions are sometimes overlooked. I shook my head and she grinned. "Typical man." She leant across the desk and grabbed one of the directories and thumbed through it, flicking from page to page, but to no avail. "Not in this one anyway," she said taking the next one from the shelf. Same result. Not one to give up, our Gill. She picked up the phone, punched out a number and I listened to her try and wheedle the information out of the operator at the other end. No luck. She hung up, a resigned look on her face and didn't say anything for a moment, then clicked her fingers, her eyes lighting up. "What about looking up the 'Who's Who'?" A great idea and I told her so.

The school library was well stocked with all sorts of reference material and it didn't take me too long to first find the appropriate book and then the appropriate name: Grey, Baron cr 1975 (Life Peer), of Welwyn in Hertfordshire; Ronald Charles, b 10 April 1932 . . . . . .

I glanced down all the other information until I came to the bit I wanted. I read the address. The Orchard House, Ayot Green, Welwyn Garden. I knew of it. Certainly knew the little green: Tree enclosed with a sporadic dotting of houses and a pub tucked up in the corner. A very pretty little slice of rural Hertfordshire. Not too far away, in fact on my way home. There was nothing else for it but to take the bull by the horns and drop in on him.

The evenings were drawing out a little more which was just fine by me. A little more daylight recharged the batteries a bit. It was still light enough to see reasonably clearly, as I edged the car along the rutted road. No name plaques, but I was fairly convinced that I knew which one it was. I just didn't feel like stopping to see whether my guess was right or wrong, so turned and headed back in the direction I had come, pulling up in front of the pub. At that time of night it wasn't very busy and the barman was friendly enough to inform me that my guess had been right, that Lord Grey was a frequent patron of his pub, was a fairly decent old chap, the same not able to be said for his sons, more is the pity. I thanked him, refused his offer of a drink and drove back to the large 'cottage' at the top end of the green.

The drive up to the house was impressive. A pergola type arrangement of climbing roses and clematis made a roof overhead and there were standard lamps along its length, not yet turned on. I decided to park on the road outside and walk and as I broached the entrance the lights switched on, illuminating my path. The large oak doors at the front were in fitting with the rest of the house and I lifted the brass knocker and let it thump upon the plate, the noise loud in the quietness of the hamlet. Nothing happened for a moment and I wondered whether there was in fact anyone at home, but slowly a door was opened and Lord Grey stood in front of me.

"Lord Grey, Good evening." He peered out into the growing gloom, not recognising me.

"Yes, what is it?" He answered in an abrupt manner, civil but impatient and I stepped forward so that he could see me more clearly. "What the devil . . . . . . What are you doing here?" His tone one of great affront as well as surprise.

"I was hoping to talk with you actually . . . . . ."

"Mr Sutherland, there is nothing that I would want to talk with you about. And I seem to recall that you were of much the same opinion the last time we met."

"I had just been to the burial of a colleague, a colleague from the school where you sit as Chairman of Governors, if I may remind you."

"I need no reminding Mr Sutherland. If I recall, I suggested that for the good of the school, Mr Jones' death should be put behind us." He stood, characteristically leaning forward in his hawkish manner, hands thrust in pockets. "But you wouldn't hear of it. All you did was slander the Head and my running of the school. You, who has no idea of the difficulties faced by schools, and the demands placed upon those who run them. It's easy for your kind isn't it? No responsibility, just the advantage of standing up and criticising. It must be nice."

"Fair enough, but then I am not appointed, nor paid for that position. Therefore I expect whoever is, to be able to do the job that they were appointed and paid for. It's as simple as that, and if I feel that they are lacking in their judgement or not doing things in the appropriate manner, then surely I have a right to my opinion?" I stared back at him determined to remain calm, and continued to speak before he could butt in. "In this instance, I felt the dismissal of Len Jones was appallingly handled by the Head, along with you." He attempted to speak but I cut him short. "No, no, hear me out. You cannot attempt to justify how things were done, surely? In every respect it seemed to me and others, that Len had been judged guilty by you both and that you were determined to get shot of him as fast as you could. Why?" I left the question hanging and for a moment he said nothing, but just stood there.

"As I said a moment ago," he finally uttered in a contained and measured way, "there is nothing you and I need talk about, and I would thank you if you would remove yourself from my doorstep." He went to close the door, his manner final.

"What about Peter?" I asked quietly. The door stopped closing and he reappeared, everything about him suggesting controlled hurt and anger. He stared back at me with distaste and spoke with a voice that seemed to have been choked of air.

"I beg your pardon, what did you say?"

"What about your son Peter?" He took a step back, as if recoiling from a physical blow.

"How could you know . . . .? Who told you . . . . ?" His manner now threatening, like a wounded animal, cornered but willing to take on its adversary, advancing from the sanctity of his hallway towards me in jerky staccato steps, the words erupting from his mouth, as he proceeded towards me. I stepped back. I hadn't counted on this. In the half light of the doorway, I could see his face change from its usual red to a deep purple as he continued to roar at me, shouting out meaningless words in his rage. And then he stopped, and stared with a bemused look, his mouth wordlessly opening and shutting, the colour draining from him as he sunk slowly to the ground. Bloody hell. It wasn't what I had expected. Think! On reflection, my initial impulse to get the hell out of it, whilst not honourable, was probably the most prudent course of action. The saying 'discretion is the better part of valour, or he who fights and runs away, lives to fight another day,' had probably been well tried and tested over the years.

I bent over the prostrate figure and felt for his carotid artery. Yes! There was a pulse, not particularly strong, but at least beating. There wasn't much I could do. I guessed he had suffered a seizure of some kind. I thumped the door knocker again and again, its sound loud in the quiet night air. Nothing, not even a response from my yells. Something had to be done quickly. I'd probably be done for breaking and entering, knowing my luck I'd probably be done for unnecessary stress on a Peer as well. I didn't have my mobile with me. I had left it at home, something I was prone to do. There was nothing for it. I pushed the door wider and stepped in. The hallway was magnificent, dark oak, impressive dark framed portraits lining the walls. There had to a phone somewhere. Most people kept one in the hall. No luck. I pushed open another door, taking me into the drawing room, a large tastefully decorated place of peace and scanned quickly for the phone. Nothing. And nothing in the next two rooms; kitchen and lounge. I was getting desperate. I seemed to have been stuck in the damned house forever. Another door. Thank God. The study. Better still, on the large desk, a phone. The call was made. Now it was just a question of waiting.

In most of us there is an innate curiosity. Arguably Man had progressed as a consequence. I was no exception. With something bordering on guilt, I took stock of my surroundings. The desk was piled high with various assortments of papers and magazines. Two framed photographs were placed directly in front of where one would sit. I looked closely at them. One, of a gentle looking elderly lady, her smiling face framed with white hair; the other of a fair haired dashing young man in University blazer, with an inscription emblazoned across it. 'To Father, I made it. Love Peter.' He looked nothing like his elder darker haired brother, but had obvious similarities to the woman in the portrait beside him. No doubt his mother. I could appreciate the anguish that Lord Grey must have felt when the life had been virtually extinguished from this young man. Lord

Grey! I had forgotten my mind preoccupied with the photograph. Good God. Done for neglect as well!

I had placed my jacket over him before going inside to phone, to keep some of the chill out. On the way back out I managed to find a double sheepskin rug which had lain in front of the open fireplace, what better, and draped that over the prostrate figure. An appropriate New Zealand action really. He was still breathing but in shallow breaths and the colour had completely drained from his face. Worrying.

Car lights appeared heading towards the house. But no siren. Damn. I wished they would hurry up. The car seemed to be slowing down and I watched as it drew to a halt, heard the door slam shut, couldn't see a thing. Heard running feet crunching over the gravel, heard the expletive.

"What the fuck . . . .?"

Great. That was all I needed. One of his sons, and by the sound of it, the youngest one.

"Who the fuck are you?" He appeared at the doorstep, took one look at his father, then at me and stopped, his eyes betraying the recognition. "You!" He advanced towards me, the hatred clear to read, the intention equally sign posted. "What have you done? I'll bloody have you." He looked wildly around as if hoping to find something to help him.

"What's the matter, no baseball bat this time?" I asked. "He's had a seizure. The ambulance is on the way. Why don't you sit beside him and try and comfort him."

"You did that, you bastard. You and your interfering. You have no right to be here. I'm going to fuckin' make you wish you weren't." His face was twisted, the words fighting their way out as he advanced, a slavering gargoyle, eyes full of malevolence. No listening to reason. He was beyond that. Round three. I wasn't going to stand on ceremony this time. He stepped in and I feinted with my left, and as he drew back, stepped forward and toe punted his groin, this time connecting with some force.

He grunted in pain, but to give him credit continued to come forward. I had a fleeting desire to step back into the house and slam the door shut, but pride overcame common sense and I stood my ground. He moved quickly, dodging under my swinging punch and hit me close, up under my ribs. Shit! Not again. He struck again, same place. Painful. I tried to roll out of his way but he blocked my moves, directing his punches up towards my face. I ducked and twisted, angered at my inability to do anything, this guy a practiced brawler. I was taking a hammering. Taking a leaf from his book, I dropped low, surprising him and delivered a short hard jab in the same place that I had kicked him, and before he could anything, drove in another one. He did more than grunt this time, doubling over in pain, and before he could draw breath I pulled his head down to my knee then let him drop to the porch floor. I was breathing hard, blood was pouring from my nose and my ribs were back to their aching best.

When the ambulance arrived, its lights lighting up the darkness in incandescent blue, there was momentary confusion as they looked from one to the other of us. From where I was sitting, nursing my nose and hugging my ribs, I pointed to Lord Grey and tried to tell them what had happened. They were quick to put him on a breathing support, and soon had him on a stretcher and into the vehicle. One of them looked back at us as he closed the door and spoke.

"You look as if you need a bit of attention too mate, and the other guy. Sorry we can't oblige. This guy's priority. I'll put a call through if you want?"

I shook my head, slowly and mumbled that I would be okay, but he must have put some kind of call through, for before too long we were joined by a police car and its two occupants, both with whom I had a passing acquaintance.

"We meet again Mr Sutherland, once more in dubious circumstances." D.C. Carmichael at his best. He looked about him while his colleague checked Lord Grey's son who was starting to show signs of life again.

"Are you the only policemen in these parts?" I asked, trying to smile. He cast me an almost disparaging look before replying.

"No more than you are the only casualty. It just seems our paths cross on occasion. Now, what has happened here? This is the home of Lord Grey. What brings you here? And who is that other thug? Do you know him?" He paused, at last, staring down at me with nothing that suggested sympathy.

"I can answer all those. First off, the thug as you call him is the youngest son of Lord Grey." His face registered mild surprise. I coughed, the cool night air beginning to make me shiver, and spat out a mouthful of blood. "Yeah, hard to believe that the noble classes spawn the likes of him eh?" He said nothing, his face impassive, then spoke.

"In this job, nothing surprises."

I continued. "His son thinks I was up to no good. He happened to arrive on the scene after his father collapsed, put two and two together and made five. Wouldn't listen to reason and set about trying to rough me up."

"Succeeded too, I'd say," he replied dryly.

"Pretty much so, although if you asked him how he felt he'd probably say he wasn't feeling the best right now." I looked across at the thickset young man who had tried to give me another beating and wondered whether or not to say anything to the police. I could prove nothing, yet. You always got your chance in the end, my mother used to say. I would leave it for the moment. I watched as he looked across at me, his hands massaging his groin, like a cricket bowler without a ball, or in his case, very badly tampered ones, watched the hatred in the eyes, the unspoken threats and smiled at him, read the words he was mouthing. A pleasant person. D.C. Carmichael had also been studying him and turned to me.

"You've not won yourself a friend there. Did you know him before?"

"We've met." I proceeded to tell him about the incident at the pub and left it at that. He shook his head.

"You know Sir; you seem to have the misfortune of being at the wrong place at the wrong time." I couldn't have agreed with him more.

"That bastard had no right to be here." Grey's son spoke out loudly and coarsely. "Hey copper, do you hear me? Do you know who I am?" D.C. Carmichael turned back slowly and asked.

"Are you addressing me Sir? Because if you are, then I suggest that you address me in the appropriate manner. And for the moment I would prefer if you said nothing, but just sat there and waited." He gave him a withering look and turned his back on him.

"Listen copper, that prick tried to hurt my father: Lord Grey. I'm not someone to be ignored by a flatfoot like you. You bloody arrest him." He snarled, an ugly man in an ugly mood.

"Sergeant Coombe, can you instruct our friend over there, that the less said the better. Ignorant yob." He muttered under his breath. "May I enquire as to why you were calling on Lord Grey?" he asked me.

"Lord Grey is Chairman of the Governors at the school. There was something that I needed to see him about."

"It must have been pretty important, judging from the impact that it had," he observed matter of factly, raising his eyebrows. A sign for me to explain but I refrained. "Come now Mr Sutherland, there must be something more that you can tell us. I mean, it's rather unusual for a teacher to go out of his way to visit the Chairman of the Governors, surely?" I shrugged and he continued. "So what was it that was so important? Did it have anything to do with the dismissal of your colleague last year? You're not still trying to sort that out are you?" He was reasonably astute, this policeman.

"If by sort out, you mean trying to establish the truth, then yes I am," I replied. "Everything about the dismissal of Len Jones, and the subsequent actions that followed, stink." I could feel the anger of injustice firing up in me again. I knew my words had carried to Lord Grey's son, for he had gone still and was listening intently. Sod him, sod the lot of them. D.C. Carmichael asked a very simple question.

207

"Did you lay a finger on Lord Grey, or man handle him in any way?"

"No," I replied, "it's not the sort of thing one does to one's employer. At least ways, not whilst they are wishing to remain in their employ."

"And are you?" he asked.

"Yes."

In the end, he suggested that we both accompany him down to the station to fill out incident forms, allowing us to stop at casualty on the way to get seen to. He promised to get us a ride back to our cars once things were sorted out.

As luck would have it, Peter James, the doctor from the rugby club was on duty and gave me preferential treatment, bundling me into a cubicle and seeing to my ribs, commenting rather exasperatedly that it was all well and good getting sorted out on the rugby field, but that it was becoming all too frequent on the street. And anyway, these ribs were developing more cracks than a crazy paving.

When we were finally finished at the police station it was fairly late. They had checked with the hospital to find out whether there were any suspicious marks or otherwise on Lord Grey, 'just routine Sir' they had informed me. Lord Grey, they said was in a satisfactory condition, but had suffered a minor stroke. They had informed his eldest son, who they said was at the hospital now. D.C. Carmichael added that they didn't sound too chuffed about it. I had to laugh. I could imagine him strutting about demanding this and that, and moaning about one thing or another.

"Have you met him?" I asked. He nodded and raised his eyes in exasperation.

"Unfortunately yes. A boorish man. Too full of himself. Heaven help the constituency if they vote him in. Heaven help the force too. He's all for cutting the numbers down and introducing some form of civilian patrol. God almighty, I don't know where they get them from. We'd have all the vigilantes out for action. I can see it now. Gun clubs would flourish as they recruited more and more of the ordinary but frightened public." He shook his head in despair. "But then, who am I, but a dumb flatfoot. Anyway, for the moment there is nothing else we need from you, so you might as well get yourself home." I looked at him and he stared back. "Oh yes, you need a ride don't you. I'll get that fixed up. I think it would be prudent if you went back separately. I don't want a rematch. I'll give you some advice for nothing; keep away from that family for a while, for ever if possible, for your own health," he added as though knowing what I was thinking. "I think that for one reason or another, you may have put two and two together yourself and come up with a similar answer as that hot head did. Rushing in making accusations is hardly subtle. Leave the police work to us. That's an order, not a request. Quite frankly I'm seeing too much of you. My wife will get suspicious." He laughed out loud at his attempt at humour. One couldn't help but like the guy, but I wasn't convinced that they were particularly motivated towards finding the culprits for Len's death.

"Did you people get to hear about Mrs Jones's suicide?" I asked. He looked at me speculatively and said nothing. "Well, I got a letter from her; posted on the day that she took her life. She was crying out for help, and no one was able to do anything for her. I don't like thinking of that, so, it may be too late now, but I made a promise that I would do my utmost to see that the truth was uncovered." He could hear the passion in my voice and paused before replying.

"Let me just remind you again, Mr Sutherland, that it is a criminal offence to interfere with police proceedings. I understand how you must feel, I truly do, but if there is anything that you feel we should know, then I most strongly urge you to tell us."

I said nothing. For a moment I thought that he was going to say something else, but he turned on his heel and strode off in the direction of the car pool to organise my lift home. I wasn't flavour of the month in a number of circles.

TWELVE

"*You* did what?" Lucy's response to my actions fell well short of admiration. "Mike, you really are stupid. Tampering with police investigations will only get you into further trouble." There was a long pause at the other end of the phone and I could hear her breathing deeply. Woman. Often too logical. It seemed that the circle was widening.

"Oh c'mon Luce. What was wrong with what I did? Since when is it considered stupid to confront someone to find the truth? It's what you do isn't it?"

"Michael, don't start telling me what I do. It's completely different. There are rules to follow, protocol to be observed. It's a job, its law," she retorted, the little bit of Irish in her accent coming to the fore as it always did when she was irked.

"What! What are you saying here?" I replied. I quite enjoyed playing the devils advocate at times. "Do you mean to tell me that the only people who can tell the truth are those that do it for a living?"

"You know exactly what I'm saying, so don't try and twist my meaning Michael Robert Sutherland. Dad told me that he spoke to you about the Greys. Truly Michael, you cannot afford to take them on."

"I tell you what Lucy; I couldn't give a diddly squat about who they are. You didn't read Lara Jones's letter. She was used. Len Jones didn't do anything. You know that, and I know that. I want to know why. What's behind all this?" I paused, before reading the message to her and there was silence at the other end and then. . .

"Those poor little girls. Oh Michael, that is so awful. When did this happen? Why didn't you tell me?" I went on to explain about the newspaper clippings, about Peter Grey's unfortunate accident, about Lord Grey's reaction, about the photograph, everything, and didn't feel a great deal better at the end of it. The thought of someone running around Scot free while others had suffered so, deeply affected me.

"There is one thing Lucy I could do with a bit of help with. I wondered whether you could look into where Peter Grey was hospitalised? He must be in a private home somewhere. You could do some checking through your offices more easily than I, and with less questions being asked." I wanted to meet this man, to see what he was like. For all I knew, he could be the instigator of it all. Lucy agreed and by the time we had rung off, I had received an invitation to Gavin's eighteenth, to be held in the big barn, for the younger party goers, and the house for some of us more senior ones. It would be good. Hadn't been to a party for some time. It was just a pity that there was a funeral in between. Odd how that the word funeral was an anagram for real fun. I had never yet been to one where that had been the case. That was the other thing, I was getting to go to too many, the black tie I wore most frequently now was not a bow tie. Thank God for Alison's wedding.

Briefing in the morning aroused almost as much interest as my entrance into the staffroom. I entered into a quiet room, late, the effort of rising, showering and shaving, taking that little bit longer. I should have been used to it. It felt like a three weeks on, three weeks off type of scenario. Fields was midway through his delivery, in his ponderous, self pontificating manner. . . . . . . "and it seems, ladies and gentlemen, that our chairman Lord Grey, suffered a stroke." . . . . His delivery faltered as he looked up, spotted me, saw my face. Chris, obviously another late entrant, whispered. "Been at it again eh Mike." I winked.

"More than you realize mate. It seems to be becoming a habit. Still, you should see the other bugger." He grinned.

"Mr Sutherland, as you are late," Field hung heavy emphasis on the word late, "your lack of decorum can perhaps be excused, but as I was telling the rest of the staff, we have received some very sad news concerning Lord Grey. I have just received word that last night he suffered a stroke and was rushed to hospital. I am sure, that you along with the rest of us will be disturbed with this news. Lord Grey has served this school for a number of years with distinction. We can only hope that he makes a full recovery and is soon back at the helm." He took one final look at me, before sweeping back out, his deputies close on his heels. I was tempted to tell him what had happened but common sense prevailed.

"Whoa, the things we do to get noticed." Robin had moved beside me. "What was it this time? Fists, knife, or car crash?" He laughed. "Or did you walk into a door, something more normal like the rest of us would do?" I shook my head.

"No, unfortunately your first guess was the best."

"What the heck is it with you? You seem to be in some kind of incident every other week. You got a death wish?" Chris, who had gone to check the cover for the day, had returned and was listening in, asked what had happened. I told them. Their reaction was comical: "what, you mean Old Grey was your doing? . . . . . . jeez, he was going to hit you? . . . . . . .His son? Bloody hell Mike. What gives?" By the time I had finished telling them everything, I had quite an audience listening, and found that I had to repeat things several times. There was a degree of mirth over the fact that Fields hadn't known, but they were concerned enough about the welfare of a fellow human, even though he wasn't that well liked. As Brian put it:

"I don't like the old sod, but I wouldn't want to see him die like that. God knows why?" he seemed genuinely puzzled by his own feelings. I wasn't so sure that I mirrored them. Anything connected to that old sod or his family was causing me a lot of grief.

TWELVE

The rest of the day was lost in the usual goings on of school. It seemed less and less strange to me that while on the one hand I was teaching and instructing children, there was another world beyond the gates, which had encroached what had once been a sanctum of learning, a place of the real world but somehow apart from it. And now the two were forced to become as one and I seemed to be caught in the middle. And I didn't like it. There was a lot happening to the teaching profession, a lot of it good, but a lot of it not so good, simply because the world beyond its gates was in fact gate crashing. Litigation had become the watch word. What it simply meant was that there were less and less activities that one could do with students. The fun was going from the game. And of the other game, Fields had yet to make a final decision but I held out little hope. Still I wasn't going to let it lie and with that in mind and a lesson free made my way towards the school office in the hope that he might see me. Fat chance. Mrs Pringle smugly informed me that Mr Fields appointment diary was completely filled for the day and he would not be able to see anyone. Please add my name to the diary for the next day, I asked, and without a great deal of fuss a time was found that was convenient to us both.

By the end of the day I was feeling pretty jaded. I had planned to head straight home, put my feet up and relax. But the best laid plans of mice and men . . . . and so forth. Thoughts of Jimmy McKay came unbidden as I drove past the Crooked Chimney pub, and the conversation with his mother followed in my mind, so that I turned off in the direction of their house.

Stephen McKay answered the door bell, with an almost accusing, where have you been look, took a second look at my nose, before ushering me inside, in towards the sitting room and offered me the customary beer. I didn't much feel like one, but accepted it all the same.

"Belinda," he yelled towards the kitchen, "get us two beers, will you love?" There was no reply from the kitchen but I could hear some movement. He turned to me and smiled an explanation. "Her Mum's out shopping, getting the weekly food in." Obviously Stephen McKay's household was not yet truly sexually liberated.

213

I hadn't seen Belinda since my confrontation with her in the P.E. office at the start of the term. Whilst she had looked fairly withdrawn then, the child that entered into the room carrying two cans of beer and a couple of glasses, gave me something of a start. Her movements were deliberate, almost automatic, no visual animation evident.

"Hello Belinda, how are you now?" I asked. No response. Her father sat forward and took the cans from her.

"Belinda. This is Mr Sutherland from school. You remember him don't you?" She nodded. "Good girl. He was just asking how you were. The last time he saw you, you weren't too well, but you're much better now, aren't you love?" She nodded again.

"Well I'm pleased to hear that, and look forward to seeing you back at school." I could have been speaking to a door for all the response I got. Stephen McKay's face had crumpled slightly, the face of a father who was suffering for the one he loved. He cleared his throat before speaking.

"The doctor thinks she is making good progress and should make a full recovery. We can only trust in his assessment." I murmured some appropriate reply as he handed me a drink. "Off you hop then Pet. Mum will be home shortly." We both watched her move mechanically out of the room. Still a heck of a long way to go, I thought.

"Have you heard from Jimmy?" I began for a starter. He shook his head.

"Only the once, as my wife told you. He phoned to apologise for the grief he had caused the family. Said he wanted to put things right. Said that after talking with you he realised that there was no end to his actions, and the sooner he managed to get it all sorted the better. I tried to tell him not to do anything rash, but he didn't seem to want to listen. Not that I'm surprised, he hasn't wanted to listen for years." He wiped a furrowed brow with the back of his hand. "This time though he seemed hell bent on doing the right thing. I tell you Mr Sutherland, it's not very nice being at the other end of the phone and hearing your son break down, not nice at all." He stopped for a moment, took a long pull at his drink, wiped his mouth and went through his familiar routine of preparing a cigarette.

214

Finally, with it lit he continued, "I was pretty certain we would hear from him again, if only for him to tell us he had thought better of himself and wasn't going to do anything. I mean, that was usually the pattern of the past, so I've been expecting a call. But nothing."

"Have you tried ringing him yourself?" I asked.

"Of course, but all the time, all we get is the answer phone telling us that he is unable to come to the phone and to leave a message. What do you think has happened?"

I didn't know the answer to that, didn't like to guess. Jimmy McKay had got himself mixed up with some pretty nasty characters. I just couldn't think how it would be to their advantage to get rid of him, for should anything happen to him, then there was no reason for his father to remain quiet any longer.

"What sort of work does he do, is their any chance that he has had to go off on business, overseas or anything?" I asked by way of an answer.

"He has on occasion, but we usually hear from him just before he sets off, normally as a way of gloating about how successful he is." What a nice guy! "But nothing this time. I mean, the girl he lives with seems to have vanished as well." I remembered her voice; perhaps at long last she had wised up and seen the light.

"Well it does seem to be a puzzler, but more likely than not there is an obvious answer to this. Time usually unravels these sorts of things." He didn't seem to be too convinced.

"I have to ask, you know, what has happened to you?" he said, changing the direction of the conversation.

"What do you mean?" I replied.

"Your nose," he said, pointing to it. "It looks like it met with a fist."

"It did." I went on to explain all that had taken place since my meeting with his son at the pub. He seemed genuinely shocked that I could have been deliberately driven off the road after speaking with his boy, the enormity of it not escaping his attention. I could virtually see his mind ticking over, putting some very nasty conclusions together, conclusions I too shared. When it got to the part about confronting Lord Grey he sat bolt upright in his chair.

"Lord Grey?" he demanded. I nodded, intrigued. "The Lord Grey who lives over at Ayot Green?" I nodded again. "Bugger me, that's a coincidence. He owns the company Jimmy works for."

Bugger me as well for he now had my full attention. Coincidence? Bollocks. It was all too neat, all to complete. There had to be a link, a connection. "What's the matter?" Stephen McKay asked. My face must have been advertising my thoughts yet again.

"It all seems a bit too cosy don't you think? Jimmy, Len Jones, Lord Grey. All connected. There's no coincidence there I reckon. And then Belinda. Everything nicely packaged for someone out to destroy a life."

"But why, why would they want to hurt that art teacher? What had he done?" I told him, and watched the look of disbelief blossom. "No, surely not. All this because of an accident. Sweet Jesus, no." The enormity of it overtook him and he lifted a trembling pint to his lips. "My little girl destroyed because of a friggin' accident. That poor teacher's wife, he was married wasn't he, I remember you telling me? She has lost a husband, all for a mistake, a simple rugby accident. I don't feel proud for what I did, for letting Belinda carry the weight of her brother on her shoulders, or the death of that teacher. I don't feel proud at all. I can't expect her to forgive me, but I hope one day I can meet with her and explain how it was. I know Belinda wants to desperately."

"She died last week," I went on to tell him about the letter.

"Dear God, what a tragedy." He said nothing else, but I could tell that the news had shocked him, knew that he felt responsible No one could turn back the clock.

I said my goodbyes to Stephen McKay, promising to keep him informed of any developments. Hoped that we would hear about Jimmy. In the

216

short time I had been with him, he seemed to have aged, the weight of the world bearing down on him, too much for him to carry. The domino effect seemed to be claiming another victim.

"Come in Mr Sutherland." Field's voice answered my knock, and I stepped into his office. He had moved his desk slightly, but it still stood at the same height. "Sit down won't you." He gestured to one of the empty chairs and I complied. "Mrs Pringle has told me that you want to speak to me about rugby. I take it you are referring to our decision to remove it from the school prospectus." He smiled one of his obsequious smiles.

"So the decision has been ratified then," I asked.

"Oh no, not yet, but it really is a formality. The board meets in a couple of weeks time and that is first on the agenda. I can't see that there will be any problem. Lord Grey and I are very strong on this. Poor man, I know he won't be there, but the board will know his views." I loathed the little man.

"Why?"

"Well Mr Sutherland, it doesn't take an intelligent person long to realise just how brutal the game is. Incidences hit the newspaper frequently. As such, I consider it in the best interest of the pupils to protect them from the possibility of such accidents."

"Those incidents are fairly few and far between," I corrected him. "Life itself is a risk. You can't wrap all the kids up in cotton wool and protect them from everything that is going on. Good God, what sort of society will we create?" I stopped in disgust.

"I understand your concern. You're worried about your job." I went to say something but he waved me down. "No, no. Let me finish. I can see no reason why you can't stay on as Head of the Department. Your results at G.C.S.E and A level have been adequate. But you and Mr Williams will have to get yourself on to a course in the summer to learn the art of soccer coaching." He smiled magnanimously, resting his face on his hands, elbows on the desk.

"I'm not worried about my job, but I am worried that you can wipe out a century of tradition in this school without as much as a flicker of concern. Were you to frequent the playing fields, you would see just how much interest the game has and what it has to offer. Sure it's tough, but then, so's life. How do you propose to protect them from that?"

"My concern is with them whilst they are being schooled here. What happens afterwards, Mr Sutherland, has nothing to do with me." He stared back at me, sure of his footing.

"I thought we were given the responsibility of preparing them for life. Whatever the case, my concern is still that you are forsaking years of good tradition, for nothing more than a silly whim at best, or a Governors sad decree, at worst." He stiffened, colour coming to his cheeks.

"I beg your pardon? What was that you said? How dare you call my decisions for the school to be nothing more than silly whims. You've overstepped the mark. Lord Grey will have to be told of this. Quite frankly, Mr Sutherland, I've had enough of your manner, your criticisms. If you're not happy here, not happy with my leadership, then I will not stand in your way as you look for another position. In fact, I would recommend that you do so!" His voice had risen considerably, but I remained seated, took a deep breath and replied.

"Now that you bring it up Ian," I had wanted for some time to call him by his first name, "I actually don't think you have done a wonderful job for this school, but because you have such a great staff, it has survived. I can't forgive you for the hurt you caused Len Jones, and I won't forgive you for his wife's suicide. If you made more decisions for yourself rather than being steered by Lord Grey, then things might have been different. This last thing is just another example, isn't it?" He said nothing, just sat there looking stunned. "Lord Grey wants rugby banned at the school because of the accident that happened to his son Peter. You knew that, didn't you?

And did you know that the man his son tackled was the very same person that you saw fit to suspend on the grounds of misconduct." I could see by the shock on his face that he hadn't known.

"How do you know this?" he demanded. "What proof have you got?"

"Enough about Len and his rugby. Lord Grey's response to my questions seemed pretty conclusive as well. I was with him when he had his stroke the other night." That shook him.

"You were speaking to him?" he uttered in astonishment. I nodded. "I think you overstepped the mark there. The consequences of your actions have been devastating. Lord Grey is in a poor state at your doing," he accused.

"Not quite so cataclysmic as your actions." I retorted. He stood up and came round from behind the desk. An angry and troubled man.

"I don't think we have anything more to say to each other Mr Sutherland. Except this: Given the move by the school to introduce association football next year, your contract will not be renewed. Good day." I stood up, and looked down at him.

"Getting rid of me won't stop the questions being asked you know. I'll make certain of that." I gave him a last withering look then strode from the room, the fire inside burning like a furnace.

Damn it to hell and high water. I'd gone further than I bloody intended. Said more than I had meant to. When would I learn to hold back? I had given Fields the very opportunity he was looking for. What a fool I was! Well, I wouldn't go lying down, of that I was certain. The odd thing about it all was that I didn't feel too bad. It was like a decision in my life had been made for me and I knew what the next chapter was going to be. New Zealand beckoned, and the thought of it filled me with excitement. Time for a change. God, I hoped Lucy would come as well.

"You're looking thoughtful Mike," Chris's voice interrupted my thoughts as he stepped into the P.E. office. "Problems?"

"Depends how you look at it Chris. Fields has more or less fired me." His reaction was brilliant.

"You what? He can't do that. What for?" He thrust his face toward me, anger and aggression clearly evident. I told him what had taken place and got the predictable response. "The guy's a plonker. Out and out dick head. And you're not much better yourself," he said rounding on me. "What the hell did you provoke him for? You know more than anyone that he can't stand being challenged." He shook his head in disgust.

We were interrupted by the arrival of Jane, sweeping into the room, face slightly flushed. "Phew, I'm getting a bit old for gymnastics . . . ." she stopped, looked from Chris to me and asked, "Have I interrupted something? What's the problem? Mike?" Chris answered before I had a chance, his voice vibrating with anger.

"Mike has gone and provoked Fields to the extent that Fields has told him that his contract will not be renewed next year."

"Is that true?" Jane looked shocked, colouring visibly. I nodded. "Oh Mike," she took hold of my hand and squeezed it, her face a picture of sadness and concern. I told her, as I had told Chris, about the decision to replace rugby with football, about my reaction and then my comments to Fields. She shook her head slowly in disbelief. "You never did know when to hold your tongue."

"I know, my Mum used to say the same thing," I replied giving her a smile. "Come on guys, it's not the end of the world. In the face of adversity lie the seeds of an equal or better opportunity."

Chris groaned. "Christ, even now he finds time to quote one of those slogans. It's sickening. At least we won't have to put up with them for much longer." Jane sniffed, laughed, cried and laughed again. I gave her a hug.

"Just think, if you had married me we could be planning a life in New Zealand now."

"That's all I'd need. A husband without a job, me without my family, and living in the sticks in a country it's not possible to be further away from. Great."

"I take it then, you have no regrets." She smiled slowly, looked directly into my eyes, those wonderful open windows, and said softly.

"I didn't say that Michael." I was aware of Chris humming something that sounded like 'Love me Tender' in the background.

"Give it a rest." I threw a tennis ball at him and he ducked, plucking it from the air with his left hand.

"Still got the reflexes boss." He gave a big beaming smile. The mood had changed, the moment lost. It was just as well.

Lara Jones's funeral was as every bit sad and final as Alison's wedding was happy and promising of life. The circle of life. I had once been caught up in a funeral procession, looking with some amusement at two dogs copulating as the hearse drove slowly by. It seemed to encapsulate the whole function of being, in an odd sort of way.

The wedding took place at St Mary's church in the centre of the village, a stones throw from where we lived. Alison looked radiant, beaming at friends and relatives as she walked down the aisle towards a proud Andrew. Having given her away, I took my seat beside her mother and Lucy and enjoyed the rest of the ceremony. The reception afterwards was a bright affair, a good band playing easy music. As honorary 'father of the bride' I got to dance with her as soon as her husband allowed.

"I'm going to miss living with you Mike," she giggled. "Not many quiet moments with you."

"You're not going to have many anyway in a few months time," I reminded her, giving her stomach a tap, "and don't think you can drop the little nipper off when you've had enough of him for the night."

"Oh, be a sport. Seriously though, what's going to happen? I've been rushing around headlong, and we haven't really spoken much about your problems at school. Will it be alright? What does Lucy say? She's a really lovely person Mike. I hope you two can make things work out."

I held her at arms length. "Steady on Alison, let's just enjoy your wedding for now eh! As for school, I just haven't had time to tell her. I'll let her know tonight." I could see Andrew waiting impatiently at the side of the dance floor so steered our way towards him, handed him his bride and went looking for Lucy, and found her in the middle of the floor with an elderly gentleman who seemed intent on doing a John Travolta sequence. Watched her silently plead for me to rescue her, gave her a big grin and the thumbs up, before turning toward the bar to get a drink, turning back to see her face screw up and read the threat she mouthed. She was as Alison had said a lovely person. I would hate to lose her.

The flat was quiet. Another stage of life had passed by. The house to myself. It would be different. Lucy moved to the kitchen. I could hear the sound of water running as she filled the kettle. "Do you want anything to eat?" she yelled.

"No thanks," I replied. She came back into the lounge carrying two mugs of coffee and we sat back sipping at the hot drinks in silence, no need for words. This was going to be hard.

"Lucy?"

"Mmm?" She threw a long leg over mine and wiggled her toes. "That was a lovely night wasn't it? I thought Alison looked beautiful."

I mumbled in agreement and took hold of her free hand. "Listen, I want to tell you something and I don't think you're going to be too chuffed." That had the desired effect, and she turned to me, giving me one of those calculated looks, as if looking through me.

"You've had a problem at school haven't you? A run in with the Headmaster." It was uncanny, almost nerve wracking. Never underestimate the Alexander women. I nodded. She removed her leg from mine and sat up straight, waiting for the story to be told and when I had finished remained quiet for some time.

"What does it mean then?" she asked quietly.

"It means I'm out of a job come September," I replied.

"Give me some credit Michael, I think I am capable of working that out for myself," she answered laconically. "I was referring to the Len Jones case. I mean, it does seem reasonably conclusive that there was some sort of conspiracy against him. I do think the police should be informed." She was back to being business like, the lawyer now, not the lover. I knew this was her way of dealing with the situation. Putting on her professional hat put her personal emotions on ice.

"I can't, not just yet. I've made my own promises to people, as you know. I can't let them down now. It would be like you betraying a client's trust."

She snorted in derision.

"Hardly."

"Whatever, it is to me. I can't go back on my word. I wouldn't have thought you would want me to."

"Well I do, you're out of your depth. . . . . . Oh Michael . . . . .I don't know. . . . ." she faltered, the professional hat was slipping and the Lucy I knew and loved was coming to the surface. She bit her lip, trying to hold back the tears, but there was no contest, and the tears began to fall. "I don't want to lose you Michael. You're going to go back home aren't you? I know you are." She wiped her nose with the back of her hand and sniffed. I didn't say anything for a moment because I didn't know what I could say. Instead, I pulled her towards me and cuddled her and for a moment she resisted before yielding with a muted whimper, clutching tightly.

"I would hate to lose you too, you know," I whispered. "Let's just take it a day at a time and see what happens eh? Anyway, Fields may have been bluffing and I might still be there this time next year. Worrying about it won't change anything." She snuggled closer before replying.

"I know you're right. It's just that New Zealand is so far away. It's not like we could meet for a meal is it." I had to concede that point. "Or anything else," she said with a wicked laugh, her hands exploring. God, she was right there.

We made love passionately, with an intensity that took our breath away, leaving us drained and glowing and several hours later rekindled the fire and gently explored each other leaving us once again fulfilled. With the arrival of the morning Lucy slipped out of bed, a lithe nymph, her blond hair tousled but still creating a vision of beauty. I watched as she slipped out of the room, heard the taps in the bath run, then heard her call me. She was lying stretched out in the bath foam, and sat up as I entered, beckoning me to join her. We sat facing each other, soaping each other, talking and caressing, adding more water as the bath turned tepid, carefully, for I had the tap end, until with great reluctance it was time to get out and get on with the day. While Lucy dried her hair, I made the tea and buttered the toast and we sat in quiet companionship reading sections of the newspaper.

"Would you come with me if I went?" I asked looking up from the sports section. We hadn't spoken about New Zealand or anything remotely connected with my job since last night, but it had been hanging over us like a cloud and it was time for the downpour. She lowered her paper, the happy carefree face of earlier dissolving into a troubled sad expression.

"Oh Michael," she sighed, "I haven't thought of much else for most of the night. I couldn't. I want to, but . . . . . it's just my parents, Gav, my job. This is where I belong, and yet I want to be with you." She stopped; a face that seemed to carry the weight of the world looked across at me. I tried to smile. I understood how she felt, had pretty much known that that would be her answer, but it had had to be asked.

"I love you, you know."

"I know, I love you too. That just makes it worse doesn't it. Will you really go?" I shrugged and handed her the letter that had been waiting for me when I arrived for Dad's funeral. I knew it off by heart. Had read it enough times.

'Dear Mike, (I knew his hand so well, bold vertical slopes with strongly formed lettering) if you are reading this before we get a chance to put an end to our stubbornness, then I've gone and popped my clogs well before I intended to, damn it!

Son, I've missed you, I've always loved you. Unfortunately, you've inherited my stubborn side. Whatever the circumstances, you'll not bow down. God lad, I used to watch you when you were a little nipper and delight in the way you would not give in when the sheep had to be penned, hay baled, or dogs trained. You just had to win. Then you took that onto the rugby field. Mike, you should have been an All Black. I'm sorry you didn't get the chance, sorry we haven't had the chance to put things right. Iain agrees with me: the farm is as much yours as it is his, so, if you can bury the hatchet, come back to where you belong. You would make an old man very happy, albeit in his grave! Whatever, Son, I have always been proud of you. Remember IF. DAD.'

Lucy sniffed, taking a kitchen towel from the roll on the bench before blowing loudly.

"That's sad Mike. I'm sorry." I shrugged; there wasn't anything for her to be sorry about. I had spent enough time myself telling my father how sorry I was. I hoped he could hear. "What did he mean, remember If?"

"Dad was a great one for poetry. Said they had to learn it off by heart when he was at school. He could recite all manner of poems, but Rudyard Kipling's If was his favourite. Mine too." She looked quizzically at me. "Don't tell me you don't know it, I thought everyone did." She shook her head. I quoted the opening lines," 'If you can keep your head, when all about you, are losing theirs and blaming it on you, if you can trust yourself when all men doubt you, but make allowance for their doubting too.' . . . and on it goes. It's what Dad used to live by. I think it says quite a lot."

"It has pretty close parallels with you at the moment, doesn't it?" she responded.

"That's what makes it so good, you can apply it to yourself." I agreed.

And so the rest of Sunday was spent in lazy companionship, the topic of New Zealand, of us, of work, all pushed to the side, unresolved but a little better for having been spoken.

THIRTEEN

The photographs arrived through my door just as I was heading out to work. Inside the envelope was a hastily scrawled letter from Anne Wilson, Lara Jones's sister. She had found them under the bed whilst cleaning out the house and didn't know what to do with them. I took another look at the six prints. Sex prints would have been a better description, for they showed in graphic detail, pictures of naked young girls with Len Jones, himself naked as far as one could tell, although the prints caught him from the waist up. Given the content of the photographs it seemed pretty conclusive that he would be completely naked as well. I could imagine the shock and horror both Lara and her sister must have had when they viewed these for the first time. It pretty near bowled me over, and left me wondering whether I had been wrong about Len Jones all this time. I felt repulsed. No wonder his wife had had him beaten. I'd have done the bloody same. On the back of some of the photographs were hand written comments, made worse by the fact that his sister in law identified the writing to be in his hand! Jesus. It got worse. I read the first inscription 'a great little girl, lively and cooperative' The next read: 'Mary really enjoys her 'work'! - I do too!

They were all pretty much like that. Enough to sicken the strongest minded. Mrs Wilson had gone on to say that she refused to believe that they were true, didn't want the police to see them, for they would only go on to say that they had suspected Len all the time and this was only further proof. Could I do something? I wasn't sure that I wanted to. Give me a baseball bat and I might become like one of those who had done him over. The dirty bastard deserved what he got. Photographs didn't lie, did they? And yet his wife, who had suffered so much doubt, had been driven to such despair that she had virtually sanctioned his beating, had realised at great personal cost that she had been wrong? Why? What conclusive evidence did she have? How could anyone blame her? I realised that she didn't have any, only a belief. A belief that had wavered in the first instance but one which had grown strong with the passage of time. I had been told by Belinda McKay that she had lied. I had the proof. And I still felt disgusted.

I spent the day in turmoil, my mind working on automatic pilot, lessons taking place, without conscious awareness. Who would have sent those photographs? And if they were fake, how were they done? I had to find out the answers, but didn't have a clue where to start.

"How did the wedding go?" Robin's voice interrupted my thoughts. I'd skipped lunch, having decided to grab a coffee and relax in the relative quiet of the staffroom. That was where he found me. "Do your part properly?" he enquired.

"Yep, didn't even trip. It was a good do. Went without a hitch." I replied.

"You don't really mean that, surely it went with a hitch," he countered.

"Very droll. It was a good day. Makes a change to have something positive happen," I reflected. He nodded in agreement.

"Yeah, I guess so. Things can't get a lot worse for you can they. No sign of Fields making abject apologies to you, I take it?"

"Pigs will fly before that happens."

"Before what happens?" Jane eased herself into the chair next to mine and looked intently at the both of us.

"Before Fields apologises to Mike and offers him his job back," replied Robin.

"Oh," she flared, "I don't see him as one who will ever apologise, right or wrong. He's so arrogant. I can't stand him. And Mike won't go and apologise to keep his job. He's too stubborn. Would rather leave on his high horse than try and get the head to accede to let him stay. It's all a matter of principle isn't it Mike? I mean, the fact that you haven't got a job to go to doesn't matter does it. You just won't be seen to be beaten, isn't that right?"

"Hey, what gives here?" I stared at Jane, offended by her attack. "You think it's the right thing to go and apologise, to crawl back to him? He's the one who should be apologising to me. He's the one who has overstepped the line, not me."

"I know Mike; it's just that you are so blasted proud. None of us want to see you go. Surely it's worth eating a bit of humble pie to keep your job?"

"Mike eat humble pie," snorted Robin, "You must be joking I thought you knew him better than that."

"Do I get a say?" I interrupted them. "I have no intention of talking to Fields about my position in the school. I will fight him all the way concerning the playing of rugby here. As it stands I have absolutely nothing to lose."

"And there speaks the voice of one of God's chosen ones," mocked Robin, "conversation finished and all that sort of thing. At least I can start looking for a decent geographer at long last."

"Thanks mate, it's nice to feel valued."

"You know, none of this would have happened if it hadn't been for that incident with Len," said Jane somberly. "It's just not fair. Why you Mike? You seem to have carried the load all by yourself?"

Robin cut in before I could speak. "Because he likes to feel needed. It's that Boy Scout in him I bet."

"You're wrong there. Never was a boy scout. Boys Brigader, that was me." I answered.

"That's what I mean, sure and steadfast and all that sort of thing," he quoted. "He's continued it right through." He patted me on the back.

"You one yourself then eh?" I countered. "You must have been to know their motto. Well, well, wonders will never cease. Blair a Boys Brigader. Doesn't bear thinking about." He acknowledged with a nod of his head before speaking.

"Yeah, but at least I grew out of it. Adulthood makes most of us a little more cynical."

"If it hadn't been for me digging out Len's address, maybe it would have all just died out. Maybe he wouldn't be dead." Jane looked shocked at the possibility.

"Rubbish. We just happened along once everything had begun to take place," I told her. "It had all been set in motion for whatever reason."

"Perhaps he was guilty after all," Robin suggested.

"No way," Jane exploded. "Absolutely not. He was set up. Mike and I heard Belinda Mckay state that. He was set up, for some reason and no one has done a damn thing about it apart from Mike. I feel ashamed that I haven't done more." Robin looked pensive, no doubt reflecting that he too felt impotent, unable to find the right sort of action. While I had done something, I hadn't in fact achieved a great deal, apart from break the odd rib or two and alienate a whole family. Nothing especially productive there.

"Look, none of us should feel any guilt with this. The police haven't managed to do much, so why should we feel bad? All I've managed to do is stir up some bad feeling and bash up against a few brick walls. I can't really say I've managed to sort anything out. But I'd like to. Let's just let the matter lie for the moment. If I come across anything which I think is important I'd be the first to let you know. The truth will out in the end you know. You have to believe that." Jane nodded, but Robin looked less than impressed.

"Who are you kidding?" he grunted. I ignored him, and turned to Jane as she spoke.

"Change of subject. How did the wedding go? What did the bridesmaids wear? How did the bride look?" I attempted to answer her questions as best I could, leaving Robin to excuse himself, stating that girl talk wasn't his sort of thing. It wasn't mine either. When it came to the photographers, I was completely flummoxed. I didn't think anyone would be that interested in who they were.

"You're useless," countered Jane. "These are important issues. Every girl wants to know all the details." I apologised for my lack of knowledge and said that if it was really important I would find out for her. She laughed and said not to bother. But it had got me thinking.

"Yes Sir, can I help?" The girl behind the counter of the photographic shop looked about sixteen, fresh faced, not too much makeup. I had used the shop occasionally, it being convenient to work, even though it sat back from the main street and was partially hidden from view by the other larger shops which commanded the high street. She waited expectantly.

"Thanks, yes," I hesitated not exactly sure how to continue. "I actually want some information about films, or the processing of them." I paused and she waited, "Are you the person I should be talking to?"

"Well it depends what it is exactly that you want to know?" she replied looking inquisitively at me, "I might be able to help."

"It's a bit difficult really. But let's say that I wanted to merge some prints together to make them look like they were one shot, how would it be best done?"

She looked at me for a moment, then replied. "I think Mr Clapp would best be able to help you. He owns the shop. He's good at those sorts of things. He's not in at the moment but if want to leave your name and telephone number I'll make sure he rings you. He's my Dad actually," she added smiling shyly. I thanked her, leaving her what she needed and left.

"Mr Sutherland?" Hesitant, unsure of himself. "It's Jimmy McKay."

"Jimmy, where the hell have you been? Where are you now?" And why was he ringing me?

"It doesn't matter where I am. I'm just ringing so that you can tell my parents that you have heard from me. I can't ring them again. I don't want them to go through anymore. Shit, I've certainly given them enough of that." His voice was shaking. "I can't turn one way or the other. Everywhere I go I run up against some obstacle or other. It's impossible!" His voice had risen in near hysteria. A man at the end of his tether. "They've got me by the balls no matter what I do. They even said that they would know if I rung you and that you would be in for another sorting out. Oh God I'm sorry. But they won't know I've called. Not from here." He paused for a moment as if worn out by his tirade. I waited for him to continue, my mind racing. What was happening? Someone had certainly put the frighteners on him in a big way. It didn't take a lot of guessing to work out whom. He started speaking again. "Dalton Murphy told me later what they had done to you. How they had run you off the road after you spoke with me. I didn't know anything was going to happen like that. You must believe me!" Again the voice had become shrill, desperate. I told him I did. It had the effect of calming him down a little, but not much. "Murphy said that you were lucky to be alive, that if you interfered anymore you would end up like your friend. Now you've gone and done something else, because Craig went ape shit. Says he's going to make sure you never surface again. Something you did to his Uncle?" I couldn't believe what I was hearing. "It's hopeless. There's nothing I can do. I said that I was going to go to the police and to hell with the consequences. In some ways it would be good. I hate having to live with the thought of that poor girl on my mind. Craig told me that if I did, something nasty would happen to Belinda, that she might get a bit of what I did to the girl. Can you believe

232

that, my own sister?" His voice had risen with the anger and shock that something like that could happen. Unfortunately I could. "I've seen her you know. I went to the hospital. Pretended I was a distant relation. Oh Christ, she just lay there, almost lifeless. Didn't respond to the nurse, to anything. What have I done?" It was a bit late for remorse, but I guess he had been fairly high at the time and pretty well urged on by the others. But there was no denying that he had destroyed a life. "I said that I would do away with myself, but they just laughed and said good idea but they would still screw Belinda and Julia whether I was dead or not."

"Who's Julia?"

"She's my girlfriend."

"So why haven't you rung before?"

"I haven't been able to. I was scared. When you left me at that pub Dalton took me back to my flat in London and he and Paul Marshall started on me. They wanted to know what I was doing meeting up with you. What had you said? I told them that you hadn't said anything really, that you were concerned about my father. Dalton didn't believe it for a moment. He got Paul to hold me while he hit me. He just kept hitting me. My nose broke and I lost some teeth. They just laughed. I begged them to stop but that just made them enjoy it all the more. Then they grabbed Julia from the bedroom and said they were going to screw her, both of them if I didn't tell them all about our conversation. They pulled her clothes off until she was naked and threw her to the floor. She was screaming so loud so they hit her until she stopped. Then they hit me again and again. I couldn't think straight. Dalton had taken his belt off and before he tied Julia's hands together he hit me across the back so many times with the buckle I started to faint. When I told them what they wanted to know, what we had spoken about, they strapped Julia, threatened to cripple me if I said anything to anyone. I've been too frightened to do anything. I thought you might be dead anyway because Paul said your car looked a mess when he came down past it on the motorway."

I was stunned. The information I was listening to was like one of those gangster style movie scripts. Is this what happened to bullies who left school? The thought of the guy driving past my crashed car, dispassionately observing the wreckage incensed me.

"Bloody hell Jimmy. Is this for real? I mean, Jesus. I don't know what to say. You're taking a bit of a risk then, aren't you, ringing me now. If all you say is true, how come you've managed to give them the slip?" I managed to keep my voice level, camouflaging the anger I was feeling.

"I had to go in to work, there was something needed sorting out in my section. I had been off for several weeks following the beating, and then I was made to go out of the country for a while. Craig Holden came with me, so I couldn't do anything anyway. And they had warned me about Julia. I was just sitting at my desk, not really wanting to go back home when I came across your number. I had put it in my personal organizer after I met you, when Dalton went out to watch you leave the pub. Just seeing it there on my desk reminded me. . . . . ." His voice tailed off. I wondered whether they had his phone bugged. I presumed it was a fairly simple thing to do.

"What do you expect from me then Jimmy? I don't see how I can help you." Actually, I felt as if I was sinking into an abyss, getting deeper all the time.

"Uh, I'm not sure. It's just that you seemed to have everything in control when you spoke with me, like you knew everything, and everyone. Then when you spoke with Dalton and didn't appear to be frightened of him, I just thought you might be able to help me." He sounded desperate. He had to be if I was the only person he could think of as being able to help him! Lara Jones had thought the same way. It hadn't done her much good. Stephen McKay thought I would sort everything out. Why me? Didn't they know I was just bumbling along, going from one crisis to the next?

"Look Jimmy, I don't know what I can do. This whole thing seems to have exploded into a nightmare. I have absolutely no idea why my questions have had such catastrophic consequences."

"But you will try and do something?" I grunted a reply, and he blurted out his thanks, far too effusive for the help I thought I would be able to give him. "Dad said that you would get things sorted. Said that you were not the type to back down from anyone. And Dalton virtually spat your name out, said he was going to get his own back for you breaking his nose. Gee, no one's ever done that to him." Far too much admiration for what I had done, considering I had been scared witless myself.

"Listen Jimmy, you said that if you went to the police or told anyone, then there would be repercussions. That's right isn't it? Then what if I went to the police and told them everything? They couldn't blame you then. And as you said yourself, the way you feel at the moment, you don't care if the police prosecute for the rape as long as those guys get done as well."

"Yeah, but . . . . they said that if the police started nosing about regardless of whether or not I had told them, then Belinda would not be a virgin for much longer. Even if things went wrong for them, they have connections. You have to believe that." His voice had risen again. The false hope somewhat shattered for the moment. Back to square one. I left him with the promise that I would do my utmost to see that things were sorted. It was all I could say. Deliverance might prove to be more difficult.

In fact it was two days before I received the call from the photographer, but credit due, he had bothered to call back. He started by way of an apology, stating that his daughter had taken down my particulars but had forgotten to include the dialing code, and as I hadn't bothered giving my full address, it had proved somewhat difficult to find me. I thought one good apology deserved another and offered mine.

"So what is it you want from me Mr Sutherland?" he asked. I liked his voice. He had a soft northern accent, or so I guessed. Better still, I liked his perseverance. I attempted to explain to him what it was I was after and he seemed to see it as being straight forward "Pop in sometime and I will demonstrate," he added. "In fact, we could make a time now, to avoid us missing one another." That sounded a good idea so we confirmed a time early in the next week and I rang off.

Gavin's eighteenth fell on the Saturday, which was two weeks before we broke up for the Easter holidays. His father had done him proud: the barn decked out like a beach party, with imported sand, surf boards and beach bars. For the wrinklys as Gavin referred to us, it was a much more sedate affair. Sad to have to admit to enjoying the sedate over the lively. There was a mix of people, so I was to find out, straddling all layers of society, from the titled, and the landed, to the untitled and the landless. Lucy steered me towards various gatherings where we conversed politely and unthreateningly. My reply to the oft asked question of what I did for a living, brought a variety of responses, mainly depending on whether they fitted into the titled, landed or otherwise category. Lord Alexander 'borrowed' me for a while, as he put it, suggesting to Lucy that she keep her mother company or check in on Gavin, do the big sister act to make sure that they were all behaving themselves. "Threaten them with the law courts if anything looks untoward," he said. She wrinkled her nose at him, telling her father not to keep me for too long as she wanted me to herself for a while. "Lucky devil," her father whispered conspiratorially giving me a nudge, fondly watching his daughter sweep out of the drawing room towards the barn.

"Now, Michael, let's sneak out of here for the moment and grab ourselves a cigar and a drink. I want to know what's been going on. Lucy has given me a brief rundown, but I would like to hear it from you." He motioned towards his study, pulling the door behind us. "No one will miss us for a while. Actually, it's quite nice to escape and not have to make conversation all the time with some of them. Virginia will kill me if she notices," he added, like a little boy doing something naughty. He moved across to the big walnut roll top desk, rummaged in a draw and pulled out two tubed Havana cigars, motioned to the small statue of a cow which sat above the fire place, informing me that it was in fact a lighter, and so I discovered after one or two attempts: you twisted the horns and the flame came out of the mouth, poured two large measures from the crystal decanter on the coffee table and eased himself into one of the two large chairs that occupied the room.

"Well?" he said, waiting expectantly, "What's been happening?"

I did my best to fill him in with anything that seemed relevant since last we talked. He had a good idea of most of it, having heard from Lucy, but wanted again to get the 'lowdown' as he called it, on my meeting Lord Grey and the resultant discussion with the youngest son.

"Nasty piece of work, from all accounts, that one," He had said. I didn't disagree. I told him that the nasty piece of work had more or less admitted being responsible for my first attempts at being a baseball, which brought the expected reaction: George's choice language would have turned the milk of his prize herd of cows.

"You know," he added, having returned once more to the well-bred man that he was, "it is a terrible thing, but it had totally slipped my mind that Grey had another son. Terrible." He shook his head in irritation. "Fancy forgetting the only good thing in that family. No, that's wrong. Mildred his wife was a fine lady, but alas she passed away. They reckon she died of a broken heart. Couldn't bear to see her son wasting away in a hospital, confined to a long inactive life. Just destroyed her." He paused, looking reflectively into his whiskey. "Mind you, I can imagine how she must have felt. Perhaps it wouldn't have been quite so bad if it had happened to one of the other two boys, but Peter was the golden child. That must have been heartbreaking."

"I wonder how he found out about Len?" I couldn't see that he would have employed him had the connection been made and said so to George. He shrugged.

"Perhaps the penny dropped later, or he wasn't on the selection committee. When did he become Chairman anyway?"

I wasn't certain, but it had probably been for five or six years which meant of course that he might not have had anything to do with Len's appointment in the first place. If that was the case, it must have come as a shock to him when he read his CV.

George grinned. "A helluva shock I'd say."

I told him about Jimmy McKay's phone call and the trouble he was experiencing. George wasn't altogether sympathetic but was once more infuriated when I told him what Jimmy had said about Dalton Murphy and Paul Marshall.

"You should get the law onto them, immediately," he fumed. "Thugs like that can't be allowed to walk around free."

"And what can I tell the police?" I asked him, "That I had been run off the road by so and so, or so I believed. They need concrete evidence. On top of that, I don't want any more harm to come to Jimmy's sister."

The door of the study was pushed open, interrupting any further conversation, and Lucy stepped through.

"So this is where you've gone and hidden," she said accusingly. "Mum's not impressed, Dad."

"Oh dear, looks like I could be in for a torrid time," he inhaled on his cigar, rolled the smoke around in his mouth, before exhaling deeply.

"What was so important that you both had to hide away, anyway?" She looked at me for the answer.

"Nothing really, it was just that your Dad wanted to get up to date with everything that had taken place. This seemed the best place to do it. You know most of it."

"If it's any help Michael, I did manage to find out where Peter Grey is. I was going to tell you later, but this seems as good a time as any. What do you think Dad? Should he go and see him?"

"Can't see why not Luce. Michael may get to learn a little more, and if not then what harm can it do?" I agreed. Apart from anything else I was interested in finding out just exactly what the fellow was like. I was about to add that it would be nice if Lucy accompanied me, but didn't get the chance, for the door swung open again and in waltzed the other Alexander woman.

"Excuse me Michael," she said, turning back to her husband. "George, this is not good enough. We have a whole room full of guests and they are starting to wonder where you are. What can I tell them? That you have gone and hidden yourself in the study? I want you back out there now. Let these two young folk spend some time together. Have you checked on Gavin yet?" She stopped for breath, hands on hips, still looking lovely even in anger. George eased himself up from the chair with a resigned sigh.

"Well all good things must come to an end. I suppose I have to go and socialise." He looked at me and grinned. "Whoever said that Man was master of his own destiny obviously wasn't married. Come on then my dear, let's hit the scene. And Michael," he added turning back to me, "be careful. These fellows appear to be playing it for keeps. If I can do anything let me know. Did I mention to you that Eric Grey wasn't at the Governors meeting that time?" I shook my head and thanked him and they disappeared to join the rest.

Lucy slipped her hand into mine. "Hi ya. We haven't exactly had much chance to be together have we?"

"Nope, but we're alone now." She snuggled closer and stretched up towards me. I kissed her lightly on the lips, and she screwed up her face.

"Is that the best you can do?" She looked closely at me, scrutinizing my face. "What's the matter? Michael, what's wrong? What have you and Dad been saying?"

"Oh it's nothing like that. Lucy, I think you're wonderful. I'm in love with you and I don't know what to do about it. I hate the thought of losing you."

"Trust you to bring in the doom and gloom. Don't. Not now Michael, let's forget for the moment and take each day as it comes, please!" She implored. "Come on, let's go and party with Gavs lot. Let's show them how." She didn't give me the chance to say no, but ushered me out unceremoniously and headed us towards the barn and the noise. Topic closed. Finished.

FOURTEEN

*D*onald Clapp met me at the door of his shop. He had obviously been waiting to let me in. A 'closed' sign hung on the door, and the room was in darkness, apart from a small lamp which glowed dimly at the back, illuminating the basic shapes of the shelves and counters through which he lead me. We threaded our way through to the back room, brightly lit, spotless. Negatives hung from brightly coloured plastic clips, along lines which stretched across the bench down one side of the room. There were other bits and pieces and paraphernalia which didn't mean a great deal to me, except that they were all obviously connected with photography.

"So Mr Sutherland," he said, "what exactly is it you want to know? You said over the phone that you were interested in altering images on film. Is that what you want?" He looked enquiringly across at me. An intelligent face, sandy hair falling over a wide brow which swept down to a aquiline nose upon which perched a pair of horn rimmed glasses.

"Something like that. And its Michael," I added. He nodded before replying.

"Donald." Pointing to himself. "You have some sort of accent Michael, New Zealand?" I nodded. "Thought so. Lovely country. Visited it a few times in my younger days. Used to be in the merchant navy. We called in to various ports. Which island do you come from?" I told him. "So you know Timaru and Port Chalmers then?" I told him I did. "Lovely part of

240

the world. Would liked to have lived there. Would have done if I hadn't married. My wife Susan couldn't be convinced that it was the place to go. She felt that it was in the back of beyond. One of the reasons that I liked it. She had aging parents, didn't feel she could leave them. The opportunity just slipped us by. Then I got the chance to make a business out of a hobby and here I still am today." He stopped talking, appearing surprised by the amount he had said. He struck me as a very taciturn man, not given over to unnecessary talk. Then asked the question, so often asked.

"What on earth are you doing living over here when you come from such a beautiful country? You must be mad." I had never found an answer that seemed to convince those who asked the question. Beauty was in the eye of the beholder. I liked this country. Missed the matter of factness of the genuine kiwi, but had found enough genuine folk to convince me that it was not really a country thing, more an individual one. Donald dismissed my views with a shake of his head. "I'll get out there one day again, if it's the last thing I do. Just a holiday. The kids are too involved with their own lives now, education and everything else." He sighed. The inward frustration coming close to the surface. Like so many of us, trapped in situations of our own making and not really able to do much about them without causing devastating consequences. One of the ironies of life. He suddenly galvanised into action, shaking off thoughts which got him nowhere. All business like. "Right, let's get started. You tell me what it is you want to know and I will try and see if I can help." I attempted to explain, telling him that I wanted to know how I could put a face of one person onto the body of another without making it look obvious. He stared at me with a calculating look but said nothing, just waited for me to continue. I didn't have much more to say.

"Why?" he asked.

"Why what?" I answered.

"Why would you want to do something like that?"

"I don't, I just want to know if it can be done, and if it can, I would like to know how. I know it can be done by cutting photographs up, photocopying and reprinting, but I want to know how it would be done professionally, and in colour."

"I think you are telling me only part of the story here, but you strike me as a fairly decent chap." I ducked my head in thanks. "Seriously, I've been asked some pretty strange things in my time. There are some weird characters out there. Some of the negatives that have been sent in to be developed would curl your hair. There are some pretty odd characters about." He didn't need to convince me. I knew already. "Let's see now. Basically it depends on how hi - tech you want to go. Today, anyone with a decent computer could go into digital retouching and image manipulation." How appropriate I thought. There had certainly been a few images touched up and manipulated. I wasn't particularly au fait with what he was saying but let him keep going. I could see that he was enjoying the opportunity to talk about his life. "You would need really good printer software plus an adobe illustrator, adobe photoshop, quark xpress etc. Basically you are talking Art Studio or colour lab. Is that the sort of thing?" I shrugged. I didn't have a clue and told him so. He wasn't deterred. "Well, to put it simply, with the right equipment, computer generated, you wouldn't be able to see the join. So the head would belong to the body, right?" I guessed so. It was another language. I had a long way to go. "Then you take the two images, blow them up, increase the pic cells, check them, bring them back to the size you want, back them onto photographic paper and bingo." He looked pleased. I felt confused. "You don't look convinced."

"It's not so much that, it's just that I haven't got a clue what you are talking about. Way over my head I'm afraid. Could the average Joe Bloggs do what you're saying?"

"Pretty much so, yes. Particularly if they were into digital cameras and the whole set up. As I said, it is so easy today with all the computer programmes that are available. You could do it yourself. Have you got a computer?"

I nodded. "Well there you go then. You go to one of the computer outlets and tell them what you want and bobs your uncle, they will tell you what soft ware you need. It would cost a bit, but it's available."

"I would imagine that the guy I'm thinking about wouldn't have too much trouble finding the necessary cash."

"Well then, I've probably answered your question. The finished product would come out looking just like the real thing. So, I guess you have the information you need. You can do all this without having to go near a photographer. But I have to ask, what is this all about? My curiosity has been aroused."

"How about it being just a teacher's desire to further his knowledge?"

"Yeah somehow I doubt that. And is that what you do?"

"For my sins, yes. At King James."

"Good school from what I hear. Unfortunately my first daughter didn't get in. We didn't quite make the grade on one or two entry requirements. Still it didn't turn out too bad. She went to the girls school and did very well. Her mother and I were very pleased and the other two followed on in her footsteps." His face glowed with pride. Obviously a father very much in touch with his progeny. I reckoned that I had found another genuine bloke. Had nothing to lose.

"It's to do with King James school," I said quietly.

"What is?" he asked, coming back to the immediate.

"All this business." I gestured around the room. "The photography, the questions." He said nothing. Just looked and waited. "Do you remember an incident that took place at the school. About half a year ago now. One of the teachers was suspended. It wasn't probably widely known, but in a community this size, word probably got around the town. Right?" He nodded slowly. "Yeah. Well, this guy was basically set up, although the police say there is no proof. But I know. He died as a result. His wife committed suicide; he left behind two wee kids. All for nothing. Well not quite. There is a motive, but it had nothing to do with what he was suspended for." I paused. The injustice of it all still burned deep; only when I spoke of it did it fan up like a fire again.

"And it had something to do with photographs did it?" Donald enquired softly.

"Indirectly yes. There were some pretty damming pictures. They would have turned the most supportive person against him."

"But not you eh." he mused, "why not."

"I had the advantage of knowing a bit more than the others. Even so, they almost got me going. Here take a look for yourself." I handed over the prints that Lara Jones's sister had sent me and watched his face crinkle in distaste, his head shaking in disbelief.

"He was the teacher yes?" I nodded. He read the back of one of them and slowly handed them back. "Not very nice are they? And you say he was innocent of all this?" I nodded again. "Well, it seems a pretty odd business, and those photographs should be handed to the police, in fact the police should be dealing with it all."

"Well, that's probably right Donald, but things don't always work out the proper way, and there are circumstances which have to be taken into account. And to be honest, I can't really elaborate." He sighed.

"You're asking quite a bit."

"Yes," I agreed.

"Not very nice are they?" he said again, turning the print over to read the back. "His hand writing I take it?"

"Mmm."

"Read like a school report don't they. Typical teach jargon," he added smiling. I laughed.

"I would guess so, but out of context they appear pretty awful don't they?"

"Yeah. You think his face was put on that body? It's certainly a good job if you're right. I guess there are those out there that would get a kick out of it. You see enough about it in the newspaper. All I can tell you is that reputable firms wouldn't do anything with this sort of stuff. In fact they would be duty bound to inform the police if it was passed to them. So again, at a guess, this would be done at home by computer."

"Bit like you eh?" I said, knowing full well how he felt. He said nothing for a moment, then spoke.

"Well I would if you hadn't been up front with the story behind them," he said, "but I don't like the idea of a family being destroyed by someone, and I could see how it affected you. That wasn't an act. It gets under your skin doesn't it? Tell you what," he said changing tack, "there is a simple way of doing things that a half decent photographer would be able to do given the right equipment. What say we try and do it for ourselves?" I could see he was getting into this.

"Have you got the time?"

"No problem. Should be a bit of fun. And I haven't done it for quite some time. Will be a challenge. Actually, I'm not that certain I can do it now." He pottered around the benches, sorting out the various bits of equipment. "Okay. I've got a roll of 35mm here. My daughter wanted me to develop it. Don't think she'll mind if we use a couple of shots." He chattered away as he worked, keeping me informed of what he was trying to do. It came down to exposing light to sensitive film, removing it and putting it into a tank to create the difference between light and dark. I had to admit to being in the dark myself, but he was right into it now. A man on a mission. His face slightly aglow in the eerie red light of the darkened room.

"What I'm doing now is putting it into a stop bath for a certain amount of time to settle the negative image," he said at one stage. It seemed that he then had to wash the film for about half an hour and whilst he was doing that he pointed out where the cups were and the kettle and I made myself useful, doing something that I felt I was able to do. "Thanks," he said when I handed him his tea. "Perfect." He bent over the bench and picked up some paper, gently licking one side of it. The paper stuck to his lip and he carefully placed it down.

"Was there a reason for doing that?" I asked, as it had seemed that he was being pretty particular.

"Yes. This is light sensitive paper. One of the reasons we are floundering away in the dark. I have to make sure that I face the correct side to the light. The paper is coated in bromide. I want to use the side that sticks to my lip. Sometimes you can see the sheen off the red light, but this just makes it a bit more certain." He stopped talking and took a large gulp at his tea.

Bromide. What a laugh! I hoped it wasn't potassium bromide. Mates in the army swore that it was put in their mashed potatoes. Kill cock, had been the popular name for it. It seemed strangely incongruous that it existed in this red light area. I found myself laughing. Donald looked over inquisitively and I did my best to explain. He chuckled.

"No, I think I'm pretty safe. Can't say I've noticed any side effects!" There was more to this man than first met the eye. He continued to work away, enlarging the part of the negative that he wanted, using two negatives at the same time, telling me that he was working with a white background and a black background. The black background would supercede the white and the two figures would print on the same paper. I took his word for it and waited. Donald went on to say that there were several options. One could print part of the photograph and 'dodge' out the bit that one wanted to modify then work on that part. In the end he tried using two enlargers focused onto white paper. He dodged out one part while printing another, then reversed it and went through the rigmarole of agitating the sensitive paper again. After what seemed an eternity he switched on the lights and presented me with a photograph of a horse with the face of a young girl. No signs of a join or any other tell tale feature. Impressive, and I told him so. He beamed with delight. "Actually I am pretty pleased with it," he admitted. "You could do more than this you know. You could in fact use any image, take a negative from a magazine, such as a porn magazine and voila! A bit frightening really," The possibilities of it suddenly becoming too real.

Without a doubt, Donald had found a method to incriminate Len. I had to somehow find the means of proving that it had been done. As hard as it had seemed to me, Donald's task now seemed infinitely easier than what I had to do.

We chatted on for a bit, tidying up and leaving it ready for the next days work. I invited Donald for a pint and he seemed pleased at the prospect. We crossed the high street to a small pub. Smoke stained ceiling, flagstone floor. Good beer here, Donald had said. Didn't make a lot of difference to me. Most of what I drank came out of a bottle, chilled, went down well and tasted how it should. I left Donald, his pipe and his beer much later than intended and headed back home with lots of information, lots of thoughts in a turmoil in my mind. All a bit of a maze that I wasn't convinced I could find my way round.

A week of school left then the Easter break. So much had been happening around me that one of the priorities of my life had been taking a back seat. The Oxford Sevens was possibly the last chance for me, for the school, and for the lads to figure in a game of rugby. The prospect appalled. Whilst training had been on going, it hadn't really been at the intensity I felt comfortable with, but then I had always believed that fitness was the priority for this type of game. And so it proved. A Saturday, bright and warm for so early in April, perfect weather for this simplest of games. The lads were very much up for it, so much so that I wondered whether the bush telegraph had been at work again. They played with purpose and flair, more focused than in the tournaments running up to this one, and we came away from the final with nothing but credit and the reversal of a defeat that had been meted out to us at the National Sevens by a competent Welsh side. An elated Danny Boyd confirmed my suspicions when he stepped over to me; sweat drenched and tired, like the other six who had just finished the game.

"That was for you Boss," he said extending his hand and shaking mine firmly. "We know there are some odd things going on. We've heard that Fields, sorry, Mr Fields has decided to put an end to rugby, we have heard that you might be without a job next year. We thought this would at least be some kind of consolation prize." He stopped, not sure of what next to say. I wished he had kept going; I was becoming far too emotional for my age. The spontaneous applause from the others finished me and I turned and walked away, unable to control my feelings.

The presentation of the cup provided an ideal platform to inform the school rugby world what was about to happen at King James, and a hush descended over the gathering as I spoke. I could see faces that I recognized in the crowd, men like me who had devoted their time to giving back to rugby some small measure of the pleasure they had got from it. They voiced their concern afterwards, one or two suggesting that there would be openings at their school should I be looking?

On the way back home, the boys in a jubilant mood, I finally managed to let them know how proud and pleased of them I was. For the majority, it was the last time they would represent the school. There couldn't have been a more fitting end.

Briefing on Monday seemed to overlook the victory, but before the entourage had time to disappear I quickly informed them of the result. Many of the staff, less politically aware burst into applause, not so the senior management team. What a pity, I informed them all, that that was to be the last time King James would be represented at any occasion like that. I looked across at Fields and shook my head in disgust. He was not a happy chap, and left the room bristling, whilst I fielded the many questions which followed. The demise of rugby would not happen without a fight or a maul of some kind!

The address Lucy had given me was for a private nursing home in Essex, in the village of Saffron Walden. I got their number from Directory Enquiries and rang through to a pleasant sounding lady who after a moment's hesitation informed me that Peter Grey would be pleased to receive a visitor. It seemed that he seldom had anyone visit him, and whom should she say would be calling? Just friends, I had replied. We would like to surprise him. I let her know that we would be calling on the Saturday, about midday and she replied that we should ask for her, Mrs Craven. She would be on duty that day and would look forward to meeting us. I thanked her and rang off, then rang Lucy who said she would love to come. Perhaps we could stay over somewhere for the night, had been her parting shot. The idea had merit. The first Saturday of term was about the only weekend that I had to myself before the cricket season began in earnest.

It proved to be a perfect day, one of those magical spring days which seemed to forget that it wasn't yet summer and sent the population into a frenzy of activity, while the managers of garden centres rubbed their hands in glee.

We sped up the M11, lowering the soft top, the wind streaming by. catching the mood of the day. I turned off the motorway and drove up one of the minor roads into the old market town. Lucy read out the directions which took us through the high street, a delightful tangle of 15th and 16th century buildings. She pointed out a pub sign and we drove into the car park, deciding to eat before visiting.

"Have you any idea what you are going to say to him?" she asked between mouthfuls of the most enormous ham salad.

"Not a clue," I replied. "I'll just see what develops."

"His brothers may have warned him about you. He may not want to see you."

"Well he can't exactly march us off the premises can he?"

"Oh Michael, that's awful. The poor man has probably lain there for the best part of his life. He could be all bitter and twisted. What if it was his idea to get back at Len Jones? What if he suggested it to his brothers? What will you say?"

"That he's a bastard, probably," I replied. By the time coffee had been drunk, the afternoon was no longer a new thing. We rather reluctantly departed, for the pub exuded a plethora of ambience, so much so that I booked us a room for the night. The wife of the landlord escorted us upstairs to view the accommodation before we left, opening the door to a tastefully decorated room, a quaint mixture of old and new, full of rural charm.

"Will you be wanting supper?" she enquired. We informed her that we would, without a doubt, and drove off, following her directions to the nursing home, finding it with little trouble up a wide sweeping drive, lined with laburnum trees, an imposing entrance to what was an imposing red brick building, set amidst large grounds. Peacocks, in all their finery strutted nonchalantly by, their eerie calls like cries for help, echoing through the trees. Mrs Craven met us at reception. A comely lady, about ten years older than me, at a guess, with striking red hair.

"Hello," she said extending a slim hand. "I'm Margaret Craven. I'm right in thinking that you are the ones who have come to see Peter?" I nodded, and introduced ourselves.

"How did you know?" I asked.

She smiled a dazzling smile. "Oh it's not too difficult. One gets to know most of the regular visitors, and there are very few others. You are somewhat of a novelty. How do you know Peter?" She looked questioningly at us.

"We don't." Lucy was quick to reply. I had been struggling to think of an appropriate response. "We know his family and knew a man who told us about how good he had been at rugby before he met with his accident."

"Oh," she replied, "well I'm sure he will be pleased to meet you anyway. He hasn't had much in the way of company of late. It's unlike his father not to call, or write. I think Peter is about to give up on them all." I said nothing, "Not that I would blame him," she added with some feeling, then remembering her professionalism turned and apologised. "I'm terribly sorry. That was extremely rude of me." Colour flushed her neck and cheeks. Not a woman to mince words. I liked her even more.

"Peter is a delightful man. He is a gentle person trapped inside a wasted body, yet he bares no one any ill feeling." We turned into a bright, airy room, decked out in light blues. Classical music quietly played from a sound system in the corner, the music suiting the atmosphere, if not creating it. I recognized it as the music which used to accompany the Hovis bread advertisement on television. In the centre of the room, and commanding it, was a large bed, pale blue sheets, a white bedspread, and Peter Grey, propped upright, watching.

"Peter, you have some visitors," Margaret Craven spoke quietly, her voice betraying the affection she had for the man.

"So I see. Thank you Margaret." His voice was soft, barely rising above a whisper. "Who are they?" He stared, his eyes the most intense I had seen, looking from me to Lucy, then back again, then back again. She stared back, smiling uncertainly.

"My name is Michael Sutherland. This is Lucy Alexander."

"Excuse my not getting up," he replied sardonically, "I've been trying for years but haven't quite got the hang of it yet." Lucy murmured something; I couldn't quite make it out.

"Well, don't try on our account, it's an informal visit," I replied.

"Thank you. They seem okay Margaret, thanks. I think I can manage them on my own." He smiled, his face lighting up, robbing the words of any unintended hurt. Margaret Craven turned to Lucy, said that she would be back at the front desk should any of us need her and removed herself from the room.

"She is a peach, that one. I'd have married her myself if I had had the opportunity. Would have been a life of bliss eh? Never out of bed. Sorry, shades of self pity coming through here, and I don't even know you. Who did you say you were? Margaret said something about friends of the family. I'm sure I don't know you."

"You don't. It's Michael, Michael Sutherland and my friend is Lucy Alexander. As for being friends of the family, that's not strictly true. I know of your family. I've met them, but friends, no."

"You say that with more feeling than you intend Mr Sutherland. And what about you Lucy Alexander. Have you met my family?"

"No I haven't Mr Grey, although my father has. I'm afraid neither he nor Michael speak particularly highly of them."

"Whew, you don't mince your words. But fair enough. What about me then?" he countered.

"I'm sure an intelligent person like you would not want to be judged on such a brief encounter. I'll reserve my opinion until the end."

"Well, at least you give me the benefit of being intelligent. You seem to be able to make that judgement rather quickly."

"I'm afraid that was based on prior knowledge," Lucy responded. "I'll be able to see for myself how reliable the information was." Peter Grey began to laugh, a quiet, dry, slightly wheezing sound, his head nodding. Eventually he stopped. "I guess I'll have to be on my toes," he paused, "figuratively speaking, that is. Grab those two chairs and pull them closer to the bed. I don't seem to have the voice I used to have. You two certainly intrigue me. Not many people have the temerity to visit and criticise my family at the same time. Why have you come? How can I possibly be of interest?"

This was the crunch really. I had no idea how he would take what I had to say. "Well, it's a bit of a long story, and not a particularly happy one on any front, and you seem to be the pivot around which it all revolves." I paused and looked closely at him, sensing his interest.

"Oh yes?" he answered, "what could I possibly have anything to do with Mr Sutherland. I have been in this home for the past fifteen or so years. Let me assure you, nothing particularly interesting has happened. I don't get to be wheeled further than the grounds." He said it with feeling and I couldn't help but feel sorry for him.

"Tell me," I added, "what does the name Len Jones mean to you?" He stared back at me unblinkingly, stared, saying nothing, completely motionless now, as if his face had suddenly become paralysed as well. I waited. Lucy stirred restlessly in the chair beside me.

"Len Jones," he replied quietly, his voice trembling with suppressed emotion "was a gifted rugby player. Did you know that?" I nodded. "He had the lot. Balance, flair, pace and power. They used to say that about me too. Said we were destined to higher honours." He snorted. "It didn't happen for either of us did it?" I said nothing, just let him talk. "I got them to write to him you know. Dad wouldn't. He blamed Len for my condition. I told him he was not being rational. It was a freak accident. Did you know?" I nodded again. "The doctor wrote to Len on my behalf, urging him to play. Telling him he was not to blame. He wrote back. Said how sorry he was, and how there was no way he would ever play again. He hated the thought of anything like that happening again. What a waste. And he wasn't to blame, you know. Sometimes accidents do happen. God knows, I've run that moment by thousands of times and there was no way of knowing what would happen. Len caught me at an awkward angle, as I hit him head on. I felt my neck, actually heard it, snap. Hell of a loud noise you know. Great sound box the old head. And that was that. Poor Father, he couldn't come to terms with it. It really got to him. My mother too, although she understood. Broke her heart. But bless her, even she wrote to Len, telling him what a wonderful player he was and that he must continue to play. She was great, but in the end I think having me lying here was too much for her and she just withered away." His voice had begun to go quiet, the emotion draining him. I could see him choking back the tears, heard him utter a single expletive in despair. "Shit." I looked at Lucy; saw that she was affected by his anguish. She stood up and moved to the side of his bed, taking a tissue from the box on the bedside cabinet, then proceeded to gently wipe away the tears, like a mother with her child, completely natural, a woman's desire to comfort. I walked to the window and looked across the open grounds. To be robbed of the chance of a normal life was too much to contemplate. I knew how angry I had been when I had had to stop playing. "I'm sorry." His muffled voice brought me back. "It's a bit of a bugger when you can't even blow your own nose or whatever. Thank you," he said to Lucy. "So why have you asked me?"

"Len Jones died last year. Did you know?" He said no. "He died because he had been beaten to death."

"How do you know this?"

"Because he was a colleague of mine. We worked at the same school."

"That is awful. I am truly sorry to hear that. Why on earth would anyone want to kill him? Was he mugged?"

I shook my head. "As I said earlier, I think you are the reason." I watched the words take effect, watched as he closed his eyes, his face screwed tight shut, head shaking back and forth.

"Dad," he whispered, "You fool, you . . . . oh Dad, surely not." He breathed deeply. "Did my father have anything to do with it?" He looked imploringly towards Lucy, then me.

"I honestly don't know Peter. We wondered whether you knew anything about this. Like you, we thought that your father could be involved. I'm pretty certain your brothers were."

"Stupid, so stupid," he interrupted angrily. "What help have they been? They've been more trouble than anything else. They never supported Dad, not even when Mum died. Eric was so wrapped up in himself, his own importance, his so called political career, he hardly gave any thought to the funeral. As for Aaron, what a waste of space. I'm sorry Mr Sutherland, as you can see; I have very little time for my brothers." He paused, shook his head sadly and added. "About as much time as they have for me. I think they would prefer that I didn't exist. Dad still listens to me, holds back from doing some of the hair brained schemes they want to tie him into." He explained. "And now you think they have something to do with the death of Len Jones. Why?"

I tried to answer him as best I could, stopping at times to explain things over again when the thread became tenuous, answering questions that he posed, Listened as Lucy described the car crash, watched the horror blossom in his eyes as I told of Lara Jones's suicide, and the letter that went with it. Watched as he listened silently to my account of the meeting with his father, his subsequent stroke and my encounter with his younger brother again.

"Do you know how my father is?" It was all he asked, his voice drained.

"Have you not heard?" Lucy's voice couldn't hide her surprise. He shook his head.

"No. I wondered why Dad hadn't called in. He usually tries to see me at least once a fortnight."

I cut in. "The last I heard, he was doing okay. Although he has had a bad time of it, I think he'll come through alright." It didn't seem fair to say otherwise, and I was pretty sure I was right.

"My brothers," he said scornfully, "don't bother coming to see me. Of course, writing or phoning would be too much of an effort. My father would have asked them to get in touch. I guess they said they would." He stopped for a moment. "Do you really think they had something to do with Len Jones's death?" I knew he had accepted the inevitable, knew that he knew they would be capable of it, yet understood his reluctance to confront it.

"I'm sorry Peter."

He inclined his head in resignation. Defeated.

"My father always said it was criminal that the two of them were so mentally weak, and I was confined to a physically weak body. It ate away at him. I imagine he's got at them and used me as an example, told them how useless they were, and that I was the only one who had anything going for him. He used to do it when we were little. You know my father. Not one for tact. I guess when he found out that Len Jones was the same man who he held responsible for my condition, he berated them even more so. Aaron would only see one solution. Eric would come up with the mechanism. Christ what a mess."

I had one further question to ask. I wasn't sure that he would answer, it was a difficult topic. But it had to be asked. "Did your brother have any dealings with photography?"

He said nothing for some time, just lay there staring into space. Lucy looked at me and raised her eyebrows. I winked at her and she relaxed, a smile flitting across her lips. At last he spoke.

"That's not just a simple question out of interest is it?" I shook my head. "Jesus, what a bloody mess. You're asking about Eric. I know that. Eric, my illustrious brother. You know, even as a little boy he had peculiar tendencies. He liked to see things get hurt. He would get all excited." He looked at Lucy. "It's not very pleasant opening up the family closet and revealing all the dirt. I'm ashamed that you have to hear this." Lucy squeezed his hand.

"Mr Grey, I need no longer reserve my opinion of you. I think you are a very decent man, a very kind and caring man. Whatever your brothers happen to be, you are you, and I like what I see."

"Thank you," he whispered.

"You're welcome," she replied patting the hand that lay in hers.

"You asked me about photography," he said turning toward me. "Eric was always interested in it. It was his hobby. He has a dark room at his home so my father tells me. In fact Dad has hired him sometimes for promotional work. It was one of the few times Dad would speak proudly of him. But of course Eric manged to put an end to that. Seems he was found with some pornographic pictures. Dad didn't say much but Aaron boasted about them. Gloated that Eric had given some to him as a present. Apparently Dad had to pull a few strings to keep it all hushed up. There were photographs involved in all of this weren't there." It was a statement more than a question. I told him what I had seen, told him what I had found out regarding the printing of them. "I'm sorry Peter." I was. I meant it. Perhaps if fate had been a little more selective none of this would have happened. If. Dad's favourite poem. Bloody big word. All the world's casualties had hung in its balance. If Peter Grey had remained unscathed, perhaps he could have kept the family together. No bitterness eating like a cancer in his father, the chance to keep his younger brother in tow, to retain the fabric of the family. If life was fair. Well it bloody wasn't and that was that.

256

"It seems as though you have got all the answers to your suspicions. I guess you will now involve the police. It will kill my father you know. The shame of it all."

"Well it isn't quite that simple," I replied, "there are other's involved and going to the police isn't really an option at the moment."

"You have certainly landed yourself an unenviable task Michael," he replied when I had finished speaking, using my name for the first time. I took it as a sign of his trust. "I wish I could help."

"Thanks, but she'll be right. I'll muddle through this somehow."

"She'll be right? You sound like one of those characters from Neighbours. You're not Australian by any chance are you?"

"Good grief Peter, you'll have him doing a haka on your bed in a moment," Lucy interjected. "That's tantamount to an insult as far as he is concerned.

"New Zealander then. All Black?" I shook my head.

"No but he would have been if he hadn't been injured," Lucy piped up. "He was pretty good."

"Well, that's grand. I don't get to meet many rugby players anymore. What position did you play?" He could hardly contain his enthusiasm. The desire to quiz me on all aspects of the game, to get my views on the new laws, to see what I thought of the Southern Hemisphere teams, the Super Fourteens. It all came bursting through. He said they didn't have Sky TV or cable so he was unable to watch some of the games. I promised to send him recordings. Did he have a video? Yes he said, his delight bursting out of him. I made a mental promise to send him some of my collection and to look into setting up Sky for him. I couldn't understand why his father had not done that for him already. Lucy told me later that I should have been a social worker. I told her the pay was lousy. What, more lousy than teaching, she had countered?

We left him with the promise of keeping in touch. I gave him my phone number, told him we were staying overnight in the village and that we would call in before we left for home. He thanked us profusely. Did we mind if he didn't walk us to the door? A game of self mockery he seemed to enjoy. I told him yes, but for this visit we would let it pass, and left him chuckling in the dry sort of wheezy way that he did.

Lucy seemed preoccupied as we drove back to the pub, finally voicing the thoughts that had been whizzing around my head.

"So what now Mike. What happens now? I mean, he's more or less told us that it must be his brothers, but what can you do?"

"I wish I knew Luce. I haven't got a clue? I mean, it's not like I can go back to them and say that we know what's happening, is it? Somehow, I don't think they would be too chuffed."

"What about seeing their father again?" she asked.

"The last time didn't prove too successful. Who knows what sort of state he is in? I don't know, it's all a mess." It certainly was. Every turn seemed to be check mated.

"What would happen if Peter told his father what has been said today?" Lucy continued. "Perhaps that would help."

"It might," I conceded, "but the chances of that seem pretty remote at the moment. I mean, his old man is lying in hospital somewhere, unable to communicate with anyone, Peter didn't even know he was ill, so how on earth is he going to be able to contact him? It's not as though he is in regular contact with his brother's is it? Hell, they seem to despise each other. Their father seems to have made it pretty clear that Peter was everything they weren't. Once he dies, I wouldn't count on their support too much if I were Peter."

"I know, it's awful isn't it" Lucy's voice was sad. "And all he can do is lie there. It's not fair."

258

"Life's a bitch, as they say, and then you die," I agreed. We said little else. There wasn't much to say, finishing our journey to the pub in mutual silence, preoccupied with our own thoughts.

We sat in the lounge, Lucy nursing a white wine, me a pint of lager.

"Australian," she snorted. "Things must be bad." I had to laugh.

"Fair do's," I replied, "they do make good lager, and their red wine is pretty good too. Credit where credit's due."

"Well, that's a turn up. You must be losing it Sutherland."

We ate a superb supper of venison in red wine, accompanied by a fine red, Australian naturally, to prove I was more than just talk. Lucy agreed that it was indeed pleasing to the palate. Good food, good wine, good company. It tended to mellow one, and thoughts of the afternoon drifted away. We finished late, savouring the delights of a fine sweet and finishing with a coffee.

"Fancy a stroll round the block before bed?" she asked.

"Sure thing. Mind if I take a cigar along?"

She grimaced, before grinning, adding with a resigned sigh, "if you must."

We stepped out into the evening air, the quiet of the town enveloping us.

"This is beautiful Mike," Lucy said slipping her hand into mine. "So peaceful. So different from the hustle and bustle of London."

"Why not set up in business over here then?" I asked.

"Precisely because it is so quiet," she replied. "I would have nothing to do."

"Sounds pretty good to me."

"Maybe, but it doesn't pay the bills," she answered.

"There's always a down side, life never lets you have it just right does it?" We were walking down a narrow street, the only people on the road. Not even a fast food store in sight. Bliss.

FIFTEEN

They came out of the darkness, four of them, moving quickly towards us. Hooded. Sinister.

"Lucy," I screamed, "For God's sake run, run." I pushed her away from me, my brain urging her to get away as quickly as possible, willing her to evaporate, praying that she would be safe. She needed no second urging, kicking off her high heels, speeding away from the immediate danger. One of the four peeled away towards her, running in long strides. Oh Christ, he was bound to overtake her. Then no time to worry. They were upon me, fanning out to encircle me, no hesitation, purposeful. Nothing said, everything understood. As if on an unspoken command they rushed in, swamping me, fists thumping, thudding, jarring. The intention to constrain rather than to destroy. The blows rained in and although I tried my utmost to retaliate, it was all rather futile. Arms grabbed mine and pinned me from behind. Tape was quickly wrapped around my hands, then unceremoniously wrapped around my mouth, and over my eyes, pulling at my hair. I had once read that blindfolding a horse was the best way of gaining control over it. If it felt as vulnerable as I did, I could well understand how it worked. I could only swallow, couldn't spit the blood which filled my mouth. Tasted its metallic flavour. Struggled to breathe, my nose blocked with blood and the effects of a cold. Fought off rising waves of panic. Dear God, don't let me suffocate. Lucy! What about Lucy? Please don't let them harm her.

"Where the fuck's the girl?" A voice I recognized.

"She got away." Unknown. I tried to picture the person to match it. Conjured up an image of a weedy weak looking character. The voice lacked substance.

"You useless prick. Can't you do anything right?" A voice loaded with contempt.

"I couldn't help it," whined the other, "she had some sort of spray. It went into my eyes. It bloody burnt like hell. I couldn't see a thing. She got away." One of the others snorted in disgust.

"You always were a pussy Craig. Shit useless." Not a voice I knew, but the name he had mentioned left me in no doubt as to the company I was keeping.

"We got Sutherland at least. If his bit of stuff knows what's good for him she'll shut up. It mightn't hurt to give her a reminder." Dalton Murphy. His voice belied the nature of his intentions. I should have realized what he was like. The tape around my hands gave way, but before I could do anything my left hand was grabbed, fingers spread, then the most sickening, intense pain. Oh Christ, the bastard had cut off my little finger. I could feel the vomit rising, couldn't shout, couldn't scream. Felt like my eyes were about to explode from my head. Swallow, damn it, swallow. Oh God the pain! I heard someone retching. Could appreciate the need to.

"Jesus Dalton, you sick bastard, you cut off his finger !" Disbelief, shock in the voice of Craig Holden. Heard him spitting.

"Yeah, so what. He deserved it. Been nothing but trouble right from the start. Always getting in the way, always managing to get out of trouble. Shit, Paul should have finished him on the bridge but he got out of that as well. Well not this time buddy." He squeezed my hand, pushing into the stub which had once been my little finger. "Like that?" he sneered. "Here Grey, you take the finger and mail it. Let her know it won't be the only thing we'll cut off if she gets the police involved. Tell her he won't be good for nothin', that she will have to find a proper man if there is any trouble." he laughed out loud, and one of the others joined in, making ribald comments.

I was pushed roughly from behind, pushed and dragged. Hands once more taped in front of me. One of them had stuffed my handkerchief over my hand to staunch the blood, and I cursed my weakness for feeling grateful.

We didn't walk far, before I was bundled into a car, crammed in between two others. Whilst I tried to pick up sounds, or any other clues, my mind was constantly reminding me of the throbbing pain, so much so that I couldn't detach myself from the immediate. At some stage the journey ended and I was maneuvered somewhere, the tape covering my mouth was torn off allowing me to breath deeply for the first time.

"Not such a clever clogs now are you," sneered the voice of Dalton Murphy, "You think that artist guy had it bad, you just wait and see."

"Remove the tape over my eyes and I might be able to," I replied.

"Still got the answers eh, still the big man. You wait mate. You wait and see." The tone of his voice did little to reassure me.

"You're one tough guy, Murphy. You and your cronies. Good in a crowd, good when you can outnumber someone. Been like it all your life eh? Haileybury must have celebrated the day they got rid of you and your mates." There was a sharp intake of breath, then a voice.

"Jesus, how does he know your name? He's not meant to know anyone, or see anyone. How does he know?" Rising panic. Criag Holden, very much the weak link.

"Marshall was right," I continued, "You are a pussy."

"Shit." The expletive carried a great deal of pent up feeling. Paul Marshall was equally disturbed.

Murphy spoke again, his voice loaded with contempt. "Who gives a toss if he knows us. It won't do him any good. I knew McKay would crack. He's as weak as you are Craig. I'll sort him out. Stupid prick. All these years he's thought he screwed that girl. What a laugh. He couldn't even get a hard on. We did her good and proper though eh Paul? Gave the bitch a good seeing to."

The enormity of what he said was too much to contemplate. Left me gutted. Jimmy McKay had carried the guilt of his behaviour that night, for so many years. The family had been exploited, his sister had been put through a nightmare, a friend had died as a consequence. For no reason. It need not have happened. It was almost too much to take on board.

"You bastards," I whispered.

"Yeah aren't we," smirked Murphy. I flinched in anticipation, and was rewarded by a blow to the kidneys. After the finger it was almost an anti climax. Still, at least I was getting to know my adversary.

"Leave him. He'll not be so full of it after a few days." The voice of Lord Grey's youngest son. "Truss his hands behind his back again so he can't get at the tape. And wrap it round his mouth. I'm sick of listening to him." It was duly done and I was shoved to the floor, feeling the dampness of the bare earth underneath me. Where the hell was I? Voices died down, fading into the night. Heard car doors slam, heard the sound of the engine start up then disappear. Alone. What a bloody shambles. Alone to thank the being who watched over Lucy. Took some comfort in the knowledge that she had escaped. Couldn't bear to think of the anguish she must be feeling. Willed my mind to send subliminal messages to her.

Felt like I was in a time warp. How long I lay there I had no idea. Wanted to nurse my hand, to comfort it. Useless. Exhaustion numbed my mind, seeping in at the edges, fuzzing reality with make believe until I succumbed, drifting off into a fitful sleep, a sleep which conjured up images of violence, of naked children, of me, naked and abused and bleeding, until I woke up screaming in my head, sweating and confused, unable to utter a sound. My shoulders ached, my hand caused me to flinch every time it rubbed up against the other one, and I desperately wanted to see, to have some control. How long had I been asleep? My internal clock suggested it was early in the morning. My bladder suggested it was later. Couldn't bear the thought of humiliating myself. Couldn't see any other option. Tentatively flexed my wrists, tried to work against the tape, tried to ignore the sharp messages my brain was relaying, concentrated on twisting my wrists, straining against the resistance. Seemingly hopeless, or did it give a little? I had to believe it gave a little. Had to. Strain, relax, strain. How long I kept it up I couldn't tell. Didn't seem to be making much difference. Heard noises, voices. Wanted to stand. Rocked over onto my side, then onto my back, the floor digging into my hands, which lay beneath me. Painful. I was sick of pain. I could feel my anger rising, rolled back onto my side, the momentum allowing me to twist onto my knees and get to my feet. Better. But now what?

"What the hell did you bring him here for?" An angry voice. I'd heard it before. Would know it anywhere.

"What else could we do?" Whining voice. Poor old Craig. Didn't seem to be too popular with anyone.

"I don't understand why he had to be brought anywhere. Dalton should have just sorted him out." I heard the sounds of keys in a lock, heard the door creak open, heard them in the room. "He doesn't look to be too much of a problem now though, does he?" Heard Craig snigger. Waited. Soft footsteps on the floor, a voice whispering in my ear, his breath offensive. Would have liked to have breathed through my mouth, couldn't, so suffered. "So Dalton removed a finger eh? Good for him. One less to put in the pie. Let's see. This one wasn't it?" I knew it was coming, but it didn't help much. Still the same red hot stab of agony. Couldn't stop my body tensing up, too involuntary to control. Knew his type would be pleasured by the response, knew he would do it again. Waited, felt the explosion of messages, felt my back straighten, could feel my jaw clenching, teeth grinding. Heard him breath deeply in satisfaction. The others were thugs, this one was perverted. Dangerous. Got off on other people's pain.

"Hurts doesn't it. Every time I do that! Look at the way his back arches." His voice trembled with suppressed excitement. Almost throaty. "It must really hurt him. Take the tape off his mouth. Let's see what he sounds like when it hurts. Go on, do it." Impatient now, his voice rising in expectation. Hands on my head, then the tape was removed. I could smell the smoke of a cigar. Oh God. I knew what he was going to do. Wished the tape was back over my mouth. Wasn't going to give the sick bastard the satisfaction. Couldn't control my breathing. Waited for it to happen. Bit deeply onto the inside of my lip, willed my mouth to stay shut. Smelt the flesh burning, felt my senses going. Don't. Don't give in please. In time it receded. My head seemed to be on fire, about to burst, as if all the blood had rushed to it and needed to escape, thumping and throbbing.

"Did you see that. Look at the sweat on him. Pity he didn't scream."

"Yeah, sorry about that. Didn't want to get you too excited. You might have blotted more than your copy book." Silence. I'd probably over done it. What next. Heard him breathing deeply. Close enough. Lashed out with my foot. Caught him somewhere soft. Lashed out again. Connected again. Great. Hopefully that would take his mind off his sick thoughts. Was about to kick again. No chance. Thumping blow to the side of my head. Not a fist. More like a lump of wood. Again. Legs gave way. I hit the floor. Felt the boot come in. Heard Cigar man coughing and moaning.

"Leave him," I heard him gasp, "I want him." It didn't sound too good. Heard him shuffle across. "Want a cigar?" I didn't answer. Couldn't answer. The burning end was ground deep into the wound. Couldn't hold the scream which tore from my throat, a scream so primeval, wrenched from the very depths of my soul. Heard it come to a shuddering stop, as though it were a part of me yet beyond me.

"Did you hear that Craig? Like a wild animal." His voice had thickened again with emotion.

"You're one sick person," I croaked, my voice catching in short ragged breaths. "Where did they let you out from?" I didn't want him to do any more burning, didn't think I could stand it. Wouldn't let him have the satisfaction of begging him to stop. No answer.

"What are you going to do with him?" An uncertain Craig. "Let him be." A good question. I wondered myself.

"What do you think Craig, mm? He knows who most of us are. Do you think we should let him go?" His voice was patronising, a bit like a teacher with an erring child. "I'm afraid poor Mr Sutherland has come to the end of his teaching days."

"You're not going to do it now?" Rising alarm in Craigs voice. He really wasn't cut out for this.

"Jesus Craig, you could be a liability. Murphy was right. You're weak. How the hell you're a friggin' relative of mine beats me. And no, not now. We'll let him stay here for a while then arrange a little accident. Make it look real. Like the sound of that Teacher boy? Just think, you can lie here and wait, knowing that there is no way out, knowing what the end will be." His voice had started to tremble again.

"You're a bloody fruitcake Eric. Should make a good politician. Why don't you do everyone a favour and put a plastic bag over your head and throttle yourself. By the sound of things it could be your second coming." I had thought of keeping it to myself that I knew who he was. Didn't see much point in it now. He let out an expletive.

"Shit! See what I mean Craig. A very dangerous man is our Mr Sutherland. Seems to know everyone and everything."

I wasn't expecting it; the force of the kick to my stomach temporarily winded me, my breath whooshing out. Felt my bladder give up the fight.

"Didn't know that was going to happen though did he. Look, the poor bastards so frightened he's pissed himself." He started to laugh.

"Leave him before he stinks the place out. Better place the tape back over his mouth. Not that anyone would hear him out there, but best to be on the safe side. Watch where you step though." The tape was roughly pressed on; there was the sounds of footsteps receding, the creak of the door, the jangle of keys, the door slamming and lock clicking into place. Then all was silence again. Alone once more, infinitely preferable, safer and less humiliating. The only thing which didn't ache was my bladder. One had to be thankful for small mercies. What a mess. How on earth was I going to get out of this? I had to think that I would. Anything else was too horrific to contemplate.

Help came from the most unlikely source. I had spent lonely hours desperately trying to remove the tape which securely bound my hands, thinking that I was making progress, but in reality getting nowhere. Having managed to get back onto my feet, I had bumped and collided with various obstacles in a vain effort to find anything which could be used to cut my bonds. All I had succeeded in doing was to add to my collection of bruises. I had come to the conclusion that I was in fact well and truly stymied. It was not a pleasant feeling. When the sound of footsteps became audible, then the rattle of keys in the lock, I experienced the coldness of fear. Knowing that there was nothing I could do to prevent the inevitable filled me with intense feelings of anger, frustration and sheer panic. I didn't want to die. There was too much to live for. Oh God, help me. The door creaked open. Silence. The sharp sound of an indrawn breath. "Bloody hell." Not a voice I knew. Who was this? Had they hired someone to do their dirty work? I could sense him coming closer. My senses razor sharp. 'Come on you bastard.' 'Give me just one chance to lash out.' I wanted to go down fighting. Not just give up and be blown away. The door! It was still open. I was on my feet. A chance. Had to grab it. I ran. Knew nothing stood in my way. Had found that out at least on my various attempts to manoeuvre myself around whatever it was I was being held in. My movements were so unexpected to my assailant that I collided with him, my shoulder jarring into him, and I heard the whoosh of his breath as I struggled to stay on my feet, the impact spinning me away to the side. Hoped I was back on course, running free. For the first time, thoughts of escape seeming possible. Short lived, as I careered into something sending me spinning to the ground. Cursed as I felt hands hold me down. This was it. Where was my life? They always said that it flashed before you. I wasn't going to even get the benefit of that.

"Jesus You gave me a helluva start. Whoa. Stop struggling. I'm not going to hurt you mate. For Christ sake, lie still!" he ordered. He had his knee in my back, and I felt his hands tugging at the tape wrapped around my mouth and then over my eyes. I could sense the light, for the first time in what had seemed an age. Then I could see! What a relief. It was like feeling more whole once again. I struggled to twist round, to see who it was that had me pinned to the ground. Pinned to the ground in what was obviously an old tractor shed of some kind.

"Who are you?" His voice was deep, a west country accent easily discernible. It went with the territory: A big chap, brown weathered skin, deeply lined with wrinkles, eyes partially hidden by large sandy eyebrows. But not the eyes of a killer. Of that I was pretty sure. "Well?"

"My name is Michael Sutherland." I left it at that and waited.

"You don't look too good Michael Sutherland. What's happened? Why has someone done this to you?"

"Who am I talking to?" I asked.

"Fair enough, I reckon I owe you that. I'm Colin Penreeth."

"Well I might shake your hand, but you have the advantage. I can't."

"True. Let's just leave it like that for a little while longer. I'm not up to fighting you, and from where I am this all looks a little strange."

"So you're not with the others then?" I asked, trying to keep the hope out of my voice.

"What others?" he replied "Who's done this to you?"

"Let's just say that I ran into some pretty nefarious characters. I thought you were one. I mean, how did you get the keys for this place. Who does it belong to?"

"I've had these here keys for years. They belong to the shed, which belongs to me. So that explains that. But it doesn't help me at all. How come you've ended up in the state that you are, in my shed?"

I told him as much as was needed. There was no point in going through the whole thing. Half way through he undid the tape which bound my hands, looking with concern at the mess which had once been my finger.

"They do that too?" he asked, anger visible in his movements. I nodded. He shook his head in disgust. "You know who they were?" I nodded again, but said nothing. "You're not going to tell me then are you?"

"Not yet," I replied. "I've got to think it all through. I don't know what's best at the moment. They've thrown a couple of curve balls at me which have completely knocked me sideways."

"I think I should call the police anyway," he added. A natural reaction, but not the one I wanted, yet.

"No don't do that." He looked at me oddly, and I hurriedly tried to reassure him that it was all okay. He wasn't convinced.

It transpired that Colin had lived in this neighbourhood until a couple of years ago. He was still undergoing the slow process of moving house, or in his case, shed. He had been allowed to store some of his junk in the shed and this was to be his last trip. Business had brought him back this way and it seemed the ideal time to pick up what was left, before heading back to Taunton. I looked around the shed, heard him chuckle.

"I can see you are not impressed," he said. "The look says it all." I mumbled an apology. "No need," he replied, "unless you're a keen blacksmith type person you wouldn't think anything of the junk that remains. I've got an old forge down at my home, drives the wife crazy. I tell her it beats golf, at least she's got me close by. And she gets the benefit of some of my creations. She's not so convinced. Says she's got so many pokers all she needs now is an open fire!" He stopped suddenly, looked keenly at me again then spoke. "This is bloody madness. You're sitting there in Christ knows what state, and we're passing the time of day as if nothing has happened. So tell me again. Some guy that you know just cut your finger off and left you here. And you can't tell the police? I'm damn sure I would!"

Why not go to the police? I'd heard enough now to know that Jimmy was innocent of any rape charge. Heard Murphy admit that it had been him and Marshall. Knew that they intended to get rid of me. So why not the police? Carmichael couldn't deny the fact that my finger had been chopped off. That was proof enough. Or was it? I hadn't seen their faces. I couldn't testify that I had seen them. Only that I knew their voices. No doubt some sharp lawyer would be able to swing that in their favour. And then what? They'd murdered Len Jones. His wife had died, his kids had gone through hell and so had I. For what: Some sick prick with a half baked idea of winning his father's favour. Someone who was hoping to go on to higher things. Sod that. I wanted to get even. The police couldn't do that. I said nothing.

He stared back, waiting, then slowly shook his head in resignation, breathing a sigh of defeat.

"I've got to say that I'm not happy about this, but you obviously have your reasons. What are we going to do with you?" His eyes wandered back down to the bloodstained cloth covering my hand and he shook his head again. "Just cut it off. Jesus, what an animal."

"Where exactly are we? I couldn't work out how long we were in the car. It didn't seem too long."

"Much Hadham. It's a little village southwest of Bishop Stortford. Do you know it?"

I said I didn't. Bishop Stortford I knew because of rugby, but not really the town or the surrounding area. "There's a hospital there. I think you should get that finger seen to." I went to object but he wouldn't have it. "Listen, it has to be cleaned. When was the last time you had a tetanus injection?" I couldn't tell him. A few years ago perhaps. "Just tell them you caught it in some sort of machine." He knew what was bothering me. "They're used to it in these parts. There's always a farmer doing something like that. Come on. Let's get you into the car and out of here." He leant me his arm in a friendly gesture, I was grateful for it, and we made our way to his Volvo estate. I was suddenly aware of the tension draining from me as we distanced ourselves from the little shed, away from death.

"Lucy," The tone following her recorded message had finished. They had been kind enough to point me toward the telephone, at the hospital, my mobile had gone missing following the scuffle, letting me ring before attending to my hand. "I know you will be thinking the worst, but don't worry. I've managed to get away. I'm at the hospital in Bishop Stortford. They should have done with me pretty soon and I'll grab a lift back to the house. I love you."

I wandered back to the waiting room and bided my time. Colin had his head immersed in a magazine, but looked up as I sat down.

"Any luck?"

"Answer phone," I replied.

He shrugged. "Better than nothing at all I guess, but a bit unsatisfactory all the same." I had to agree.

The doctor who attended to me was puzzled by my delay in getting attention. Wasn't impressed with the burning around the wound. I explained that the accident had happened last night, I hadn't been able to find the finger, thought there was no point in wasting everyone's time until the next day, so had decided to leave it. He gave me a good old dressing down, lecturing me on the importance of immediate attention, the danger of septicemia and other such complications and made me promise never to leave something for so long again. I could see that he was a little skeptical, but given the fact that outpatience was heaving he let it lie. Giving an address wasn't the problem I thought it would be. They simply accepted that I was visiting, and took my own home address. Colin said he had nothing better to do and would be glad to drive me back to the pub to pick up the car.

The fact that it wasn't there, simply confirmed my belief that Lucy had managed to get it started and drive it home. Unfortunately that belief was shattered when I stepped inside to talk with the landlord. He looked surprised to see me, then slightly annoyed, asking where we had gone and informing me coolly in the same breath that I owed him the price of an evening meal for two and the cost of the room, for we had left our

272

clothes in it. "Hadn't my friend sorted that out," I asked? "No Sir," he had replied. He had seen neither of us since we went for our evening stroll. He provided me with a key for the room, the other one having been lost in the fracas, and I found my wallet lying on the bedside table, exactly as I had left it. None of Lucy's stuff had been taken. Colin raised his eyebrows at that, but said nothing. I knew what he was thinking. I felt the same. While Colin packed up all our bits and pieces, I fed coins into the payphone and dragged George Alexander from his living room repose, to gently enquire as to whether Lucy had been in touch.

"Why?" Typical George. Straight to the point. "You had a bit of a bust up?"

"No George, nothing like that. I was just wondering whether she had been in touch or not?"

"Not good enough Michael. What gives? You're not thinking of doing something honourable are you?"

"You're making me feel bad George. It's just a harmless question." I tried to convince him.

"You're not doing a very good job Michael. I know you too well now my boy. So what gives?" George in a more determined mood now. Whilst I hadn't wished to alarm him, it seemed that I was in fact doing just that. I took a deep breath and launched into the explanation, stopping to feed in more coins, hoping that I had enough to finish the conversation. George, now most concerned, took my number and rang back. I could sense his anxiety. Could understand it. Felt terrifically guilty.

"How about you?" he asked at one stage, "did they do anything to you?" I told him as matter of factly as I could. Told him that it was possible that a small parcel could arrive addressed to Lucy and that he should get rid of it.

"The bastards," was all he had to say.

"It doesn't feel right George. I'm worried about Lucy. She hasn't been back for anything. The car's gone. It might or might not be her. But I would have thought her first action would have been to get in touch with you."

"Yes," he replied, "I agree. Lucy would not go to the police, knowing that you didn't want any fuss made. You had made that pretty plain." It sounded like an accusation, but I knew George well enough to know that he was simply stating a fact and meant nothing more by it.

"I wish she had," I answered. "There might not be a problem now." There was a long pause before he replied.

"I'm not going to worry unnecessarily Michael. Lucy's a resilient girl. She'll not be beaten easily. But, I think it's time the police were brought in. Don't you?"

"Yes." The knowledge that Jimmy McKay was innocent of rape had done more to deflate me, than the beatings I had taken. And now if Lucy was in danger. All my intentions of getting even, of making certain that they were found guilty, seemed insignificant now. Nothing could happen to Lucy. I could have kicked myself for not having involved the police more in the first instance. None of this mess might have happened. "I'll get in touch with the policeman who has been dealing with the incidents. Not that he will be too pleased. He'll probably attempt to do me for withholding information."

"I wouldn't think so. If he does, I'll have a word with the Chief Constable. We go back a bit. No doubt you will tell me it's all part of the privilege thing again." I didn't care. I just wanted everything sorted. I wanted Lucy. "I'll pick you up," he continued. "Give me the address." I did so and hung up. George was a great man in a crisis.

"You've looked better." I looked up as George strode through the entrance to the bar, purpose and energy vibrating from him. Just as well he hadn't seen me before I had showered. He looked me over critically, gently taking my left hand in his, looking at the bandage which covered the gap where my finger should have been. "Bastards," he said it again. It

274

was fast becoming one of his favourite words. He looked intently at me. "You okay?"

"Yeah, I'll get by," I replied. He scrutinized my face, seemed satisfied with what he saw and turned to Colin who had kindly waited with me. George made his own introductions, thanked him for all he had done, listened to Colin tell him how he had found me, looked closely at me again, told me that I had missed one or two details out on the phone. I shrugged. No sense in alarming people. And anyway, things weren't that bad. They both snorted. "Well, what do you consider bad then?" George asked. I told them.

"The poor bastard," George uttered his word for the day again. "What an existence."

"Peter Grey." Colin uttered his name out loud and nodded his head as his mind clicked things into place. "I know of him. My wife has a friend who works there. She used to say he had had such a tough break. A bright mind trapped in a useless body."

"Margaret Craven, by any chance?" I asked. A long shot, but one of those which seemed right. He nodded, a shade surprised. "I met her when we went there yesterday. She just seemed to be the logical choice," I tried to answer him. He smiled.

"Yep, Margaret would see an angel in the devil. One of life's positive people."

"Very protective of her patients." I replied. "Wouldn't want to see any further harm come to her children."

"You've got her in one," he laughed. "It's a small world, I'll say that." He turned towards George and extended his hand and shook George's. "Nice to meet you. I'm going to make a move. I've still got a couple of things to collect before heading off." He turned back towards me, "it would seem you have a lot to sort out. I don't think I'm any the wiser as to why this has all happened. But by God, I don't think I could be so matter of fact as you appear to be. You're a hard one. I don't fancy that guy's chances should you ever meet up with him again, that's for sure." He grinned a big grin, shook my hand and made to leave.

"Colin," I called him back. "Thanks." He looked at me and winked.

"For what? You just get it all sorted. Let me know what happens eh. And look me up if you're ever down my way. I've given George the address. Cheers." He turned and strode out of the bar, not looking back.

"A good bloke, that," George commented watching him leave. "You were lucky having him turn up." I nodded. More grateful than any one appreciated. "So what next?"

"Let's get out of here," I replied. "I think it's time I saw D.C. Carmichael and confessed."

We said very little on the drive back, both of us preoccupied with our thoughts. Thoughts that were pretty much about the same person I would imagine. What on earth could have happened to her?

As luck would have it, D.C. Carmichael was on call. He came out from one of the rooms behind the glass reception area, ran his eye over me, stopping briefly at my hand, said nothing, pushed a button and beckoned us to come through into one of the interview rooms, the door clicking back behind us. He gestured for us to sit down.

"Cup of tea?" We both nodded. He got up, called the sergeant from the reception desk and put in an order for three cups of tea. "Sugar?" George nodded, I shook my head. "Two with, Bob," he yelled at the disappearing sergeant. "I know you well enough Mr Sutherland, well enough to know that I never see you in good health. As appears to be the case today. But I have not met your companion before."

"George Alexander," George replied.

"Lord George Alexander," I informed him. He looked a little surprised, but said nothing. Just nodded his head a couple of times. "I'm a friend of his daughter," I explained.

"Right. Now to coin an old expression, what seems to be the problem? You look to have been in the wars again. No doubt it has something to do with that deceased teacher. Yes?" I nodded. He sighed. "I thought I told you to leave all that to us, last time we met."

"You did, but this time it was all fairly innocuous, or so we thought." I took my time telling him. Told him everything. Went right back to our first meeting at Len Jones's house. Told him that I too had been given much the same treatment. He smiled a knowing smile and confirmed my suspicions that his bumping into me that night had not been an accident. I told him so and politely suggested that he was George's word of the day. Told him about Jimmy McKay, about my promise to his father. He sighed again and informed me that I was in fact admitting to withholding information. I asked him whether he wanted to hear the rest or not and if so just to listen, otherwise I would withhold the bloody lot, but as Lord Alexander's daughter was now missing, probably abducted, I would rather he listened and got some results. That had the desired effect.

"What do you mean, abducted?" he asked sitting forward in his chair.

"Exactly what the word implies," I replied. "She's missing. I can only assume the worst." I went on, telling about our meeting with Lord Grey's son, and our confrontation with the four in the evening, told him who they were.

"Can you be certain it was them?" he asked. I could. Said that although my blindfold had not been removed, I had managed to identify them.

"Pity you hadn't seen them, it would make it all a little easier." He looked disappointed. I shrugged, told him to look at it from my angle. I hadn't liked being trussed up like a chicken. He didn't seem to be too concerned. "What happened to the hand," he asked. I told him Dalton Murphy had felt compelled to remove a finger. "You certain it was him?" was his concerned response. I told him I had no doubt. Third time round. I was getting to know him quite well. He took the point. I reeled off the other names, and he wrote quickly into his little diary, looking up with surprise when I mentioned Eric Grey.

"Are you positive it was him?" he asked again.

"Without a doubt." He looked up from his writing, the intense dislike reverberating around the small room.

"That's interesting," he acknowledged. "One of them cuts off your finger and you tell me in a pretty matter of fact way. But boy, you don't have much love for Eric Grey. What the hell did he do?" I looked across at George. The question had obviously interested him as well. What could I tell them? That the humiliation of having wet myself hadn't exactly endeared me to the fellow? Nor his perverseness? That was my business, my personal concern. I shrugged.

"Let's just say I don't like the fellow and leave it like that."

"Fair enough Mike," George answered.

"So what about your friend, your daughter?" D.C. Carmichael enquired looking to George. I explained that we had separated in the street and that she had seemed to have escaped. All I could think of was that they had gone back to the hotel and waited for her to show up. I could see that he thought so to. He excused himself, leaving us alone in the room for a short time, and returned saying that he had been in touch with the constabulary in Saffron Walden and that they were getting things moving. He had given them a description of Lucy and of the car, along with that of Eric and Aaron and asked me to describe the others. I did my best and he went back off to ring them again.

There was nothing more that I could do. D.C. Carmichael gave me his by now regular lecture on leaving police work to the police. I was too tired to argue. He told George that he would do his utmost to ensure that everything was done to find his daughter, then excused himself from the room, leaving us to make our way out. Not really satisfactory. I guess it couldn't have been anything else.

SIXTEEN

The next few days were hell. No word, no nothing, just the parcel containing the bloody remains of my finger, and a lurid note attached to it, threatening. George had decided to stay at Lucy's flat for the week just in case anything cropped up. The parcel and the note did much to inwardly destroy him, tangible evidence of the type of people who had his daughter. Virginia remained at the farm, quietly strong. Gavin was not to be told just yet, she had stated. His A levels were fast approaching and he had to be given a chance to concentrate on them. George hadn't liked the idea, but knew better than to oppose his wife at this particular time.

"We'll get her back," I had told him over the phone. We had to. The last couple of days had gone by in a daze. Everything automatic, emotions and senses on hold. Tried not to let my imagination take control. Found unbidden images would fleetingly appear: Naked legs, Satin white body, the thrusting image of Dalton Murphy. Bodies coupled in violence. Knew then that I would kill him. Without a doubt I would kill those who harmed her. To hell with the police. What did they know, what did they feel? Somehow I would get to them.

I told George that, Wednesday night, both in need of company. A bottle of Black Bush fast disappearing, sitting in Lucy's flat. Told him that with tears running down my face. Told him how sorry I was. Felt him embrace me, heard him quietly speak.

"It's not your fault son. Not your fault. There's no need for guilt. We'll get her back."

The police had been quick to pick up Eric Grey. He had been helpful with their enquiries, but as there was no real crime to hold him to, they had been forced to release him. Thinly veiled threats of what would happen when he came to represent the constituency did not go unnoticed by the officer conducting the case. As for the others, no sighting had been made of them. It was just a question of time. Time! There wasn't any.

They had also visited Stephen McKay. I had rung him on Monday to warn him of their visit, and to tell him the good news. He had broken down on the phone.

"Are you alright? I know it's a shock, but it's good news eh?" I said.

"All those years. What a waste. Years of guilt. For nothing. It's criminal!" he said between gulps.

"You could say that," I replied wryly.

"Yeah." That had brought a trace of a laugh into his voice. "It's just time that you can never get back. Mistakes that cannot be undone. Just think of the consequences of it all. None of it might have happened if the truth had been told in the first place."

"People like them never tell the truth in the first instance. It is not a natural choice for them. There would have always been something going on with them. There still is. We just happened to be the unfortunate victims who got in their way. If it hadn't been us it would have been someone else."

"I guess you could be right. But think of the number of people who have been caught up in all of this. That teacher's wife. Why did they want to destroy her husband? It doesn't make sense." He had a point. Perhaps it didn't have to make sense. Life didn't always. I said that to him, but he disagreed.

"No. What they did had a purpose. There was a meaning to it. There has to be a reason."

He could be right. But I had yet to find the trigger: that one factor which had sparked such a chain reaction. God knows, I had racked my brains enough, just in case there was. I couldn't believe that Peter's accident had been the sole reason.

"Whatever, just let Jimmy know. But warn him as well. They are still out and about. They see him as a weak link. Although it's all a bit academic now I would have thought."

"Why?" he asked.

I told him what had happened. Didn't go into all the detail.

"You were lucky," was all he said.

I guessed so, but again I didn't feel it particularly. Still that was another story and I didn't feel like telling it. I rang off, leaving him to sort out his life, his family. And wished him well.

Thursday. Or so my diary said.

"What gives Boss? You're not the happiest person that's for certain. You're going around like someone who's suffered a death for God's sake." Chris with his usual subtlety dallied with his coffee mug and waited for me to answer.

"What is wrong?" Robin chipped in. "Hell, you've found out who was responsible for all the goings on and you look like death, or like someone you know has died. I'm sorry about your finger Mike, but it's not the end of the world, surely?"

I hadn't told them about Lucy. Wanted the hurt to be all mine. I wanted to suffer. Didn't want anyone else to know. It was a punishment.

"They've got Lucy." There was silence. No one said anything for a moment. I felt Jane's hand on my arm. Felt her squeeze it gently. Chris mumbled something which sounded like an apology. He hadn't known.

I told them what had taken place, aware as I spoke that someone was banging the teapot lid for silence. The usual way to get our attention. The room went quiet. I looked up to see Fields standing in the middle of the room, smiling benignly. I hadn't even known he had joined us for break.

"Good morning Ladies and Gentlemen. Good news. I felt I should share it with you. I have just heard that our Chairman of Governors has been allowed to go home. Seems he has made a complete recovery. I know you share with me a great sense of relief and thankfulness." He looked around the room, nodding away at the murmurs that greeted his news. I watched him look my way, then hurriedly move on. I couldn't resist it.

"I hope he doesn't get too comfortable. With all the goings on of the last few days, I wouldn't count on him staying there too long." I stared back at Fields and watched the usual shades of colour rise to the surface. If he hadn't had the complete attention of the staffroom before hand, he certainly did now.

"Your lack of respect is appalling Mr Sutherland. Absolutely disgraceful. Whilst I can overlook some of your colonial vulgarities, I'm afraid you overstep the mark by a long way this time. Tasteless. Utterly tasteless. The Chairman of Governors has suffered an illness and all you can do is make some meaningless remark suggesting that he will probably end up back in hospital. I will not have you speaking like that whilst you are in his employ!" he barked, his anger clearly evident to all in the room.

"I don't wish him any harm at all. You've got the wrong end of the stick. What I said was that he will probably end up back in hospital given the news of his son's behaviour."

"I have no idea what you are talking about Mr Sutherland. And neither do I find this to be the right place to discuss Lord Grey's family." He turned back to one of his deputies, conversation finished. I could feel my own anger building up. What the hell did he know?

"Then let me enlighten you Mr Fields!" I could hear the anger in my voice, the words coming out much louder than intended. He turned round sharply, displeasure etched on his every feature. One or two of the staff shifted about in obvious discomfort, caught in the cross fire. Sod the lot of them. What did any of them know. Fields made to speak, the colour once more spreading upwards from his neck. I beat him to it. "Your Chairman of Governors has a lot to answer to. The sons he spawned are in no small way responsible for the death of Len Jones!" I could hear one or two sharp intakes of breath. Robin muttered something. I couldn't make it out. Didn't care. Things had to be said. "Further more, unless I'm way off the mark, I think underneath it all you knew that."

"How dare you," he spluttered. "How dare you accuse me of knowing anything at all about the death of Mr Jones. I will not have such slanderous remarks made. Be careful Mr Sutherland. Your opinions could land you in a lot of trouble."

I heard myself laugh. "That's rich. Ever since Len Jones died. No, I tell a lie, even before he died, I have had nothing but trouble. And most of it from Grey's two disturbed sons. I've been beaten, knifed, run off the road and this." I held up my disfigured hand. "You see this! Lord Grey's eldest son had much delight stubbing his cigar out on it. The bastard even laughed. So don't tell me about trouble." You could have heard a pin drop. The staffroom resembled a painting, figures caught in various postures, faces etched in comical relief. It was an image which initiated another set of independent subliminal impulses, which set about organising and connecting the two: Comical figure, painting. It fell into place. Good God. Len Jones had captured for life, his life, the unseating of Lord Grey. I could see the painting clearly. Should have seen it clearly a long time ago. Couldn't see its importance. Had dismissed it as an interesting fact. Could appreciate the irony. Len must have had such a laugh. "And as for slander, Mr Fields. It is only slander when it is an untruth. Should you wish for confirmation, then ring D.C. Carmichael in Welwyn Garden. He'll be glad to inform you. Or better still, ring a good friend of mine, Lord Alexander." I could name drop with the best of them. "He'll tell you that his daughter is missing, presumed abducted by Lord Grey's youngest son simply because she was with me. But don't tell me to be careful of my opinions!" My hands were shaking. Jane grabbed them and held them.

Fields stared back speechless, his mouth moving as though he were about to speak, then turned away and walked out of the room. As the door clicked shut, the painting came to life. Voices raised in excitement, people scurrying across to talk, bombarding me with questions.

"Well, you did yourself a lot of good in there Mike." Chris and I sat in the P.E. office between lessons. He tossed a cricket ball up in the air and caught it, repeatedly, while watching me.

"You're right," I acknowledged, "my Achilles heel. I resent authority. Particularly when it comes from weak people like him. I think I'm too old to change my ways." An unbidden image of Lucy lodged itself in my head, not the image I wanted. The same scene which had rerun itself time after time, driving me to despair. I had to control it. I willed it away, physically shaking my head to scatter the horrific scene.

"You okay?" The ball had stopped. Chris was looking on concerned.

"Yeah. Just a horror show running through my head. I can't keep it at bay." God, I had to share this with someone. It was driving me to the edge. Chris seemed to be the perfect choice. It wasn't something one could share with the father, although I had almost done so. Too personal. Too painful for him. I looked at Chris and told him and watched the understanding grow. Watched him struggle to say the right thing. Was there a right thing?

"You poor bugger. Look it won't do you any good mate, punishing yourself like that. You'll end up going out of your mind. That's what happens to nutters. You know, worrying away at a problem, almost masochistic like."

"I can't help it. It's just there. I wake up at night with the same nightmare. Can't get it out of my mind. I can't just sit waiting for something to happen Chris. I'm going out of my tree. I've got to do something."

"Like what?"

"Lucy's held somewhere. The police have no leads. I think it's time for another visit to Lord Grey to see where his son and cronies hang out. He might know something."

"Want a hand?" As simple as that. No big deal. He tossed the ball in my direction.

"Thanks," I said as I caught it.

"When?"

"Tonight?"

"Sure thing. Pick me up." He said nothing else, just got up from his seat and sauntered back out to the gym. It was done.

I had spent many seasons trying to impress upon the lads that I coached, that the secret to success on the field was to be proactive, rather than reactive. It gave you the control, the time to make the decisions, whilst the opposition could do little but react to them. It was time I applied this to my own personal life. I was stumbling from one calamity to the next, acting when it was too late. Life doesn't wait, it passes by quickly. It was time.

George had left a message for me to phone him. I dialled his number and it was answered almost immediately.

"Yes?" A very abrupt, curt George.

"George, it's Michael. You left a message."

"Michael." Relief came through to me clearly, "We've had a message." I could feel myself tensing, waiting for his next bit of information. "They've got her. They say that she will suffer your fate and much worse if the police are informed of any more. They want to meet with you." There was a long pause at the other end, then his voice spoke quietly. "They want to do an exchange Michael. You for Lucy." His words filled my mind, caught up with the relief of knowing that Lucy was alright and the fear of knowing what my outcome would be. "Michael!" I was aware of George's voice once more.

"Its great news that she's okay George," I answered.

"You can't do it Son. You know as well as I do, what they will do to you."

"I don't really have an option. Neither of us will allow anything to happen to Lucy. I tell you George, they will do as they say. You're her father. You couldn't look at me the same way if she were to suffer, and I couldn't look at you. They've got us by the balls."

"Michael, I can't ask you to do this. It's suicide. You're the only link back to them. They know that," he said, his voice heavy in defeat.

"It's not a question of asking. I'm volunteering. I love your daughter. I wouldn't have any harm come her way." I stopped, then asked the dreaded question. "When?"

"They are going to get in touch with all the details. I'm so sorry." His voice choked off into silence.

"Michael," the voice so soft, it gave me a start, so similar to her daughter's that for a split second hope surged through every vessel. "Michael, I just want to tell you that we have always thought the world of you right from the beginning. Whatever you do, we will always see you as being the perfect choice for our daughter. I understand how you must be feeling. There can never be any blame. I just wanted you to know that Michael. You are a fine man." The phone went dead. Dead. The word chilled me to the core.

I picked Chris up, suitably dressed, just after seven o'clock, my one and only chance of saving everything rested with this.

Ayot Green. The signpost said. Left across the bridge over the A1. Parked the car at the back of the pub carpark, where I had first gone to find out where Lord Grey lived. "Fancy a quick half?" he asked hopefully. I shook my head. There wasn't any such thing as a quick half and anyway the demons in my head were once more taking shape. I wanted them gone.

We walked purposefully up the road, why with purpose I had no idea. I literally had no idea. Chris asked the question which had obviously been on his mind.

"What's the plan?"

I looked across and smiled. "Plan? The plan is, that we make it up as we go along. Sorry Chris, the only plan I have is to find Lucy. This seems as good a place to start as any. I don't like the old bugger, he might just be the key to all this. What about you, any ideas?"

"Mike, you're a constant source of comfort. Me? No. I've got no ideas, but I'm not too happy at the prospect of walking straight up to the front door and asking whoever is there if they know where she is. Somehow I don't think that will be too healthy. Do you?" A touch of sarcasm laced with exasperation. I couldn't blame him.

"Sorry mate. I wasn't intending knocking on the front door. I've done that once before. It's not a stroke I want to pull again."

"You know Sutherland; you have a bloody terrible sense of humour." All the same, I could see he was grinning. "Why don't we try the back way this time?" I agreed. And anyway, I didn't want to be walking up the drive only to have the lights come on and announce us to all and sundry. I couldn't be certain that Lord Grey wasn't harbouring them all.

It was easier said than done, as we discovered. Down one side of the property stretched a long high brick wall, which whilst affording excellent cover, posed problems for scaling. Along the other side of the gardens a more natural barrier in the form of a blackberry tangle, interspersed with elderberry bushes and other such uncultivated plants, among them a copious number of stinging nettles, as we were to discover. Whilst not proving ideal, it offered us the best chance of getting to the back undetected. Chris's perpetual murmured curses, occasionally punctuated by a slightly louder and more pointed expletive as a nettle stung or bramble dug in, dispersed the nagging demon, that grotesque puppet dangling image of Lucy that had somehow grown real, my Lucy being jerked about as if on a string, blond hair tangled and disarrayed, dancing to the thrusts of the evil Dalton Murphy. The mind could be extremely cruel and punishing.

"Thank Christ for that," Chris's heartfelt statement brought me back to reality and I realised that we had passed through the problem and were now in the clear. A lawn and trees lay before us and the house. "No dogs, I hope," Chris murmured. "I hate dogs. Especially the type they are likely to keep at a place like this."

"Not that I know of," I whispered back. "There weren't any last time anyway."

A light came on from the back of the house, one of those house floodlights. It bathed the area immediately surrounding the back and the carport.

"That's not what we wanted," Chris grunted. "I wonder why they turned that on?" As though on cue, the back door swung open and a figure stood bathed in the light. Whilst it was not possible to identify who exactly it was, I could feel the hate welling up, could sense my breath quickening. Jackpot! So I was right. They were here. We watched as the figure stared out into the growing night, saw the flare of a match. He had stepped outside for a cigarette. As simple as that. We could do nothing but wait. I imagined that I knew which one it was. Would have bet on being right: Paul Marshall. My old driving pal. We lay still, for sound travelled in the quiet night air. As if to prove a point the figure passed wind, the sound clearly audible from where we lay.

"Just as well he went out for a smoke." Chris rolled over onto his side and grinned at me. "I don't know which would have been the more damaging for the others."

A moment later we watched the figure throw the butt down and turn back indoors. The night light went off, and the darkness became more real again.

I stood up. If I didn't move now, I was concerned I might never. Chris looked up.

288

"Time to go then eh?"

I nodded. I made for the first tree, then the next. The safest route seemed to me to be the out buildings behind the carport. It meant breaking cover and sprinting across the exposed lawn. I pointed to where I was intending to go and Chris gave the thumbs up. Nothing for it but to go. Heart pounding, legs pumping, we made it without arousing any interest. I was more out of breath than I should have been. Put it down to nerves.

"So far so good."

"Next move?" Chris asked, hands on knees, bent over, slightly out of breath. Good. It was getting to him too.

"What about a poke around these sheds? It's as good a place to start as any." I wished I had had a torch. But then that might have given us away. We stepped gingerly towards the first of the large outbuildings. The door was unlocked, which in itself suggested that nothing of any consequence would be in there. I half hesitated. Didn't want to waste my time. Chris bumped into my back and I lurched through the door.

"Sorry," he whispered, "I thought you had gone in."

"No harm done," I replied. "Not that we can see much in here anyway. Look out the side of your eyes, you get a better sight in the dark that way." I was doing it myself, trying to look without looking directly at anything. It sort of worked. Not that there was very much to see anyway. A bench, a tall wardrobe arrangement, a petrol lawnmower, you could tell by the smell, and a few other odds and ends.

"Nothing in here," I whispered. We manoeuvred our way back out, and turned to the next shed, slightly larger. It had big imposing doors, the sort that were hinged, and would fold in the middle. The sort that looked like they would make a lot of noise were they to be moved. "This doesn't look too helpful. You can't see a side entrance can you?" I asked. Chris headed off to one side. All was silent. Just the soft muted sounds of traffic on the highway in the distance. The quiet was suddenly shattered by an explosion of sound. A thousand possibilities raced through my head, my heart pounding, all systems working to put my body into a heightened state of readiness, for flight or fight.

"Fuckin' hell, a pheasant. Scared the shit out of me." Chris appeared beside me, his breath rasping. I could just make out the shocked look on his face.

"Didn't do me a hell of a lot of good either."

"There is a side door, but it's locked," he added. "Short of breaking it down, I can't see how we are going to get in."

"Forget it then. It's probably empty." I replied

"How about a window? There might be one we can prise open. Just in case," he suggested.

"Okay. You go back the way you came and I'll do the other side. If you get anything come and tell me, and I'll do the same."

I headed towards the side of the shed, not convinced that there was any point. The first window was stuck firm and anyway was far too small for either of us to have got through. There was another not too far along the wall. A good enough size. I ran my hand around the edge of the frame and pulled. There was initial resistance and then suddenly it gave, so quickly that the window almost came away in my hand. Hell, how much noise had I made? Chris appeared, running, his face once again registering shock.

"Chris, what happened?" he asked in a rush. I gestured to the window, held firmly in both hands.

"Guess what? We've got ourselves an entrance." My attempt to be nonchalant failed.

"Great. We've probably got ourselves company as well. It sounded like a bloody gunshot from where I was." He replied accusingly.

"Couldn't help it. Bloody wood must have been rotten."

"Either that or you're on the steroids," he replied, a smile beginning to form, only to be wiped quickly from his face. "Shit!" The outside light had come on, swathing the area in bright light. I felt like an actor on centre stage, fully exposed.

"Quick, inside," I urged. He dived through the window and I followed as quickly as was possible, trying desperately to wedge it back into place behind me. I had no idea what it looked like from the outside. Just prayed that it would pass a brief inspection from a distance.

"Can you see anyone?" Chris whispered.

"Yeah, the guy with the wind problem." I had been right: Paul Marshall. I watched as he lit another cigarette and peered out towards us.

"Not a thing." I heard him say, in obvious response to a question. "I'll have a wander."

Great. I watched him head towards us, stopping to look into the shed we had just previously been in. Closer now. There was a sudden commotion from behind us. I twisted quickly, expecting the worst. Couldn't make out much in the darkened area, the bright light having put paid to my night vision. I heard Chris breath out a heart felt expletive. Watched as he moved deftly out to meet whatever was in the garage with us. My heart was hammering away. Marshall had obviously heard the noise as well. He had disappeared from sight. Whatever had made the crash had stopped. No sign of Chris. The light in the shed came on without any warning. I hadn't even heard the door being unlocked. Too late to hide. Turned, and watched Marshall's face dawn with recognition. Ten foot away, not much more. And no prettier.

"You?!" At least he was surprised.

"Absolutely. Thought I'd drop over and see how things were. I hear you chaps have been asking for me."

"Very good," he sneered, "except you should have come via the front door and not tried to sneak about. Well, well. Cocky bastard aren't you." A statement, not a question.

"Whatever. There's just one thing Paul. Only you know that I am here. So the way I see it, if it stays like that, then I should be okay for a while."

"You reckon. The others know that I'm having a look round. If I don't go back then one of them will come out for a look. And quite frankly, from what I've seen, you don't look like you pose too much of a problem." He grinned, a slightly lopsided grin, and puffed himself up. A guy that fancied his chances. He pulled a flick knife from his pocket and edged forward. Stupid really. Had he turned and run, yelling at the top of his voice I would have been in all sorts of trouble. "Remember this?" he asked, waving the knife out in front of him. "This little number got rid of your little pinky. Hurt didn't it? Can you feel it, all that pain. And then there were nine. Shall we make it eight? Balance things a little. Get you dangling with your mate. See how you like it."

"You really are a cretin Paul. You had the chance to turn and get help. That would have made it very difficult for me. But like the big, moron that you are, you fancy your chances. Well right now I quite fancy mine. I'd like nothing better than to smash the smirk off that face of yours."

"What's stopping you then," he sneered, beckoning me with his finger.

"Me!" Chris's voice, quietly menacing from behind the door that had been opened. Marshall swung round, turning slap bang into the plank of wood Chris was wielding. He uttered a grunt of pain, or it could have been surprise, before sinking heavily to the floor.

"Nice one partner," I grinned.

"You were right, the guy is a dick. Gee that felt good." He breathed out in a release of tension, leaning on the very weapon that had done in Paul Marshall. "He looks a bit of a mess though, hope I haven't killed him." He bent down to feel for a pulse.

"I shouldn't bother. Scum like him don't die easy. Let's get him trussed up." I looked about for something suitable, with the light on, everything was visible. "What the . . . . !"

"Oh yeah, that's the guy that made the noise just before your pal came in. Sorry, forgot to mention it. He must have kicked a bucket or something," Chris said matter of factly.

"Jesus," I had trouble forming any words, the sight almost incomprehensible. "Get the poor bastard down." I grabbed the knife that Marshall had been wielding and stepped over to the bloodied body of Jimmy McKay. They had obviously had their fun with him. Stripped to his boxers he had cuts all over his body and visible burn marks from cigarettes or cigars. His face was puffed and severely bruised, his nose pushed to one side, bloody tape covering the mess that was his mouth. In places skin hung flacidly beneath raw angry cuts. It seemed of little consequence that he was two toes short. Chris gingerly supported his weight as I cut the cord which had bound his arms together and left him stretched almost off the ground, the cord wrapped around the centre beam of the shed. As we lowered him to the ground he writhed in pain as his feet made contact with the concrete. Chris took a brief look and I watched the metamorphosis from detachment to emotional closeness. He shook his head in disbelief, his voice catching.

"They've slit his soles. Jesus wept. From toe to heel. What sick prick would do that? Not just a scratch Mike. But deep." We lowered Jimmy as best we could, seating him on an improvised stool. With that done Chris walked back to the prostrate figure of Marshall and swung his foot into his unprotected body, twice! "I sincerely hope that does some damage," he said to no one in particular. He took the cord from Jimmy's arms and wrapped them none too gently around the hapless Marshall whilst I tended to Jimmy, doing my best to carefully remove the tape without hurting him too much. He was in a bad way. Hung up like that must have made it difficult to breath, a bit like a crucifixion. The fact that they had removed toes and slit his feet had been particularly sick, the pain of trying to support his weight to give his arms a rest must have been pure hell. He had yet to open his eyes, just sat immobile as I removed the last piece of tape.

"Jimmy, can you hear me?" I spoke into his ear. No response. "Come on Jimmy, answer. Come on mate, you can do it." I looked across at Chris, who was struggling to drag Marshall across the floor, positioning him in the spot once occupied by the unfortunate Jimmy. "He's not doing too well Chris. We have to get him to a hospital as quick as possible."

Chris looked across, concern etched on his face. "I know," he grunted, "but that makes things difficult. If we shoot off for help there's fat chance of getting the rest of these pricks, not to mention Lucy." He stared intently at me, but the point hadn't been missed. Catch twenty two really. If this was the fate suffered by Jimmy, my mind was screaming with vivid scenes of what was taking place with Lucy. But the fate of the young chap in front of me was all too real as well. One couldn't just leave him. He had suffered enough already.

"Get them." Two words. Hardly audible, whispered through swollen lips, but conveying such intensity of feeling. I looked down at the face, one eye half open, the other obviously unable to open. Watched as Jimmy McKay slowly gave the thumbs up, very controlled, almost slow motion.

"Jimmy, you can hear us," I said. He nodded deliberately. "Do you think you can hold out for a while?" He nodded slowly again.

"Just get them," he whispered, breaking into a racking cough, his face screwed up with pain.

"He's in a bad way alright," Chris said watching with concern. The coughing subsided. "Jimmy," Chris raised his voice a bit, "we've got one already." He pulled the cord tight raising the body of Paul Marshall into view, mouth taped securely, but eyes beginning to function. Chris pulled harder. "Lend a hand mate." We tied the rope to a hook on the wall and turned back to Jimmy.

"Did he do most of that?" I asked pointing to the cuts.

"Mainly Murphy," he mumbled. Damn right it would have been.

"How many in the house Jimmy?" He thought for a moment

"Three or four." His face crumpled. "Oh Christ, they've been raping her. She's like a rag doll." He tried to say more, but his emotions overwhelmed him and he sat quietly crying, very broken. I was watching him, but not really taking it in. Nightmare revisited. Now real, there to haunt me, virtually tangible.

SIXTEEN

"Before we go rushing in to things," Chris counseled, no doubt seeing the look on my face, "I think we should hang about here and see if anyone comes looking for our friend there. That way, we might be able to work the odds a bit better." He didn't wait to see whether or not I agreed, but walked over to the shed door, closed it and turned out the light. "That's better, let's see what eventuates." He put a hand on my shoulder giving it a brief squeeze. There was nothing to say. "You alright mate?" he enquired of Jimmy. Jimmy slowly nodded. And we waited.

"Paul?" A voice from the house, an uncertain voice, the very same voice I had last heard when he visited me with Eric Grey.

"Craig Holden," Jimmy mumbled, proving me right, the loathing in his voice very clear.

"Where are you Paul?" the same wheedling intonation. "Paul, what are you doing? Murphy sent me out to find you. He wants some time with the girl. Aaron is trying to sort his old man out. Come on Paul, where the hell are you?"

"Turn the light back on," I said to Chris, "Let him think he's in here." Chris grunted in agreement and felt his way over to the door, the brightness once again lighting up the interior. "You any good at impersonations?" He looked at me and shrugged.

"In here," He yelled. It didn't particularly sound like anyone, but then it didn't sound welsh either so it probably did the trick.

"You took your time answering." Holden's voice getting closer. "Gives me the creeps having to stand out here everytime you or Dalton want your bit of fun. It's not fair. How come I don't get a bit? Poor bitch is shagged to pieces. Just lies there. Dalton said he had an interesting way of livening her up." There was a dirty snigger, the voice very near the entrance now. I had gestured to Chris that I would deal with him, the hatred inside barely contained, so much anger I could feel myself shaking. The door swung open. "Giving old James a . . . . .shit!" He had taken just a couple of steps inside, the image in front of him finally taking shape, wild panic as he turned for flight. No fight in this one, self preservation and fear his prime

295

motivation. The shock of seeing his friend strung up instead of Jimmy, who was seated staring at him, all too much. As he spun round I could see the look of horror blossoming as saw me. His mouth silently formed the word 'You'.

"Too bloody right," I answered kicking the door shut. "You're going nowhere you piece of slime. Except prison I hope. There's no way you'll get out of it this time. You low life. Blackmail, rape, kidnapping and grievous bodily assault. I'd say life, wouldn't you?"

"I haven't done anything. I had to. Dalton would have done the same to me as he did to Jimmy." His voice had risen in alarm.

"You keep pretty lousy company boy," Chris appeared from behind a partition. Holden jumped, turning to face the new threat, and seeing the burly figure approach him. He took a couple of steps back, and realised that he could go no further.

"What are you going to do with me? Please don't hurt me. I hate pain. Please. I haven't done anything. I haven't raped her. You must believe me." His face took on a pleading look.

"You're a real low life Craig. Happy to go along with whoever seems the strongest." I took a step forward, and he shrunk back, knocking into Chris, the contact causing him to visibly cringe. "Well, guess what. You have finally made the wrong choice, because we're going to sort things and see to it that none of you ever do anything like this again. I have this theory that if you remove vermin or their offending parts, you negate the threat that they pose. And you buddy are vermin. And don't give me any of this crap about not raping. I know for a fact that you raped a girl at University and for all I know, you probably raped the same poor girl that Jimmy was supposed to have raped. Except he didn't. He was so far gone he couldn't do anything. Marshall and Dalton saw to her." I heard a gasp from behind as the news sunk into the listening Jimmy. The poor guy had been carrying that guilt for years. Holden had sunk completely. To be confronted by someone who seemed to know everything about him had deflated him completely and he stood there staring, shocked. I turned to Jimmy for a moment.

"The only crime you were actually guilty of Jimmy, was getting involved with such scum in the first place. They used you boy. Your so called mates blackmailed your parents, destroyed their life, Belinda's life and yours. And Holden knew it all along. Didn't you?" I said turning back to him. He shrugged, said nothing, perhaps his best form of defense. "Chris," I nodded. Holden knew what it meant and broke into a panic.

"Yeah, yeah...... I knew. But what could I do ......?" There were answers, but what was the point. All a bit academic now.

"So it's Murphy and Grey left eh?" I said to him. He nodded. "What about Grey senior? How come he's allowing all this to happen? I wouldn't have thought it was his sort of thing."

"He doesn't really understand what's going on. He hasn't been too great following that attack he had. The one you were responsible for," he added accusingly. "He gets in a muddle a lot of the time. Aaron, that's his son." I nodded. "Well he looks after him in his room and pretty well keeps him confined to bed." He tailed off.

"So what about you then?" I asked. "What are we to do with you?" He looked up, alarm spreading across his features once again, the conversation seemingly having lulled him into a sense of false security.

"I won't do anything. I'll just stay here. Please! You have my word."

Chris snorted. "Your word. That doesn't mean an awful lot. We'd go; you'd let Marshall free, probably work Jimmy over again, then come and get us."

"No, no I wouldn't," Craig protested. "I'd just sit here and wait for you to come back." He looked across to me, then back at Chris, hoping to see us nod in agreement. I nodded to Chris, seeing the relief on Holden's face, watched it change as Chris, understanding me, grabbed Holden's arms from behind, dragged him across to the watching Marshall, and began to tie him up with the same rope. He began to yell in distress, so much so that we had to tape him up much like his colleague. I told him that we would not hurt him, that it was just a precaution and he relaxed, his legs no longer flaying about. "However," I added, "What Jimmy does while we're away I'm not responsible for." The legs began to kick out in desperation again. A vain struggle to get away. Pointless really, for his weight was then supported by his arms only, and he soon tired, only his eyes rolling with fright. I could see in Jimmy an awakening of interest. Vengeance is sweet nourishment. Good on him, he had suffered enough under them.

"All right then," Chris mimicked, "there's nothing else to do but go and visit our illustrious Governor. I hope this isn't going to end up getting me sacked."

"If you're lucky." I replied. I couldn't think of anything else to say. "Here goes" and stepped out into the night, the light from the house swathing everything in its unnatural glare. I moved quickly, feeling uncomfortable and exposed. Wanted the surprise to be on my side, not the other way round. Could hear Chris just behind, slowed as we reached the door, but entered on the burst. Nothing in the laundry room. Bright and light. White walls, bench running along one side, sink and washing machine, tumble dryer. Every housewives dream. A passing thought. Next room: kitchen. Large pine farmhouse table, food scattered across it amidst a pile of unwashed plates, large dresser against one wall, red aga along the other. But no one. Two doors led off in opposite directions. Had been here. Continued in the direction we had begun and stepped into the hall. Familiar territory. Same dark wood. The words of an old Crosby Stills Nash and Young song came unbidden to my mind. 'If I had ever been here before I would probably know just what to do . . .'. Deja vu. Except it wasn't, I had and I didn't. But at least I had my bearings. The sitting room was straight ahead, study off to the side, stairs heading up. Aaron heading down. Shock. Utterly flabbergasted, his mouth forming words which bore no sound. He had stopped rooted to the spot. Uncomprehending the totally unexpected. Chris was acting on the 'he who hesitates is lost' policy and was half way up to greet him before Aaron came to his senses, movement and speech returning in a flurry of words and a desperate effort to turn and run. Too late. I was confident that Chris could deal with anything the young Grey could dish out and moved on, the need to be expedient upper most in my mind. It seemed most probable that Lucy was being kept downstairs. Murphy would be with her. From the hall, beside the study door was another door and I pushed it open, surprised to see a narrow set of stairs leading down sharply. I moved quietly to the bottom, finding myself in a largish cellar, come basement. A couple of large metal containers dominated some of the space, which on closer scrutiny proved to be ash collectors for the open fires above. An ingenious system. To the back and in the gloom I could make out the thudding rhythmic sounds I had been dreading, the occasional grunting and a more desperate whimpering. I moved quietly forward until I could see. Could see the pale naked body of a woman, her back showing visible signs of ill treatment, stretched over what appeared to be a church pew, her head hidden, but her blond hair hanging in view. Could see Dalton Murphy thrusting brutally from behind. The bastard. I moved forward, desperate to get behind the grotesque coupling: Shakespeare's beast with two backs. There seemed little danger of being seen, so intent was Murphy on what he was doing, eyes screwed tight, uttering obscenities, urging Lucy to take a more active part. I pushed Marshalls knife none to gently between his open legs, heard his cry of pain, and held it there.

"Make one more move and I'll castrate you, you fucking animal." I dismissed any doubt from his mind with a further application of pressure. "We know this knife cuts off little pinkies don't we Dalton. I'm sure it can cut off one more little one."

"You!" He uttered a string of obscenities. "You won't get away with this. The other's will see to that. And then I'll fucking slice you from head to toe you prick, do away with you once and for all." He went to turn but thought better of it. Sod it, there were more important things to be dealing with for Christ's sake than to listen to him. Wine bottles lay within reach from the dusty rack to my left. I stretched across, grabbed one by the neck, a familiar label, full bodied, and swung it down on the back of his head. He fell heavily, his face colliding with the inert body underneath him, before sinking to the floor. She didn't move. I felt sick with fear. Sick with the thought of all she had gone through. And angry, not just with the hurt she had suffered but because I couldn't rid myself of the unbidden thoughts I was having. What kind of person was I? Used merchandise.

Wanting to leave, not wanting to leave. Just walk away. Who was guilty of the most inhumane act then? Get a grip. This is the girl you loved. Loved? Past tense? Love. I do love her. Forget the abuse. Wounds mend. Mental scars heal over. For us all. Time. I shook myself, willing the guilt away, physically moving towards her, the kinetic activity dispelling the potentially negative thoughts.

"Lucy!" Her name ripped from my lips, realisation finally acknowledged: This was the woman I loved. I gently untied her bound wrists, seeing the way the cord had cut into her skin, turned her over, to cradle her in my arms. Wanting to cover the hurt, looking with horror at the cigarette burns across her breasts, seeing for the first time that the woman I held was . . .was not Lucy. Not Lucy!

"Mike?" Chris's voice boomed down the stairs, "Everything alright? Need any help?" I could hear the uncertainty, understood his awkwardness. He would not know what to do, unsure of what he might be coming down to.

"Yeah. Yeah, it's finished. Bring a blanket down with you, or something to throw over the poor girl."

"Okay," he acknowledged. I could sense the puzzlement in his voice, as though the expression poor girl didn't quite fit my finding Lucy. That was rich. The sense of relief had been more than I cared to admit to, but the question still existed. Where was Lucy? I sat still. Thoughts racing away, guilt tripping back and forth. Relief and worry strange companions in my head. Looked at the swollen face of a once pretty girl. Who was she? Felt inadequate. Nothing could make up for the hurt she had endured. Hurry up Chris. Let her have some dignity. After what seemed an age I heard his heavy footsteps thumping down the wooden stairs. I whistled to let him know where we were, watched as he took on board the sight, the scant regard for the prone Dalton Murphy, the concern for the girl I was holding, the second look, as though to convince himself that he had got it right first time.

"That's not . . . ." he began.

"No it's not Lucy. I have no idea who it is."

"That bastard's given her a rough time." He stated. "Caught him at it eh?"

"Yeah, a severe case of coitus interruptis." I gently placed the settee throw over, over her body, and positioned her as best I could on the floor. My mind was in a turmoil. I had expected to find Lucy here. Hadn't wanted it to be her when I found them. Couldn't bear her being so brutally raped. But now? What now? What had happened to her. Perhaps she had suffered. Perhaps they had got rid of her. Christ. I was no better off. There had to be answers. "I'm no better off, no fucking better off!"

"We'll get some answers Mike. Someone knows where she is. They'll tell us." He grabbed Murphy's arms none too gently and wrapped some rope that he had found, around his wrists, behind his back and down to his ankles so that he was completely hog tied. "That should do him. What now?"

"We'll take him to the shed to join the others. We'll let the cops sort him out. What about Grey?"

"Looks a bit the worse for wear. Didn't look too good before I hit him anyway, just looks worse now." He grinned, and held up his right fist so that I could see the red rawness of his knuckles. He blew on it before adding, "bloody hurts."

"Let's get this poor girl out of here. We can lift her upstairs into the living room. You go and get Jimmy and bring him across."

Jimmy's response on seeing the blond haired girl took us by surprise. I guess it shouldn't have really.

"God," he had cried in anguish on seeing her inert body lying on the sofa. "Julia. Oh Lord, is she alright?" He had looked imploringly up into Chris's face, caught in the incongruous position of being carried child like from the shed. Was she alright? How could one ever answer that? How tough was the human spirit? It depended on the individual. The poor girl had certainly had more than her share of horror. Chris didn't answer, but looked across at me, and Jimmy's eyes followed. "She isn't dead is she? Don't tell me she's dead." His lip trembled, tears forming. His girl. It made sense now. Why he had been so upset when we first found him.

I answered as gently as I could. "She's had a pretty rough time of it Jimmy, but she is alive. She'll need you to help get her through it."

Chris placed him as best he could beside the girls body, his body still shaking from the pain and the distress at seeing her. I knew he had heard me, but he hadn't responded. What was there to say? I looked down at the two pathetic figures. What had they done to deserve such a fate? It seemed to me that life didn't pick and choose. The most God fearing person in the world could still end up as they had. It didn't make sense. Where was Lucy? That didn't make sense either.

"Now what?" Chris asked the obvious.

"The police I guess. Ambulance for these two. We can't let this drag on any longer. Lucy has to be somewhere. We'll get her." I spoke with a great deal more confidence than I felt. Chris looked sideways at me, not at all fooled.

"I don't know. You have to believe me. They didn't tell me anything about her." I had none to gently ripped the tape from his mouth. He had been lucky. Jimmy had obviously not made the painful journey to repay his transgressor. I watched him as he struggled to find a comfortable position to relieve the weight on his arms. Without much luck. "She sprayed something into my eyes when I chased after her when we first caught you. I didn't see her again. She just kept running, and my eyes were hurting me." He sounded as if he wanted understanding or an apology. I gave him neither. "All I know is that later on, as Murphy put it," his eyes darted to the now conscious Murphy, swinging slightly, two bodies down from him and thought better of talking anymore.

"As Murphy put what Craig," I spoke quietly, close to losing it. "Tell me what he said." Craig vigorously shook his head, the fear of his friend visibly evident. "Tell you what then Craig, I'll go and do some damage to your friend over there, and when you feel like telling me, you just sing out. Because as you know I owe him a few return hits. But don't worry. I'll leave him so he can recover and come back and get hold of you sometime. Or perhaps I should just give you a taste of what they dished out. Seems to me you've been hiding behind their apron strings too long." I bent down a picked up a length of four by two planking. "This will do the trick nicely. Not as good as a baseball bat, but should even the score." I hefted it in my hands and swung it towards Holden's legs so that it landed with a nasty crack on his kneecap, hard enough to hurt, but not hard enough to cripple. More luck than judgement. He let out a long drawn out howl and began to plead in desperation. I waited for him to stop, told him he could end it for himself and then gave him another reminder of what he would be putting an end to. It was enough.

It seemed that Murphy had told them that after leaving me in the shed, he had gone back to the pub and had come across Lucy about to leave in the car. He had followed and had been surprised when he, as he put it, 'saw where the silly bitch was heading'. Holden was unable to elaborate, for it seemed that was all Murphy had said. However, he did go on to say that Murphy had looked very pleased with himself. Everything falling into place.

"Are you sure that there is nothing more you can add," I asked him. He shook his head. Not even the threat of another swipe of the plank got anything more out of him. I looked across at Murphy, noted the smirk on his face. Knew I wouldn't get anything from him. Lashed out, All the hate welling up in an uncontrolled fury, his nose crunching and splitting under the contact. Blood gushing out. No smirk now you prick.

"Mike. Mike!" Through the rage I could just make out Chris's voice. His hand was on my arm, restraining. "No more." I tried to shrug him off, but he hung on and slowly the blindness of anger subsided. I stepped back and took a couple of big breaths. "Okay?" he asked. I shrugged. I still wanted to destroy him, the same way he had destroyed so many others. I wanted Lucy. I needed answers. It seemed hopeless. Or was it? Perhaps I was going about things the wrong way. Brute force had been met with the same. Why not apply a little Archimedes principle? Roughly translated 'given the right lever, anything could be manoeuvred.' Time was of essence. The police would hardly allow me the liberty of conducting my own interviews.

SEVENTEEN

A large bed dominated the large room, the small figure in the large bed stirring and then sitting upright at the sound of my voice.

"What is the meaning of this?" he whispered hoarsely. "You're not Aaron. Who are you? One of Aaron's friends are you." The contempt in his voice was plain to hear. He fumbled about the bed clothes searching; his old hands shakily scrabbling to find his glasses, glasses which I could see were well out of his reach. Hardly the tour de force he had once been. See how the mighty have fallen. Quite a shock, all the more so, for I feared it was down to me that this man now no longer vibrated with the energy that had once driven him to the top, secured him a title and amassed a fortune along the way. He had gone quiet, the effort of searching seemingly tiring him, and he sat still, peering in my direction, waiting.

"I'm not here to hurt you," I continued, surprising myself at my own words. I had actually spent a lot of time wishing him exactly that. Circumstances change. He no longer seemed a threat. "But there are a few questions I need to ask you and as your son is tied up for the moment perhaps you could answer for me."

"Do I take it that that is a literal, rather than a figurative statement Mr Sutherland?" I heard rather than felt my breath draw in. Pathetic he had seemed, but his brain was obviously still sharp. "That colonial accent gives you away." He wheezed. I knew he had deliberately emphasised the colonial. The old buzzard was still capable of goading.

"The faculties still work then," I replied.

"Some of them. And some intermittently. I am entombed in a decaying body. It gives me no pleasure and a great deal of pain."

"Like Peter," I replied, watching him flinch, as if physically having been assaulted. But this time there was no outrage, no demonic indignation, just the resigned acceptance. He sighed, a long shuddering sigh.

"Yes, like my son Peter, the only good thing I had. And that was destroyed." His voiced tailed off, the loss still so very pertinent. His hands clenched tightly over the duvet, clenching and releasing.

"You realized that Len Jones was the same man who had denied your son a full life didn't you?" I asked quietly. I stared at him and waited, then acted upon the compassion that I felt and placed his spectacles in his tautly skinned hands. He nodded his thanks, shakily placed them on his head and stared back at me.

"You never gave up did you? Like a dog worrying a slipper, you wouldn't let go. Yes. Yes I did. There, is that what you wanted to hear?" His voice had risen from a wheeze to a more normal sound. "If I had been Chairman then, he would not have been appointed. That man ruined my son's life and was happily going about his own. Married to a pretty woman, able to have children, able to live a normal life." I could hear the anger vibrating in his voice. Anger that was not logical.

"Are you married Mr Sutherland? No, of course you're not. You have that lady friend. Alexander's girl," he corrected himself. "Well let me tell you something young man. Should you ever get married and have children, you will fast learn that they are an extension of yourself. You have made them, nurtured them, moulded them." He stopped to cough a long hacking cough, before continuing. I could sense the energy in his words. "You watch them grow, you suffer their disappointments with them, revel in their successes. You are them, and they are you. And when one or two of them let themselves down, they let you down." His voice trembled with resentment. "But there is a bright star, someone to pin your hopes on, then it withers, cut off in its prime. Pain and loss is not logical Mr Sutherland, it's right there," he beat his chest with his hand, emphasising the hurt he had suffered. Peter had been an acute loss, more so because of the disappointments that were his other two sons. "I know Len Jones was not deliberate in his actions. I know that!" he cried, his rheumy old eyes filling up with tears. "But Peter was my pride and joy, the only good thing I seemed to have made. And then he was gone." He went silent and I waited, and after a moment he let out another long shuddering sigh. "I guess it came to a head about a year ago now. I found it increasingly hard to see him about the school. I resented him and detested his presence in my school. I could only see Peter lying in bed wasting away, every time I saw this healthy young man striding about the place with his long hair. I suppose I wished him harm," he continued quietly. "I seemed to have lost everything." He paused, staring into space, his old hands shaking above the covers, a tear wetting his sunken cheek. "I miss my wife. God only knows, she was the only one who seemed able to keep us altogether. She was one in a million. I'm not sure I let her know that, Mr Sutherland. Like everything else, it's all too late."

"So what happened then, for something did happen didn't it?" I prodded gently, moving closer to his bedside. He took a moment to reply, as if uncertain to continue what he had begun.

He spoke, his tremulous voice pouring out the chain of events which had led to the sadness which had followed.

"He seemed to be everywhere. I seemed not to be able to move without coming across him, constantly being reminded of his presence. I don't even think he knew who I was. If he did he never let on. I ride you know, well I did until this last bit of nonsense." I could detect the pride in his voice. Knew where he was heading. "Nothing wrong with the sport: fox hunting. A dammed fine tradition, part of our heritage in spite of what the damn fool Labour party think." I felt he was waiting for me to challenge him on that, but I let it pass. There seemed very little point. There were more pressing issues to consider. "And there he was, his damn pony tail flying about, holding a stupid placard, frightening my horse, causing it to rear up and unseat me." I could hear his indignation. "What do those do gooders know? Anything for attention. And then he was laughing at me. Laughing as I lay on the ground with the damn beagles cavorting around me." His voice was loaded with indignation. The affront must have been extremely difficult for him. "If that wasn't enough, the blasted man painted the scene on canvas! And showed it for all and sundry to see and laugh at me." Outrage. Pride goeth before a fall and all that sort of thing except in his case it had gone with the fall! His face had flushed a purple unhealthy colour. Sure sign he was agitated. It reminded me of the last time I had spoken with him. Hoped like hell he wouldn't over do it. Knew we were getting to the crux of it all. I nudged him on.

"Then what?" I coaxed.

"Where's Aaron?" he demanded, changing tact, not yet willing to give up his information. "I need my medicine."

"I'll get it for you." He muttered in irritation, not happy at having his routine upset. After a moment or two he somewhat grudgingly pointed across to a tall boy and indicated that the pills he needed, in fact it was a puffer of sorts which I read was used for angina attacks, were on the top in a small straw plaited basket. I took it across to him and he took the necessary. After what seemed an age, where I looked about the room and fidgeted, he spoke again.

"Peter was the only one I could talk to. The other two would not have cared a jot. He didn't say much, just told me not to let it upset me. He seemed to think that very few people would take much notice anyway. It was as though he was implying that events are easily forgotten, hurts quickly overlooked. I think he was referring to himself. Didn't at the time, but I see it now." There was sadness in his voice.

"What happened?" I asked.

"Fields rang me up about a month later to say he had received a complaint from one of the pupils alleging that Mr Jones had sexually assaulted her, and what should he do. I'm no better or worse than anyone else Mr Sutherland. This was like manna and I grabbed at it and advised Mr Fields. You know the rest."

I did that alright, but it was what was between the lines that I was missing.

"Do you think the manna came from heaven, or was supplied by someone a little less godly?" I asked him.

"At the time I didn't give much thought to the matter. It was only when things began to turn nasty that I did wonder whether or not someone was out to frame him. Your persistent questioning did cause me some concern, but I wasn't too bothered, felt he deserved everything he got."

"Even death?" I asked quietly, "then that of his wife. Do you feel all that was justified?" he didn't answer. "For Christ's sake, you must have known that your sons were implicated. Did you not think you should stop them?"

"I didn't want to think about that. I did ask if they knew anything about what had happened. Aaron just laughed and said he wished he had. Said he would have enjoyed helping out. As for Eric, violence was never his scene." He stared defiantly at me ready to defend his sons against any ill spoken word. He needn't have bothered. What he was saying was true. I was sure of that. But they had got involved, there was no escaping that. Old Lord Grey had set in motion a chain of events which seemed to have been destined to happen since that fateful day on a rugby field so long ago. Destiny, fate? I didn't believe in them did I? Logic however, was another matter and there was little time to act on it.

"Pulling wings off butterflies may not be violent, but it suggests some pretty odd tendencies," I replied. He didn't say anything, just inclined his head slightly, a small gesture of resignation. "Peter told me about him a while back." That got his attention. He didn't know that I had met him. "But it goes further doesn't it?" I pressed on, noted the look of anguish in his eyes. "He also has peculiar sexual tendencies! That's true isn't it?" I didn't expect him to answer, knew it would be paining him. "Did you never once consider that it could have been your son who was instigating all the rumours about Len Jones? Surely it must have crossed your mind?"

Still nothing, but the eyes said it all. "I think that you did. I think that you knew he had the facility to doctor films, but you put it to the back of your mind. You didn't want to acknowledge it because it didn't suit your purpose. Good grief, have you any idea how many people have suffered because of that?" The question was left hanging in the air. Damn it, the man was guilty, guilty of not acting on his better judgment. "Did you know that your son Aaron has been entertaining some of his friends here? Have you not heard them?" He shook his head. "One of the guests has been severely beaten and cut up by your son's friends. Whilst his girlfriend has been repeatedly raped."

"I didn't know anything about it. If what you say is true then I am ashamed."

"I had thought that the girl was Lucy, George Alexanders daughter." He looked up in surprise as if to ask why. "Someone has abducted her. They did so the same night I was caught by your son and his friends." I lifted up my hand. "They removed that finger. Eric enjoyed stubbing his cigar out on it!" I could see Lord Grey wince with horror "Did he not tell you that the police questioned him about this?" He shook his head, continuing to do so, the realisation of what he had started overcoming him.

"What have I done?" he asked quietly, "what have I done?"

"I don't know the answer to that, but I have seen some of the results and I need to find Lucy Alexander again."

"Let me speak to Aaron." He started to cough, a long series of racking coughs that took over his whole body, his bed shaking with the intensity of them. After a while he subsided, sinking back into his pillows exhausted. There was no point asking him if he was fit enough to go downstairs. It was a case of bringing the mountain to Mohammed, a rather surly, demoralized mountain.

"So, once more you let me down. Yet again you and your brother set something in motion. God knows I've tried. What a let down you both have been to me," the old man whispered, fixing his son with a look of disdain. "Can't you ever do anything right?"

"What would you know?" his son snapped back, "You've already taken his word for everything. How do you know he's not lying? You've always done that, always made it plain that I was no good, couldn't live up to your expectations. Peter this, Peter that. A bloody cripple, a bloody do gooder. I've hated him since we were kids. You doting on him, hanging around him like he was a bitch on heat . . . . ."

"Aaron!" his father interrupted, his voice reverberating with shock and anger, "how dare you speak in that way."

"How dare I? Who the hell do you think you are talking to? I'm not some kid that you can push around now. And think about this. Once you're gone, your favourite son will be all alone because you can be as sure as hell that neither Eric nor I will be bothering to go to him. He can rot in hell with you for all I care." The outburst of emotion silenced his father for some time.

"What have you done with Lucy Alexander?" His voice was calm, devoid of any emotion.

"What, his bit of stuff?" he answered looking in my direction, a sneer spreading across his face. He shrugged his shoulders. "Nothing."

"Where is she?" he asked again. "Aaron, I demand that you tell me. This has gone way too far."

"You're in no position to demand anything. And anyway, it was you who started all this," his son accused.

"What? How did I do that?"

"By telling Eric that you had been humiliated by that Jones fellow. Eric took it upon himself to sort things out. I think he saw it as a way of getting your gratitude!" He laughed. "I told him there was fat chance of that."

"But I never told Eric. I'm sure I never told him," replied Lord Grey in a puzzled way. "I know I told Peter, but I don't think he would have said anything to him. He said that he hadn't seen you or your brother for a long time." I could see he was curious.

"Who else did you tell then?" I asked.

"No one. I can't think of anyone."

"Then perhaps we should go and ask Eric for ourselves. He might just have the answers we need." I looked across at Aaron, who stared back, blank faced. Not much given away there. Then again, I hadn't expected anything.

We left Jimmy with a telephone and instructions not to ring the police for at least an hour. Did he think that he could survive for that long and Julia too? He said yes, and not to worry. Everything would be alright. We weren't too convinced but there seemed little other choice. Lord Grey had furnished us with Eric's address.

Harpenden was an attractive town lying to the north of Hertfordshire, very close to the Bedfordshire border. This was commuter country, the town having grown as access to London by rail and motorway had improved. I had been here often enough. It boasted a number of fine pubs and eating places, some of which I had frequented. The rugby club, on one of the roads heading out of town was surrounded by homes that most of us dreamed about. It was in this direction we headed. The quality of the environment didn't pass unnoticed.

"How the other half live eh?" Chris spoke for the first time. "Not teachers that's for certain. Whew, look at the size of that place over there." He pointed to a large brick mansion, surrounded by tall cedars and a sweeping drive leading away from an impressive entrance guarded by two white lions sitting atop the concrete pillars.

"That's it. Number 18. Not bad eh?" I looked across to my companion. "Only the best for us."

"What! This is the place? Bloody hell. It's a bit daunting. Seems different to going up to a small terraced place somehow." He stared at the house, as if willing it to transform into something more manageable and shook his head.

"Big house, little house. Come on Chris. Think of it this way. The guy that owns it is still a prick, regardless of its size." I looked across at him and smiled and he returned it, his mouth creasing into a big grin.

"You're absolutely right old chap," he mimicked. "Let us dally no longer." With that he climbed out of the car and began to walk purposefully down the drive, briefcase in hand. Very much a salesman. I locked the car, and followed, keeping to the lawn and pretty much out of view. I wanted it to look like there was only one of us. Chris made it to the door and rang the bell. After a short wait, the door was opened and I caught my first view of Eric Grey. I could taste the hate welling up inside me. Watched as Chris went through some sort of patter, saw the irritation in Grey's manner, watched as he turned abruptly and went to close the door. Watched as Chris chose his moment to perfection, his body angle perfect as he drove into the retreating body of Eric Grey, every bit the hooker that he was. I must remember to compliment him, I thought. When I arrived, he had him spread eagled on the floor, face down. Eric was mouthing threats. Chris looked up and grinned again. He took the tape I quietly handed him and unceremoniously wrapped it around Eric's head, covering his eyes. I realised my hands were clenched tightly, the nails biting into my palms. I was reliving the moment, feeling the helplessness and horror. Stuff it, he deserved it.

"What are you doing?" The first hint of panic. The first question amidst the torrent of threats and abuse.

"Just wrapping you up a bit boyo," Chris answered matter of factly. "Now, now. No struggling." He pinned the arms back and gave the figure a gentle nudge in the kidney area. Grey grunted in pain and lay still. "That's better. You're a quick learner. Good."

The tape was wrapped securely around his hands. He was trussed up and helpless.

"Who are you?" he asked. Chris didn't answer, but pulled him to his feet and led him towards the living room area.

"I said, who are you? What do you want? I don't keep a lot of money here," anxiety evident in every word.

"It doesn't matter who I am. You just be a good boy and stop talking. I'll tell you when you should speak," Chris replied. He pushed him onto the white leather settee and quickly bound up his legs.

"Do you know who I am?" demanded Grey.

"Oh I do that Boyo, which is a pity really as far as you are concerned, a big pity." The words hung in the air.

"But I've seen you. I know what you look like. So you cannot expect to get away with anything." Grey blustered.

"Well, that's a pity as well. I can't have you knowing who I am now can I? Perhaps for you that is a tragedy." He played the part beautifully. In Grey's position I would have been extremely worried. Eric Grey said nothing; obviously the implications of Chris's comments had struck home. "However, if you play your cards right, there is a way out of all this," Chris added. "I have a couple of things to ask you. You give me the right answers and who knows, we might be able to sort something out. What about it?"

"What sort of things?" A more cautious Eric Grey. Who knew what was racing around his brain. Chris looked up at me and raised his hands in question. I beckoned him into the dining room and told him what he should say and he walked back to the living room. One didn't need to walk quietly in this house. The carpet was so deep you couldn't do anything else. To give him his due, one had to admire Grey's taste: a deep red carpet, deep blue curtains, leather furniture and deep mahogany side tables and book shelves. Simple yet tasteful ornaments decorated the various tables, complimented by expensive table lamps, whilst on the walls a variety of beautiful paintings completed the overall effect. Very nice. I moved through the dividing arch to join them.

"How's your father Eric? I hear the poor old fellow took a turn for the worse?" Chris asked the question nonchalantly. I watched Eric stiffen momentarily as the information sunk home: His captor knew more than a little about him.

"My father has nothing to do with you. He is an old man. You leave him out of this," Eric demanded.

"Fair enough for the moment," Chris conceded, "but what about your younger brother, Aaron, where's he? I haven't seen him for a while." "None of your bloody business," Eric replied. I thought I detected a hint of concern.

"Well now, according to the rules of this game, it may in fact be exactly that. My business that is. So how about reconsidering?" Chris asked softly, his voice loaded with unspoken threats.

"Well how the hell should I know? I don't know what he does from day to day."

"Okay. When did you last see him? Or hear from him?" Chris asked.

"I don't know. A week or so ago. I don't log our contact times," Eric replied sarcastically.

"Do you own a computer Eric?"

"Yes.... what? What does that have to do with anything?" a puzzled reply.

"Nothing really, I just wondered. Let's see. Where were we?" Chris looked over and winked. I had to smile. I could see he was enjoying himself. "Right, your brother. Bit of a thug from all accounts. Likes to rough it up a bit doesn't he?"

"What my brother is or does is his own business." Eric replied. Then more impatiently, "Look, I can't believe you have come here to discuss the why's and wherefores of my family, so what the hell do you want?"

"You're right, even though they are an interesting family: A titled father; Pity it's not hereditary; Bet that hurts. A violent brother, a cripple and

314

you. Quite the odd bunch. But as you say, that's not the real reason for the visit. What have you done with Lucy Alexander?"

No reply.

"That's not good enough Eric. I like answers." Again the jab, a little harder this time. When he wanted to, Chris could mix it with the best. I watched Eric double over and start wheezing.

"I don't know. I told you that. I don't know." His voice rose in desperation.

"But I think you do. Think about it Eric," Chris demanded. He jabbed him again, same rib. "Remember the rules now. You speak when told. Otherwise that old rib is going to crack. Could get painful. You're not one of these guys that gets off on pain are you? That would be too bad. You might end up in a mess."

"No."

"No what," asked Chris.

"No I don't like pain." He answered.

"Well, not yours at least. Still that's by the by for the moment. Now listen old chap, I do need an answer. I need to know where Miss Alexander is. So try and think. And no silly answers. I won't leave until I'm satisfied."

Nothing.

"Oh dear," Chris sighed resignedly and jabbed again, much harder. Judging by Grey's reaction the rib must have snapped. I watched, as the sweat began to pour off his face. His moans filled the silent room. I could see Chris was suffering too. This was new territory for him, but to give him his due he remained focused.

"Hurts doesn't it. Did you ever see that Rocky film where he was in the freezer smacking dead carcasses? Impressive. I'm no Rocky, but I reckon I can see off a few more of those ribs, unless you start coming up with the goods. So where is she?" The question hung in the air, waiting. But no reply. I could see Eric tensing. Chris moved behind the settee and pulled him upright so that his body was stretched over the back of it, then punched quickly. The rib snapped. Eric groaned out loud.

"No more, please, no more," he pleaded his face ashen and drenched in sweat.

"Then you know how to stop it. Just answer the question," Chris demanded. He looked over and quietly mouthed his distaste. I nodded in understanding. "Listen Eric. I don't care what happens to you, and that's the truth. You and your brother and his dubious collection of friends, have messed up a good friend of mine and I aim to even the score a little. One way or the other, I will find out what I need to know."

"Sutherland. That's it, isn't it? That bloody interfering teacher. He's got you onto this hasn't he? Wasn't he man enough to do this himself? He'd probably wet himself at the thought of it," he laughed, the sound totally incongruous for the occasion.

"Perhaps you would like to ask him yourself?" Chris said.

"No need, I heard him," I said stepping forward. "Hand me one of those cigars off the table will you please. I know how much Eric enjoys a good cigar, Don't I Eric?"

"You!" The realisation sunk in and his head dropped.

"Yes it's me. I reckoned I owed you a return call. The other one was so unsatisfactory, at least as far as I'm concerned." Chris handed me one of the cigars. "Thanks." I looked about the room for a lighter and spied an onyx one on one of the small coffee tables. "You having one?" I asked. Chris shook his head.

"Can't stand them. Horrible things." His lip curled in disgust. I flicked the lighter and inhaled, drawing in the smoke before blowing it in the direction of Eric.

"I much prefer to smoke them, than have them ground into my finger. I need answers. You will end up telling me. I have no doubt about that. You shouldn't either." I could hear the coldness of my voice. It matched my mood. "You have something I want. Where is she?"

No answer. "Eric, this is for keeps. I don't have time. The police may have let you go. I won't." Still no reply. Damn. I knew I couldn't burn him. I wasn't in that sort of league. "Damn you," I punched hard into his face, his mouth splitting under the impact, blood streaming from, and over his cut lips.

"Tape his mouth up," I croaked to Chris. "Unlike him, I don't get off on other peoples pain. I don't like hearing it." Chris looked on with concern, not moving.

"Jesus Mike. You could kill him. His nose is a mess; he might not be able to breath. He could choke on his vomit for Christ sake."

"So what. The bastard only has himself to blame. I told you I would kill anyone who harmed Lucy. I mean it. Here give me the tape. I'll do it myself." I grabbed the tape from his outstretched hand and picked away at the edge of it. I didn't dare think too far ahead. Couldn't contemplate my actions. Got the tape to unwind. Began to wrap it around the back of his head. He moaned, tried to lash out, desperate to prevent this next phase. I cuffed him over the head and told him to sit still.

"Don't do it," he begged, "please don't tape my mouth. I can't breathe properly through my nose. You've broken it," he added accusingly.

"Where is she then?" I asked again. Nothing. I continued with the wrapping. He started to breathe convulsively, trying to suck the air in, in large whooping breaths, his efforts becoming less effective as the tape covered his wide open mouth.

"No!" He screamed in a long drawn out cry. I stopped and waited. Chris looked on a trifle perturbed, but not interfering. Sweat drenched Grey's face. "I'll tell you." I stood stock still, hoping against hope, my heart in my mouth. "She's in the attic." He slumped forward, defeated.

"I hope for your sake she hasn't been hurt in any way. Keep an eye on him Chris. I want to check this out on my own." He nodded, understandingly.

Access to the attic was via a fold down metal ladder that appeared once the hatch had been opened. All was in darkness. I groped for a switch and was eventually rewarded. Lucy lay directly in front of me, semi clad, a blind fold covering her eyes, her ears covered with some form of ear plugs. The bastard had obviously not wanted to be seen or heard. I moved quickly to her and she stiffened, before lashing out with her legs in all directions, her arms unable to move because of the ties that held her down.

"Keep away from me," she screamed. I pulled the plugs from her ears.

"It's me Luce, it's alright, it's over now, it's me." I continued to remove the tape as gently as I could, my hands shaking with emotion until she was looking up into my face. She crumpled, sobbing, clutching me desperately once I had untied her, clinging to me as though afraid I would up and leave her.

"Michael," she whispered. To hear her voice was my undoing. I felt myself shaking uncontrollably, felt the hot tears running down my face, tasted their saltiness. What a hero! "He told me you were dead, that there would be no escape for me, that he had other plans. He showed me pictures, vile pictures, of little children being abused." I didn't have to look too far to see what she was describing. All around the room were blown up prints of them. It would have sickened even the hardened. She shuddered with the revulsion that I felt. "Said that whilst he didn't want anything to do with me, he had friends who would. Oh Michael, you're alive."

Someone once wrote that it is better to have loved and lost than never to have loved at all. As far as I was concerned, it was better to have loved and lost then refound that love. She kissed my tears, kissed me, slapped me on my back, laughing, crying, kissing, touching. The nightmare ended. God it felt good.

Chris met us in the living room, a broad grin etched upon his face, slightly embarrassed but positively buoyant. Her captor sat deflated and I watched Lucy look across, waited for the outpouring that never came. Just a hand squeezed more tightly in mine. Knew that I could not deal with violence in that manner. I led her on to the hall to the telephone and listened to her make the call to her parents, took over as she broke down again, cuddling her as I spoke to George.

"Michael, we are forever in your debt." His voice cracking. "Thank you. It's marvellous. Is she alright?"

"She's great, all things considered." He wanted clarification. I said I would tell him in person before the night was out. And what about me he had asked? Me? I was over the moon.

The prudent thing to have done was finish it there. For in many ways it was. I had got what I most wanted: Lucy. She was safe, I was fine, we could all live normally again. And yet, it wasn't quite. The pictures on the attic walls bore testimony to that.

I rang Lord Grey's home. Didn't know who answered. But it wasn't Lord Grey, nor Jimmy. Asked for D.C. Carmichael on the off chance that he was still pursuing his lines of enquiry, (sarcasm) and was rewarded eventually, having disclosed my name, with his reassuring abstemious tones.

"You have left us an interesting collection here Mr Sutherland. It seems you have had a very busy night." A long pause. I guessed it was my turn to talk.

"I think you will find that Jimmy McKay has some interesting stories to tell. Lord Grey is up stairs in bed if you haven't visited him yet. He has a fair idea of what's going on, but not the whole story."

"Bit like us then I guess," he commented dryly. "When do you think you can avail yourself to us or are you still doing our work?" It seemed he was adept at the sarcasm too. I ignored it.

"You might like to know that Miss Alexander is now safe and sound."

"Indeed. That is good news. With you now no doubt. Where did you say you were?" he probed.

"I didn't, but I will. I have what I want for the moment." I replied.

"Oh yes. But why for the moment? As you say yourself, you have got what you want."

"You forget that I pursued all this to clear a colleague's name. I know I have done that. I've got the proof with me now."

"We would like to discuss this with you in person Mr Sutherland. We have quite a few lines of enquiry which need to be closed." I smiled.

"Talk to some of those characters who are hanging in the shed. They have a lot of the answers. For the most part that is the lot of them. Those are the guys that have beaten, knifed, driven me off the road, raped that poor girl and assaulted the young chap in the lounge."

"Your handling of them was a little rough," Mr Sutherland. "That sort of thing doesn't sit well with lawyers acting on their behalf I'm afraid." He admonished.

"With all due respect, I couldn't give a shit. You just make sure that you make everything stick. Photograph the girl. Have you seen what state she is in?" I paused, breathing deep. "How would you feel if she was your daughter? Think about that. Are you married, do you have children?"

"I'm not expressing a personal point Mr Sutherland. If it was left to me I would lock them all up and throw away the key. Scum like that shouldn't be let out on society. But, there seem to be enough so called decent lawyers out there willing to express the rights of human kind, for the right price of course. I just don't want my pitch queered, and yes, I am married, and yes I do have young children."

"Then you wouldn't like what I have here," I replied.

"Oh yes?" That got his attention.

"Yeah, seems like the guy I'm with now has more than just a passing interest in children. In fact judging by some of the pictures in his attic I'd say his interest was pretty unhealthy. I would guess that if I searched around long enough I would find the very photographs that were used

320

against Len Jones." There was silence at the other end for some time, then I heard him let out his breath in a long sigh.

"Where are you?" I told him. Told him I would wait for him, with Lucy, and rang off. Offered Chris the opportunity to go before the police joined us, but he would have none of it. I marvelled again at the quality of true friendship. A truly solid guy. The prospect of hanging around until the police arrived was not that appealing, especially now that Lucy was safe. All I wanted was to get her home, away from this place. The excitement of the nights activities were wearing off like a painkiller, the mental equivalent of lactic acid building up, sapping away at the senses. Chris complained of being hungry, and that Eric kept a lousy larder, having already had a snoop around. He wasn't the only one, so we got on the phone and ordered a couple of pizzas from the local pizzeria and hoped they would arrive well before the boys in blue, otherwise they would all be digging in.

"Got any games on this thing?" Chris pointed to the computer in the corner of the room and looked back at the silent figure of Eric Grey. Nothing.

"Yes or no?" he asked again, flicking the switch, setting the machine humming.

"I've got something better than games." He spoke in a low voice, almost as if he was reluctant to be saying what he had started to say. We looked at him intently, not wanting to say anything, but intrigued as to what he might have to say. Lucy looked across with an expression of loathing on her face. He looked quickly away from her and back to Chris. "I'm not the only one in this game."

"What game is that?" Chris asked. "We've got your brother and his pals. Is that what you mean?"

"No."

"Then what? C'mon Pal, what are you on about?" He had our attention now, reluctantly even Lucy's. What a girl. She had been stuck away in an attic, left to wonder what would become of her, and here she was sitting here taking an interest as though nothing had happened. Amazing. Truly amazing. I loved her the more for it. Watched her look across at me and smile a little smile, that simple action overwhelming me with emotion. Knew I couldn't be without her. My brother's offer would have to wait. I didn't mind too much. Realised all this in such a fleeting moment of time. Eric Grey was speaking again.

"If I give you some names will you help?" he asked looking at me. I wouldn't help him, not in a million years. I told him so, told him that I had got back what I wanted. Suddenly everything was clear. I didn't want to hear any more. I had had enough. A chunk of my life had been wrapped up in this and I wanted out. As far as I was concerned the reason behind all that had happened had now been unearthed. I would make it publicly known that Len Jones's murderers had been caught, that he had been framed for a crime he did not commit. And all because of a painting and the sick minds of one of our so called noble families. Anything else he had to offer was of no interest. I asked Chris to keep an eye on him, took Lucy's hand and walked out of the room into the clear fresh night air.

EPILOGUE

'*O*h what a wicked web we weave . . . . . .' How true!

D.C. Carmichael informed me much later of the events which followed. He hadn't said much on arriving at Grey's house. Had muttered something about getting used to being one step behind, paid scant attention to Eric Grey although looked twice at the tape and the state of his nose, not to mention the way he sat all scrunched up, hugging his knees, and shook his head in resignation. I thought I caught him saying something about familiar carnage. I didn't care. He came back down from the attic very quiet, looked at Lucy for a long moment, said nothing, just breathed deeply. Nodded in recognition to Chris who hadn't bothered getting up from the computer, deeply entrenched in a game of solitaire, and beckoned me into the dining room.

"Well Mr Sutherland, what can I say?" he paused to scratch his chin, then continued. A rhetorical question. "You were right, weren't you? Your colleague seemed to have had the misfortune of falling foul of a pretty dire lot. Bad luck on his part." Did everything come down to that? Len knew where he was going with what he did, he just didn't appreciate that there was more baggage attached to what he was involving himself with. I shrugged. "Miss Alexander kept company with some pretty terrible scenes," he continued, his mouth down turning in disgust. "Mr Grey has a lot of questions to answer, the depraved bastard." His professional detachment crumbled, his voice one of loathing. I liked him the better for it. "I wish I could go and take a poke at him," he added with great feeling. I laughed, and his anger evaporated and he smiled a resigned smile. "Ah well, maybe not."

"I think if you question him appropriately he might just have some information of interest." I told him what Eric had started to tell us. The professional instinct returned and he strode off in the direction of the living room, turning at the door.

"Thanks."

"That's okay," I replied.

"No, no. Not just for this, but for everything. We were floundering. Nothing to go on. But for you they would probably have got away with it."

Injustice has always been my Achilles heel. Life's not fair. I'd grown up saying it, believing it. But I'd grown up. I'd had the chance, the good fortune to live. Len Jones and his wife were not so lucky. They wouldn't see their little girls grow and flourish. Life wasn't fair, but death was even less fair. It would take me a long time to come to terms with all that had happened. And for what? That was the rub. Pride? Anger? Sadness? They were the main emotions, but there were plenty of others attached to this as well. The very emotions that made for life. Funny old world. Yet there hadn't been a great deal of laughter.

Laughter and tears came with Lucy's family reunion. George threatened to dislocate my shoulder with his pumping up and down handshake, pulling me into his den once the initial family bonding had taken place, holding a whiskey tumbler in my direction and unwrapping a huge cigar. There wasn't a better time to ask him for his daughter's hand. He had thumped me across the back in pure delight and said that hell, considering she had been sent my finger, her hand seemed fair exchange.

I was marrying into a comedian's family! Virginia just hugged me tight, my own special bonding. Life might not have been fair, but life was good.

I hadn't even got the question out to Lucy. Had started to ask her as we dropped Chris off at his house. There was light in the sky, the sort of light that signalled the hope of a brand new day. A new start. I had tried to thank Chris. It sounded all so lame. The guy was a one hundred percenter. D. C. Carmichael had said that without me the case might not have come to fruition. Without Chris I knew for certain that it would not have. Lucy had kissed him lightly on his cheek and squeezed his hand. Her tears had almost been his undoing. When he saw mine he called me a typical kiwi poofta and no wonder the 'hard' New Zealander's had trouble beating the English at rugby. But his handshake was firm, the glistening in his eyes speaking volumes. What a friend. A best man.

Lucy had started to doze as we sped towards her family home, the past activity taking its toll. My own mind was a turmoil of thoughts, of mixed emotions: the good ones. I knew I wanted to return to New Zealand, to be with a brother and his family. Reunited and in partnership. But in my heart of hearts, I knew that I wanted to spend the rest of my life with the lady beside me, that without her it would be empty. It was as simple, as difficult, as that. Whether she would come to New Zealand or not didn't in the end come down to anything. I would be happy with her wherever! It was still academic. I had to ask. Be proactive Sutherland. I noticed in a detached somewhat amused self deprecating way that my hands on the steering wheel were becoming damp. Was glad Chris Williams was no where around to witness that as well. My street cred was already plummeting! Talking of plummeting.

"Lucy?" I watched as she stirred, said her name again and gently shook her leg.

"Mmm?" A lazy sleepy lovely sound as she stretched awake and looked at me, her eyes clear and steady. I went to speak, but she put her finger on my lips to silence me then put her hand down onto my left hand, covering the scar where my finger had once been. "Michael, I love you. I would love to marry you." I looked across at her. Speechless. "I don't know. It's just sometimes I feel I know what you are going to say. I wasn't wrong was I?" she asked, her face turning pink, hand going up to her mouth.

"No," I reassured her, "but I'm going to ask anyway. Lucy, will you marry me?"

"Yes. Yes Yes!" She had answered unbuckling her seat belt and flinging herself across.

The Vice Chairman of the Governors had called an extra ordinary meeting for the staff about a week after Lucy had agreed to marry me. There had been a good deal of gossip going around. Funny how the old band wagon had changed direction and most of the staff were backing Len's corner. Pity they had cornered too late! Even Mary Streeton had sung his praises, telling one or two of the new staff how she had always believed him to be a fine Christian young man. And what a tragedy had befallen him.

"Talk about a full circle," Robin sat propped against the corner of the staff room, one leg resting on the arm of the chair, the other extended in front of him. John rested on the arm, Brian sat on the bench. "She can't help herself. Women, they're all the same. You'll find out mate, now you've entered the marrying stakes. Mad." The others grinned. Chris sauntered across, catching the last of the conversation and giving me the thumbs up.

"So what do you reckon this is all about then?" Brian asked. They all looked in my direction. I shrugged. "Come on Mike. Let us in on it. You know what's happening. I can tell. Has it got anything to do with Fields being away?" I said nothing. Just thought back to my last visit with D.C. Carmichael a couple of days ago.

He had called me at home early in the morning, asked how I was, asked after Lucy. I told him we were engaged. He congratulated me, and then in his more business like way requested that I call in at the station before going to work. Didn't say anything more.

He met me at the front desk and showed me back up to his office. Not really familiar territory, but it brought it back to me. Seemed an age ago, another lifetime, Lucy missing, my life in tatters.

"Cup of tea?" I'd love one. With that duly done he began to tell me what had taken place once we had left Eric Grey. All off the record. He just felt I deserved to know. A decent chap.

". . . . . . so it was as you said. He ranted on about doing a deal. That he had information which we might find interesting. I told him we weren't in the business of doing deals and that there was enough on him to keep him out of circulation for some time, not to mention politics. When he saw that we were not going to be forthcoming he just came right out with it. Gushed like a well. Said he wasn't going down for the pictures on his own. Said that he knew someone else who had shown lots of interest in them. He said that they had come off the Internet but that he knew who else was receiving them, for he had passed some on." He paused to sip his tea and dunk a biscuit.

"I didn't think you could work out who was who on the web if the person didn't want anyone to know," I countered.

"Hmm. That's what I thought as well, but as you and I are hardly computer whizz kids, it seems there are ways of finding out things. And it seems Mr Grey had more than a passing knowledge. He told me that he had hooked up with someone on the IRC: the Internet Relay Chat," he added in answer to my raised eyebrows. "It's a chat room. Kids are on it all the time. Mostly harmless but you do hear about the few who start conversing with strangers and end up meeting with someone who has pretended to be a young person. That's where the paedophiles come in to it. It's an easy way to make a contact. It appears that on this system there are groups of users who are all on line at once. This particular cosy little group were in the habit of distributing charming pictures of little children to one another. There was a slight risk in this, as e-mail pictures could be relatively easily intercepted. The normal course of events was to give the address of the web site on which access to the right sort of pictures could be gained. Well, Grey being the devious type of person that he was, after all, he was in politics!" That was a bit of a shot from the broadside and I told him so. "True though," he countered. Who was I to disagree. "Anyway, Grey did a couple of things which enabled him to find out who he was conversing with in his little group. Just in case it might come in handy sometime. He struck gold with one of the names."

"So how is it possible?" I interrupted him.

"There are a number of ways. I think Grey did what they call 'social engineering'. He rang through to the company operating the net and told them that he knew the guy with such and such a user name but had lost contact and could they help? Seems like the fools did just that. Security conscious? That's a laugh. Still, to be fair, that was a couple of years ago. It wouldn't be as easy now, they tell me. He told us that he had also managed to hack into the company as it was a relatively small one and confirmed the information. Bingo. And when the time came, he called it in and your Mr Fields danced to his tune." He said it so matter of factly that the name almost went past without recognition. Then it hit and I found myself sitting upright. Ian Fields had been part of the game plan. Not a player as such. More an observer. But guilty as hell. He must have known, known that what was happening to Len Jones was all a put up job, yet had done nothing because he feared exposure for what he was: more indecent than the man alleged to have actually done something. Ironic or what? Or downright sad and unjust!

"Good afternoon Ladies and Gentleman. I have called this meeting to inform you of some unfortunate news. Sadly Mr Fields is no longer able to carry out his duties as Headmaster. He is unwell . . . ."

Unwell? What a joke. The guy was out and out sick.

It was Thursday afternoon and the staffroom was buzzing.